Parallel Prairies

PARALLEL PRAIRIES
STORIES OF MANITOBA SPECULATIVE FICTION

EDITED BY DARREN RIDGLEY
& ADAM PETRASH

Copyright © 2018 Darren Ridgley and Adam Petrash

Enfield & Wizenty
(an imprint of Great Plains Publications)
1173 Wolseley Avenue
Winnipeg, MB R3G 1H1
www.greatplains.mb.ca

All rights reserved. No part of this publication may be reproduced or transmitted in any form or in any means, or stored in a database and retrieval system, without the prior written permission of Great Plains Publications, or, in the case of photocopying or other reprographic copying, a license from Access Copyright (Canadian Copyright Licensing Agency), 1 Yonge Street, Suite 1900, Toronto, Ontario, Canada, M5E 1E5.

Great Plains Publications gratefully acknowledges the financial support provided for its publishing program by the Government of Canada through the Canada Book Fund; the Canada Council for the Arts; the Province of Manitoba through the Book Publishing Tax Credit and the Book Publisher Marketing Assistance Program; and the Manitoba Arts Council.

Design & Typography by Relish New Brand Experience
Printed in Canada by Friesens

Limestone, Lye, and the Buzzing of Flies by Kate Heartfield was previously published in *Strange Horizons*, February 2015

LIBRARY AND ARCHIVES CANADA CATALOGUING IN PUBLICATION

Parallel prairies : stories / edited by Darren Ridgley & Adam Petrash.

Issued in print and electronic formats.
ISBN 978-1-77337-003-3 (softcover).--ISBN 978-1-77337-004-0 (EPUB).--
ISBN 978-1-77337-005-7 (Kindle)

1. Short stories, Canadian (English)--Manitoba. 2. Canadian fiction--21st century. I. Ridgley, Darren, 1984-, editor II. Petrash, Adam, 1984-, editor

PS8329.5.M3P37 2018   C813'.010897127090512   C2018-904158-7
                                                 C2018-904159-5

ENVIRONMENTAL BENEFITS STATEMENT
Great Plains Publications saved the following resources by printing the pages of this book on chlorine free paper made with 100% post-consumer waste.

TREES	WATER	ENERGY	SOLID WASTE	GREENHOUSE GASES
8 FULLY GROWN	620 GALLONS	3 MILLION BTUs	26 POUNDS	3,350 POUNDS

Environmental impact estimates were made using the Environmental Paper Network Paper Calculator 4.0. For more information visit www.papercalculator.org.

Canadä

FSC
www.fsc.org
MIX
Paper from
responsible sources
FSC® C016245

Table of Contents

FOREWORD 7

THE UNCANNY ROAD
S. M. Beiko 9

THEY JUST WANT TO PLAY THE GAME
Sheldon Birnie 29

THE COMMENTS GAZE ALSO INTO YOU
David Jón Fuller 45

HUNGER
Christine Steendam 54

COD LIVER OIL
Lindsay Kitson 67

VINCENT AND CHARLIE
Patrick Johanneson 81

SEVEN LONG YEARS
Jennifer Collerone 104

REASON 4,286
J. M. Sinclair 124

ALL THAT COLD, ALL THAT DARK
Keith Cadieux 134

WE DRAW THE LINES
Will J. Fawley 147

JUDITH
 Jonathan Ball 160

EATING OF THE TREE
 Chadwick Ginther 168

A FISTFUL OF WOOL
 Darren Ridgley 189

INSECTUM
 Adam Petrash 206

LIMESTONE, LYE, AND THE BUZZING OF FLIES
 Kate Heartfield 214

WISAGATCAK'S JOURNEY
 Wayne Arthurson 226

ANNE BLAINE
 Craig Russell 241

SUMMER FRIEND
 Chris Allinotte 258

MY MOTHER'S FAMILIAR
 Gilles DeCruyenaere 274

ABOUT THE CONTRIBUTORS 282

ABOUT THE EDITORS 287

EDITORS' ACKNOWLEDGEMENTS 288

Foreword

When we set out to assemble *Parallel Prairies*, we weren't quite sure what to expect.

We knew from our travels that Manitoba wasn't without its speculative fiction writers, but we weren't sure just how large the community was. Finding a wealth of talent with deep ties to the province, and putting all those authors between two covers, felt like a worthy endeavour—but would we find enough people for a whole book? If we put the call out, would anyone answer?

It turns out, we had nothing to worry about.

Manitoba is a province with a long history of mutual support, and we should have known better than to doubt it. The speculative fiction writers of Manitoba showed us who they are with this project, in print and in spirit. And for that, we are grateful.

Speculative fiction tends to get bogged down with labels. Yes, there's "fantasy" but what kind? Urban? Portal? Epic? Yes, there's science fiction, but is it hard sci-fi? Space opera? Looking at what we have in this book, we are less interested in what slot you'd put them into, and more about what they have to say.

To us, good monster stories aren't really about the monsters. They're at their best when they reveal something about the human condition. A dragon is a visual feast, with its hard scales, fearsome talons and steel-melting breath. But it's the knights in those stories, grinding their boots into the mud and drawing their swords against tremendously bad odds, who teach us about valour. A ghost is terrifying and gruesome, but it's the paranormal researcher (or unlucky homeowner) creeping through the halls, revealing only what a flashlight's beam allows, who teaches us about fear.

Real life, while full of its own wonder, slips into mundanity, with each person preoccupied with the day-to-day. A forest trail is pretty, and the air is fresh, but it becomes something more when one's eye can imagine spirits, gnomes and elemental beasts hiding just beyond the ridge, or under a leaf. Speculative fiction is unlike myth in that its status doesn't shift from accepted truth to fiction over time. But the messages remain.

That's what we tried to do here: to rip open the portal to those other worlds and inject that magic into our own humble prairie province. What you'll find in here runs the gamut: Stories of hidden faery worlds, of realms crossing into our own, of deals with the devil gone wrong; stories of far-flung futures where Canada's Indigenous peoples congregate around a great fire among the stars; simple stories of love and loss under circumstances not like those of our world. Forget the categories. What you'll find here are stories that are exciting, frightening, sad, and at times funny. They have things to say about who we are as individuals and as a community.

In Manitoba, we find ourselves in a geographic centre, standing at the crossroads of a continent. Who knows what we might find at that intersection?

Sincerely,
Darren Ridgley and Adam Petrash
Editors

THE UNCANNY ROAD

S. M. Beiko

Judging by the crowd of passengers that had gathered in the bus terminal, it was going to be a hot, cramped, three-hour horror show of a trip back to Brandon. The place reeked of almost thirty bodies in their end-of-week sweats. Not that Kate was surprised or even put out; general discomfort had always been her norm, stench notwithstanding.

The sun was already low by the time the Greyhound pulled into bay four, everyone anxious to queue up just so they could be shunted into the rat cage on wheels. Kate could feel her shoulders bunching at her ears and hugged her bag in a death grip as a pasty tweaker with face tattoos bumped into her, too preoccupied lighting his smoke to give a shit about order.

"Sir, you can't come through here without a ticket," came the station agent, stepping into his path seconds before the gob of spit hit his face. Kate's hand went bloodlessly tight, and the crowd moved aside while security came in and dragged the screaming guy back into the bus terminal, skater shoes flailing.

Winnipeg.

A gentle tone sounded over the intercom, underscored by the bus's pneumatics as it knelt to the platform. It was hot out, even for August. A breeze sighed past, but it was more a gassy breath than anything, stealing the weak waft of A/C escaping the bus.

"Attention passengers: now boarding the eight P.M. shuttle west, Winnipeg to Vancouver, with stops in Portage la Prairie, MacGregor, Carberry, Brandon …"

The placid voice rattled off regional stops as people shuffled forward, eyes on phones or pavement. Kate flicked out an earbud to shake her head at the driver as he came to grab everyone's luggage. Luckily, she only had her shoulder bag; the guy's eyes were red-rimmed, and he was coughing, sweating. Too bad her hoodie couldn't hermetically seal.

She took the stairs two at a time and headed all the way to the back, to the window, pressing herself in. She should've booked the airport shuttle, but the idea of asking for the extra fifteen bucks from her parents made her shrink deeper into herself. Especially with the funeral and all. She clutched her grandmother's locket under the confines of her T-shirt. She'd just plug in and zone out and be thankful for the sliver of grocery money she'd saved … even though it would go towards more Mr. Noodles. Not like she would be cooking anything in her roommate's filthy kitchen. *Just get through your Masters, and get out. Everyone has student debt. No matter that there's no job market for a postdoc in folklore. No matter that you've spent the last five years in the middle of nowhere with few friends and your existing ones in Winnipeg getting further and further—*

The doors clapped shut with the last passenger, the bus pulling away from the platform. Kate squeezed her eyes shut. She'd sleep this ride away. *Tomorrow will be better,* Nana used to say.

As the bus left the lot, Kate took a last look in the fading light. The man with the face tattoos was standing there, back straight, eyes bright. He seemed to be looking right through her.

They turned the corner and he was gone.

✦

When they pulled into Portage la Prairie, the bus lurched so hard Kate was nearly thrown into the rainbow-patterned seat ahead of her. Dazed, she blinked around her, trying to re-establish where she was. Her dreams had been blank; her head kept bobbing, neck snapping, and all she could recall was watching a rush of dark shapes coming for her.

"Jesus Christ," a guy a few rows down muttered. People filed out for a bathroom-slash-smoke break, but the driver was rooted to his seat, coughing so painfully that Kate could easily visualize his lung slapping meat-heavy against the windshield. No one asked if he was okay on their way out.

Kate didn't see the point in getting up. She shifted uncomfortably, jeans chafing her thighs. God it was hot. She was sweating from every cranny and it was only nine PM. She wasn't getting back into town until eleven, maybe midnight. That meant sneaking in and trying not to wake Audra, so no shower until morning.

"Sorry."

Kate blinked up at the guy in the seat in front of her.

"Sorry?" she said. Classic Canadian roundabout.

The guy held up his phone. "You wouldn't happen to have an Android charger, would you?" He waggled his cracked-screen behemoth at her.

Before even thinking about it, she rummaged in her bag. "Oh yeah, sure..." She passed it over. Growing up in a house full of loud cousins at Nana's had conditioned her to share automatically, even if it was against her will. A flash of *what if you don't get it back?* pinged through her, immediate regret for trusting so easily, but he'd already taken it.

"Thanks so much!" The guy had turned back to face her. *God I am not in a chatty mood.* "Where you headed?"

"Brandon." Kate was awful at small talk. Awful at interactions that weren't planned months in advance. She remembered to be polite. "You?"

"Going *all* the way," the guy huffed. "Vancouver."

Kate shuddered. "I've only been on this bus an hour and I want to die."

He laughed. "Yeah, it's a long haul." He drummed his fingers on the seat. Kate felt her chest contracting, unsure what to say next. He was cute. She had didn't know the steps to this dance.

The doors clapped shut again. "Off we go," the cheerful guy chirped. "Thanks again for the charger. I'll give it straight back."

"Sure." Kate quickly looked back out the window, thumbing in her headphones. The sun was already setting, and shadows grew long claws past the Tim's as they pulled away.

She thought she saw—

The driver erupted in a coughing fit so bad that suddenly the bus pulled over to the side of the road. The passengers were silent. Finally, someone—not Kate—asked: "Are you okay to drive, man?"

He took a racking breath. Kate saw him turn around and grin weakly at everyone, sunken cheeks deepening. He looked like death.

"Sorry folks," he rasped. "Haven't been able to take a sick day in a while." Soon they were back on the road, heading for the exit to the Number One West again.

As they sped up and changed lanes, Kate realized her heart was hammering behind the locket there. It felt warm.

Kate forced herself to look out the window after exchanging a glance with the guy in the seat ahead. In the distant sky, the full moon was rising.

✦

Kate dreamed.

"Be careful," Nana was saying. Kate was small again, but her mind was still its twenty-three-year-old self. They had been shelling peas in Nana's tremendous garden. A place of wonder. And of poisonous things.

Kate had plucked a flower. *Hensbane*, Nana called it. "If you don't know what it is, don't eat it. Caution will save you. Canniness will protect you."

Kate raised the flower to her. "Is this what killed you?"

Nana shook her head.

"I had my time, child. I went into death's arms gladly," she said. "But that's not to say I didn't avoid him many times over."

She passed little Kate the locket. It was copper, faded and tarnished from years of being held tight. Nana always wore it. She said it kept her from harm. That inside was something the world should never see again. She told Kate that one day, when she was done in this world, she would pass it on to her. The day she took it off, she died.

Now she clasped Kate's chubby hand around it, clenching her old, gnarled fingers tight. They seemed to dry and crumble the longer she held on, but her eyes were intent.

"Do not let him have it," Nana said.

The garden faded. Kate was running. She had been aware of things on six claw-legs skittering after her, mouths huge and hungry.

Come away, o human child …

The darkness rushed by. Ahead, a silver procession of gauzy men and women astride horses passed in front of her. She tripped and flew right through them, the tinkling of musical laughter over her head as she landed in the dirt.

They turned their gaze on her, revealing empty sockets. Their mouths slackened, and they decayed as she watched.

To the waters and the wild …

The woods were all around her now. The boles of the trees loomed skyscraper high, choking out the world. A prison closing in, the moaning screams of a fearsome rage at her heels. She got up to run, but tripped again, gasping, trying to pull herself away from the brink of a chasm at her feet, opening up to a deadly pool.

The chain's locket at her throat tightened as someone caught it, pulling her back. Choking out her life.

✦

When Kate woke, the bus was dark. The world outside was dark. She couldn't tell where they were, but she'd only shut her eyes a moment. Her heart struck her ribs and her chest burned. She couldn't move. All she could hear was the driver's violent coughing and some passenger chatter at the front of the bus.

She felt the air crackle. Was she still dreaming?

As if underwater, the guy with her phone charger turned around and looked at her. She watched his eyes widen, saw his lips move, but couldn't quite make out the words. Her neck whipped to one side as the world suddenly swerved, and she was thrown rag-doll limp across the aisle as the bus caromed off the exit ramp.

Suspended in the air like a firefly in a shaken jar, Kate loosened and relaxed. She was floating. Everything would be fine. Her hand was around the locket.

The bus collided with the ground and Kate collided with unseen bodies in the dark, and everything went blacker.

◆

Someone was crying. Kate tried to roll over, her stiff, trembling hand moving over her body to check for injuries. She turned her head. Nothing was broken. Here, wedged between a seat, legs tangled, face pressed to the crushed window underneath her, she was alive.

The crying ebbed into a pitiful *hah hah* of spent breaths. Aside from this, it was startling how few voices there were. How quiet it was. Kate dragged herself up. She crawled over the seat in front of her, tried to heave herself over to see the state of the rest of the passengers.

The bus was empty. Save for the man who had her phone charger.

He was breathing hard, but he was breathing, and wedged, as she had been, between his seat and the glass.

"Hey," Kate rasped. "Are you okay?"

His eyes were startlingly white in the dark, his face streaked. He'd been the one crying.

His hand came up weakly. His mouth parted, but he didn't speak. Kate crawled over to him, and as soon as she came around the inverted seat, she saw his leg was twisted. She froze, seeing the bone sticking out of the shin.

There was no way she could move him.

"Okay," she said, because there wasn't much else to say. "Okay."

She had to calm down. She had to get help. She patted her sweatshirt, but her phone was gone. She could crawl around in the dark for hours and never find it, and she barely had minutes. Then she remembered.

"The charger." Kate squinted; the little light that came from outside afforded only impressions. She reached for the outlet in front of the guy's seat, did her best not to press into him, and found the cord. Dangling from the other end was his phone.

Kate yanked it free, turned on the screen, swiped. Aside from the original crack, it wasn't damaged, but there were no service bars. She tried the emergency call function.

"Fuck," she squeaked. It wouldn't connect. The guy had been staring at her all this while. Kate couldn't tell if he was growing paler, but it was likely.

"What ... what's your name?" she asked. She was very close to him, but there was nowhere else to go. His mouth was still parted, and she heard him swallow, heard the sound of the lips pressing together to form words in barely a whisper. "What? I can't hear—"

His hand gripped her shirt, pulling her closer. "Don't. Let them. Hear you."

Kate felt a stone in her gut. "Who? Who do you mean?"

The bus was empty. Kate hadn't fully processed that. Where had the other passengers gone? Had the emergency crews been and gone and just missed them? Had they all gone to get help?

"They took them." He pressed his mouth to Kate's ear, and she had no room to shy away. "They'll come back. They—"

A grunting sob of pain overtook him. Kate pulled away. "Look just ... I'm Kate. Okay? I need to get us help. There's no service in here. If I go outside—"

His grip tightened, both hands now, teeth clenched. Kate felt the spit on her face. "Don't leave me."

"Stop. Please." Kate's protest was as helpless as she felt. "Just tell me your name."

This close, she could see his terrified eyes. But only a bit. "Alex."

"Alex," Kate repeated as she unhooked his fingers from her shirt. "I'm just going outside. I'll be right outside the door. I'll be right back. Okay?"

She climbed off him, finding purchase by leaning on the seats. It was still hot. She took off her hoodie and put it over his twisted leg. When she looked into his face, it was tight with fear. The tears still streamed.

"I'll be back," she promised, tucking the phone in her jeans as he buried his face in his hands. *What the fuck had happened to scare him so bad?*

Kate scaled to the front. The door was open and facing the sky. That small bit of light coming in on top of them had been the moon, crystalline and sharp in the black vault. She awkwardly pushed herself out, scrambling until a misstep lumped her onto the grass.

She let out the breath she'd been holding, got to shaky legs. On this side of the bus was an open field, bright under the caustic lunar glare. There was a breeze wrinkling the tall prairie grass, and beyond that, trees. *Maybe some kind of wild animal had come?* She tried to think of the most plausible explanation for Alex's terror. But that didn't explain the rest of the passengers. There had been at least twenty. Had they left on their own steam? Or had something really taken them?

Kate's body ached. Limping to the other side of the bus, she knew she needed better bearings to get a hold of anyone. Maybe she'd have better luck flagging someone down on the highway. After all, it was a Friday, and traffic would be decent heading west, so her chances …

But there was no highway.

Kate blinked, looking ahead and behind the wrecked bus for the direction they'd come. She did a full turn and tried to stop her heart from slamming. No highway. No road. No streetlights. No cars. There was nothing. And no one.

She saw the tire marks the bus had left as it careened and crashed here, but they seemed to start from nowhere. The bus was stranded in the middle of a field that went on for miles into black nothing. In the silence and the dark, she could only guess at where they'd ended up. She could barely remember what the last stop had been—Portage la Prairie? Kate's spine stiffened when a howling moan filled the air. She flattened to the ground, pressing into the wreckage. Something had scuttled by. The tall grass shivered, and it wasn't the wind. The sickening howl came again and closer, and Kate realized she'd heard it before. All she could think of was Alex's warning. Could see his eyes cutting into her, begging.

Please don't leave me.

Kate swallowed a scream as she lurched onto all fours. A crab-clacking sound shivered over the crushed metal of the bus's side. She crawled to the back wheel, jaw tight, and hid in the wreckage's shadow.

Something huge and hulking scurried out of sight.

Before she could move, the shape fell on her, legs, arms—she couldn't tell—slashing. She shut her eyes, flailed, and screamed.

Her leg crunched into the shape's hard body, and there was a scream that made her blood run cold. She rolled out from under it, unable to get her legs under her. She could make out few details: six razor-sharp legs, glinting like polished bones. A heavy, gnarled body. And a twisted face with too many dead eyes.

Something sharp—a spear?—plunged through its heaving, jittering chest. It writhed on the point as it went back out and in again like a sewing needle. Kate counted six punctures before the thing collapsed on its carapace, its six legs now stiffened into claws.

Holding the spear was a man. His eyes were a painful blue.

"Are you all right?" he asked.

Kate was insensible, eyes locked on the spear blade dripping black gore. "It ... what ... I ..."

But the man was at her side, strong hand lifting her to stand. She stumbled and he steadied her. He'd stabbed his spear into the ground near the dead thing that was nearly the size of a polar bear.

"What's your name?" he asked, gently. Her pulse was so close to the surface, Kate felt it move the locket.

"Kate," she replied, maybe too willingly.

The stranger's eyes darkened, moving down. He stepped back. "I am sorry I was too late."

Kate staggered, still unsteady but trying not to lose control. "Too late?"

He went back to reclaim his spear, wiping it clean in the grass. "For the other passengers."

Kate looked from the dead monster to the bus. "There are ... more of these things?" Kate understood Alex's terror now. "Shit." Kate whirled to the other side of the bus. *Alex.*

She scrambled back inside, clumsy and tripping over the inverted seats, but something inside her already knew what she'd find when she got to the back of the bus.

Alex was gone. All that was left was her sweatshirt.

"Shit," she hissed, mouth twisting. But how? Had that thing gone in, extracted Alex, and passed him off to another monster she hadn't seen? What the good fuck was going on?

"Your friend?" came a voice at Kate's shoulder, and she let out a yelp. The stranger was balanced perfectly between two seats as if this whole situation were a common occurrence.

"He ..." Kate struggled to answer. "He's hurt. I have to—" What? Find him? Save him? Why? Kate didn't know him. Didn't know anyone else on this god-forsaken bus. She just wanted to go home to her shitty student life in shitty dead-end Brandon. She screwed her eyes shut. *Wake up.*

"Come," said the stranger, and Kate allowed herself to be led back outside.

Once there, she collapsed to the ground, trying to overcome a panic attack. The stranger moved off and let her cry it out.

"I just," she sobbed, "I just don't *get it*. What the fuck is going on? Where are we? What are those things?"

The stranger sighed, examining the spear before sliding it into a sheath across his back. "An unfortunate accident," he said. Did he mean the bus crash?

"I just want to go home," Kate moaned petulantly into her hands. A voice from somewhere buried whispered, *and what about the others?*

"You are farther from home than you think." The stranger was beside her, crouching. His face was all smooth, sharp planes. The eyes were like a lake reflecting sky. Like they were made of glass. They turned on her, pinning her in place. "How did you cross over?"

The tone had been so kind and coaxing, but Kate saw it for what it was—an accusation. "Cross over?"

Then there was a smile. It did not look at home on those features. "You are in the Uncanny Realm, Kate. Do you know what that is?"

Nana had lots of stories. Too many to catalogue. But tales of the Otherworld, the dwelling place of faery lords and terrible monsters, had been her main fare.

Kate barked out a laugh so harsh it bounced off the bus and dissolved into the abyss around them. "Are you *high?*"

The stranger made no noise, but his eyes narrowed as he stood to his full height. He was tall. Too tall.

"Doubt if you must," he said. "But here you are. And if you know not why or how, then getting you back will be difficult." He walked away to the other side of the bus, and desperate for answers, Kate followed.

"What does that *mean?*" she hissed, as she skirted the punctured corpse. She tore her eyes away, gazed back onto the bus. Only now did she notice that the exterior was shredded with gashes, blood streaked from the door down to a straggling path that led to where the stranger gazed.

The woods.

He looked down at her then, not unkindly. "This is a dire place," he said, "and has been for fathomless ages. Perhaps you think this a dream. Any human that arrives here thinks the same. Time here does not intersect with your world. You could be under the hill for a day and years will have passed elsewhere, and all you love could be dead and gone. Perhaps you think this a tale told to children in bedtime shadow. Imagine, then, a beautiful realm plunged into eternal night, ruled over by a malevolent king, who will stop at nothing to spread his darkness to your realm."

He looked back at the woods, quiet now. Kate exhaled a rattling breath. If this were one of Nana's stories, or a myth she had to interpret for a paper, she could guess the ending. *Caution will save you. Canniness will protect you.* A faery king who wanted to go into her realm? There was always a price.

Kate stared into the woods where she presumed Alex had been taken. "It's a trap."

The stranger appraised her with a surprised, bemused respect. "Yes."

"But it's the only way to get home, right? To bargain with this … king." Kate looked back at the bus. Even if she could somehow push it back upright, she could drive forever and never find help. She could be here forever and never wake up again. Maybe she was already dead.

"I am Cabal," the stranger said suddenly, in his lilting voice of changing tones. "I will help you find your way back."

Without waiting, his long stride cut towards the dark trees in the distance, and before she could think, Kate followed.

✦

They walked in silence until they reached the threshold into the trees. Cabal went ahead, nearly melting into the shadows, but Kate held back, tilting her head up to find where the massive trees ended. They seemed to blend into the upper dark of the sky. It was then Kate realized there were no stars.

"What is it?" asked Cabal, and Kate started. He was standing close, and she hadn't heard him. He held out a hand to her.

Caution, came her grandmother's voice as Kate forced her hand down from taking his. It pressed into her chest where still hidden under her T-shirt, the locket touched her skin.

"I'm fine," Kate lied, but she didn't move. "You're sure this is the way?" What other choice did she have?

"The king has taken your friend." That kind voice, those gentle, strange eyes. Otherworldly. "The king is no friend of mine. I will see you home safe."

Kate wondered if Cabal could see inside of her. That the purpose in her stride had nothing to do with saving Alex, a guy she'd exchanged less than ten words with, and more to do with getting out of here. Waking up. Because this had to be a dream. No matter how real the sensations were. How heavy her legs felt. The crushing headache and the gnawing at the back of her mind that she'd missed something.

She didn't take his hand. But she did cross into the woods. A breeze nipped her heels like a heavy sigh. As Cabal led her into the deep, moonless trees, there was no wind.

✦

"Tell me about your world."

Kate started. Had she fallen asleep on her feet? Had she zoned out so deeply? She blinked at the mossy ground beside a stream bed.

"Uh." Kate rubbed her face to get the feeling back in it. "There's not much to tell." The faeries in Nana's story had been beautiful creatures of desire and pleasure and joy. There were benign gods and spirits and there were evil ones. Very few liked humans or felt inclined to help them. Most of the time, humans were the enemy of the natural world. The cause of its suffering. But in the dark of Cabal's woods, anything would be an improvement.

"I would tell you of mine, but this is only a shadow of its glory," Cabal grimaced, again, reading her too well. "Gauzy processions of the most beautiful lords and ladies. Open pathways between realms to welcome humans in our revelry and pay the Fey back in kind. Now there is only shadow and the monsters that inhabit this place. Ever since the Uncanny King lost his power to a human." Cabal glanced at Kate, measuring, as if she was to blame.

They came to an incline and climbed. Kate straggled behind. Cabal was all grace and lithe balance; she was awkward and miserable and too bewildered to exert herself properly. When she pinwheeled her arms and nearly fell backward down the steep rise, Cabal reached out and grabbed her, holding her close. Too close.

For a moment, his hands squeezed her arms sharply before releasing her again.

"What does any of this have to do with me?" Kate asked as they moved on. "Why does it have to be me?"

Cabal regarded her carefully with his painful gaze—full of memory of the beautiful forsaken world he'd recalled to her. *Gauzy processions of lords and ladies* ... something tugged at Kate's memory the longer she stared back at Cabal. Then she finally tore her eyes away.

He simply shrugged then, that giant spear on his back levelling with his movements. "No man can say," was all he said. "But you are human. The king will try to stop you. Or worse, follow you. Come. Through here."

Kate's marrow chilled. Nana's stories about faeries were always about riddles and bargains. And the high cost of freedom.

Not looking where she went, Kate tripped and fell over a rock. Cabal was far ahead, and when she got back up on hands and knees, Kate realized she was in a clearing of stones, and they were shuddering.

No, not shuddering—unlocking. Unfurling. The rocks stood up and suddenly had arms, legs. Faces. They encircled Kate, eyes piercing.

"Go no further," said one closest to her shoulder.

"Turn back. Leave these woods," warned another.

A hand went heavily to her shoulder. Kate met its eyes—they were full of the sorrow of an age.

"Do not let him have it," the creature begged.

Suddenly Cabal was there, sweeping the small golems aside with his spear as if they were toys. He hoisted Kate up by the forearm and threw her behind him, drew his weapon out. "Stand aside," he said quietly. "These woods are filled with creatures that will deceive you."

The rocks chittered and hissed, showing square-filed teeth. "Turn around!" they said again, speaking as if Cabal wasn't standing in front of Kate. "Leave here now!"

Cabal's spine stiffened, then he turned to Kate. He handed her the spear. "You must do it."

She balked. "What the hell do you mean?"

"They will never let us pass if you don't defeat these creatures yourself. It is a test." It hurt to look into his eyes. But Cabal stood aside then, leaving the spear in Kate's hands.

The woods were heavy with silence. One of the rock creatures broke the circle and came forward, lifting a heavy hand to the spear and levelling it at its eyes.

"We are already doomed," The creature said.

Kate's body shook. "I can't. I can't do it."

"You must," said another rock creature, baring its stony teeth. "Or else turn around and leave this place."

She clenched her teeth, clenched every muscle in her tired body. This wasn't happening. *It's just a dream*, she thought, the pressure behind the spear building as it pressed into the creature's old, sad eyes.

✦

"You did well," Cabal was saying as he rubbed Kate's back in one even stroke. The gesture was over-familiar, but as she retched up the last of her stomach's contents, she was grateful.

She nearly did so again when Cabal handed her the two glinting stones that had been the creature's eyes. "Take them. You'll need them for what comes next."

Kate opened her hand and they fell into her palm. They were weighted with cost.

They walked until they came to a calm, impassive lake. Kate still clutched the stones in her hand, and squeezed harder still as she felt a burning on the skin under the locket's chain.

Cabal appraised her again. "You think it was cruel."

Kate still couldn't fathom how the piles of rocks that surrounded her afterward had been breathing and speaking to her only moments before. "They were trying to warn me," she said.

"The Uncanny realm tests every human who crosses the border. They will want to keep you here in their thrall." Had he just clenched his hand around the spear? If he had, it was relaxed now. He gave her that unnatural smile again. "Come to the water."

Kate obeyed without thinking. The pool was like glass, reflecting any light that struck it. They'd been walking for hours, and no sun had risen. Kate knew deep down it never would.

"The eyes will show you the way," Cabal said, indicating the stones in Kate's hand. "I have a feeling you know what to do."

Kate was suddenly elsewhere—pants rolled up to her knees while she waded through the enormous spring puddles around Nana's Charleswood house, throwing rocks. The water shimmered in unseasonable sunlight, proving winter's hold wasn't forever. Kate had thought there were other worlds at the bottom of those puddles.

In the Uncanny forest, she lifted her hand as if in a trance, and dropped the stones into the water.

The ripples were subtle, then all at once devastating, as if she had shattered a crystal window. The reflection went dark and changed. Before her was a cavern, pulling her in. At the end stood a bright pavilion, bedecked with leaves and summer berries. The curtain parted.

"But how do I—"

The image went dark again, and suddenly before her was a set of stone stairs, leading down into the dark. The lake drained away into it—or had it been there at all?

Cabal didn't move.

"Well?" Kate asked.

He shook his head. "You must lead, now," he said gravely. His handsome, sharp face seemed too bright. Too earnest.

Kate looked down the stairs. *Just a little farther. Then this will be over. Then you'll wake up.* She took the first steps and went down.

✦

The cavern was long, and wound its way through the core of this strange world. Kate felt like they'd gone miles down. Her head swam. "This king really lives deep underground?"

"The dark gives him strength in his weakened state," Cabal answered from somewhere behind her. There were only sounds: their footsteps shuffling against rock, hands sliding against wet stone to guide them. A moaning wind ahead. "It is all he has."

This close to the end, and only now Kate decided to ask questions. "What's in this for you?" she whispered, the moaning putting her in mind of the creatures that took Alex. "Why are you helping me?"

Cabal was so quiet that Kate wondered if he'd disappeared. In fact, without seeing him, she couldn't tell if he even breathed. "I am a great enemy of the Uncanny King. The sooner you are away from his clutches, the easier I will rest."

But you're delivering *me to him,* Kate wanted to say, but she was tired, so tired. "How did he get stuck here, anyway?"

This Cabal answered right away. "The Uncanny King managed into your world, once. But he was foiled almost immediately by a human woman. She trapped his power inside a locket, one of the King's ancient treasures. He has sought it ever since."

Kate froze. She wanted to turn around, to run back up the steps and all the way out of the woods. *Do not let him have it.* Was she going to have to trade the one thing Nana had left her for a way out of this? Cabal pressed into her, gently at first, as if coaxing a terrified sheep.

There was light ahead. Kate went toward it like a moth heedless of the heat. As if it always had been there, a pavilion stood steps ahead.

A hand went to her shoulder, and Kate remembered the warning of the stone creatures whose eyes she'd taken. But the hand now was Cabal's. She suddenly knew she couldn't turn around. "This is where I leave you," he said. "This next part you must do alone."

Kate swallowed. Of course. Her favourite: confrontation. And with a faery king no less. Whatever. Soon this would be done, and she would wake up on the sweaty, stinky bus, and Alex would return her cell charger, and she'd go home to her crappy place near the train yard, and Monday she would work through her dissertation notes, and maybe one day she'd turn this whole thing into experimental fiction.

She took a few steps and found herself at the curtain. She turned around, but Cabal was gone.

The curtain parted for her. A scent like lavender and rotting leaves hit her, then curled around her neck and led her in.

"Finally," said a voice. It was lilting and gentle. There was one lantern on a table in the centre of the tent, which was grand and enormous inside. Servants without mouths and eyes were nailed to the floor and held up trays of rotting food. At the far end was a dais, and on it reclined a tall figure clad in shadow. Kate couldn't see his face.

"Please," she said. "I want to go home."

"Don't we all," mocked the voice. Kate swore she saw sharp teeth glint in the little light.

"Please," she said again. What else did you say in dreams?

"You ask a great deal," said the voice, the Uncanny King. "Why should I let you leave? What do you offer?"

Kate kept her hands still. She knew he wanted the locket. That her grandmother could be the woman from Cabal's story seemed both unreal and the only explanation. Nana never talked about the past. That she could be the hero in her own story seemed a bitter celebration now she was dead.

But this was just a dream. By now Kate had forgotten even Alex's face. Forgotten about the other passengers who had been dragged away in blood. What did it matter now?

She lifted the chain over her head and held out the locket. "This is what you want, isn't it?" The locket was burning in her hand. This dream was too real. "Your old power. Send me home and you can have it."

The pavilion was silent. The servants and the rotting food vanished. The king was standing on his throne. Kate thought she saw him shaking.

"You offer it willingly?" His voice was full of both greed and shock, as though he'd been expecting a fight. But Kate was no fighter. She was no hero. And none of this was real.

"Yes," Kate said. The moaning came again, this time so close it made her shiver. It was the Uncanny King. He was laughing.

"Very well," he said, and stepped into the light.

Kate should have been surprised to see Cabal standing before her, his hand over the locket as he took it from her. Now his grin looked like it belonged there—wide and full of sharp, barbarous teeth.

An afterthought: "What about Alex?"

Cabal's eyes tightened onto her. "I already dispatched him," he said, waving his hand and throwing down the spear, still covered in black blood. "You were there. I needed you alive." But he wasn't talking to Kate, he was lovingly stroking the locket.

Kate's stomach tightened. He had turned Alex into that *thing*. "What about the deal? You'll take me home?"

Cabal snapped the locket in his grip and smiled that serpent's grin. "Of course," he said. "It is a pity that after all this time you gave this up so easily. But it is fitting. Not all humans are the same."

"What..." Kate started, but she felt herself being pulled forward, like a hand was caught tight in her shirt, the fist of the wind. The locket was open in Cabal's hand, and it was pulling her to it.

"No!" Kate cried. "You promised I'd go home!" She struggled against the current, but there was nothing for it. She was suddenly aware that she was awake. That she always had been.

"The Uncanny King never reneges on a bargain," he said, but to

Kate's horror, she realized that the king was changing before her—he was changing *into* her. "But we will go *together.*"

The wind howled, but the locket snapped shut, and the darkness that had plagued Kate's journey swallowed her whole.

✦

"Kate?"

Kate's eyes fluttered open. Above her was a bright light—no, it was sunlight, streaming in from a window. Her breath came in hitches. She tried to sit up.

"No, don't. Just rest," came a voice. A woman's voice. It must be her mother, whose face was swimming into focus.

There were tears in her eyes, and she was grasping Kate's hand. "There was an accident, honey," she was saying. Something about a bus disappearing, about Kate wandering on her own up the Number One Highway.

"It's going to be all right," her mother said, "Everything's going to be okay."

Kate turned her head, looking from her mother out the window. The sun was setting. The moon was rising.

She smiled, a hand on the locket around her neck. "Yes," she said.

THEY JUST WANT TO PLAY THE GAME

Sheldon Birnie

When Jake Shipley up and disappeared the weekend before the annual Manawaka Golf Tournament, word around town was he'd done a nose dive right off the wagon. Course, nobody'd say as much to his face when he turned up on Monday, sober as ever and without a hint of hangover. Still, everyone kept on talking behind his back like Jake had run a bender. It's a small town. What do you expect?

Me, though, I wasn't so sure. I've known Jake nearly ten years now, and I don't believe he's had a drop in all that time. I just don't believe it. There had to be something else to his disappearing act. Sure, it wasn't like him to make himself scarce, to miss work without notice. Heck, it's not like him to miss work, period, much less at the busiest time of year. So I figured it had to be something serious.

But when he told me he'd spent the night of August 21 aboard an alien spacecraft, I thought, "well, I guess old Jake's done lost it," traded in all his marbles and bought the banana farm, after all. I thought, "he's gone plum crazy". Now I'm not so sure.

As we worked our way around the eighteen holes of the Manawaka Golf & Country Club on the crisp, clear morning of August 27—the morning before the tourney got going for real—he filled me in on his version of the events of that night.

"Wasn't like in the movies," he said after I'd chipped a shot out of the rough up towards the third green.

Jake's ball was already sitting pretty after only his second shot. He'd sink her for a birdie, while that chip in had been my fourth, and I'd finish off the hole with a double bogey.

"Wasn't like the movies at all."

Me, I didn't say nothing. Hadn't said much all morning. When Jake first got going on this alien business I thought he was just pulling my leg. I didn't know what to say so I just grunted and kept moving on down the course.

"Weren't no bright lights to be seen," Jake continued. "It was dim, warm. Kinda like a fancy Italian restaurant or something. A massage parlour, maybe."

"You don't say, Jake," was all I could muster as I put my nine-iron away, pulled out my putter, and gave my lie a good, long once over.

I'd never been in a massage parlour, but I had been to a couple hoity-toity restaurants in my day. I found myself picturing it, this spaceship of his, as we walked up to the edge of the green.

✦

Around here, the Manawaka Golf Tournament is just about the biggest deal going. The tourney draws golfers from across Manitoba, Saskatchewan, and northwestern Ontario. Might be a few folks coming up from the Dakotas, even. For weeks leading up to it, the course is swarming with duffers looking to get the lay of the land before the qualifying scramble. While he don't really need the practice—he's been the tourney champ four of the last ten years and always in the top ten—it just ain't like Jake to up and take off a couple days before the whole thing gets going.

For starters, he's the club pro and has his hours to put in, and those are doubled come tourney time. Besides, if he'd had some other place he had to be, he'd have just about bent over backwards trying to get out of whatever it was he'd got himself into rather than leave the club high and dry.

Even if he *did* run off for a couple days to soak up the sauce and run wild in the mean streets of Winnipeg, the Wheat City, or Grand Forks, it ain't like they'd ever fire him. The dang course has been in the Shipley family since near day one.

✦

"That there's right where I was standing when it happened," Jake said, pointing with his five-iron to a slight rise in the fairway of the sixth hole, just off to our right and up about twenty yards.

I looked at the spot, raised my eyebrows, and waited for Jake to hammer his ball down the stretch towards the pin. Instead, he shook his head, staring at the nondescript patch of grass with a look of wonder on his tanned, lined face. After a moment, he looked back my way with a shrug.

"I was trying to sneak a quick nine in before dark. That's as far as I got."

Jake lined up his shoulders, glanced up the fairway, and took his swing. Sure enough, the ball sailed through the air a dozen feet above, fading ever so slightly at the end to drop, bouncing, just shy of the green.

Dang.

I whistled, shaking my head. Jake, he didn't even seem to notice his near perfect shot.

"Weirdest feeling I ever experienced," he said. "Bar none, Roy. One second, there I am, gauging the wind and squinting through the dusk, the next, I'm lying flat on my back, frozen in place in a goddamn spaceship a mile above the clouds."

Again, I didn't know how to respond. It wasn't that I didn't understand the words he was saying. It's just—how's a man supposed to respond to such a thing?

Instead I picked up my pace, angling hard towards my grass-stained Calloway. That's pretty much how she went as we made our way through the front nine. Jake kept on with his tale between strokes, and I just mumbled and nodded, hoping he'd change the subject.

"You tell anyone else about this?" I asked him after a while.

Jake just shook his head.

"Nah," he said, looking sadly over the rise in the fairway at the flag hanging off the pin. "Better the town believe I had a little dance with the demon rum than think I've lost the plot, eh? Remember what happened to that guy over Rivers way who said he'd been abducted by aliens? Oh boy. No, thank you."

"So why you telling me?"

"Heck, Roy," he said, breaking into a smile. "We're pals, ain't we?"

I liked to think we were, so I just let him talk on. And talk on he did.

"Dangedest thing is why they told me they done it," Jake said at one point. "Why they chose me, of all people, to beam up."

"And why's that, Jake?" I said with a sigh.

He'd already explained how these aliens of his didn't really *speak* so much as *transmit* their thoughts straight into his brain. I was lost on the particulars of just how they pulled that trick, but it didn't seem no wilder than the rest of Jake's tall tale. Besides, if these guys could fly across the universe, I reckoned they'd have a lock on making their *parlez-vous a ding dong* understood by a good ol' boy from the backwoods. Otherwise, what was the point of the trip?

"Dangedest thing, Roy," Jake repeated.

Off in the bush, a magpie set to squawking up a storm. I squared up to take my shot, waiting on him to finish.

"Said they wanted a crack at winning the Manawaka Golf Tournament. Said, more than anything, they just want to play the game. Ain't that something?"

Once again, I didn't say nothing, but as I swung my driver back to take my shot I caught myself thinking that was just about the first sensible thing Jake had said all morning.

+

By the time we wrapped up the round danged if Jake didn't have me thinking he might not be so far off his rocker after all. Now, it's not that I *believed* he really got himself beamed up into an UFO and roped into an intergalactic mission to win the Manawaka Golf Tournament.

That's just crazy talk, but I didn't fully disbelieve him, neither. Not completely, anyhow.

According to Jake, these extraterrestrial buddies of his wanted in on the thrill of a hard-fought golf championship on a heritage course. Only their bodies don't hold up under Earth's gravity, Jake explained, so they couldn't beam themselves down and hit the links. They might have eight arms and giant brains, but their bones turned to rubber under our atmospheric pressure.

"Plus," he added. "Our air's like poison to 'em. Pure poison."

That, Jake said, is why they had to install some sorta radio-transmitter doohickey into his spine that allowed the green guys to tap straight into his skull and, as he put it, "come along for the ride".

Heck, Jake even showed me the mark the installation left behind his right ear.

"That ain't nothing but a mosquito bite, Jake," I told him, though I had to admit that it was awful inflamed. "Quit itching on her, and she'll be gone day after tomorrow."

"They can't quite control what I'm up to," he continued, ignoring me. "But they get to feel it, see? It's like I'm locked into them, and they're locked into me. Kinda like, half virtual reality, half like those dang video games, see?"

I didn't have a clue as to what either of those things was, not outside of the movies, anyhow. I'm an old man, and my boys never got into such things, thank goodness. I just nodded, let him go on with his tale, though I couldn't help but ask a couple questions now and then.

"Why here? Why Manawaka?" I asked. "Why not Augusta, or the old Links at St. Andrews? Why not Pebble goldang Beach, Jake?"

"Can't just abandon their post, can they Roy?" Jake said without missing a beat. "They got orders from the home planet not to leave the zone until the mission's accomplished."

"What's the mission?"

"Never did tell me that," Jake said with a shrug. "Must be classified."

"What about Falcon Lake?" I wondered. "Ain't that in their 'zone'?"

"Dangit, Roy, Manawaka's a fine course," Jake bristled, familial pride firing him up enough to nearly flub his putt. "Dang fine. Besides, they tried Falcon Lake once. Didn't work out for 'em."

We dropped it, and then finished up the eighteenth hole. When we arrived back at the clubhouse, Jake headed for the pro shop while I sidled over to where my old Lincoln was parked.

"Hey Roy," Jake called out as I dumped my clubs in the trunk. "See you tomorrow?"

"You bet," I nodded. "I'll be here."

"Right on," Jake said with a grin. "We're gonna give these spacemen a ride they won't soon forget."

•

Me, I haven't put my name into the Manawaka Golf Tournament for years now. I was only ever a weekend duffer until I retired. The couple times I did enter, in a fugue state of vanity I'll admit, I never made it past the first round, but I do enjoy the hustle and bustle of the course when competition's in full swing. The past couple years I've caddied for Jake. It gets me right in on the action. Even though I ain't been with him when he's won one, it's a treat to watch a pro like Jake on top of his game. I guess, in that way, I ain't much different than Jake's little green buddies, hitching along for the ride.

The first nine holes here in Manawaka were built back in the Depression by guys who were on government relief. A make-work project, but she was designed by the famous Stanley Thompson and she's about the best between the Rockies and southern Ontario, though the courses at Falcon and Clear Lake might give her a decent run for her money.

The Shipleys, they've owned the course since Frankie Carlson, the fellow who commissioned Thompson to design the course and rooked the government into paying for her, up and died rather suddenly before the back nine were much more than cleared. Heart problems, some say. Others add that the boozing and the whoring on top of a bad heart might have had more to do with it. Anyhow, the Shipleys scooped it up at a bargain before Carlson was even cold in the ground. In time, they finished up the back nine to be near as nice as the front. They've been at the helm ever since.

It was Jake's granddad that done that deal, John Shipley Sr. He had himself two sons and a daughter, all of whom were quickly roped into various aspects of course and club upkeep and management. John Jr., the eldest, he eventually took over managing the books, while Jake's father, Al, got the run of the grounds. The daughter, Sarah, she kind of got squeezed out of the deal, moved out West years back, though I hear she still owns a third of the place, which must put some walking around money in her purse every year, no doubt.

John Jr. still runs the place. Jake's father died more than a few years back. John Jr. didn't have him any sons, but his middle daughter, Jane, she runs the grounds crew now if you can believe that. An only child, Jake seems happy enough running the pro shop and beating the pants off just about all who come to any of the corporate and charity tournaments the club hosts each year. But it's when the annual Manawaka Golf Tournament rolls around that Jake really shines.

If there really are spacemen stationed above these empty prairies with a hankering to hit the links, I guess they done their homework when they homed in on the Manawaka Golf & Country Club and beamed up Jake Shipley. I'll give 'em that much.

◆

The first day of the Manawaka Golf Tournament was crisp and clear, not even a touch of wind. You could taste autumn in the air. Jake was golfing in the opening flight, a 6:45 A.M. tee time. I arrived at the course at quarter after six, but Jake was already there itching to get at it.

"Great day for some golf, Roy," he said.

"Sure is, Jake," I told him true.

I was relieved that Jake never said nothing about the aliens, but of course, that didn't last long.

We set off in due course, paired with some blowhard from Melita by the name of Johnson. This fellow Johnson wasn't a half bad golfer, but he wasn't no Jake Shipley. Still, Jake fell a couple strokes behind, and didn't look near as in control as he usually did, flubbing a couple putts he'd put down a thousand times with no trouble at all and duffing a couple into the rough. After the sixth hole I couldn't stand it any longer.

"What's up, Jake?" I asked him.

"Nothing to worry about," Jake said, eyeing up his next shot and giving his five-iron a practice swing. "Guess I'm getting used to these green guys being so up in my business."

"Dang it, I'm serious," I said, nearly losing my temper.

"So am I, Roy," Jake said. "So am I."

Sure enough, as we wrapped up the front nine, Jake's game started to come together. He missed another long putt he would have normally sunk, and his drives weren't quite as on the money as they ought to have been, but by the time Jake and Johnson teed off on the ten, they were even. Jake just kept getting better as they worked through the back nine, finishing a modest two under while Johnson choked, ending up four over.

"Told you not to sweat it, Roy," Jake said as we made our way to the clubhouse to grab a lemonade and see how the rest of the competition was shaking out. "Just had to get used to being synched up to the mothership, was all."

When the field had come in early that afternoon, Jake was sitting just shy of the top five.

"Right where we want 'em," he said, rubbing his brown, sun baked paws together.

Two of the top five were local guys, decent golfers who'd had good opening rounds but would no doubt fall off as the weekend wore on. Jake was familiar with two of the others, a fellow from Wawanesa by the name of Patches Boyd and another from Hartney way, Benny Blood. Both boys regularly finished top ten at the Manawaka each year. Neither had ever won the dang thing though, and their best years were behind them. The man currently holding the lead was unknown to us, a young man out of Regina by the name of Kyle Esterhazy.

"Could be a dark horse?" I said.

Jake just shrugged, unworried.

✦

See, Jake gave up drinking when his wife, Lois, left him. He'd been a big boozer, a real hard living, good timing man, up until the day he crashed his Pontiac Parisienne on his way home from the Manawaka Golf & Country Club. He must have driven that route drunk a hundred times or more, but this time he took the corner a quarter mile north of town just a little too fast. He hit the ditch before parking the Parisienne partway through a farmer's fence and upside down. Nobody got hurt, but that was the last straw for Lois. Once the divorce papers were signed she left town and that was that. Last I heard she was living out in Cheyenne, Wyoming, or someplace like that. That was ten years ago, nearly to the day, actually, now that I come to think of it.

The way Jake tells it, getting sober wasn't a way to try and win Lois back.

"I was in a dark place," he's said time and time again. "It was the only thing I could think of doing that would save my life. I don't know where I'd be if I'd kept drinking. Dang sure I wouldn't be here, living the dream, anyhow."

In the years I've known him, Jake's weathered plenty of tough times without hitting the bottle. When the Little Saskatchewan flooded out his basement and he wasn't insured for it, Jake never took to drinking. When his father died of cancer and then a stroke took his mother the next year, Jake dealt with his grief sober as a judge.

That's why I say it just don't make no sense for a man who's kept to the straight and narrow ten solid years to slip up over nothing. I just don't believe it.

•

Jake kept at it through Friday and Saturday, and by the final round on Sunday, he was sitting in second place. He was two back of Esterhazy and three ahead of our buddy from Wawanesa. He hadn't let up on the space talk, neither.

Sure, he was driving them balls the distance, setting his shots right where he wanted 'em and sinking those long putts like the Jake Shipley from Manawaka we all knew, and if I whistled, or complemented a particularly sweet shot, Jake would just grin and say something like, "Who knew Martians could golf so good?", but in between shots, or sitting at the clubhouse over afternoon Arnold Palmers, he would get reflective.

"Of course, they ain't really Martians," he said at one point, staring out across the fairway and up at the blue sky above. "We'd call 'em Glieseans, after the star their home planet spins around, which is Gliese 832, see. Course, they got their own name for it. Couldn't pronounce it if I tried, though."

"Is that so?" I said, watching the leaves on the aspen trees that lined the eighteenth hole dance in the breeze, gauging what speed the air was moving at. "You don't say."

•

Of course, I knew Jake Shipley by reputation before I ever got to really know him personally. That's just the way it goes in a small town like Manawaka.

I've been here most of my life with the exception of a couple years over in Yorkton and down Medicine Hat way. Me and the wife, Shirley, we never really took to any of those places, so we moved back home just before our first-born, James, came around. It's a good place to raise a family, Manawaka. A decent one, at least, and decent's always been good enough for me.

James grew up, and so did Frank, our second, and they went onto university down in Winnipeg. James is still there. Frank's out in Calgary. Shirley, well, she passed away too soon. Cancer, a dozen years back now. Since then, I've just kept going, I suppose. A few years ago, I retired, and I've been spending my summers on the golf course ever since.

I never did squirrel enough away to head south come winter, else I'd be a snowbird, golfing twelve months of the year. Those dark winter hours can get lonesome, sure, but I tinker away in my basement workshop, keep up with the curling on the TV and down at the club most Friday nights. Time, she passes quickly nowadays anyways, and before I know it the crocuses are out and the course is open again.

I never was much of a drinker and I guess that's how I got to know Jake. Not drinking in a town full of lushes, that is. I've got nearly twenty years on him, but we get along well enough. Better than most, truth be told. Jake, he's never been one to string me along before. Even though I can't wrap my head around the idea of aliens from across the galaxy wanting to play a round or two at the Manawaka Golf & Country Club, I figure there must be *something* to Jake's story about the Glieseans. Why would he tell it to me if there wasn't? For a laugh? No, sir. Not Jake Shipley.

✦

Sunday morning dawned grey and cold. There would be no short pants or sleeves out on the course for the final round. Rain was on the way.

Jake didn't seem to mind a bit, though. He was just a grinning, raring to make his run for the cup. He still had to overtake Esterhazy, but Jake didn't seem bothered by that, neither.

"Any day she's not snowing is a decent day for golf," he said, well-worn Manawaka Golf & Country Club windbreaker zipped right up beneath his chin. "Besides, them Glieseans are hot to trot. They can feel the win, Roy. Can you?"

"Sure," I said, and I did. That's a fact.

Jake's game had only been improving since his little disappearing act, and I didn't see no reason why he couldn't catch this Esterhazy. Unless he choked, or the transmitter stuck in Jake's neck went haywire on him. "You got this."

"No," Jake said with a tip of his Manawaka Mohawks ball cap. "*We* got this, Roy."

The two of us lit out for the first tee when the rain started coming down. Not hard, just enough to get the grounds nice and wet. Esterhazy, dressed in a brand-new Titleist rain slicker, joined us. He was accompanied by an older caddy, a surly-looking guy about my age hauling a set of golf clubs that liked to have cost more than my car did off the lot.

"Howdy, boys," Esterhazy said with a curt nod as we approached the tee, waiting for the round to begin.

"Beauty of a morning for a round, eh?" Jake joked.

"Goddamn delightful," Esterhazy's caddy grunted, and then spat on the wet ground.

"Good luck to ya," Esterhazy said ignoring both the caddy and Jake's jape. "You'll need it."

"Mighty sportsmanlike," I coughed.

"Got a good feeling about this, Roy," Jake muttered as I handed him his driver, just loud enough so I could hear. "We're gonna show these Queen City sons of bitches just what we're made of here in Manawaka, Manitoba."

True to his word, Jake Shipley done just that. He drove with power and accuracy. While Esterhazy seemed to lean heavy on the power as well, his balls never seemed to drop where he wanted them to. By the time we'd finished the front nine Jake was two up on Esterhazy. The Queen City Kid was starting to lose his temper, but Jake, he just kept on grinning. He hit par on the tenth and eleventh, and birdied twelve while Esterhazy played a dang fine birdie on ten, but bogeyed eleven and only made par with a heck of a putt on the twelfth, cussing a blue streak under his breath the whole way.

"Dang, Jake, you're on fire," I told him, grinning myself after he chipped in and sank her off the pin on the thirteenth green.

"Don't it feel good?" Jake said, pointing his putter up to the sky. "The spacemen are eating it up!"

Jake had a little trouble on the fourteenth hole, a long narrow fairway that takes a hard dogleg to the left after 200 yards. He knocked the ball about 150 yards down but sliced it off to into the rough. It was the first time he really slipped up all round.

"Feels like we might get a bit of an electrical show here later," Jake said, looking up at the dark clouds and rubbing the red mark on the back of his neck. "Signal's getting some interference or something."

With a powerful stroke out of the long grass Jake finished the hole one over par. For a change, Esterhazy was on his game, smacking his shot straight and true for nearly 200 yards before she started peeling off to the left, setting himself up for a straight shot at the green. The Saskatchewanian nailed that one, too, sinking a long putt to birdie. On the fifteen Jake shot fine, earning the par three, but Esterhazy pulled out some of the fine work that must have got him to the final in the first place. He got to the bottom of the hole in three swings himself with an amazing chip in from twenty yards out.

"Mighty fine shooting," Jake told him.

Esterhazy just grunted, shoving his nine-iron at his caddy and huffing off to the next tee.

By then the sky was dark, clouds that had been grey had acquired a nasty, blackish hue. Far off, you could hear what could only be thunder. The rain had died down, though, while the wind whipped at the flag 180 yards away.

"Storm's coming," Jake said, rubbing at the red mark on his neck.

Meanwhile, the course marshals were on their radios checking with the clubhouse and Environment Canada on what the heck they should do.

"Think they'll pull us off the course?" I wondered aloud, figuring it wasn't looking good.

"Nah," Jake shrugged. "She'll keep away. Long enough to wrap this puppy up, anyways."

Sure enough, the marshals said just about the same thing, waving Jake and Esterhazy up to the sixteenth tee. Using a five-iron, Esterhazy smacked his ball up and over the little creek that cut across the middle of the fairway, settling just on the edge of the rough with a clean shot at the pin. Jake wasn't so lucky, depositing his ball straight into the drink.

"Dang interference," he cursed. "Keep losing the signal."

Down a stroke and on the wrong side of the creek to boot, Jake lined up a decent shot just shy of the green, while Esterhazy plunked his ball a gimme from the hole. Jake chipped in beautifully, coming within a hair of sinking it himself, having to settle two over for the first time all round. Still, Jake held onto the lead with only two holes to go.

Thunder rolled over the prairie as Jake and Esterhazy teed up on number seventeen, a 420-yard, liver-shaped monster, and the flag just visible behind a copse of aspen off to the right. Jake took a couple practice swings, stepped back and rubbed his neck again, all the while staring up at the sky. He took a couple more swings, gazed out across the fairway, then stepped up to the tee and whacked that ball like a son of a gun. She sailed through the air, whizzing like a spaceship herself, curving with the course. She come to rest not far from the green, an easy chip on for a straightforward putt and the birdie.

"Dang, Jake," I said. "We got this."

"You said it, Roy," Jake said, looking up again at the clouds and whatever was hovering up beyond them. "Heck, yes, we do."

To give him credit, Esterhazy also blasted a mean drive off the tee, but she did not hold as true nor fly as far as Jake's. He got on in three, and sunk a long putt for par. Jake, as predicted, sunk his putt on the third shot. He walked into the final hole up four with a smile on his face and never looked back.

◆

Not five minutes after Jake drained his final putt to win his fifth Manawaka Golf Tournament, the skies all around Manawaka lit up with a late summer lightning display that nobody who seen it will soon forget. Once the electric show had passed through, the clouds dumped rain for days. It was something, alright.

When all of the hullabaloo around the presentation of the trophy, cash prizes and the like was all done and dealt with everyone retreated to the club lounge. I stood there in the lobby waiting in vain for a break in the rain to make a dash to my car. Jake was standing with me staring out at the sheets of water that were just pouring from the clouds. We hadn't talked much since Jake was hustled off the course and into the winner's circle, me at his heels carrying his clubs.

"We did it, Roy," he said finally, so quietly I could barely hear him over the roar of the rain splashing down in the gravel parking lot. "We showed 'em, just like we said we would. Showed 'em good."

"Sure, Jake," I said, smiling.

Down the hall behind us the roar of golfers getting drunk issued from the lounge. Grown men yelled lies at each other about how well they'd played over the past four days, but here I was, standing quietly in the hallway with the winner, the man who'd just won the whole dang thing. He'd just said we'd done it together, as though I had anything to do with the magic out there on the course. As though my hauling his clubs around and nodding my head when he worked out a shot had contributed to Jake's mastery of the links in some mysterious way; as if I were anything more than a hanger-on, there for the ride, only to get a taste of the thrill of it all.

"Sure we did," I said.

We stood there, Jake and me, silent for a moment, the lightning still flashing up in the black sky to the east. Jake grinned and gave me a quick pat on the shoulder.

"Wait till they hear about this back on Gliese," he said, as the thunder rumbled in over the empty prairie. "That'll give them spacemen something to talk about eh?"

"One for the books, Jake, One for the books."

THE COMMENTS GAZE ALSO INTO YOU

David Jón Fuller

I never set out to be a "hero"—in fact it was the newspaper now posting this that started all that, and it's part of the reason my career is over. I just called my avatar The Herald, no relation to *The Winnipeg Herald*. There's a deeper reason for it, but of course my enemies online and in life only want to tear me apart for superficial things. (I suppose if I'd called myself The Star, people would assume I'd been inspired by *The Winnipeg Star*? Would they want to kill me as badly, then?)

But never mind; it's over now. You few out there who really care (no, I won't name you; I know you'll want to comment on this before the pixels are dry, but good luck with that) can rejoice, or be sorry, you won't have The Herald to kick you around anymore.

For obvious reasons, I'll skip going over what I do in "real" life. Where I work, how I live, who I associate with. I never trusted the worst of you, and the trolls proved me right.

I can tell from this newspaper's coverage over the last year and a half that what they really want (because it's what they think their readers crave) is an origin story. That would fit the narrative of the superhero, if I had a dramatically appropriate tale. But the truth is, I've always hated assholes and that's about it. The fact I can do what I do is beside the point. I could have used my talent to become rich (I'm not) or famous (does infamy count?), but the fact it seems to work in the nebulous world online, not just in person, is what gave me the opportunity to make a difference.

I'll admit, I also wanted to scare the hell out of bad people, just like the flashier cape-wearing vigilantes you've read about in comic books. I'm not sure now whether I did, really—and that's what led to it all going to shit.

So, an origin story? Try this one on for size: In the comment sections of too many media sites in this prairie town, I saw a few people spending most of their time trying to hurt others, and I got sick of it. I created a new username and avatar—ta-da, The Herald! (No, I won't tell you how I came up with that pseudo-medieval face, red hat, and blue collar)—and decided to take on the trolls.

Let me add, since it's the subject of endless speculation: no, I didn't go after people I merely disagreed with. I didn't even care whether they were violating the commenting policies of the sites I found them on. That would mean going after a lot more people.

The first time I killed a troll—virtually, anyway—was when I was just about ready to log off for good. Didn't matter which sites in this wonderful and diverse but also hateful and xenophobic city I went to, I saw the same toxicity. Thousands of comments, usually by a minority of users, often on multiple sites under different handles but with surprisingly similar patterns of idiom and axes to grind, that attacked everything. Yes, I read that study on trolls and sadism. It wasn't news to anyone who's been their target. I decided to live by the new wisdom: Never Read The Comments. "Logical argument"? Hah! "Spirited debate"? Please. Even the moderated sites were bogged down in shouting matches, and the unmoderated ones were a trolls' sandbox. I'd had enough.

But a good friend of mine IRL knew what I could do—had seen me do it from the time we were kids. I can't explain it, but I've always been able to "suggest" things to people. Most often I just ask, quietly, for them to tell me the truth. I have to be very direct, and Lord, didn't that ability make junior high even more of a minefield than it should have been. You don't know temptation until you're 13 and you can find out what people really think about you or anyone else, straight from the horse's mouth. (And yes, I can hear all you confident I-don't-care-what-people-think heroes: in my experience, you either already hear often enough how awesome you are that the stings of criticism bounce off your forcefield, or you are among the most desperate to find out. Who do you think started coming to me all the time when word got around I knew the score better than anyone else? That's right: all those paragons of "I'm the best" and "I'm beyond caring about such petty things.")

And I'm not psychic, by the way. I think that would have driven me insane.

Anyway, my friend (no, I won't tell you my friend's gender here—or mine, even though my many nemeses couldn't keep themselves from endlessly theorizing) suggested, as an experiment, that I try the same thing online.

It was the usual free-for-all in the *Star's* unmoderated comment boards. The story was one of many pro-Tory-provincial-government articles, this one about the new tax breaks. I ignored the howling from the one or two NDP die-hards in the comments—they'd been Dippers since before the previous government fell. No, what I was more interested in was a new user, comeonlefties. His (yes, his) handle alone gave it away: a "clever" double entendre meant to enrage supporters of both parties. That, and his comments, which tilted at the right-wingers *and* the left-wingers. Personal attacks about their intelligence, upbringing, ethnicity. He kept going at them until somebody took the bait—NeverendingTory, I think. Trying to rebut comeonlefties with data on overspending under the NDP and of course the usual arguments over the PST. Flame-worthy stuff! Anger, facts, opinion, all mixed together until the poster can't tell them apart. Well, comeonlefties kept up the attacks—on NeverendingTory's hypothetical trust fund, his whiteness (N.T. bit down hard on that one, averring Chinese ancestry), his gender ("so what if I'm male?"), and his weight, calling him "Fat Cat." All data trolling, of course, and the more NeverendingTory argued back, the worse the attacks became. I noticed that comeonlefties then piled on more attacks on any comment NeverendingTory made anywhere on the site, a barrage of insults and relentless attacks that drowned out any actual argument.

So, I created my new avatar and user ID, logged on, and made a single reply:

"Hey comeonlefties, why don't you tell everyone the truth about yourself?"

Then I logged off and went to bed.

The next morning, I didn't think to bother checking the *Star's* website until after breakfast. When I did, I saw that the first few responses, from other commenters, were as deep as could be expected: "What, are you a therapist, The Herald?" and "Looks like the competition is trolling *The Star*" and "WTH does that have to do with anything". No, I've never worked for the *Herald*, not even as a newspaper carrier (they're not paying me for this, either).

But then there was this response from comeonlefties:

"My real name is Josh Kyrczuk. I live alone and spend about 16 hours a day online when I should be working. I'm known as spunkygrrl on the *Herald's* site, Catas Trophy on the CBC site and I have about 20 other aliases." Then he posted an URL that listed all his usernames and which sites they were for. "I don't give a shit about the government I just like to make people angry. BTW those missing dogs the *Herald* did a story on three months ago, it was me that smothered them and cut them up." Then he posted his address. And his phone number.

I found out in the news coverage that day that he'd posted the same comment on just about every site he'd ever used, including social media networks and in an email to the police.

I should have quit right then and there.

It was weeks before I engaged another one of the trolls. Of course, in the media—social or otherwise—the discussion veered away from trolling in general and zeroed in on the specific case of Josh Kyrczuk. Why he had lashed out online at so many; whom he targeted for abuse and why he in particular wouldn't quit. There were articles here and there about safety in online spaces, but I can't think of one that wasn't full of advice on how to avoid trolls and protect oneself, without any mention of what would or could or should be done about the trolls' behaviour itself. How to stop it.

So, I tried again.

I lurked in the comments on any story to do with Winnipeg Mayor Degvan, because you could be sure, despite the fact he was a practising Sikh in his private life, that the usual comments raging against "Islam" would crop up. Or the more veiled posts "concerned" about the effects of religion on public officials—and where, exactly, were these concerns about past mayors, Christian, Jewish, or undeclared? Oh right, nowhere. The fact he was an unpopular mayor made for comment fodder, but there weren't many people doing more than decrying tax freezes or tax increases when they weren't trying to fill up their card for racist bingo. Maybe I should have stayed there, been a different kind of do-gooder, and fought racism. In Winnipeg that would be a full-time occupation.

But I didn't.

It was in the comments on a piece on the legacy of the Idle No More movement, its effects, and how people were taking action in new ways. Of course, you had the usual racist comments there, too, but in Canada it seems white people really, really want to be concerned either about the welfare of Indigenous people or about how much money from Ottawa is going to First Nations. So there were a lot of easy targets among the commenters for the trolls.

I recognized HappyLand as a troll when he went after Justicenow. Justicenow had previously self-identified as a mother, and HappyLand lit into her when she commented on the lasting effects of residential schools and poverty. HappyLand lambasted her for "white guilt" and a "saviour complex" and then went on to insult her children's intelligence. I had already decided to confront him, but before I could, he really crossed the line. Sprinted over it, really. He posted the address of her kids' school.

I don't know how he got it. I didn't care. I saw the comment before it got removed by the *Winnipeg Herald's* moderators. He tried to post it multiple times, and I knew they would ban him from their site. But that wouldn't stop him, of course.

I made sure mine was the next reply to him: "Tell us all about yourself, HappyLand."

He did. Thirty-six and still living in his parents' home, admitting that while he was ostensibly taking care of them he was actually unable to hold down a job that would support an apartment or house, even in this city's astoundingly cheap housing market. He had flunked out of an engineering degree because he spent all of his time trolling people online. HappyLand went even further. He not only admitted his real name, his address, where he was currently working (a Subway, nights, in St. Boniface), but also that he didn't care whether his online targets lived or died, but kind of hoped they lived and were dumb enough to come back for more abuse, again and again, because that's what he really enjoyed.

He also listed his other aliases (fifty-three of them), many of them on the same sites, which he used to gang up on his targets. HappyLand also said he'd never felt any guilt over harassing people into doing something drastic, because if it were him in their shoes, he'd just walk away before it got to him.

I wondered.

So I replied to him again. "If all this is true, HappyLand, just end it."

He made no reply, there, or anywhere else online. But the newspaper didn't report on his suicide until the police decided to look into my comment.

I logged off for more than a month. I couldn't look at news sites, social media feeds, even the headline tickers on the news networks, without usernames jumping out at me, as if any of them might be HappyLand, suddenly pleading, "What did you do to me?" But I knew the trolls still out there wouldn't suddenly leave other people alone; I couldn't leave the trolls alone, either.

And that's when things got interesting.

Why am I telling you all this? Why post this here, publicly? Never mind that this piece is online-only. I have my reasons. Mostly, to tell something of the truth before it's all over. Which should be any minute now, really.

Three things started to happen. I had to become a lot more careful in how and when and where I made comments to the trolls; hundreds of users started searching me out for help, and the trolls began vehemently denying my abilities and my existence.

There was the social media page (now shut down) that people set up to attract my attention and ask for help. Teens wanted help with online stalkers. Parents seeking lost children. Enraged customers trying to track down contractors who'd stiffed them. People who hated emoticons. When I didn't respond, the mods of the new page realized I would never be able to interact with anyone there without leaving a trail for the RCMP's cybercrime division to follow. So the pleas became more explicit. Details on where to find the alleged perpetrators online. I didn't really do much with the information when I got it, just asked each troll what was becoming my de facto slogan. And the cyberstalkers and abusers and even one abductor started blowing their own covers, keeping the RCMP, the FBI, and in one case, even the Policía Federal Ministerial, busy enough that I hoped they wouldn't bother coming after me.

And you know what? For a while—a couple of months, at least—the trolls kept quiet.

It was astonishing. Oh, sure, there were the same racist, sexist, classist, homophobic comments being made on all the news sites, the clever ones that phrased things to get past the moderators; but no one was being harassed. The "discussions" were at least civil.

Then came my would-be nemesis. "Doxxor Doom" they called themselves.

It wasn't one person. They knew with a single reply I could expose any individual, so they kept making comments, a different person each time, while dribbling out the personal information they'd dug up about me. IP addresses. Webmail. A few guesses as to my physical location at certain times of the day that were too close for comfort. And when I tried to uncover them by replying, "Why don't you tell us the truth about yourself?" there was nothing but silence. The dozens of people they must have enlisted to be Doxxor Doom is astounding.

Then my house was burned down.

I wasn't home at the time. I was at the—heh, almost said where, didn't I?—I was at another place, trying to get hold of the tail of my would-be nemesis (nemeses?). I'll be honest, I didn't sleep much for a number of weeks, so I was actually getting ready to call the police, when I heard the news. An anonymous email popped into my inbox saying: "You'll have to find somewhere else to sleep tonight :)".

Obviously, it was a way to get me to physically go home, so whoever they had waiting could verify my identity. I didn't know how much they knew. I still wonder whether they were sure of my address, or just sociopathic enough to burn down someone's house as a test.

Then I found out my webmail accounts had been hacked.

The images on the news of my house burning nearly to the ground that frosty autumn day left me with no choice.

I asked a friend—a very, very good friend, the one who had nudged me in the first place—to see if they could retrieve my car from the parking pad behind what was left of my home. They came back a long time later, with a small remote camera they'd found mounted in a tree across the street, and a report that they couldn't drive the car back because they'd thought to look underneath first and had seen something attached to the chassis that had no place on a working automobile. They were shaking as they told me. They'd called the police and left the scene.

The bomb was found by the cops before anyone else had a chance to remove it or set it off.

Then I found out that a message attributed to Doxxor Doom on every media site and social network you could think to name led off with "Hey, The Herald, why don't you tell us the truth about yourself?" And then it listed off everything about me: name, gender, social insurance number, age, place of employment … you name it.

The fact the police were ostensibly on the case of the car bomb and the arson was cold comfort when there was a knock on my friend's door. They knew where I was. Everyone did.

Which leads us to today.

I don't claim to be much different from Doxxor Doom and everyone behind it, except to say I went after the sociopaths. There's an old saying: don't feed the trolls. Except nobody acknowledges that *that doesn't solve the problem*; it doesn't stop them. Think of the first two Billy Goats Gruff: they declined to feed the troll, passed the buck, and were lucky enough to get away with "nothing more" than a death threat. But as in current society, getting to live in fear is a poor consolation prize. It took the third Billy Goat Gruff to deal with the problem: kill the troll.

I didn't actually want to kill anyone; I thought maybe, by heralding a person's true identity, I could at least be the sunlight that turned those trolls to stone. Maybe they would learn, and stop doing it. But I underestimated just how much trolls hate the taste of their own medicine. So I've had enough. I have an "offer" from, well, one of the police forces—I can't say more, except it's a chance to help bring some of the worst offenders online to justice. But … in return I have to get people to stop talking about The Herald. So here goes.

I chose to write this for the *Winnipeg Herald*, an exclusive, because they, at times, tried to deal with the trolls on their site. And you won't see it in print, because I'm posting it from their offices, online.

I'm sure you're wondering what I'm going to do, now that all my privacy has been destroyed. Well, I'm going to ask for help, and then no one will see or hear from The Herald again. It's going to make for an awkward, strange exit from this newsroom, I'm sure.

Thanks for reading, all of you, right to the end. Now why don't you burn and delete what you know about me, and forget all about this?

HUNGER

Christine Steendam

Justin walked into the elevator and pressed the button for the lobby. "Hold the elevator!"

He knew that voice. He stuck his hand out to stop the door from closing, and a moment later Maddie joined him. They'd lived in the same building for five years now, and he liked to think they were, at the very least, friendly acquaintances.

"Thanks."

"No problem."

The scent of vanilla filled the elevator. Her scent. She usually took the stairs, but looking at her now, he could see why she didn't today. High heels showed off her long legs, and a tight skirt and tank top didn't leave much for the imagination.

"Going out?" he asked, trying to fill the silence.

Maddie looked up. "Huh?"

Then understanding lit her eyes. "Oh, yes. With Vanessa."

Justin offered her a smile and the elevator dinged their arrival at the lobby and the end of their short-lived conversation. "Well, have fun."

"We plan on it."

He let Maddie leave first, then followed her outside. He turned down Bannatyne toward King Street and the King's Head, a popular local pub. Maddie walked in front of him, so he jogged to catch up. "It seems we're going in the same direction. Mind if I walk with you?"

Maddie glanced over and smiled one of her bright smiles that seemed to light up the room. "Sure. I wouldn't mind an escort during these uncertain times."

Uncertain times—she must be referring to the series of attacks that had been happening lately. They filled the news, yet no reasons for the attacks had come to light. They didn't seem to stop people from going on with life, though.

These things don't happen to me, they happen to other people—that seemed to be the mindset.

They walked in silence for a time, the roar of traffic making up for the lack of conversation.

"Well, looks like this is where we part ways," said Justin, stopping at the intersection of King street. "Be safe tonight."

Maddie chuckled. "Always." But her face looked uneasy. Maybe she was scared of the attacks.

"Hey, you've got nothing to worry about. Just some crazy people."

"I know. Thanks for walking with me."

She turned away, continuing down Bannatyne while Justin waited for the light to change so he could cross to King.

Walking alone was a bit more unsettling than walking with Maddie. Pedestrians milled about on the sidewalk outside various establishments.

Was there a hockey game tonight?

Judging by all the Jets jerseys, there must be. He waded through the people, going in the opposite direction of traffic flow, and pushed through them and into the King's Head Pub.

Inside was dimly lit, but loud with voices. Justin paid his cover and walked up the stairs and into the main area of the pub, looking around for his friends. He found them sitting at a few tables pushed together.

"Can I get you anything?" asked a waitress almost as soon as he was seated.

"Bud Lite."

"Sure thing."

"You come here, with all these beer choices, and order a Bud Lite?" asked Joey, one of his friends.

Justin shrugged. "It's a safe choice."

"Boooooring," cooed Katie.

Justin rolled his eyes. "I don't judge you for your choices, don't judge me for mine." He looked pointedly at the girly, fruity drink she had sitting on the table in front of her.

"Oooooo, someone is feisty tonight," cut in Dan.

"Just don't feel like putting up with your crap," he countered.

They bantered back and forth for a while. Justin's Bud Lite came and went and another replaced it. He lost track of time and drinks consumed with his friends. They milled about the bar, playing pool, chatting, and passing the time.

I wonder what Maddie is up to now, he thought, taking another sip of beer and waiting for his turn at pool. *Probably dancing the night away with Vanessa.*

She seemed so carefree, so young, though he was sure she was close to his thirty-one years of age. Maybe a bit younger. She certainly didn't act in her thirties, though. It was refreshing, to not see someone slowed down by age or the exhaustion of a daily grind. They'd been living in the same building now for five years, nothing more than acquaintances who shared the occasional elevator ride or chatted at the mailboxes. And that was fine. But he couldn't deny that she intrigued him.

"Earth to Justin! You're up," said Joey, lightly punching him in the shoulder.

"Oh, thanks, man."

Justin lined up his shot and hit the cue against the white ball, sending it careening into the solid red and then the red into the pocket. He lined up his next shot and tried for a second sink, but the ball bounced off the corner of the pocket, just shy of sinking it.

"What the hell?"

Joey's voice made him look up. Some girl was all over Dan while Katie gave them death glares from where she sat a little too close for comfort. She'd been holding a torch for Dan for years but never did anything about it.

Damn, it's gotta hurt to see him sucking face with another girl.

"Let the guy have fun, someone has to like Dan," said Justin to Joey. "It's your shot."

"But seriously, could they get a room? That's disgusting. They're not eighteen."

Justin looked over again. "*She* might be. Dude, you can't blame him."

Joey sighed. "No, I guess not."

They turned back to the pool table and took a few more shots, the game dragging on due to their lack of skill.

"Dan!"

Katie's scream broke through the din of the bar and Justin spun to see what was wrong. Dan sat in his chair, a guttural howl escaping his mouth, his hand pressed to the side of his head. He could see blood streaming between Dan's fingers and down his face. On the ground—apparently dumped there—sat the girl he'd just been making out with. Her mouth and chin were covered with macabre red and she grinned. Something bloody and flesh coloured lay on the floor beside her. Was that an ear? Justin could feel his knees going weak.

"Dan! Dan! Someone, help!" Katie continued to scream.

Almost in slow motion, Justin watched the girl on the floor stand up and turn to Katie.

No! thought Justin, but he couldn't move. He clutched the pool cue tighter in his hand and tried to convince himself to take a step, to fend off the crazed girl, but he couldn't. He could only watch as she turned her attention to Katie, leaping at her and wrestling her to the ground.

Katie's screams made the hair rise on the back of Justin's neck and down his arms. He sprung into action, spurred on by his friend's panic. He hit the girl over the head with the pool cue, dropped it, and with the help of Joey, pulled her off Katie. She struggled against them, swearing and spewing blood and spittle. Katie sat up, scooted backwards on the floor until her back hit a wall, and curled up in a ball. She hugged herself tight. Scratches covered her face and arms and blood seeped from what looked like a bite wound.

"Someone, help!" ordered Joey, trying to hold the crazed girl with Justin. She lunged away from them, trying to jerk out of their arms, and then changed her tactics and lunged toward Joey. Justin hauled her away, keeping her gnashing teeth away from his friend's flesh.

What the hell is going on?

What seemed like hours later—though in truth it was only minutes—cops poured into the bar and walked over to the group of friends, the crowd parting way like the Red Sea to allow them through. They grabbed the girl out of Justin and Joey's arms and threw her to the ground, slapping on handcuffs and what looked like a muzzle made for people instead of animals.

Justin watched in silence.

Who was this girl and why did she target Dan? Did he choose the wrong girl to get cuddly with? Or was there something more at play here?

A cop knelt by Katie, not touching her, just talking in smooth, even tones. "Are you bit?" he asked.

She just stared blankly ahead.

Justin walked up and sat down beside her, placing his hand on her hand. She jumped, pulling away and looking at him, her eyes wide and wild with fear.

"Hey, it's just me," he said. "The cops need to ask you some questions. Think you can answer them?"

She swallowed hard and then nodded.

"Thank you," the cop said. "Now, can you tell me if you were bit?"

Katie nodded her head, a sob escaping her throat.

"Okay. The paramedics are going to be here shortly. We'll get you some help."

The cop then turned to Justin. "You're her friend?" Justin nodded. "Can you stay with her? I need to go talk to the other guy." Justin nodded again and held Katie's hand tighter, stroking his thumb across the back of her hand in what he hoped was a soothing motion.

"What do you mean I can't see her?" he demanded. The nurse looked at him, her face firm and her eyes hard.

"She's in isolation."

"Okay, so what about Dan? Daniel Gilbert."

"I'm afraid he's also in isolation."

What the heck was going on?

"Look, they got bit. Dan lost his ear, Katie is terrified. They should see a friendly face."

The nurse pressed her lips together and shook her head. "I'm sorry. The police have ordered that no one visits them until we can get answers."

"Answers? What do you mean, answers? They got attacked. It's pretty straight forward." Justin's blood boiled, and he clenched his hands together. Why couldn't he just see his friends? This shouldn't be so complicated.

"I'm afraid it's not that simple. They both reacted badly to the bites, and for the safety of everyone, they're in isolation."

"Can I see them through a window? Just see how they're doing? It would make me feel better."

"I'll see what I can do, but I doubt it'll make anything better."

What was that supposed to mean?

The nurse walked away. Justin paced the hallway in front of the nurse's station and waited. What was wrong with his friends? Why would the police order the *victims* of an assault isolated? It made no sense. Something was wrong, very wrong, in this city. He'd read the news this morning. Both the attack in the King's Head and a few others, including one in the night club, Area, were reported. The pages of local newspapers were filled with speculation as to the case, with theories ranging from something in the food, to a mysterious virus. It had people scared. More scared than they were a few days ago. Justin had noticed it on his walk to the Health Science Centre. There were fewer pedestrians than usual in downtown Winnipeg, and those that did walk seemed to be glancing over their shoulders, peering into dark alleys as if the boogeyman from childhood would jump out at them. Even Justin found himself on edge, but he had to see his friends. He had to make sure they were okay.

The nurse returned and shook her head. "I'm sorry, I tried, but you can't see them."

What were the police hiding?

Justin sighed and nodded. "Alright. Thank you."

There was no sense in fighting, no sense in getting mad at the nurse when she was only doing her job, only following orders. He'd come back tomorrow and try his luck then.

Bang!

Justin spun to face the noise. It came from down the hall.

Bang! Bang! Bang!

He looked back at the nurse, her face pale with fear. He took off down the hall at a jog towards the noise. The banging continued, picking up in speed and ferocity. He turned a corner and at the end of the hall saw police at a door yelling through the window. "Step away from the door!"

The banging only continued.

One cop put his hand on the handle and gave a signal to the other cop. They both drew their guns and, on three, threw the door open and burst in. Screaming and growls filled the hall. Shouting from the cops echoed out the open doorway, and Justin's feet carried him forward toward all the noise.

He stopped and stared. Dan struggled against cops as they attempted to restrain him in his bed. He continued to shout and scream and growl. He then lunged toward one of the cops, biting at his neck. The other cop yanked him away, but not fast enough to prevent Dan's teeth from sinking in and drawing blood.

The bitten cop yelled out: "Damnit! Get him down!"

They threw him onto the bed. One cop held him down while the other strapped down his arms and then his legs. Dan bucked against the restraints and yelled out in anger. Justin's feet remained glued in the doorway, and he stared at his friend. If he didn't know better, he'd be unrecognizable. He'd never seen Dan so violent. *What the heck was happening?* He'd been fine last night. Besides the attack and losing his ear. Justin had expected to find him recovering in bed, in pain, but okay. Not like this.

"Hey!" one of the cops yelled. "You can't be here."

Justin looked at the cop who walked toward him. "I just came to see my friend."

"You can't be here," the officer repeated. Both cops exited the room and closed the door behind them. "It's not safe."

"What's going on?"

"We can't talk about that."

Justin tried to peer past the cops and into the window. He couldn't see anything, but he could still hear Dan. He seemed tireless in his anger.

"Why is he like that?"

"We can't talk about it."

"I just want some answers."

"We'd love some answers too. But you need to leave. Now."

There was no room for argument in the cop's voice and Justin slowly nodded. "Alright, but do you know where my other friend is? Her name is Katie. I'm told I can't see her either. Is she—is she like that?"

The cops both looked solemn and the bitten one gave a sympathetic shrug. "I'm sorry, I really am, but we can't tell you anything. All I can say is you're better off leaving and not trying to come back."

"Are they going to be okay?"

"We don't know."

Justin closed his eyes and breathed in deep. What was going on? Could Katie be like this too? Sweet, gentle Katie? Not her. Of course, he thought Dan would never be capable of this and yet, he'd seen it with his own eyes.

"The bites. Is it some kind of rabies?"

"We don't know."

Nothing. No information. Just nothing. Justin nodded again and turned away from the door and walked back down the hallway. The sounds from Dan's room chased him away as his heart pounded in his chest.

✦

Justin rushed down the street toward his apartment building. It was getting late, the sun was beginning to set, and he hated the idea of being out after dark. His heart continued to pound, not slowing down even an inkling after leaving the hospital. If anything, it beat faster. He looked around, jumping at every sound, every honk of a car horn, and every rustle in a back alley. What seemed like a doable walk before seemed much too long now.

Maybe I should flag down a cab?

The thought of getting in an enclosed space with a stranger seemed more terrifying than walking out in the open. So he continued to walk, stopping only when he came to an intersection. Finally, he turned onto Princess Street.

Almost home.

Almost safe.

He picked up his speed, his long legs stretching further and covering the ground as fast as he could. He passed a parking lot with a few cars parked; the setting sun made it dim and sinister.

Did he just hear a growl? He paused and looked around, then continued walking, cautious, peering between vehicles and into the shadows. He could see a metal bar of some kind leaning against a dumpster and he walked to it, picking it up. He didn't know what he'd do with it, but he felt better having something to defend himself with.

This time he heard the growl clearly, and he spun around, his grip tightening on the metal in his hands, looking for the source of the sound.

Please be a dog, please be a dog.

He searched desperately for something, anything, that would let him know where the growling came from. His eyes settled on a shadow about twenty feet away at the entrance of a path between two buildings.

"Stay away," he called out. "I'm armed."

He held out the bar in front of him in warning, but the figure took a few more steps toward him. He backed up. Blood thundered through his ears. Not now. Not like this. Could he run? But terror kept him from turning his back on the shadowy figure. It continued to move toward him and stepped into a light that illuminated part of the parking lot. It was a woman, her shirt torn and bloody, her chin a darker shade that could only be more blood. She growled again and Justin shuddered. "Please, stay away," he pleaded, taking a few steps back, trying to keep the distance between them.

She seemed to pause, and then sniffed the air. Her actions reminded him more of an animal than a human. Her eyes met his and a deep, guttural growl rumbled out and picked up in volume until it could only be described as a war cry. She lunged forward, and Justin lifted the metal bar and swung just as she reached him. It connected hard and loud with her head and she reeled away. Justin couldn't help but be thankful for all the baseball he played every summer, making his swing strong and sure.

That swing should have been enough to knock her out, but instead she turned back to him, her head now bleeding. She lunged again. He swung again. This time he took no chances when she stopped, stunned. He hit her again. She fell to her knees. He swung again. Then again and again and again until her body crumpled to the ground. He breathed heavily, his chest rising and falling. His lungs protesting the adrenaline that coursed through him. The bar dropped from his hands with a clatter against the pavement and he stared at the lifeless body.

What have I done? What have I done? What have I done?

He backed away from the body and then spun on his heel and ran. He could see his apartment building and he slowed to a walk. He needed to get away. He needed to get to his apartment and clean up. He needed to scrub every last ounce of evidence of what he'd done off of him and out of his mind. He paused to pull his key card out of his pocket, but the door burst open before he could use it. A woman, a figure in tight jeans and a loose, flowy shirt ran past him.

"Maddie?" he asked, but the figure didn't even pause, as if she couldn't hear him. "Maddie? Are you okay?"

She kept running.

What's going on?

His mind seemed to scream at him. He put his hands on the door and swiped the key card to unlock it. Entering the brightly lit lobby, he looked to the elevator and then to the staircase. He didn't want to be in the metal box, but he couldn't take the stairs. He'd never make it up the ten storeys to his apartment. He walked to the shiny metal doors and pressed the button, waiting for his ride. A bang made him swing around and he looked straight in the eyes of a man panting, blood seeping down his hair and face from a head wound. He paused and looked at Justin, tilting his head to the side much like a dog would.

Why did I drop the bar?

He reached behind him and pressed the button for the elevator again.

Hurry up! Hurry up! Hurry up!

The elevator dinged and he turned, leaping into the opening doorway. A scream erupted out of sight and he pressed the close door button, but not before a hand reached into the doorway and stopped the door's motion. He kicked out at the hand, but it was too late, the man entered the elevator, looked Justin up and down and then lunged at him.

Justin yelled and tried to fend off the man as he fell to the floor of the elevator. The man bit his arm and this time a scream of pain, not fear, erupted from deep within him. He grappled with the man, refusing to give in. The man was much stronger, but he struggled to bring his mouth to Justin's neck. Justin brought his legs up, trying to push him away, but to no avail. The man's teeth closed around Justin's throat and bit down, tearing away flesh and muscle and vein as he pulled away.

The scream that ripped through Justin felt foreign, only the pain and the warm, wet blood filled his mind. *Not like this*, he thought, but he could feel his body slowing down, his arms losing all strength to fend off his attacker. Everything felt quiet and distant. He could see the man returning to his prey and he stared. It seemed almost unreal, like he was an impartial party, watching it happen. The man descended on him again, and everything went black.

⁘

Light filled the elevator, though its doors remained closed and still.

Justin looked around and sniffed the air. He was alone. Silence told him that—that and the lack of anyone's scent but his own. He stood and walked from wall to wall inside the metal box, looking for an opening.

Ding.

He whipped his head around, looking for the source of the noise.

So hungry.

A whirr drew his attention back to a wall as it opened.

So hungry.

He nearly ran out, but the scent of vanilla stopped him in his tracks. He waited.

So hungry.

In stepped a woman. Her eyes met his and she froze. He sniffed again.

Hungry. So hungry.

The woman screamed, dropped something, and spun around.

Justin leapt at her and they both crashed to the ground, him on top of her.

So hungry.

She struggled against him, but he felt nothing. Only hunger. He grabbed her arm and sunk his teeth in, tearing away at the flesh.

COD LIVER OIL

Lindsay Kitson

Ten years I've been married to Marie, and ten years she's been pale and sickly. Not healthy enough to bear me a single child.

Perhaps that's why I gave in to her when the new railway brought the carnival to the Red River Valley.

Between the bearded lady's tent and a gypsy fortune teller's wagon, the doctor hawked his green glass bottles under a sign that read "Doctor John's Amazing Elixir."

"All that ails you," he called from a table with a red checkered cloth, "bring back your health, your strength—your youth even. Cod liver oil, my friends, God's gift."

Then he tipped his black beaver top hat at Marie as if he could pick a naïve buyer out of a crowd. He probably could.

Marie's hand tightened on my arm. "Giraud, do you think I could …."

It was nothing but snake oil, surely, but perhaps it would make her try a little harder around the house. I looked down at her, all brown eyes with dark circles under limp strands of mousy hair. "You'll make a proper supper tonight?"

She glanced back at the doctor. The glass bottle in his hand glinted in the sunlight. "I could … would you like a fish steak?"

A proper roast or a chicken would be more like it, but I said, "That'll do, I suppose."

"Would you like to put a little spring in your wife's step, sir?" The doctor leaned forward, inviting us to approach the table.

"What is this concoction?" I asked.

"Cod liver oil, sir, bottled by the ocean, with a bit of my own herbal additives for good measure, and a lemon in each bottle for taste. Sunshine in a bottle, they call it by the ocean, sir. Puts a sparkle in your eye and strength in your hands, practically a cure-all. Would you like to read some testimonials?" He held up a bottle, and in the sunlight I could see sprigs of flowers, leaves and bits of bark settled in the bottom of the bottle.

"No, no," I didn't have the patience for that. "One bottle," I said. "For my wife," I added because I couldn't bear to have anyone hear that it was me who took him for anything but a mountebank.

"Very good sir, it's fifty cents, or forty each if you want two."

"One, please," I asserted. "Five crowns, who pays that, that he can make a living at this?" I muttered.

"Oh," he said, wrapping a bottle in brown paper, "word of mouth, it gets around, you see. One person tries it, and they tell their friends. You do have to give it few weeks to take effect, mind, but if you will look over my testimonials; letters from customers—"

"No thank you," I said. No doubt every one of them was written in his own hand.

Doctor John tied a string around the bottle to hold the paper and held the package out to Marie. "There you go Madame. Take one tablespoonful by the mouth, each day."

"Yes, sir, thank you," Marie said, with a shy smile that made me jealous. She hadn't smiled at me for years, but she flashed one at this trickster. Oh well, fish steak for supper.

We saw the rest of the Carnival, Marie walking with her brown package clutched to her chest. I made her stay at least for the main ring show to see the tigers jump through their hoops of fire and the elephant stand on a tiny ball. I took her on the Ferris wheel where we could see the whole city from the top, but I could tell all she wanted was to get home. If she'd had a tablespoon with her, she would have tried the stuff right there at the top of the Ferris wheel. I had to remind her three times on the way home that we had to stop at the market.

There was a fresh catch of cod just come in on the riverboat at the market, an uncommon thing this far up the river. "Don't let them give you a skinny one," I told Marie as we approached a stall.

"Poor things," she said, glancing over the fish strung across before us.

"Just pick one and come on," I said. "You need a lemon, too, don't you?"

The moment we got back to our childless little apartment, she went straight to the kitchen. When I got there, the green bottle sat open on the counter. Marie stood with a spoon in her hand, making a face as if she'd just tasted something terrible.

"What did you expect?" I said. "It's medicine."

"I know."

"Now don't you forget that fish," I said.

"Yes, Giraud, I'll start on that now."

The fish was all right.

The next morning I woke to an odd smell. It was almost like bacon, I thought. Perhaps the neighbours were cooking and it was wafting in through the window. I opened my eyes to look, but the bedroom window was closed. Odd.

I rolled over to rouse Marie—she was always a slow riser.

Marie wasn't next to me.

I heard a scraping in the kitchen. Could that be Marie, frying bacon?

I climbed out of bed, too curious to take the time to dress, and went to the kitchen in my nightgown.

"What is this?" I said. "Has my wife been replaced?"

Marie jumped. "Oh, Giraud," she said. "It's not ready yet. Go get dressed."

I raised my eyebrows. I admit, I was caught off guard. I went back to the bedroom and dressed.

There were eggs on toast too, when I got back out. "The eggs are a bit hard," I said.

"I'm sorry, I'll make sure they're runny next time; it's been a while."

"I daresay. And you can fry the bacon a bit crispier next time too." At least she was trying.

A week later I came home from the factory to the sewing machine running. Marie hadn't done much more than patch my trousers and darn my socks for years, and there she was, foot working the treadle, with periwinkle blue floral printed cotton running through the machine.

"Isn't that the tablecloth your mother gave us for a wedding gift?"

"Yes, Giraud, but the edges are frayed, so I thought I might as well make it into a dress. After all, some of my old ones don't fit me anymore."

"Which ones?"

"Well, the lavender one—"

"Weren't you just wearing that last week?"

"Well, yes, but I got Danielle to come by and take my measurements, and I've gone up a whole dress size." Miss Danielle Blondet was a mature woman, not much older than Marie, with a challenging look in her eyes that I'd always found offensive. She'd divorced her husband some years ago.

Our doctor—our real doctor—had been concerned about Marie's weight for a long time, saying she was too thin, and really it was true, she was far too thin to be properly attractive without clothes on.

I looked at her now. The front of her dress had always hung empty for lack of breasts to fill it, but now it fit snugly.

I went to where she sat, and curled a finger under her chin to turn her face up to me. There was more flesh in her cheeks, and a healthy glow replaced the paleness. There was a colour in her lips that had never been there before, even before we were married. Could it be Doctor John's elixir?

"You've been taking that stuff every day."

"Every day," she said. "I think it's helping, really I do. Oh, and there's a roast in the oven, don't worry, I haven't forgotten supper again."

"Well, maybe I'll pick you up another bottle before the carnival leaves town." And I kissed those pink lips, softer than I remembered them. I reached for her breast and she pulled away surprised. I supposed I couldn't blame her; for some years I've tended to my needs elsewhere when she failed to entice me. But she was like a new woman now, and why shouldn't I enjoy my own woman?

"Oh!" she cried as I swept her up into my arms to carry her to the bedroom. She was even a little less stiff than I remembered.

I saw her take two tablespoons full of the elixir that night.

The next day I went to the carnival again after work and bought another bottle of Doctor John's elixir. His stall was busier this time. Word of mouth?

I didn't think he'd remember me, but he did. "How is that wife of yours? Well, I trust."

"She is. She'd like another bottle of your cod liver oil, if you please."

"Certainly, sir," he said, and wrapped another bottle in the brown paper. Before he could inquire further, another customer distracted him, thankfully. I handed him his fifty cents and took the package home.

Marie wasn't there when I got back; she must have been shopping for supper. I picked up a newspaper from the boy down the street and sat down in my favourite chair to read it. There was a short article on the good Doctor John, as well as his advertisement.

I finished reading the newspaper. It was nine. Marie never went anywhere but to the market and back, and she had no business being out this late. She had better have a good explanation when she got back.

I had to make myself a sandwich from the leftover roast and was about to go to bed when I heard footsteps in the hallway and a key turned in the lock. Marie opened the door and waved to someone in the hallway. "Take care, Danielle," she called, laughing. Her hair was curled and her lips painted.

"Where in Sam heck have you been!" I shouted.

Her eyes went wide. "Oh, Giraud, you didn't see my note?"

"What note?"

"On the ice box, there," she pointed. "I've been out with Danielle."

"What do you mean, 'out'?"

"At Danielle's flat; she had all of us over to play cards."

"Cards?" It wasn't proper for a woman to play cards.

"Oh, it was just a bit of fun, Giraud, it's not as if there were men there."

"That woman is a bad influence," I snapped. Here was my Marie getting uppity with me. This wouldn't do. And there was whisky on her breath. "Come here," I said, regaining control over myself. Marie frowned as I pulled out a kitchen chair and sat down. "Bend down over my lap." I said it calmly; my father had always said, when you are punishing a woman or a child, you should always remain calm, otherwise, when you calm down later, they will think you must not have meant it.

She bit her lip and lowered her eyes, but, reluctant as a child, she knelt down and laid herself across my lap on her stomach. I lifted her skirt up and over her hips that were visibly fuller than they had been a week ago. I wanted to take her like that, but there was the business of discipline to be addressed.

I pulled down her bloomers and, with an open hand, I paddled her behind as my father had taught me. Not too hard at first, just until she was red, then harder once her rump was warmed up. I used my free hand to hold her still as she squirmed against me, until finally she cried.

"You know I do this for your own good," I said when I was done.

"Yes, Giraud, I know." She stood in the middle of the sitting room, eyes to the floor.

"I know you want to be a good wife. I don't want you to visit Miss Blondet again. I want you to know that I love you. I bought you another bottle of Doctor John's elixir."

"Oh," she said, between sobbing breaths. "Thank you."

I ate my sandwich listening to her weeping in the bedroom.

Marie was sullen for days afterward. She looked well, even more colour in her face, and she did all the things a proper wife should, but there was resentment in her eyes that had never been there before. I had to spank her three more times for being disrespectful.

"The carnival is leaving soon," she told me one day as she stirred a chicken stew. "Do you think I could get enough elixir to last until they come back next year?"

I knew this was coming. Truly, I wondered if her health would fail again if she stopped taking the stuff, but I didn't think the rebelliousness she'd learned would leave with her health. Instead of a mouthy wife who made bacon and roasts and thrust up against me as I between the sheets, I could end up with a mouthy wife who didn't cook and wasn't worth a tumble.

I pulled my money clip from my coat pocket and counted bills. "How many bottles do you need?"

"I think two more would do. I could stretch it."

I counted out eight crowns and laid it on the table. "You can pick it up when you have time."

"Thank you, Giraud," she said, scooping up the money and stuffing it in her apron pocket.

When I came home, there were two more bottles on the counter, and the first two up on the shelf; the place looked like an apothecary's house. Marie wasn't home. I gritted my teeth in anger and went to Miss Blondet's apartment.

Miss Blondet lived only a block away. The doorman raised his eyebrows, not recognizing me, but when I said I was going to see Miss Blondet, he let me in without question. Miss Blondet must entertain strange men as a habit.

I came to number nine, but before I knocked, I listened at the door. I could hear Marie's voice along with Miss Blondet's, but I couldn't hear what they were saying. I knocked.

Miss Blondet answered the door. She didn't say anything to me, but called over her shoulder, "Marie, Giraud is here."

She walked away from the door, leaving it open, but didn't have the decency to invite me in. I heard a whispering and rustling, and a moment later, Marie appeared at the door, eyes down. She clutched her silk purse in one hand and held her canary yellow shawl around her shoulders with the other.

I said nothing. She said nothing. Miss Blondet watched, leaning against the counter with a look of disapproval. That woman needed someone to slap that look off her face.

But she wasn't my responsibility. I took my wife and left.

Back home, I pulled out a kitchen chair again and sat down. "Come," I said, keeping my fury out of my voice.

Marie hung up her shawl on the ash coat rack and set her purse on the counter with an expression I took for resignation. I waited patiently as she came across the floor.

But in the middle of the floor she stopped, lifted her chin, and said, "No."

I didn't know what to say. She looked at me as if she hated me. What had I done to deserve this? Cared for her, gone to work in the factory, put up with her illness—how many times had I made my own supper while she lay in bed? A lesser man would have abandoned her. I rose and paced the kitchen. "What has got into you Marie? Has that Miss Blondet put foolish ideas into your head?"

"It doesn't matter, Giraud. I will not be your servant any longer."

"Servant!" I shouted. "You're not my servant, you're my wife! I'll not have you behaving like a petulant child! What has made you like this? Is this it?" I picked up on of the green bottles off the counter. "Is this it? Has the good doctor's witchcraft put a demon inside you?"

I threw the bottle as hard as I could at the front door. Marie flinched at the crash and cried out softly. I thought that might bring her around. "Are you ready to behave?" I asked, pushing down my anger again.

"No."

I took the other bottle, and smashed it against the door. Then I took the other two off the shelf and smashed them too, one after the other. Still she stood defiant in the middle of the kitchen.

"Clean that up. I'm going to bed." I walked past her toward the bedroom.

"No."

It is not in my nature to be violent, but my anger overcame me then. I whirled on her and slapped her full across the face. She fell backwards, and I immediately felt the guilt of what I'd done. I'd never struck her face before. That wasn't how my father taught me. I went to help her up, but she scrambled away. "Stay away from me!" she cried.

I shook my head. "No, this is madness. I'll make it right. Don't worry, I'll make it right." And I walked out the door, broken glass crunching under my shoes.

I would go to the carnival grounds. I would throttle the good doctor until he agreed to set things straight.

But when I arrived, there was nothing but churned earth from many feet and garbage left behind by carnival-goers. A paper blew by my feet and I picked it up. It was a pamphlet of Doctor John's testimonials. I crumpled it in my hand. The train station. They would be there, leaving. As the sun set, I turned back to the city proper and caught the last trolley to the station. The train whistle blared as I reached the station, and the platform master called out "All aboard!"

I ran through the station to the platform as the chug of the engine started the great iron beast forward, spewing steam into the red-orange sky.

"It's too late, sir, can't let people on while the train is moving," someone said behind me, laying a hand on my shoulder. I brushed him off, watching the windows as they moved by, faster and faster. Passenger cars linked between cars carrying the dismantled pieces of the Ferris wheel.

And then I saw him. He saw me too, and leaned out the window to wave that top hat at me. "Hello, sir, I saw your wife today, she looks very well! Tell her I'll be adding her testimonial to my pamphlets, she was so kind to provide it."

I ran to the edge of the boarding platform, meaning to drag him bodily from the train. He sailed past me though, and I ran as fast as I could along the edge of the platform, right to the end, but the train moved too fast. I stood at the end of the platform and shouted obscenities that would have made a proper lady faint away.

No one at the station dared approach me, and I turned back to the street, ashamed of my outburst. The tram was waiting for people wishing well the passengers of the last evening train. I got on and rode home, seething, defeated. If the man came back next year, I would have my word with him.

At home, the broken glass crunched again beneath my feet. Marie was in the living room, mending a pair of her stockings.

"Come," I said. The time on the trolley had given me a chance to cool my mind. "Your punishment cannot wait. If you refuse to submit, you will be forced, for your own good."

I took her by the wrist and pulled her to her feet. Then I pulled her chair out into the middle of the floor where I had more room to work.

As I straightened and turned to her again, a black thing came flying at my head before I had a moment to think what it was.

When I came to my senses, I was lying on the floor next to the mantle. My head throbbed. The fire shovel lay abandoned next to me. Had Marie *hit* me? It didn't make sense; none of this made sense.

I rose up on my elbows. Marie was walking back and forth from the bedroom to the kitchen. What was she doing?

Finally she stopped in the kitchen, and I heard rustling. I climbed to my feet, fighting dizziness. Leaning on walls and furniture, I made my way to the kitchen.

Marie's peony-patterned overnight bag sat on the table, and she was packing her dresses into it, and her jewelry, and her toiletries.

"What are you doing?" I asked.

She looked over her shoulder at me as she stuffed the last scarf into the overfull bag. But she didn't say anything. Just that same look, like I'd done something terrible to her. Then she lifted the bag off the table with both hands—two weeks ago she could not have lifted anything half as heavy—and went to the door, glass snapping under her shoes. She opened the door and looked over her shoulder at me one more time.

"Good day, sir," she said. And then she left.

I know she stayed with Miss Blondet for a while, and I heard that she eventually found work in a cigarette factory. I began to think I'd never see her again.

She was gone a year, maybe more, when one day I fell ill. An ache crept into my joints, and a weakness until I could barely get out of bed to the toilet.

Someone must have told Marie, because I'd been abed only a few days when I heard a key turn in the front lock. I dragged myself out of bed in my dressing gown and made my way to the kitchen. There she was, radiant as the girl in the cigarette advertisements. She was wearing a coral dress I hadn't seen before, with a high collar newly in fashion that summer.

"'Bout time you turned up," I grumbled.

"Tsk, tsk, tsk," she said, picking my dirty socks and long underwear off the floor and the kitchen table. The maid hadn't been in for several days. "You should be in bed, Giraud. Go on, I'll make you some hot tea."

I snorted at her, but I felt a bit dizzy and thought it best if I were off my feet. Reckoning would have to wait for later.

She brought me tea, with lemon. "Has the doctor been by to see you?"

"Doctor, yes, he was here. Says there isn't a thing he can do for me. Bedrest and fluids, he says."

The next day, Marie went out and came back two hours later; what she was doing that took her that long, I don't know. "I'm running you a bath, Giraud," she called from the bathroom. "I saw a doctor, and he gave me something to help you get better."

My headache had gotten worse, and I struggled out of bed. By the time I got to the bathroom, the kettle was whistling with hot water for my bath. Marie bustled past me with it and poured the steaming water in. She brought five kettles full to warm the water, then she brought a sachet with a paper tag that said 'Epsom salts,' and dumped it in the water.

"There, now in you go," she said. "It's supposed to help draw the sickness out of you while you soak."

I eased myself into the claw-foot tub. It smelled slightly briny, with a pleasant touch of lemon. I lay for an hour, and Marie came twice with more hot water to keep it warm.

The sachet lay on the edge of the sink. I reached out to look closer at it. On the one side the tag said 'Epsom salts,' and in smaller print, 'for the leeching of toxins and disease-causing agents from the body.' I turned the tag over. On the other side it said 'Manufactured by Dr. John.'

"Marie!" I leapt out of the tub. I was immediately dizzy, however, and slipped. Water splashed everywhere, and I bashed my head against the edge of the tub.

"Oh, Giraud, what happened?" said Marie, helping me up.

"Your bloody witch doctor!" I snapped. "You had to go back to him, didn't you!"

"I don't know what you're talking about," she said, wrapping a towel around my naked body. "Now settle down, you're feverish. Come on, I'll help you back to bed."

I fell into a restless sleep and woke thirsty. I called for Marie, but she didn't answer. I climbed out of bed, steadying myself on the wall and called again, but still no answer. She must have gone out again, damned woman.

I made my way to the kitchen for a glass of water, and there it was, on the kitchen counter. She'd left it out, with the teaspoon sitting beside. The bottle of cod liver oil glinted yellow-green in the sun.

Perhaps I was out of my head at that moment, but I staggered towards the counter and lifted the bottle up to the sunlight slanting between the neighbouring buildings. I put it to my lips and took a sip. The advertised lemon flavour was barely perceptible, and if it masked anything I didn't want to know what the stuff tasted like without it. It was bitter and bland at once, and the oiliness of it was revolting. I braced myself and tipped the bottle up again.

It took three glasses of water to get most of the taste out of my mouth after I finished the bottle. I considered soap, but I didn't think I'd make it back from the bathroom just then, so I staggered back to bed.

I woke to Marie returning, and the crinkling sound of something in waxed paper. Likely supper. I was thirstier than before. "Marie, get me a glass of water."

Marie came into the bedroom with a glass. "I suppose I shouldn't have left that on the counter, should I?" she said, a condescending tone in her voice. She must have thought I'd poured it down the drain. I drank my water and asked for another.

"My goodness, Giraud, your skin is parched," she said.

It was. So dry it was scaly, even, in places.

"Come on," said Marie. "Let's get you back in the bath."

I was too weak to protest, or even to walk, and she gathered me up in her arms, lifted me up like a babe, and carried me to the tub. She brought more hot water and I soaked again. The doctor came by—the real doctor, not the crackpot—and looked at me with narrowed eyes.

"What's wrong with me, Doc?" I mumbled.

"I don't rightly know. Never seen anything like it." He turned to Marie. "You say his skin is getting worse?"

"Yes, even since this morning."

"Afraid there's nothing I can do."

The doctor left. Marie took me to bed, but I got thirsty so fast, she had to bring me back to the tub. She brought more hot water, but this time I found it too hot and made her bring a bucket of cold water to cool it down.

I drifted. Marie came in. "I went to see Doctor John, and he said to buy a lemon." She checked the water temperature. "Gosh, that's cold, I'll get a kettle going."

"It's fine," I mumbled. "No kettle …."

She went away again, and I drifted to sleep. When next I woke, I found my head under water. Someone was trying to drown me. Panic overtook me, and I thrashed about. My limbs weren't working the way they ought to, though, and I slumped down. The bathroom disappeared behind the water's swirling surface.

I wasn't drowning. I also realised there was no one in the bathroom with me. I was left to contemplate this some time before I heard the bathroom door open as if it were an echo through the water.

Marie's face appeared above the edge of the tub, wavering with the ripples in the water. She tilted her head to one side. "Poor thing," she said, her voice muffled. "I suppose now we know what Doctor John meant the lemon for."

VINCENT AND CHARLIE

Patrick Johanneson

Vincent hit the brakes, hard, and skidded to a stop.

"Huh," he said, staring out the windshield at the wounded land.

Every week or two, on his way into town or on his way home to the farmhouse, Vincent took a short detour to have a look at what he still thought of as *his* land. He'd sold the field to Roy Chambers a few years ago, when Irene was still alive. That land sale marked his official retirement from farming, but he still liked to check out the field.

He hadn't expected to see what looked like a long meteorite scar, a trench dug into the frozen earth. Black soil stood stark against the bright snow. Across the mile road, five of the trees in John Pachulak's windbreak had been sliced off low by whatever had crashed into his land. *Roy's* land. The trunks lay across the road, smouldering.

Vincent could remember planting those trees as a kid, ten or maybe eleven years old, working side-by-side with John and his brothers under the watchful eye of Ivan, the Pachulak family patriarch, kneeling in the turned earth, pushing birch saplings into the dirt and watering them, the merciless summer sun glaring down on them.

In the hazy distance, the low mountain rose from the plain, an improbable bulwark of stone deposited by glaciers in full retreat at the end of the last ice age. Clouds reared above it, heralding snow.

"Storm comin'," Vincent said aloud to no one in particular.

A wave of fear passed over him, a claustrophobic sensation of being trapped, a strange feeling in the wide-open prairie. After a second, it passed, leaving him with the sensation—the certainty—that someone needed help.

Someone in the trench.

✦

Vincent's balance wasn't what it used to be, so he clambered down, cautiously and slowly. A fading warmth came off the walls. He was already chest-deep in the ground, and the floor sloped downward.

Now that he was *in* the trench he could see what had surely dug it, and it didn't look the way he expected a meteorite would. Instead it resembled a giant silver egg embedded in the ground. As Vincent approached the thing, one hand on the earthen wall, he whispered a little prayer: "Lord Jesus, don't let this cave in on me."

A smell came to him, over and above the notes of turned earth and the sterility of the snow: roses—an impossible, impossibly sad whiff of roses.

He reached the egg. The trench walls rose up over his head now. He couldn't see the field anymore. There was only dirt to either side of him and a slice of white sky above. A tree root smouldered at waist height, thick as his thumb, sliced and cauterized by the thing's passage.

Above him in the world outside the trench the wind picked up, a gusting roar that came and went.

The egg was bigger than he'd initially thought. It stood taller than Vincent did, and he wasn't a small man.

Roses again.

Another surge of empathetic fear shivered through him. When it passed he found himself more certain that *someone* needed his help. Someone in this strange silver egg.

"You okay?" he said, not sure who he was asking.

He reached out a hand, hesitant, shaking a bit, to touch the shell of the egg.

(The *hull* of the *ship*.)

He wore no gloves, but it felt warm.

At his touch, a hole appeared in the shell of the egg, the silver material melting, puddling at his feet. He took a startled step back. The molten shell gathered like mercury shining with reflected sky. The hole grew.

The wind roared overhead.

When the hole was large enough to admit him, he entered the egg. A wave of scent, not roses now, more like Irene's orange pekoe tea, filled Vincent's nostrils.

"Hello?"

A momentary buzzing that reminded him of bees in summertime, one that he heard but also felt in his jaw.

Inside the egg was like a cavern, the walls rounded in an almost organic way. Wheat-seed lights winked on and off. A steady dim glow came from nowhere that he could see. In the centre of the cavern, he found a hammock, sort of: pale mesh that held someone in a complex harness.

The passenger, pilot, whatever, was small, skin and bones, with a head far too large for his body. Great black eyes gazed at him from a face grey as ash. Vincent tried his best not to count the fingers: three on each hand.

He did his best to concentrate instead on his, its, clothing: a tunic and skirt of dull yellow material that looked no thicker than silk.

How are you even still alive?

The pilot pawed at the harnesses, trying to unstrap himself. Those black eyes didn't appear to blink. The scent of roses came again. A flare of dark purple blotted out his vision for an instant, but then cleared.

A faint voice sounded in his head.

Help.

It sounded like it came from a long way off, a faded echo.

Those black eyes, imploring.

Vincent fished his jackknife from the pocket of his jeans. He'd sharpened it just this morning, or maybe yesterday.

Good timing, Vincent thought.

Aloud, he said: "Listen, Charlie, I sure hope I can cut those things."

If they were some kind of crazy science-fictional supermaterial, though, this rescue was doomed.

He put blade to strap. The material was stubborn, but with some elbow grease the knife would cut it.

As he sawed, Vincent said, "Hope you don't mind my calling you Charlie. Gotta call you *something*."

◆

Charlie was light, lighter than a child.

Bird bones. All hollow.

Vincent carried him out of the trench. He had to walk well past where he'd parked the truck before he was close enough to the surface to feel safe stepping out, what with Charlie's extra weight. Eventually, he made it back to the truck and set his burden down on the passenger seat. He hurried to the driver's side. When he started the truck, he turned the heat up to full. For a long moment he sat, rubbing his hands, staring out the windshield, trying to think.

"Are you cold, Charlie?"

A stink of sulfur, there and gone. Another wash of that fear that belonged to another.

Vincent looked over at his passenger. Those great dark eyes were open, staring up at nothing in particular, but his wide nostrils flared and contracted, and his shallow chest moved in rhythm with his breathing. At least he was still alive.

Vincent reached behind the truck's seat, found the ratty old pink blanket Irene always told him he should throw out, and draped it over Charlie's small form.

"Hope that helps," he said.

To the west, the mountain had vanished into lowering cloud: flurries incoming. The wind gusted hard enough to shake the truck, but then died down again.

Vincent's breath fogged in front of him. The fan was louder than the radio. The scent of roses filled the cab.

For a second he wondered where the clutch pedal had gone. With a little laugh he thought: *No, that was the old truck.* This one was an automatic.

He put the truck in gear, backed out onto the gravel road, and headed for home. The first snowflakes, small and hard, driven by a banshee wind, rattled against his windshield. He flicked on the wipers, trying to think what he would tell Irene.

✦

The car was gone.

Did she go to town?

For groceries, maybe. Vincent hoped she'd bring back fresh white bread, but lately all Irene bought was the multigrain stuff, bread made, in his considered opinion, with birdseed.

At least this would give him time to figure out how to explain all this to her.

Charlie fell from the sky. I saved him.

The wind had come up again, so he parked in the graveled yard next to the house. A blast of cold buffeted him as he opened his door. Snow, sharp on the wind, lashed his face, his bare hands. He pulled on gloves.

When he opened the passenger side door Charlie looked up at him, then slowly closed his eyes. Vincent hoped he wasn't dying.

"Stay with me, Charlie," he said.

A scent of stargazer lilies overwhelmed Vincent as he reached across to undo the passenger seatbelt.

"Stay with me."

Into the house. Charlie was light, so light. Bird bones indeed.

He laid Charlie down on the old brown chesterfield and those big black eyes opened again.

"You hungry?" Vincent said.

He mimed eating, wondering as he did it what Charlie might make of his motions.

"I have bread, cheese, probably some ham."

He went to the kitchen and returned with a serving tray: white bread, cubes of cheddar, slices of fried garlic sausage he'd found in the back of the fridge, round pucks of cucumber soaking in vinegar.

Charlie sat up on the chesterfield, old springs twanging underneath him. He picked up one of the slices of bread, sniffed it, tore a piece from it and tasted it. His face crinkled, but he chewed and swallowed. He tried the cheese and spat it out, sniffed but didn't taste the sausage, and ate every last cucumber and then drank down the vinegar. He looked up at Vincent, blinked those great dark eyes, and held out the bowl.

Vincent smelled skunkweed and flax flower.

"More of that?" he said.

Charlie looked at the bowl in his hands, then back at Vincent.

✦

He brought a chipped Snoopy coffee mug, a litre of white vinegar, and a half-empty bottle of cooking wine that had been in the cupboard long enough to have a coating of dust like a cape on its shoulders. He poured a cupful of vinegar and held it out to Charlie, who took it, sniffed it, drained it, and handed the mug back. Pink flashes flickered across Vincent's vision, little lightning strikes, heatless and without thunder. The room smelled of new leather. He poured more vinegar. When the vinegar was gone, he switched to the wine, which was dull red and smelled sour and sweet at the same time.

Charlie drank it all. When he'd finished the last mugful, he leaned back on the chesterfield and closed his eyes. Sleeping? Vincent couldn't tell.

Vincent left him to it. He washed his hands in the bathroom sink, then poured himself a half-cup of coffee in the kitchen. He sat down at the small breakfast table in the corner. From here he could still see Charlie, resting, sleeping, meditating, whatever you'd call it. The small kitchen window showed him a slice of darkening sky, against which he could just make out the skeletal black fingers of the willows in the back yard.

Stirring sugar into his coffee, he wondered what was keeping Irene.

The wind gusted, rattling the willows. He'd have to trim them, come spring, or hire someone to do it. They grew so fast. Hadn't he just had someone trim them last year? They were already scraping the shingles again.

✦

He jerked awake in the kitchen chair. His coffee had gone cold.

"Well," he said, "guess I might as well go to bed."

He poured the last of the coffee into the sink, dumped the grounds from the coffeemaker into the wet garbage pail in the porch, put the mug into the dishwasher, and started it running.

As he brushed his teeth, he listened to the wind howl outside, a beast loosed on the world. The willows scratched and scraped against the shingles. The house groaned and cracked. The window showed nothing but snow.

Charlie didn't stir as Vincent walked through the living room on his way to the master bedroom.

Vincent lay in bed, awake, for what felt an eternity.

✦

He woke up alone. The windows were dark. Irene's side of the bed was already cold. How long had she been up?

He reached out an arm, found his glasses, fumbled them onto his face. The clock read 5:55 A.M.

"Irene?" he said, but she didn't answer.

Maybe she was in the bathroom.

He rolled to his back and closed his eyes. Rainbow colours flared in the darkness of his skull, and he lay as still as he could, waiting for the migraine to start. He hadn't had one in decades, not since before he got married. Now would come the knife blade, prying open his skull, the jabbing pinpricks in the front of his brain.

But it never came.

He opened one eye, cautiously. The rainbows had dissipated.

He got up.

✦

In the living room, a small grey man, or maybe a child, sat on the chesterfield, watching Vincent with large black eyes.

"Are you real?" Vincent asked.

He received no response.

He expected to find a bouquet of roses on the dining-room table, but there was nothing.

Maybe Michael will know where Irene is.

He fished the address book out of the drawer by the phone and looked up his son's phone number.

778? What area code was that? He punched one, then the ten digits written in old ink in Irene's neat script.

The phone rang once, twice, three times.

"Muh?"

"Michael?"

"Dad?" The voice became more alert. "Is everything okay?"

"Yes. Just—have you seen your mother lately? Do you know where she is? I haven't seen her in—"

"Jesus Christ, Dad," Michael hissed. "It's four-thirty in the morning—"

"No, it's six-th—"

"Dad."

A pause, like Michael was marshaling his thoughts.

"I'm in Vancouver. You remember that, right? It's two hours earlier here."

"Of course I remember."

"Dad, Mom's not coming home. Remember? She—"
Vincent heard Michael take a shuddering breath.
"Dad, Mom died. Last year."
Vincent found he couldn't breathe. Memory crashed in: the hospital, the doctors, the nurse giving him a hug, the funeral home.
"Do you want me to come out there, Dad?"
"Michael—"
"I'll book a flight, Dad. I'll be there soon."

✦

He showered, then opened the door to let the steam clear. While he waited for the hot water to fill the sink, he caught a look at himself in the mirror. *When did I get so old?* Grey stubble, white hair. Hadn't he been thirty just last night?

He laughed, a little rueful bark, then started to shave.

A hazy blue sheen wavered over the mirror and vanished. He listened to the scrape of his razor mowing down stubble, hearing it with his ears and with his bones.

✦

The stuff in the dishwasher was clean and dry, still faintly warm. He put it away while the coffeemaker ran. He kept smelling roses but couldn't find any flowers in the house.

The news on the radio was about the storm. It had swept across most of the province overnight, from Thompson up in the north all the way down to places south of the US border. Half the roads in the south of the province were closed. Highway One was closed from the Ontario border to Saskatchewan.

The sun had come up, but the clouds hid it, letting through only a wan grey light. Snow blanketed the yard. Drifts stood thigh-high across the driveway. The pine trees lining the road were bowed and white.

"Huh," he said aloud. "That must've been a hell of a storm."

The car wasn't in the yard. Had Irene parked in the garage? He'd need the tractor to clean the yard, the driveway, and maybe even a bit of the road if the plow didn't come by soon.

The keys weren't where they belonged, hanging from their hook on the varnished pine KEYS plaque that Michael had made in high school shop class.

Shit.

He patted his pockets, looked in the junk drawer.

"Irene?" he said. "You seen the keys? The tractor keys?"

She didn't respond.

After a moment, he remembered again.

"Charlie?" he said, trying to keep from sobbing. "How about you? Know where my keys went?"

Keys.

He heard the word in his head, in his own voice, but he wasn't sure that he *thought* the word. If he didn't, though, where had it come from?

In the porch he put on his brown quilted under-jacket then pulled his old parka on overtop. In the parka's pocket he found what he was looking for: a key for a lock he no longer owned and the IH key for the tractor on a ring with a John Deere fob from Lord knew where. He smiled at the little irony.

He pulled on his old boots, a JETS toque with a missing pompom, and the padded ski gloves Michael had bought him for Christmas last year, or the year before, maybe? Things blurred together at Vincent's age.

The wind had died down, but the temperature had plummeted. It took his breath away as he stepped outside, even in the shelter of the covered deck. Snow had drifted onto the square concrete paving stones and he'd have to shovel them at some point. Right now, though, he wanted to get the tractor started.

✦

The plow went by on the mile road as he finished up the driveway. He waved to the plow driver, a middle-aged man whose name he felt sure he should remember.

He parked the tractor and then drove the truck to town. It was slow going.

First stop: the post office. Flyers, the hydro bill, and a missive from the MLA that he dropped, unread, into a recycling bin already half-full of missives from the MLA.

At the Solo store next door, he bought a loaf of white bread, a jar of peanut butter, and a jug of milk. He put the groceries on the floor of the truck.

"Shit," he said aloud.

He went back into Solo and found himself in the same aisle as the salad dressings and the ketchup. From the baffling variety of vinegars—red wine, balsamic, raspberry—he finally selected a couple of two-litre jugs of plain white vinegar.

He went through the same checkout. The girl's name tag read STARLA. He wondered if he knew her parents or, more likely, her grandparents. She chewed gum that smelled of cinnamon and wore perfume that smelled of coconut.

Back in the truck he let the engine run a while to warm it up. The sky above the store was bright and blue and cold. When the needle on the temperature gauge moved an increment off the C, he backed out onto the street then went up Main Street to the highway. He turned left and gunned it, got up to a hundred and two, and set the cruise control.

He turned two miles before his corner. Something made him want to check out the old fields, the ones he'd sold to Roy Chambers back when he'd retired from farming.

✦

Five missing trees. The felled trunks had burned away, leaving behind brittle charcoal bones. The storm winds had blown them to pieces, and the plow had scattered them from the road, spreading chunks of burnt wood in the ditches and even up onto the field.

The trench had been partly filled in by the storm so that it now looked like a shallow, soft ditch. Vincent wondered if the egg was still melting, down beneath the snow and the earth.

So Charlie is real. I'm not losing my mind.

◆

When he got home the light on the phone was blinking. He picked up the handset. MISSED CALL. 778-something. He tapped the HANDS-FREE button, then dialed his voice mail.

"Hi Dad." Michael's voice. "Okay, I'm booked on the ten A.M. flight. I get to Winnipeg at three-fifteen or so, and I've got a car booked. See you about suppertime, I guess." There was a pause. "I hope you're doing okay. Sorry I got uptight. Call if you need something. So, yeah. Suppertime, I guess. See you then." Another pause, then, "Loveyoudad," all in a rush.

Vincent rewound the message and listened again. He wrote *Michael suppertime* on the notepad next to the phone.

A sizzle of spices passed over his palate: cumin, ginger, something he couldn't name but thought he might have tasted once at a Moroccan restaurant when he'd visited Michael in Vancouver.

He caught sight of the chesterfield, through the door into the living room, and the small grey person sitting there. Charlie.

He thought of his field, flat, fallow, blanketed in thick snow. He thought of the trench, partly filled in with snow.

"I've got a question for you," he said. "I've got a *lot* of questions for you."

I understand, said a voice, one that that sounded in his mind, not in his ears.

First, I must say thank you.

Vincent grabbed one of the jugs of vinegar from the kitchen, then entered the living room.

Thank you, thank you, thank you.

A smell of lilacs accompanied Charlie's words.
Charlie sat on the chesterfield, watching him.
"You're—you're welcome," Vincent said.
Without you I would almost certainly be extinct.
"It was the right thing to do, helping you."
He poured vinegar into the Snoopy mug that was still on the coffee table, handed the mug to Charlie, and sat down next to him on the chesterfield.
"That *is* you, right? Speaking in my head like that?"
Yes. Those great black eyes blinked. *My language is not yours. But I can—I am able to manipulate your memories. Your kind's memories. I have learned to affect them. To speak.*
Charlie drained the mug of vinegar in a single long swallow.
When necessary, to hide myself.
Charlie opened the jug of vinegar and poured himself a fresh cup. Those hands were dexterous, probably more so than Vincent's hands, even if you discounted eight decades of use and the accumulated arthritic twinges.
"Psychic powers?"
No. Yes. In a manner of speaking. Your memories are—
A hesitation.
—a kind of energy. I can manipulate that energy.
"Huh." Vincent leaned back on the chesterfield. "What about the smells, the flowers? The little flashes of light, the rainbows? Is all that you, too?" *Or am I having a bunch of little strokes?* he thought, but chose not to say.
Vincent could see Charlie considering the question.
Your memories are—different. Their structures are unlike those of most members of your species. I have had difficulty in manipulating them.
A waft of strawberries accompanied the words, the thoughts. The memories, if Charlie was to be believed.
It has taken me some time to establish exactly how to speak to you with any consistency.

He spread his three-fingered hands in a gesture at once familiar and utterly alien.

Vincent nodded. "The doctors, they told me I've got—" He took a breath. "I've got the start of dementia. Mild, so far, but—" He shrugged. "Michael thinks I should be in a home."

Is this not a home?

"It's—Well, that's a story for another day. Never mind. It's not your problem."

Can you hear my thoughts? Vincent thought to himself.

He waited a moment. Charlie didn't reply, so he said, aloud: "Can you read my mind?"

I cannot. I can merely affect your memories. I am able to—make words—in your memories of the very recent past.

"Why are you here?"

Charlie waited a long moment before answering. *I am—lost. I suffered an incident. My boat lost its way, foundered, and I am here. Marooned.*

He blinked, long and slow, then continued. *I am not supposed to be here. Extended contact with your people is a—sin? Transgression? A breaking of the rules.*

"Will your people come looking for you?"

They may. It is doubtful. I have no contact with them.

Charlie drank some vinegar.

"That's sad."

It is our way. I am—You might say I am a fledgling. Finding my way.

"Will you—can you establish contact? Call for help?"

I cannot say for sure. I wish to try. I do not know what their response might be.

They sat in silence for a long moment. From the other room, Vincent could hear the *ticks* of the wall clock as it counted off seconds.

"What can I do to help?"

Charlie put a three-fingered hand on Vincent's. His flesh was dry and warm.

You have done so much for me already. It is I that owe you.

"It's the right thing," Vincent said. "You're supposed to help people. Aren't you?"

Charlie didn't say anything.

✦

The phone rang, and rang again. Vincent blinked, realized he was sitting on the chesterfield, and shook his head.

A third ring, then silence.

He wiped his eyes, trying to clear the gummy feeling from them then looked at his watch. A little after six P.M.

Wow, I didn't plan to sleep that long.

It had gone dark outside. The sky wasn't yet black, but a deep, dark shade of blue. An almost-full moon shone above the bluff of trees on the other side of the yard.

He managed to lever himself up from the sofa. Charlie watched him. Did he ever sleep? Maybe only when he's hurting. The vinegar jug had been emptied. Did he have to pee?

Vincent walked with a stiff gait to the phone. Sleeping sitting up didn't agree with him.

The call display said ROY C and the Chambers' phone number. The voicemail light blinked at him. Vincent dialed the number and listened to the message:

"Hey Vince, it's Roy. Listen, I just had a couple guys show up here askin' questions about the field and Packer's trees. Said somethin' might have come down yesterday, day before. They said a meteor, but I think there's more to it. Some kind of experimental plane, maybe? Anyways, they asked how to get to your place, and I—"

Someone knocked on the door, three quick raps. "Mr. Peloquin? May we have a word?"

His eye caught on the notepad: *Michael suppertime.* It was his writing but damn if he could remember writing it. *Still fuddled from having a nap, I guess.*

Three more raps on the door.

"Mr. Peloquin?"

Whoever it was used the English pronunciation, the *-quin* coming out like "Quinn", not the French version everyone around here would use, Vincent included, even though he spoke, at best, what they used to call Diefenbaker French.

Vincent pressed the phone's OFF button and set it down. He went into the porch and opened the door.

"Yes?" he said. "Can I help you?"

Two men stood outside, one on the stoop, the other behind him on the square concrete slabs of the covered deck. The one on the stoop said: "Good evening, Mr. Peloquin. My name is Mr. Jones, and this is my associate, Mr. Cooper. We have a few questions we'd like to ask, if you'd spare us the time."

"Uh," Vincent said.

"Thank you," Jones said, stepping forward, into the house. Vincent was forced to take a step back. Before he could say anything, both men were in the porch with him. They shed their overcoats. While they hung them on hooks, Vincent stepped into the house.

He glanced at Charlie.

Damn, he thought. *I think they're here for you. Hope you weren't lying about being able to hide yourself.*

Before he could stop himself, Vincent said: "Would you like some coffee?"

※

They sat around the big old dining-room table. The two strangers wore expensive-looking suits, Cooper in dark blue and Jones in dark grey. Jones did most of the talking, while Cooper spoke hardly at all, watching with cold blue eyes. He hardly seemed to blink.

"It's a long way from Winnipeg, out here," Jones said.

He had an easy smile and a facile, superficial charm that reminded Vincent of a shark. His smile affected only his lips; his eyes weren't at all involved.

"Further than you'd think," Jones continued. "Especially after a storm like that one. You know they closed the Number One for a while?"

"Yes," Vincent said. "I heard."

He took a sip of coffee. The other two had declined, Jones politely, Cooper with a small shake of his head.

Charlie, on the chesterfield, watched with calm black eyes. The two men hadn't seen him.

That whole memory-editing thing must be working, Vincent thought. Or else he didn't really exist; but if that was the case, what would bring these men here?

"The reason we're here, Mr. Peloquin"—Vincent resisted the urge to correct his pronunciation—"is to look into an incident affecting land that you once owned."

He held out a hand to Cooper, who handed over a tablet computer. As far as Vincent could see, it had no manufacturer's logo whatsoever.

"A meteorite." Jones turned on the tablet and opened the photo gallery app.

A long shot of a row of birch trees, all of a uniform height. Bright blue sky. A low mountain, dark in the distance. A gap in the windbreak.

"This is Mr. Pachulak's land, as seen from Mr. Chambers' land," Jones said.

Annoyingly, he pronounced *Pachulak* correctly.

He swiped the screen. A closer view, now, of the trees. The five stumps, charred and scarred.

Swipe: a view of the field, now.

"Mr. Chambers' field," Jones said.

In a thick blanket of snow, a shallow depression showed where Charlie's boat, as he had called it, had burrowed into the earth.

Vincent began, "I'm not sure what—"

"Have you been out to the field lately, Mr. Peloquin?"

"Lately?" He glanced into the living room at Charlie. "No."

Cooper, too, glanced into the living room, following Vincent's gaze. He looked back at Vincent. His manner wasn't charming; Vincent got the sense, from him, of explosive forces held barely in check.

"Hmmm." Jones swiped the tablet's screen again. "*Someone* was there today."

The tablet displayed a photo of tire tracks in the snow.

"It's hard to say there's a clear match—"

Swipe: a truck tire in close-up, brightly lit by a flash; Vincent suspected it was his, that they'd snapped the photo just before they'd knocked on his door.

"—but it certainly does *resemble* your tire tread."

"There are a lot of trucks in this neighbourhood," Vincent said.

"There are," Jones conceded.

"Drink a lot of vinegar, do you, Mr. Pelican?" Cooper said abruptly.

"It's Pel—"

"I don't care."

Cooper set a matte black case on the table. It had the general shape and size of a briefcase, but it looked like it could deflect a bullet. He pressed his thumb to a spot that, to Vincent's eye, looked no different from the rest of the case. The latches sprang open. From the case's interior he drew a shallow grey bowl, which he placed on his head, positioning it like a yarmulke or an archbishop's skullcap.

Then Cooper looked into the living room, right at Charlie. "Well, fuck," he said, and stood up.

Charlie's eyes, wide at the best of times, grew even wider. His hands moved in panicky ovals and figure eights.

Vincent started to stand, too. Jones turned to him.

"That would *not* be a good idea, Mr. Peloquin."

Help, Charlie said, in Vincent's mind.

"Is it the subject, Mr. Cooper?" Jones said, not taking his eyes off Vincent.

Cooper stalked into the living room. Charlie stood up from the chesterfield, still gesticulating.

"Got you now," Cooper growled.

He grabbed one of Charlie's bony arms with his left hand. He drew back his right, and Vincent was afraid that Cooper was going to punch Charlie, punch him and not stop.

Jones turned in his chair to face the living room. "*Is it,*" he said again, slowly, emphatically, "the *subject*, Mr. Cooper?"

"It is," Cooper said, sounding queerly subdued.

Help!

I want to, Vincent thought, but of course Charlie couldn't hear him. *But I don't know how.*

Jones said, "And you *have* it? In hand?"

"I do," Cooper said.

"No damage, Mr. Cooper."

"No. Of course not."

Cooper lowered his right hand. The tension went out of him. Vincent, in the dining room, let out a breath he hadn't known he'd been holding.

"Take it to the car."

Jones turned his gaze to Vincent. He wasn't smiling now.

"Understand that we could arrest you, Mr. Peloquin. Obstructing an agent of—well, obstruction of justice. But we won't."

His face twisted into a sneer, an expression that Vincent, even in the current situation, couldn't help but think was probably his default setting.

"Frankly, Mr. Peloquin, you're not worth the paperwork."

Cooper led Charlie out of the living room. Jones, meanwhile, reached into the briefcase for a small metal cylinder, brushed aluminum, rounded at the top.

"If you'd please focus on me, Mr. Peloquin," Jones said, "we can finish this up quickly and go our separate ways, mmm?"

"You have *got* to be joking," Vincent said.

It looked exactly like one of the memory erasers from the *Men in Black* movies. He remembered taking Michael to see it when Michael had been taking his degree at Brandon University. What were those things called in the movie? Oh, right.

"A neuralyzer?"

"Hmmm? Oh. Yes. Of course, we don't call it that, officially."

Absurdly, Jones' sneer melted into a smile, a genuine smile for once, warm and human. Not like a shark at all.

"I'm very sorry, Mr. Peloquin, but we—"

Cooper was passing Vincent's chair, still towing Charlie. His grip on Charlie's arm looked unbreakable. Those hands were fighter's hands, powerful, with big knuckles.

Help!

Vincent stuck out his foot. He caught Cooper right at the ankle. Something in his knee went *pop*, something felt more than heard.

Cooper stumbled, losing his grip on Charlie. The skullcap went forward off his head, landing with a clang on the ground.

"Fuck!" Cooper shouted.

Charlie scurried around the corner, into the kitchen, moving faster than Vincent would have imagined possible. As he passed the skullcap, he scooped it up in one three-fingered hand.

"*That*," Jones said, "was *spectacularly* ill-advised." All trace of a smile had vanished.

"I'm on it," Cooper said.

He rounded the corner into the kitchen, following Charlie. Vincent wondered if he could still see his quarry, or if he was following some other sense. Perhaps he was powered simply by rage.

After a moment, he returned, once more towing Charlie. He wore the grey skullcap again. He glowered at Vincent.

"I got it," he said to Jones. "We're good."

Thank you for trying, Charlie said to Vincent.

The others didn't seem to hear him. Perhaps the tuning he'd done to be able to speak in Vincent's memories had rendered him inaudible to merely normal minds.

"Take him in?" Jones said to Cooper. He motioned with his chin to indicate Vincent.

"You're the boss," Cooper said. "It's your call."

Jones nodded. "I'm letting you decide," he said. "He assaulted *you*, after all—not me."

Cooper considered, then shrugged.

"Fuck it. He's old. Soon enough he'll be dead. Wipe him and we'll go."

He dragged Charlie into the porch.

"All right." Jones turned to Vincent. "You're lucky. Well, if you choose to look at it that way. My associate is not usually so kind to those who get in his way."

He held up the silver cylinder and pressed something on its side with his thumb. It began to make a sound, a whine that rose quickly in pitch beyond what Vincent could hear. A red light began to wink at him, on off, on off.

"As I was saying, before your misguided attempt at heroics distracted us all: We of course cannot let you remember this."

"I've got dementia," Vincent said. "Give it time."

"Do you? My condolences."

"It's not—"

Jones thumbed another button, and everything went white.

◆

"Thank you for your hospitality, Mr. Peloquin," the stranger said.

He wore a grey wool coat over a dark blue suit. His breath puffed into vapour in the cold air.

"We will be in touch if we need any further information," the stranger went on.

"Sure," Vincent said, trying to remember what they'd been talking about.

"If you think of anything, anything at all"—he made a business card appear from an inner pocket and handed it to Vincent—"please do call."

"Sure."

The man got into the driver's seat of a glossy black sedan. Another man sat in the passenger seat, glowering. Vincent glanced at the card.

Adam Jones, Consultant

An email address and a phone number.

Out on the mile road, headlights marked the approach of another vehicle.

Rush hour, Vincent thought.

This new arrival slowed. Vincent could see its turn signal winking. Someone else coming to the farmhouse. It wasn't Irene's car; it was an SUV.

The black sedan drove slowly up the driveway, snow crunching under its tires. At the corner, it turned east. The SUV waited for it; the driveway was only wide enough for one vehicle at a time.

Thank you.

Vincent turned. A small grey man—

Charlie, some deep part of Vincent's mind said.

—stood looking at him.

When you tripped him, I had time to examine the hat he wore.

"Charlie?" he said.

I was able to disable certain devices in the hat. Enough that I was free to alter Cooper's memories, in addition to Jones.

"Who?" The names rang a bell, but he couldn't quite place them.

Cooper and Jones. Charlie gestured at the sedan's receding lights.

It came back to him all in a rush: the interrogation, the threats, the grey skullcap. Tripping Cooper.

"Oh," Vincent said.

The SUV turned into the driveway.

They have forgotten me, as thoroughly as they attempted to make you forget them.

"Why can *I* remember them? Why can I remember *you?*"

He remembered a white flash, a moment's disorientation.

Their device is tuned for normal memories. As we have discussed, yours are ... different.

"Dementia."

Yes.

The SUV stopped. Michael looked out the windshield at Vincent. His eyes passed over Charlie with no sign that he saw anything.

I must go now. Again, I thank you. With all that I have, I thank you. Never can I fully repay you.

Charlie turned and loped toward the bluff. He reached the first trees as Michael opened his SUV door.

"Dad?" he said. "Why are you out here without a coat?"

Vincent shrugged. "Waiting for you."

"God, I hope not. I planned to be here a lot sooner. They just reopened the Number One a couple hours ago."

"So I heard."

Michael nodded. "So who were those guys? In the car?"

Vincent looked toward the bluff. Charlie had vanished into the trees. Vincent wondered if he'd ever see him again.

"Dad?" Michael laid a hand on his shoulder. "You okay?"

"I think so."

"Who were those guys?"

"You wouldn't believe me if I told you."

Michael shook his head.

"C'mon, Dad," he said. "Let's go inside. We've got a lot to talk about."

"Yes," Vincent said, limping toward the house. His knee hurt. "Yes, we do."

Seven Long Years

Jennifer Collerone

If there's a word for the feeling between love and hate for your hometown, I don't know it. Every seven years I'm back in the prairie city where I was born, and nothing on Earth kills me more inside.

The skeletal trees rustle their branches overhead as cold wind presses against my cheeks. Soon they numb painfully—an oxymoron that suits this city just fine. I shouldn't be surprised it isn't happy to see me.

The rivers want revenge.

I fluff up my scarf and snuggle my nose further into the fabric. My feet crunch into the iced-over snow. The white stuff inches over and coats the inside rim of my boot liners. Damn it, that's cold. Nothing else has compared, no matter where I've gone. You'd think the city would be grateful for all I've done, but no. The houses seem to pull away from each other, so the gales pelt me harder. Even the streetlights refuse to light my way. Whatever. I'm almost there. The house I called home.

The house is large by today's standards, with a heavy bricked face and wide, wavy-glassed windows that distort the reflections from the street. Like eyes that can no longer see straight and only view the spaces beyond. When it was newer and I was young, I thought it was comforting. Now the wide-eyed stare only leaves an ache inside me that I can't quite place.

I push it to the back of my mind and try to work saliva into my mouth. Damn city is so dry. I can no longer tell if it's my body revolting against coming here, or if the rivers have somehow poisoned me too.

The veranda steps creak as I brush the snow off. It's not worth leaving a broom out here for seven years just for the one week I return. Each rotten tread bows under my weight, though I'm the lightest I've ever been. Not ideal for what I have to do, but I can't seem to eat much in the months prior to stepping foot in the city.

Rustling through the paper bag in my pocket, I draw the key out. It feels heavy. I jam it home and the lock clicks with a weary jerk. The door sways open on uneven hinges.

Smells of times past, of meals once eaten, of old, musty perfume, and the dusty odour of emptiness hit me with as much force as the wind had. Memories shouldn't hold as much weight as they do.

I sigh and regret it, since I only fall deeper into nostalgia. I close the door against the cold and pat my arms. Inside is cool, but comfortable. No point in heating a house for the dust and faded wallpaper. Shedding my jacket, I pass by my ghostly reflection in the hall mirror before parading past the front pages of newspapers pinned to the wall. 1997—*Child Kidnapping*. 2004—*Two Teens Play by River, One Missing*. 2011—*Local Man Drowns in Apparent Suicide*. 2018—*Coyote Sightings on the Rise*. I hold up the article I printed this morning and push a pin through. The printer paper doesn't have the same effect, but I can't bring myself to end the tradition. 2025—*Coldest Winter on Record*.

The light in the kitchen buzzes the same way it always has and illuminates the mint green cabinets and black and white subway tile. Mom wanted to change it, but I think grandma was right. This room is meant for vintage charm and happy baking.

"You are back." Whisp's voice floats through the silence, appearing out of nowhere like she does. "You did not call to me."

I drape myself onto a vinyl chair at the kitchen table and sigh. Then, after unwrapping my scarf, I let it hang on my shoulders. "It gets harder every time."

Her eyes appear from the dark back room, glowing as she slinks forward. The tick-tack of her claws on the linoleum sounds impossibly loud. She shakes herself and sits before me, her tongue lolling out of her mouth in a wild doggy smile. "True, but I am always happy to see you."

I nod. "You're the one good thing in this cold hell."

She huffs, as if laughing. "You lie to yourself well."

"Do you blame me?"

"Your pack needed you. And you came."

"At what price?"

Her eyes narrow. "We all do what must be done. I must hunt for food, though I do not enjoy taking a life."

I tilt my head. How often did she hunt? Like me, she seemed to age slowly, or not at all. It was hard to tell. I hadn't had a haircut since this entire process began. "You're no ordinary coyote, Whisp."

"You are no ordinary human. I do not befriend your kind often," she says with a touch of disdain and licks her ruff before training her golden eyes back on me. Once it was unnerving to have a wild animal stare at me, but now her presence is comforting.

"You win. As usual." I pluck the paper bag out of my jacket pocket and unwrap the meat from its packaging. Whisp knows she doesn't have to accompany me. But ever since the third time, she stays by my side. "I have filet mignon for you. The fifth time should be fancier than chicken giblets."

Her ears perk and her nose trembles. "I knew you had something. Fancy or not, it is welcome."

I set the paper down and flick the tape off my fingers. "Bon appétit."

Whisp needs no other encouragement to dig her snout into the meat. I set my phone on the table and tune into a local station. The crackle and old theme music stabs at my heart, but the house seems less empty when something is playing in the background. The coyote's teeth sluicing through the meat creates an odd rhythm with the voice of the radio announcer.

"Whisp, how long do you think we'll do this?"

She raises her proud head and licks her muzzle. "Until it is done."

"But why us?"

Whisp peers at me from under her furry brow. "Why not us? We do as we must."

I sigh. "You don't have to help."

"One does not leave a member of the pack behind, regardless of blood." She finishes the meat and licks the bits off her paws. "I protect what is mine."

I scratch the place behind her ear she always seems to miss. She leans into my hand and for a while we sit in the quiet as an old jazz tune hums along the edges of the kitchen.

We're only stalling the inevitable, but neither of us says anything for a long while.

◆

When you're a child, time stretches on like a road receding into the horizon. Waiting for a birthday or a meal at a restaurant becomes a test of patience. As a teen, the years pass with more purpose and the road doesn't feel so endless. Then, as an adult ... that's when time presses on with startling certainty, like you're careening far too fast with no brakes. Even if you're not ready for it. Even when the people you need stay behind. This inevitability is a piece of our humanity. It's what makes us who we are.

So, when that road disappears altogether, are you still human?

Whisp rubs her nose against my palm and brings me to. I've drifted off in her soft, speckled fur. I sit up and the kitchen draws itself into focus. The heaviness from earlier hangs over my heart. It's been so long since I've felt hope, and remembering my childhood brings memories of life passed rushing to the forefront. The linoleum is warm when I press myself up on sore knees. Whisp, while comfortable, is not a great pillow.

I massage my neck as she stretches—a perfect downward dog. With a yawn and a shake, she is up and fanning her tail from side to side.

"You should have woken me."

Whisp tilts her head, kind of a canine shrug. "Exhaustion causes errors. We learn to rest, lest we get run through by an antler."

I appreciate her caution, but the sooner we get this over with, the sooner I can spend the next year recovering. By year two, I'm shaky. Year three is better. Like a new normal. By the fourth year I've settled, but come the fifth the dread begins to creep along the edges of my life. Year six is desperate—trying to complete everything in case this is the time I don't make it out. I learned the third go around that I don't dare ignore the rivers' pull to return.

My grandfather's bright orange hunting gear hangs in the back room's closet as it always has. If I collapse, the colour will help someone find me amongst the snowbanks. As lovely a companion as Whisp is, I hardly expect her to drag my unconscious—or lifeless—body to the people she is so scared of. I step into the snow pants, fling the coat on, and slip the flapped hunting cap on my head. I cut my hair to the chin a long time ago and it still hasn't grown. As if I'm stopped in time.

Whisp sits peering out the window at the swirling snow beyond. Night has seeped into the corners of the houses, and the streetlights flicker as if they sense we're ready to move. "Well?" I offer the pony blanket I bought for her. She lifts her lip but bows her head.

I strap it on and she shudders. "I look like a common dog."

I smirk. "That's the point."

We move through the house together. I touch my fingers to my lips and press them to the third article. The one about Luca.

Local Man Drowns in Apparent Suicide.

It's not that simple. And no matter how hard this is, I must shoulder the burden. The rivers will take their due and paying it is my responsibility and mine alone. Because when I don't return … bad things happen.

Whisp and I leave the locked house and begin our trek. The moment we leave my property, the lights on the street flicker and plunge us into the true darkness of winter. Ice collects over my scarf and glues to my eyelashes. Each blink is hazed with white. I reach out a gloved hand to Whisp and she slips in beside me. It's become much easier to navigate to the rivers with her leading the way. While I can't see, Whisp was made for this.

Each step we fight against the wind and the snow that grows beneath my boots. Like sharp, cold quicksand that sucks at your feet when you walk. This is no normal snow. This is the city, the rivers, fighting me. But the city should be on my side. I'm the one that keeps it going when the world threatens to rip open, when the rivers threaten to swallow everyone whole.

"This what you want?" I ask the swirling wind and the streetlights above. Whisp tucks her ears against her skull, but adds nothing. Her acceptance softens my tone. "I give everything to save you. Is this my reward?"

The city doesn't answer. Maybe it's as scared of the rivers as I am. Maybe I'm not the champion it wants. But I swore fourteen years ago it wouldn't go through anyone else to find another.

We've walked a few blocks, but it exhausts me as if we've trudged all day. Under my hunting coat I'm sheened in sweat, but my limbs tingle with cold. A high-pitched whine hovers underneath the howls of the storm around us. We reach Main Street. Whisp pulls her lips back and snarls. Shudders rack my body.

And I step into summer.

✦

The light from the sun blinds me. Hazy flares bubble in my vision. Herbaceous cut grass and floral mock orange fill my nostrils until it makes me dizzy. Everything is too sharp, too perfect, and too undefined around the edges. The park and river come into focus in the centre of my vision like an old photograph, but seeped in tones and colours too saturated to be real. My hands are tiny; the small, rounded nails painted candy pink for my birthday. I'm seven. Finally. A big girl.

My friends are nearby, screaming with delight, playing TV tag. My brother Luca is it. Before he tags me I yell, "Simpsons!" We giggle, and he scampers off. Full of cake, I sit down beside Kimmy to admire the dandelions spotting the grass. A ring of trees surrounds the river. It's quiet and the pines look like they have secrets and treasures buried within their branches. The squeal of the wooden seesaw mixes with my friends' laughter. The wind waves the pines, so I return the gesture. Kimmy and I grin at each other.

I bite my lip and look towards the playground. Mom is chatting with Kimmy's mom while they keep an eye on everyone. We should ask if we can go look at the riverbank.

But I'm seven. I'm a big girl.

"Let's go!" I brush off my knobby knees and pull Kimmy to her feet. We skip to the first few pines. They smell like Christmas. And there are pinecones. Smiling, I pluck a long, tan one from the ground and play with the sticky sap on my fingers. They're fun to toss in the river and watch as they swirl away. Ahead, there's a pussy willow bush. Glancing back, I can still see the edge of the playground and Mom's head. The pussy willow isn't too far away. I can take a branch for mom because they remind her of great-grandma. She'll hug me and tell me I'm a big girl.

With a proud puff of my chest, I saunter over to the pussy willow. Kimmy darts further down the bank.

Everything is quiet except the rushing river.

The birds.

I can't hear the seesaw.

A puffy white cloud obscures the sun.

And a large man grabs Kimmy's wrist.

She tugs at it, but another wraps around her mouth before she can scream. My pinecones fall to the ground. I run to her and punch at the man's arms, but they whisk Kimmy away and I'm too small. He drags Kimmy from our mothers, me, crying and moaning in a way that has my heart plummeting to my feet. He's heading towards the river. I scramble to find a branch, a tree root to use as a weapon. Anything. Anything to keep her from going with him. But I can't. He's kidnapping her.

And I realize I'm not such a big girl after all.

✦

Whisp howls and I jolt. The cold slams into me like I've been hit by a driverless car. I can't see anything but darkness. Panic bubbles in my throat and a metallic tang coats my tongue. The frozen air pumps through my scarf to stab into my lungs. I bend over and command myself to slow down. I know what's happening, where I am. I'm not on the riverbank wondering if she was going to die, or worse. Luca saw us run off. He told Mom. She heard the splash and dragged Kimmy out of the river. The man let himself be taken by the current. I was back in Mom's arms within fifteen minutes, terrified. But to a child … time stretches on.

Whisp presses her nose into my hands. "It is over."

But far from done.

I stand on shaky knees. Turn on the heaters inside my gloves to bring warmth to blood that's run cold. I smooth my hands over Whisp's back and draw comfort from her solid presence. She looks no worse for wear. She never does. When I asked a long time ago, all she said was nature was cruel to those who showed weakness.

"Onwards." Whisp steps ahead, but allows me to catch up and grip the collar of her pony blanket. The storm has quieted for now. The hills of snow glitter under the full moon peeking through the clouds. The only sounds are our crunchy footsteps.

"What did you see?" I ask.

Whisp stares ahead, her eyes and ears trained on our path to the rivers. "Nothing your kind cares about." Her voice hardens.

I pause. If I press her, will she run off? I'm no longer sure if I can do this on my own. "We're the only ones who do this. Let me bear some of your burdens too."

She whines and does an odd side step, almost as if she's pacing while still moving forward.

"I see myself as a child watching my best friend get kidnapped and thrown into the river." Does she understand the concept? Whisp is fantastic, but she knows little about humans. "He took her away. He was going to hurt her."

She huffs, and plumes pour from her nose. "He removed her from your pack?"

"My brother saved us."

"A noble man."

It cuts deeper than I expect. I swallow the pain, but it simmers in my stomach. "Yes."

"I watch my first litter die again."

I stare, but no emotion shows in her face. "I'm sorry."

"It is done. I honour them every year with a kill. Humans are not the only beings who grieve."

The comment touches me. If I hadn't known Whisp, I wouldn't have given it much thought. My respect for her grows. "You're strong."

She tilts her head. "We must be, you and I."

I laugh a little though it's not funny. We really have no other choice.

Pouring forward, Whisp and I trudge down Main Street in relative silence. The world seems stopped in time, like Whisp and I are. There are no cars, no lights … nothing. Just the mournful sigh of wind that catches on the edges of snowdrifts to sculpt new ones in its wake. Our footprints disappear as soon as we make them. This part of the process isn't new, but it always confuses me. Where is everyone? Once, I asked Whisp and she seemed to misunderstand. The people were there. Couldn't I smell them?

We reach the halfway point: the corner where the two largest streets in the city meet. Here the skyscrapers stretch into the dark, clouded sky, their tops obscured by fog that drips down their sides. The windows multiply the effect, like curtains closing on a stage.

Whisp sniffs at the sky, her ears pivoting. The fog rolls down the buildings faster and faster as we edge towards the other end of the street. As we get closer, it turns to snow, falling in great sheets to the sidewalk and sending shockwaves of ice blasting towards us.

I scream over the roar, but Whisp's already in action, biting my coat arm and pulling me behind the large cement curbs that protect the sidewalks from cars that rush past. The snow slams into the barrier, rattling my teeth against one another. It flies over us in jet streams and crashes into the curb beyond. While that slows it some, it continues and shatters the windows of the building behind. The glass and snow are indistinguishable, and I can't tell what's louder—the snow against the curb beside me, or the building's curtain wall smashed into oblivion.

Everything stops.

The glass shards and ice suspend in the air with diamond-like clarity, shooting rainbows across the hills of white. They're mesmerizing, with their faded colours intermingling and shifting as Whisp and I rise from our hiding spot. She sits and howls.

The haunting call hovers over us. It's halted too.

And the world goes black.

✦

I follow Kimmy down the riverbank, my neon boots sliding along the newly fallen snow. Grass springs from under our footsteps, leaving streaks of green in our wake. It seems wrong somehow to defile the first snowfall, but Kimmy insisted. It had to be today.

My best friend is keeping something from me. While she hasn't said it, the truth is in the way her dark brows are set low over her eyes and how her petite frame descends in erratic hops.

The city is quiet this early in the morning. Geese call to one another as they leave for the season, but the sounds of rushing cars are far behind us. I slip on a buried root and Kimmy grabs my coat to right me.

"Careful."

That's more than she's said since the fevered raps against my window and her desperate whispers to hurry. "What's going on? My parents will freak if we're not back in time for school."

She turns, but looks right through me. "School?" She clamps her teeth along the side of her thumb. "What day is it?"

"Thursday?" This is weird. She's never been this absent-minded. I trot up beside her on the edge of the half-frozen water. It looks darker than normal. Almost sinister, like it's waiting for us to misstep. Her face falls and she drops her hand.

"It's fine. I'll be quick." She starts to rummage in her giant backpack for something.

"Okay, but what are we doing?"

"I didn't want to come alone."

"Obviously."

She shakes her head and grabs what seems like a random selection of items: a bunch of wheat; a bag of feathers she's been collecting for months; her diary; a paper bag that smells like rank fish; a small animal skull; and her treasure, a gold locket that has been passed down in her family for generations. I pull away from the rotting stench when she swings her armful towards me.

"What is all of this?"

"Just ... shhh ... did you bring the stuff I asked you to?"

I twist my lips in annoyance, but empty my pockets. She'd made me carry part of a Tyndall-stone brick, a coyote tail that came from her uncle's farm, pieces of pink-and-grey-spotted granite that we found by the handful our last summer of middle school, and seeds pilfered from my dad's plentiful collection.

"Why are—"

"Do you trust me?" she asks with such ferocity that I stop and gape. Kimmy isn't a serious person. She's carefree. Kind to a fault. Throw-your-responsibilities-to-the-wind. But never to the point of forgetting we had school. Or to being so intense that it shuts me up.

I nod. There isn't anything else to do. I can't leave her on the riverbank. It's dangerous. We shouldn't be here anyway.

"Good. Good." She says it more to herself than to me. One by one, she gathers her grab-bag assortment of items and lines them up.

"Kimmy—"

"Shh." She slides off her tiny boots, her socks.

"You're going to get hypothermia!" I try to hold her arm, but she wrenches away.

When she turns, her dark eyes are rimmed with tears. "Don't! Please." Her next breath is a shaky snivel. "I need you to be here for me, okay?"

I pat her back. "Okay." My hands feel weak, so I shove them into my empty pockets.

Kimmy steels herself and plunges both feet into the river. She squeaks as the water laps at her ankles.

I fiddle with a thread on my coat. This is crazy. There's no one nearby if I have to call for help. No houses I can drag her to. If something happens …

"I've brought you some stuff that you want."

I turn to her. "What?"

She glares at me, but the tears trailing down her cheeks and her teeth chattering take the edge off. "Not you."

How the hell was I supposed to know that?

"You want us to stop, right? We took everything and now we have to pay? But look, piece by piece, I can give it back." She picks up the wheat and plops it into the water. It gets swept away at a speed that makes the hairs on the back of my neck raise. That's the fastest current I've ever seen. The water begins to inch up her legs. Kimmy should not be in the water.

"This is crazy. You're going to get taken by the current."

She doesn't budge. Just grabs a few more items and sends them into the river as well. Wait. I glance at the bank. Did she really intend to throw her diary, the seeds … her necklace?

"You can't—"

"I know what I can't do. I've tried. I've tried so many times this week."

There's something weird about her. She's the same as she's always been. Blunt bangs, curls that dangle below her shoulders. An enviously small waist. I glance down. She's been getting shorter. Or, I guess, I'm taller. And wider, but not in a thick way. In an I'm-growing-out-of-the-kid-stage way. She looks similar to the way she did years ago. I thought she was just petite. My heart starts fluttering in my chest like a panicked bird. Something is very wrong.

"You need to get out of there." I dance from foot to foot, hesitating. The water moves faster now and Kimmy fights to stand upright. But she still places the items into the river. The stinky fish. The rocks. Each feather swirls on the surface before tipping into the water.

"I have to finish." She dumps seed pack after seed pack into the water and I cringe. Dad worked hard for those.

"Finish what? Dying in the river?" I grab for her, but she wades further. "Kimmy, stop!"

The current pushes against her legs, now knee deep. "Stop torturing me. I don't know what you want." She chucks the piece of Tyndall far into the centre of the river. It disappears without a splash. "I'll give you millions of things if you promise not to hurt anyone."

Confusion rattles through me, but this can't continue. I strip off my boots and socks, gasping when the cold snow melts against my feet and turns them pink. I roll up my pants. "I'm coming in."

"No!" She screeches, her eyes fixed on the water. "I didn't bring her for you. Don't punish her."

The water numbs my toes in an instant. My teeth grind together against the ice creeping in my veins. This isn't right, whatever she's doing. She shouldn't have to face it alone. I take two more steps. I'm almost to her.

A wave towers above us and crashes down on our heads.

All I remember is swirling water until nausea coats the back of my tongue and every limb is immobile. Or so cold and stiff that each inch of movement is a hard-won battle. Ice clings to my eyelashes, but they part. Bleary shapes fall into one another until my vision clears. My leg is stuck between two rocks and bent at a funny angle. There's no pain. It's too cold. The current pulls at me, but I can't go anywhere. The sound of rushing water flows in and out of my ears as I struggle to keep the black spots in my eyes from overcoming me.

"Kimmy?" I croak out. My throat feels like an ancient thing, brittle and dry. I scan for her, watching for her blue coat.

"Here!"

I crane my neck towards her shout. She's behind me, clinging to a tree root that has grown into the water. Her dark hair is tinged with frost and her lips are blue around chattering teeth.

"I'm coming." I can't be sure if I've said it loud enough. It's a chore to push myself upright and my head swims back and forth with the effort. My numb hands fumble as I tug on my leg. Am I moving fast or slow? I can't tell.

She's slipping. The tree root is slick with algae. I pull harder, but my ankle is jammed tight. We shouldn't have been here. I try again and again, my breath churning out great puffs into the air. The rocks shift, but tighten when I think my foot will be free. Instead, I turn to where Kimmy is dangling and stretch myself as far as I can.

She reaches for me. Her middle finger brushes mine.

"I'm stuck." My back cracks when I try for more length. "You'll have to swim."

She gives a frantic lunge for my hand and almost loses her grip on the root. "I can't. It's too fast."

"You can."

"The river doesn't want me to. I'm not strong enough."

I must have hit my head. That makes no sense. "You are. Reach."

The coyote tail sits next to me, wet and limp. Snatching it up, I prop my other foot onto a flat outcropping and push against my trapped ankle with everything I have. The tail gives me a few extra inches. She lunges again, grabs the tail, and tries to pull herself to me. Our hands brush. I grab her wrist, but she slips and plunges into the current. I can't tell if it's me screaming or her. The river carries her away. The last look on her face burns into my memory. Dark eyes wide with understanding, blue lips parted with fear, and the knowledge that we both share of her fate.

◆

Whisp's howl echoes into the distance and the glass falls to the ground in a sparkling waterfall, tinkling against the ice. My ankle throbs. Tears freeze to my cheeks. Kimmy never made it out. Minutes after she disappeared, the knowledge that she was gone hit me with as much force as the wave that dislodged us from the riverbank. It wasn't me realizing it. It was as if I knew for sure. Like someone whispered it in my ear, as if it were a disgusting secret. And that if I wanted to survive, if I wanted to get out, I'd give the voice what it wanted, or it'd sweep me along with her into a watery, tragic grave.

When the police dogs found me, I was fine, other than my broken ankle. The cold stayed away, but the sorrow and the fatigue didn't. They never found Kimmy. After my recovery, I convinced myself the voice was my imagination from almost freezing to death or survivor's guilt. But while everyone grew taller, I remained the same. I lopped my hair off at the chin and there it stayed. A dread grew inside me like I never knew. And the cycle started seven years later.

I rise, but my ankle twinges. I must have twisted it before I went under. "Whisp?"

"I am fine." She shakes herself. "This time, being run out of my home by fire."

I blink at her frankness, but her sharing with me helps ease the guilt I'm drowning under. "I went with my friend to the river. She never came out … she must have been doing this before me."

Whisp holds my gaze.

"She brought a tail that day."

Whisp says nothing, but dips her head once before sidling beside me.

"It's time for the hardest one of all."

She rubs her head on my leg. "We have survived before. We will again."

There's no choice. I'm bound to continue. For the river to feed itself enough on my memories for the city to live another seven years. The price we pay—the rent—for living here. Nothing on this Earth is free.

We move as a unit. Like a pack, we stand against the rivers until they remain dormant for the next cycle. One day I will break it. What's happening to me is unbelievable but real, so maybe somehow, once this is over, I will return to my time and everyone will be okay.

Where the rivers meet is hard to make out under the blankets of snow the ice storm has kicked up again. Whisp and I are covered head to toe, so that the bright orange of my coat is more of a soft peach. I draw in deep, frigid breaths so fast my head spins. Kimmy was right to say it was torture. And there's no cure for this type of mental anguish.

I look at Whisp, so poised and ready, so calm in the face of her deepest fears. She shows nothing but mild interest, even as her eyes are half shut against the wind. If it wasn't for her stalwart presence, I don't know how I'd be able to return to the city again and again. This time will be no different. I've relived the same memories over and over. The ones that are meant to break you. Those pieces of your life that are still so tender that you can't help but shove them in the furthest reaches of your mind. The ones you don't want to deal with; the ones that need the most attention.

"If this is our last, it has been an honour hunting with you." Whisp says, like she does every time.

"You brought me through." I shiver, not just with cold.

"You underestimate yourself."

I try and hold onto that thought as I pull my laser cutter out of my pocket. The beam heats the ice on the river and sizzles as it slices through. I make sure to cut the hole large enough for both Whisp and I to step in, but small enough that we can't be swept by the current. I pull off my layers of boots and socks and heaters and hope that this isn't the cycle where I freeze into the river and the silent city never wakes again.

"The hardest one of all." Whisp echoes my earlier statement.

I place a hand on the collar of her coat. The cold inches up my bare legs. We plunge in together.

✦

Mom and Luca try to convince me to return to the city for months. But I'm not coming back. I promised myself seven years ago. I deserve a normal life. Or as normal a life as a woman trapped in a fourteen-year-old body can lead. I'm a freak wherever I go, and I hate coming home and being reminded of how much everyone and everything has changed while I stay the same.

Luca begs me to return. I stop answering my phone. Ignoring news from home of boats sinking, the rivers eroding the banks as if they meant to eat the buildings residing there, is a matter of avoiding the TV and social media. The rivers are already pulling me back, I don't need Luca on my case too. I've relived my memories once already and I don't want to end up like Kimmy. Panicked, exhausted. Missing. What really will happen if I don't come back? This feeling of doom is anxiety, or catastrophic thinking, or whatever my new therapist says.

The phone rings. "Hey mom." I cradle the phone in between my shoulder and ear while dipping my watering can into pots of zinnia, sage, and dill. "Look, I told Luca I'm not coming home."

The pause is strange for my mom. As are the tears that follow. "Baby, I'm so sorry. Luca …"

My heart falls to my feet. Nothing makes my mom cry. Nothing. "What did Luca do?"

"Oh god … he drowned in the river."

The world stops as if the rivers can reach me here, all the way by the ocean to remind me I can't escape. Not really. My hands grow damp with sweat and a roaring in my ears brings everything back to focus. "No."

Mom continues on with details that mean nothing. No one knows why he went to the rivers. He suffered broken bones, but died of exposure. She is flying me in. She doesn't care for my excuses. I can stay with her. Can I please stay with her? It all rolls over me. Was it like Kimmy? Did Luca feel the need to bring things or did the rivers think they'd find their champion in my bloodline? No. It's a message.

I will always have to return.

The time between is a blur. The sights and sounds move at high speed around me. My suitcase at one point is heavy, but when I land and walk through the familiar terminal, it weighs nothing at all. No thoughts stick, just the empty, sick feeling deep inside that says it's my fault. That if I had come, Luca wouldn't be gone.

Mom meets me at the gate and wraps her arms around me. I try not to notice how grey her hair has turned or how she seems smaller.

"You look good," she tells me. But it's a lie. I look strange. Unnaturally young, impossibly old.

The ride home is silent. When we reach the house, I balk. There are too many memories here. I'm not prepared to add Luca to them. Mom pats my hand and we enter together instead. She turns to me and I can't help but see Luca's nose, and hints of the dimple he had in his left cheek. He'd use that to his advantage when he was little and—no. I don't want to think of it.

"Go upstairs and find something you'd like from his room. He'd want you to. I'll put tea on."

I pass the black and white subway-tiled kitchen and climb the stairs. The door to his room is ajar, as if Mom expects him to come home at any time. It creaks when I push through. Pieces of my brother's life jump out at me. His prized hockey gear piled in a corner. The model boat he built when he was ten, saying the real thing would be his someday. A sweater lying across the foot of the unmade bed where he threw it last. I don't want to move anything. I want to keep it like a museum display, with a notecard on the door saying, "Luca's Room, Don't Touch."

The stab comes quick and deep, and I bowl over when the grief washes over me. I sink to the ground, clutching at myself. The tears flow without a sound, but only because I'm crying so hard I can barely breathe. I lay my forehead to the carpet and smell my brother there too. There's a piece of paper under the bed, folded into a neat square. I slide it towards me.

If anyone finds this, know I love you. But these last months have left me with no choice. I see things I can't control and all of them memories that hurt too much. Why I've all of a sudden been bombarded by these is beyond me, but all I know is I have to find out what's going on. I will be stronger than this. It isn't suicide—it's to save us all.

My best, Luca

The tears don't stop for hours. My brother did what I've been charged with. He was cursed with my duty. And I lost him.

No one will shoulder this burden but me ever again. I will do this forever if it means I'll find a way to bring him, to bring Kimmy back, and restore me to my time.

✦

I gasp and slam my head on the ice. The cold has made my limbs stiff and sore, but my ice barrier holds. Whisp shakes herself off and trots onto the bank. I slide out and dive for my stuff. Shaking, crying, fumbling for heaters, my socks and boots. Damn it, damn it. Luca. I scream in my head, trying to take a page out of Whisp's coping techniques.

She curls up beside me. I wrap us both up tight and cuddle her for warmth. Her chest puffs in and out fast, though she isn't panting.

I run my gloves through her fur. "Are you okay?"

"Yes."

"And this time?"

"Is when I died."

I stop.

"I was drawn to the river too. After."

"After?" It's hard to breathe.

She nuzzles in closer. "You tried to save your friend with my tail."

"But, it was, you were …"

Whisp swishes her tail against my arm and tilts her head. A little bit of something lifts from my chest. Enough that I hold onto her tight.

A quiet clinking draws my attention. Gold twinkles against the ice and snow. I pluck it out of the water. A locket with a key on its chain lies frigid in my hand. I'd recognize the cursive *K* on its front anywhere. Kimmy. This was hers. And a key … I jolt. It's my house key. But I rustle in my pocket and pull out my key. Not mine. "Luca …"

The rivers try to break you so that you can't pay their fee. They keep you alive and feed on your memories knowing you're imperfect. That eventually you'll break and they'll move to another until someone figures out how to break the cycle, rather than perpetuate it.

I hold the locket and key close. Thinking of Kimmy and Luca keeps me strong. I will find a way to stop the rivers. To appease them and find the peace that I know lies somewhere below its dark and muddy surface. Whisp is my link to this city, the place that I both hate and love.

The city begins to crawl with life again. Waking from its slumber to find the crystalline snow unmarked, as if we had never been here, had never fought our demons so they could rest.

But some of us never get to sleep.

REASON 4,286

J. M. Sinclair

Joseph Amadeus Caleb was murdered by a woman named Shoelace on the morning before Christmas. It was an affair very business-like in its simplicity. Her knife went in. His blood went out. End of story. Maybe.

✦

The witch's assistant owned a stepladder. He was on the short side, and as the tools of his trade went, the stepladder was one of the most useful. Currently, it was propped in the snow against the side of a large dumpster. The final duty of every day's tasks—Christmas Eve included—was the disposal of the witch's kitchen scraps. As the assistant threw the first bag in, he found the body of Joseph Amadeus Caleb.

"Is that you shrieking?" shouted the witch, poking her head out of the seventh-storey window of her apartment.

"Um, yes, ma'am." The assistant was a terrible liar, so mostly he didn't try. "And, ma'am, I think you should come down here."

✦

The witch had a typewritten list of exactly four thousand three hundred sixty-nine distinct reasons why she felt it necessary to maintain the considerable expense of a qualified assistant. Dragging things of interest out of dumpsters was reason number four thousand two hundred eighty-six on that list. The witch's assistant liked neither corpses nor the insides of dumpsters, but after the witch's threat to withhold his New Year's bonus, he conceded and climbed into the dumpster, though not without considerable whimpering on his part. Fighting to not be overcome by the nausea-inducing stench, he pushed the corpse out.

The corpse landed on its head with a *thunk* before gravity took it from its headstand and it toppled over onto its back with an even heavier *thunk*. The witch, having only stated an aversion to dumpsters on her list but nothing about corpses, immediately knelt down beside it and began to rifle through the pockets of its clothing.

"You aren't robbing him, are you?" the assistant asked as he climbed out of the dumpster and made his way down the stepladder. He had accidently torn open several trash bags while inside, and from the knees down, his suit pants were damp with a mixture of lettuce slime, two-week-old gravy, and something he desperately hoped had once been berry-flavored yogurt. As he dismounted the lowest rung of the ladder, he decided that he would consider himself lucky if he managed to escape this episode without a skin rash or worse.

"It. A corpse is an *it*. Any inanimate object is an *it*. And no."

In the dumpster, there had been an unfamiliar coppery smell layered over the usual stench of rotting garbage. The assistant had also noticed that the outside of the corpse's hunter-green parka was stained with blotches of something that looked reddish-black in the evening light, but only when the witch unzipped the parka, to reveal a wash of red soaked into the dead man's white shirt and a second wave of the coppery smell, did the assistant fully understand. He reached out and leaned against the dumpster to steady himself. By now he should have been on the bus, halfway home to his own apartment in North Kildonan. But instead, Christmas Eve was quickly turning into the worst overtime of his career.

Ignoring the blood, the witch found a black leather wallet in the inner pocket of the parka and began to empty it, laying the contents out onto the dirty snow of the alley piece by piece with the deliberation of a fortune teller performing a tarot spread.

"Then what are you doing, ma'am?" the assistant asked.

He buried his face in his wool scarf, but he couldn't escape the smell. It was already in his clothes. He wondered if any drycleaners nearby were open.

"Looking for clues," she said. "Somebody might be offering a finder's reward."

The assistant was not entirely convinced. He crept out to the mouth of the alley to check for any passersby who might have heard the commotion. Normally the avenue would have still been busy with shoppers visiting the boutiques and cafés, and even the occasional patrolling police officer, but tonight everything had closed early. Even the 24-hour pizza delivery had extinguished its neon welcome sign. The street was empty except for a lone parked car that had already collected a half-inch of fresh snow.

On any other occasion, the assistant would have found the incongruity of a Winnipeg street so devoid of movement and life mesmerizing, but this time it was eerie. The streetlamps, augmented by the Christmas lights strung between them, cast strange patterns of shadows and multi-coloured reflections on the snow.

The assistant took off one of his mittens—wet and dirty with blood and garbage—to pull out his cellphone. "Wouldn't calling the police be easier?" he asked. "I mean, aren't they the professionals when it comes to things like this?"

"No! It's exactly because the police are the *professionals* that it's better to handle this privately. If they got involved, who do you think would be collecting the reward money?"

The witch's assistant put his cellphone away. He was about to say something on how he didn't think the police worked like that, but then he thought better of it. Every April when it came time to renew his employment contract with her, the witch made him read and initial each item on her list of reasons why she employed him, so he knew that pointing out the errors in her logic wasn't one of them.

"So you've got his driver's licence or something?" he asked.

The witch pulled a final card from the wallet and placed it on the snow beside the others. Then she put the wallet down in front of her folded knees. "No licence. No social insurance card. No student ID. If they were ever here to begin with, they have been taken, and the same can be said about credit cards and cash." She sounded disappointed about the money.

The assistant walked over to his employer to get a better look at what had been left behind. Some of the cards were plastic, but those that had been printed on cardstock had soaked up varying degrees of blood along their edges. None carried their now deceased owner's name. "So what do we know about him?"

"Well," she said, hovering a hand of violet-lacquered fingernails over a Celtic cross of used bus passes and frequent shopper stamp cards, "There really isn't much left, but if the cards are to be believed, our mystery corpse was probably rather dull in life and something of a cheapskate."

"I ... am ... not ... a ... cheapskate," said the corpse. He had to struggle to push each gurgling word out.

"Hey! I think it—*he*—is talking!" shouted the assistant. He pulled the dead man up into a seated position with his back leaning against the dumpster.

The witch scooped up the cards and shoved them back into the wallet all at once. Then she stood up and brushed the snow from the hem of her knee-length skirt. The assistant had donned a coat along with boots, a scarf, mittens, and earmuffs, but she hadn't bothered with warm clothes or even socks and shoes.

"Why ... can't I move anything ... but my mouth?" asked the corpse, and then to emphasize his point, demonstrated with a poorly executed series of grins, snarls, and frowns. He was missing his top right canine and he looked surprised when his tongue found the gap in his smile.

"You're dead," said the witch.

"No, I'm not."

"Or at least you should be." She pressed two fingers against his neck. "No pulse, no life. That's the rule."

"I thought I dreamt it." The corpse still struggled to speak, but the speed and clarity of his words was improving.

"Dreamt what?" asked the assistant as he looked surreptitiously for the lost tooth in the snow. He hoped that the tooth had fallen out prior to their acquaintance in the dumpster.

"Dying. Is the crick in my neck part of being dead too?"

"Sorry, that may have been me. Do you know how you died?"

"The blood isn't a hint? Obviously, it was the hole in his chest," said the witch.

"There's no hole in my chest!"

The witch pointed at the wound and at the blood on his clothes.

Joseph Amadeus Caleb touched it with his hand. "Oh. That hole," he said mournfully, "Yeah. I guess you're right after all. Hey! I can move my hand now!" He was right, but only technically. His right hand, and the whole arm with it, jerked and flopped like the arm of a poorly manipulated marionette. The left arm remained limp.

"Well that's something," muttered the witch. She offered the wallet back to the dead man, but when he couldn't close his fingers tightly enough to hold onto it, she gave up and put it back into his pocket herself.

"Do you have a name? Perhaps a message we should be taking to a wealthy relative?" she inquired.

"I'm Joseph Amadeus Caleb, but I go by Jac. No K. Get it?" He started to laugh at his own joke, bringing up fresh blood from his wound.

The assistant forced a sympathetic chuckle. He felt queasy all over again. "Clever."

"And the wealthy relative?" repeated the witch.

"Any idea how I got to be, well, not dead?" asked Jac.

"Stuff happens in dumpsters sometimes."

The assistant bit his lip nervously. Several gallons of unsold potions had expired on the winter solstice. Under the witch's direct orders, he had thrown them in the dumpster rather than calling a hazardous-waste specialist to pick them up. Although the assistant had never heard of anyone actually being fined for improper disposal of potions, it was technically less than legal.

"So you were murdered?" asked the assistant.

"It's coming back to me, but I still don't remember much of it." Jac was focused on his hands as he spoke. The more he tried to move them, the more fine motor control seemed to return. He had even managed to get some movement in his left wrist. "I think her name was Shoelace though."

The witch raised an eyebrow. "And I thought the sewer demons had some strange names. This Shoestring is your killer?"

Jac nodded. "*Shoelace.* Yeah. I think so. And you know, I'd like to be alive again, not just pretend-alive without a pulse."

"It's as if you need the services of a professional witch," said the witch.

"Yeah! That sounds about right. I hear they can do a lot these days." He tried to grin. "Do you happen to know one?"

The witch flashed her assistant a look. Then turning her attention back to Jac, she smiled, and using her best trust-me-I'm-a-professional-voice she said, "As your luck would have it, I happen to be a witch for hire."

"That is lucky. You any good?" asked Jac.

The witch's smile broadened. "I am."

In the four years he had been in her employment, the assistant had seen the witch perform many healings, even once growing a functioning wooden hand from the branch of an elm tree. She was a legitimate talent, but this task, however, seemed above even her skill level.

The assistant turned away from Jac towards the witch and used his hand to block his mouth from Jac's line of sight. "Do you think you could make him really alive again?" he whispered.

"Yeah," piped in Jac, "how about it?"

"Maybe," said the witch, "but it's a big job and pricey too." She seemed to be speaking equally to Jac, her assistant, and to no one in particular. She waved her hands as if casting off the idea. "We'll settle that later. First things first, you need to find this Shoestring and bring her to me. And I'd hurry up if I were you. There's no telling how long this is going to last."

"*Shoelace*," said Jac and the assistant in unison.

"Yes. Her."

"Well then, I guess I better mosey," said Jac. With a single, jerking movement, he swung the weight of his upper body forward and a little to the left so that his hands were both on the snow in front of him. Then he began a series of wriggling motions that ended with him on hands and knees. "A little help please."

The assistant stepped forward, took him by the hands, and pulled him to his feet. Then, because the dead man looked like he would immediately topple over again, the assistant let Jac put his arm over his shoulder. Being the taller and wider of the pair, Jac's unsteady stance also became the assistant's. If it weren't for the blood and garbage staining their clothes, standing together in the downtown alley swaying, they could have been mistaken for two drunks coming home from a Christmas party.

"Thanks," said Jac.

Jac and the assistant took their first jerky start-stop steps away from the dumpster and towards the mouth of the alley. By the seventh step, they were halfway to the street.

"How are you managing?" asked the assistant. He was afraid to let go.

"Maybe I should try it alone."

The assistant let go and retreated a few steps. The dead man swayed unsteadily on his feet. The assistant was about to rush back in to help, but the witch put her hand on his shoulder and held him back.

Still swaying, Jac lifted his right leg experimentally and then lowered it. He had limited use of his knee, so it was more a kick than a step. Then he kicked the air again and shifted his weight forward with the footfall. He remained standing. Jac and the assistant beamed at each other.

Jac took another step followed by three more in immediate succession. "Hey! This isn't so bad after all!" When he completed the walk to the mouth of the alley, he stopped and turned his head to look at the witch and the assistant. "Thanks, guys! I'll be seeing you again later!" he shouted.

The assistant waved and shouted back, "Good luck! Merry Christmas!"

The witch said nothing.

With all the rigidness and awkwardness of an inebriated soldier performing a marching drill, Jac resumed his walk, made a ninety-degree turn, and disappeared from view behind the apartment building.

The assistant followed to the mouth of the alley and peered around the building. Jac had made it past the front steps of the witch's apartment building and was almost past the parked car as well. His gait was even gathering speed in spite of its continued stiffness.

"How is he supposed to even find her?" asked the assistant.

The witch didn't answer. She had stayed in the alley and was leaning against the red-brown brick of the building.

"Do you think he really has a chance?"

"Nope."

Another *thunk* as Jac belly-flopped onto the sidewalk.

"See?" the witch said.

The assistant tried to sound casual. "Hey, Jac, are you OK?"

No answer. Not even a twitch.

"Jac? Jac!"

The witch shooed her employee with one hand. "You might as well go over there and make sure that it is really gone for good this time."

The assistant ran to the dead man, and kneeling down beside him, rolled him onto his back. Jac's brown eyes were open, but vacant. Very dead, he looked up towards the sky and at nothing in particular.

"He's dead again!"

"Technically it was never not dead," the witch said as she approached.

In the darkened shop window across the street from where Jac had fallen, Santa-hatted mannequins posed beside an artificial Christmas tree. "You don't seem very bothered by this," the assistant said.

"Why should I be? By keeling over again, it did me a favour. Unintended necromancy? My stomach knots just thinking of the potential ramifications. If news ever got out, the health code violations alone would get my licence revoked like that!" She snapped her fingers on the last word.

"Besides," she continued, her hands now moving in a way that alluded to esoteric arithmetic, "it was obvious he only had maybe five minutes left. Six tops."

Gently, the witch's assistant closed Jac's eyelids. The dead man's skin felt much colder and stiffer than it had when he was in the dumpster. The mottled purple of rigor mortis was beginning to bloom across one cheek.

The assistant's voice was quieter now. "Then why lie to him? It seems cruel."

The witch sighed deeply with her whole body. "Everyone deserves a chance, or at least to think that they have a chance. Even the people that aren't people anymore."

The witch bent down and taking the dead man by the hand, casually walked back into the alley with him dragging behind her. Then with an equal effortlessness, she picked him up and tipped him over the edge of the dumpster.

Although most of the snow in the alley was either compacted or dirty, the witch found a handful that was still an unmarred white. The far-off stare of impending magic filled her eyes; it was not completely unlike the emptiness of Jac's own eyes at the end. With a single breath, the witch blew the snow from her hand and it became a whirlwind. It grew, every snowflake multiplying countless times until the swirling cone of snow was two storeys tall. It swept through the alley and into the avenue, glittering with all the reflected colours of the Christmas lights hung along the streetlamps, and covering all the tracks and bloodstains with a new layer of snow. When the whirlwind dispersed at last, it was as if Jac had never existed at all.

"I'm going back inside," she said, "It's cold out here."

ALL THAT COLD, ALL THAT DARK

Keith Cadieux

My uncle Laird lives on a cot in a small wooden shed right where the forest starts, out of view of our house. He works on and off as a trapper. He either hunkers down in that shed, barely ever coming out or he's gone wandering through the bush for months at a time. My mother hates that he's there at all. She still looks at him side-eyed most times, but my father insists that it's a good thing to keep him around. My mother isn't the only one scared of Laird, he says, and that's a good thing out here.

He drinks and keeps to himself mostly. I can hear him snoring or cursing at nothing in particular if I get close enough to the shed, but I tend to keep a good distance away. Sometimes he surprises me, though. I like to wander away from the homestead and into the bush and I used to have a dog that came with me, but it stopped coming back to the house, probably caught in a trap or eaten by wolves or something, my father said. I was a good way from the house when I saw an old lady out in the trees. Her skin was wrinkled deep and brown, but her hair was black like it belonged to someone much younger. I jumped at first, but she didn't really scare me. She didn't come any closer but started talking in words I didn't know. They were just sounds, something like "wiiii-teee-go." That was the clearest I could make out. She made motions toward her mouth, like she wanted to eat, and then she pointed at something past me. Then a loud rifle shot hit a tree nearby and I spun round and seen uncle Laird and my father tearing through the woods at us. When I looked back to the old woman she was almost gone, a good distance away in the trees. She was fast.

Sometime later, I was still thinking about her, all alone out there. When no one was looking I grabbed a loaf of bread from beside the oven, hoping my mother wasn't counting them, and headed back out to the same spot. But I couldn't find her. After a few hours, I snuck a bite or two of the bread. I wandered a little further. Then I heard uncle Laird call out to me.

"Girl," he said. It made me stop cold, my mouth full, and when I did turn he was leaning against a tree behind me. He's a big man, but I'd gone right past him without knowing it.

"Shouldn't have come out here by yourself," he said. "What you going after?"

"Just looking for the dog," I said, trying to think fast.

"Mutt's not coming back," Laird said. "Don't know what you might find out here instead." He walked deeper into the trees and I ran home. I'd eaten the whole loaf of bread by then anyhow.

There was one other time my uncle went off on his own like that. Came back in the dead of night, tied up. Men on horses paid by the Hudson's Bay Company had been marching him for days, they said. I was supposed to be asleep, but they was yelling so loud I heard it all. They wanted money, otherwise the company was going to turn him over to the Cree, who'd be more than happy to deal with him. Had to give them something to make up for the mess he'd caused when my father settled the land, they said. The men left once they were paid, and it took my father a good hour of cutting and pulling to get uncle Laird untied. He was never allowed in the house after that, but he seems content enough in the shed.

We've had to rely on uncle Laird more and more these last months, though. The fall has been cold, and my father is sick. At first he needed lots of sleep, so much sleep, but now he can barely stand. As the leaves changed to snow, I seen him getting thin like grass, his clothes growing empty around him.

I come around the house with water from the well and see Laird and my mother talking. They never talk, not to each other.

Information is always passed to my father and then on to them. I couldn't hear at first, except one word Laird says: "consumption."

My mother smacks it clean out of his mouth. "Don't you say that to me," she says through her teeth.

I stop where I am, out of sight. They're too preoccupied to notice me.

"You're not taking my baby girl out there in the bush with you," she says.

"She's no baby, and there's no choice left now," Laird says. "I know I won't talk you into leaving him. He's my brother and I love him, but I'm not about to sit here and watch his end. He might be the end of all of us."

"He's a strong man. You saw how he managed here, even without you. He kept all that violence away from our door for years before you turned up," my mother says.

"He can't no longer talk, even," Laird says. "That bed is the end for him. You think his soul going to rest if he knows he brung her down into the dark with him?" He points, as though at me, though neither know I am near enough to hear them. My mother stays quiet now. After a moment she sits on the ground, skirt and apron right in the snow.

"It will be three months, maybe four if the winter stays hard. But she'll learn the land nearby. And you'll need the money by the time we get back. For the arrangements."

"He might get better in three months," my mother says. She stands and storms into the house.

Uncle Laird looks at the ground. "I don't think that's so," he says.

Things turn worse that night. Uncle Laird is allowed in the house, but he doesn't sit the whole time. He brings great piles of supplies outside and packs them on a small sledge. My mother brings food to my father's bed but comes back with a full bowl of thin, now cold soup. She won't let me in the room. She sets out a much bigger meal for me. Bread, some of the hard cheese I like, sausage and dried beef, which we'd normally be saving until late in the winter. And some of the soup she'd tried to get my father to stomach.

After a while she pulls the plate away from me.

"You have to learn to control your appetite sometime. You're like a dog that eats itself sick. You won't survive out there if you keep on like that." She looks ashamed of herself for having mentioned the trip aloud. No one tells me any more than what I overheard.

Late that night my mother flops down beside my bed in the dark. She has a great bundle of cloths and rags.

"I wasn't joking about your appetite. When you're out there on the land you're going to have to control yourself."

She has no candle or lantern, but I can just make out the grim expression on her face. "I know it hasn't come yet, but chances are your blood will start sometime while you're out there. It's not anything to worry about, but you'll have to be careful. I don't know that you'll get to clean anything once you leave, so take these cloths and if you have to leave them, just slip them away out of sight, deep in the snow even, so nothing comes sniffing around. And don't you tell your uncle Laird. He isn't the sort you want knowing about your womanhood." She stands. "This is your last night in a bed, so sleep. And pray for your father."

The morning comes fast, and we're gone before the dark is all the way gone. We don't say goodbye. My uncle's route goes through two territories and will take us out of Upper Canada and across into Rupert's Land; we're going to clean out traps along the way and eventually we'll meet the fur traders and local tribes at an outpost where two rivers run into each other. Laird has packed the sledge with blankets, snowshoes, a tent, his rifle, some food. As we start out, we have a few fresh things, cold meat and cheese, but also hard biscuits, dried fish, shrivelled apples. Things that keep for a long time. Survival provisions, he calls them. We're going to be hunting all along the way, he says, so we shouldn't need all that. But just in case.

The first night out isn't so bad, but I barely keep awake long enough to eat. Laird makes the camp by himself while I sit in the snow. He sets me in front of the fire and soon I'm asleep with a plate of fried bread and bacon in my hands. He leads me to the tent and lays me down on top of the nettles and boughs he's made into a bed. A little later I wake up as he comes in and lies down. It's a tight fit for the both of us. "Once the nights turn really cold," he says, "you'll be glad for the closeness."

It takes more than a week to reach the start of uncle Laird's trap route and two more days after that before the first trap. It's empty but he's not worrying about that. Over that time we manage to kill two rabbits and a duck. All of them we roast and eat rather than save. He shows me how to hold the rifle properly, where it's supposed to touch my shoulder. I pull the trigger. There's a click but no bullet, and he yanks the gun from my hands. "Your mother would never forgive me if I bring her back a killer," he says.

I try to head off into the trees. "Where you going?" he asks.

I stammer for a breath. "I have to make water," I say.

He makes a face but doesn't say anything more. I press far enough into the trees that I can't see him and pull the cloths up from my pants. No blood yet. I wad the fabric back between my legs and wonder if I'll be able to tell some other way than looking for blood on the rags. Uncle Laird stares at me as I walk back to him. He holds still a while and then spits on the ground.

"Let's keep on," he says.

The travelling is getting easier. I'm still tired something awful, but now I look forward to the dark, the dim warmth from the fire, the quiet. Most nights, after our suppers, Laird starts drooping and heads for the tent. A few times he's come back out, trying to get me to turn in too but he mainly just falls right to sleep. The night is a thing just for me and I like being lonesome for a while. The cold does more for me than sleep. I wait until the fire dies down, until the embers lose all their heat and go black. Once my eyes get used to all that dark I look up at the sky. Every night, it's like seeing the stars for the first time.

I never had much thought for faraway places or the big things around us. Like the whole of the world, everyone and everything in it. And even further than that, there are things past the earth itself, the heavens, the sun. The empty sky. And the stars. This is what comes to mind in the night out here. This is true dark, like nothing else. I sit in the cold and look up at the sky, to the far fires that have been there forever. I think, wonder, if there are fires up there that have burned out. Like the old kingdoms before Gods came to earth, before the earth even was. Right now, I feel certain that once there was only dark.

My father used to tell me stories, ones that he said his father used to tell him and Laird. But no matter what story he told, there was always ones that came before it. Stories about the sky and the heavens and the earth and God and all the other Gods before him and our very special place in all of it. Stories that it seems like people have been telling themselves for a long, long time. And under the stars, I try to imagine the stories that came even before those. How far back before the first story? And then the time before the first story. And the stars, were they there when the first story came to be? That first story that has winked out and gone back to dark. But those stars, up there, staying just the same. Unaffected by our stories.

And on this night when I look, there is blood on the rags. Quite a lot. With Laird asleep I don't have to move far off, but it's hard to pull them soiled cloths out of my pants and try to shove down more without tumbling over. I rub some snow on myself to try to clean some of the blood away. It's hard to see in the night but it looks more black than red. Then I dig a few inches down, lay the bloody fabric down and cover it over. I shiver as I sit back down, cold and wet, wishing to have the fire back. Soon I make my way to the tent and huddle into the warm bulk of uncle Laird. I wish he wasn't right about being glad for the closeness.

Weeks more of checking traps and still nothing to show for it. Some of them are untouched, old bait still there but some are sprung, lying empty. Uncle Laird is trying to make like he's not bothered, but he's not shrugging it off anymore. He starts being more careful with our supplies. We're burning through them too fast and the weather is starting to turn cold. Real, true cold.

The days are long with walking and dullness. I'm hungry most of the day now because we're sparing the food. Laird tries to pass the time by talking, usually about nothing much in particular. "It's good to keep talking when you're in the bush," he says. "Keeps bears away because they spook easy. Not so much in wintertime, though. When they're hibernating."

"What was the name of that dog you had?" he asks.

"What dog?"

"The one you went after by yourself in the woods." He stops and turns to face me. I try to take a step, but he won't let me by.

"I don't remember," I say.

"You weren't going after that mutt. He'd been gone for ages already. What were you doing out there? It's just you and me. No need for quiet now."

"That woman I saw. That you and father chased away." Laird looks at the ground quick and then meets my eye again. "Did she get away?"

"Me and your dad didn't get her, if that's what you mean. But it's hard land for someone out there all alone."

"Did you know her?"

"I know about her people. You remember when those men brought me back to the house? All tied up?"

I say nothing for a while, but he doesn't keep talking or walking so I nod yes.

"A few stragglers from one of the tribes kept coming back, poking around the land. I had to run them off. They weren't scared enough of just your father to leave for good." He turns and begins to walk again. "Where all the rest went, I don't know. Don't seem to matter none. Though looks like there are still some won't leave the place be."

There is a long quiet before he speaks again. I think he doesn't like the quiet. "She said something to you, didn't she?"

"Words I didn't know," I say.

"Wendigo," Laird says.

"That's not what it sounded like."

"I told you I knew about her people. She said wendigo." I've learned there's not much use in arguing with men like my father or Laird. "You ever hear what a wendigo is?" he asks. "It's an old story from these parts. Different tribes tell it all the same, mostly. It's a hungry spirit that eats people lost in the woods. It has antlers like a stag. Stands taller than three or four men put together. Deadly thin. Every time a wendigo eats it stretches even taller, longer, so that it's always gaunt and thin. Starving forever."

"Why would she say that to me?"

"Maybe she wasn't saying it to you. It's just a story anyway."

It's hard to keep track of the days out here. They all bleed into each other. It's been more than a month. Maybe two, walking into the cold. Still nothing in the traps. No furs or meat. They aren't empty anymore, though. We came across one just now, the metal jaws broken into pieces and strewn across the snow. Huge spurts of gore and blood. But no flesh. The red is harsh to look at after so long of seeing only white and grey. But it rumbles my stomach. Something deep inside me stirs. I know that blood should mean food. And then it comes to me. We haven't seen any creature, alive or dead, in a long while. Too long to ignore.

The mess of the traps gets to be too much for Laird and he roars. He screams and curses into the sky.

"Who did this? Thief! Rubbing my nose in it!" he shouts.

He picks up the pieces of metal and throws them, rakes his fingers through red and pink snow. He kicks at a large hunk of iron sticking out of the ground and howls in pain. He's cut through to his leg and falls hard on his duff, as though he meant to sit down especially hard. He breathes loud and ragged. My cheeks hurt from the cold. When I flex my fingers inside my heavy mittens I can feel the cracks on my dry knuckles open up, sweat getting in the cuts. Cold and sweaty and stinging all at once.

From where he sits Laird reaches out and runs his hand through the red mess again and then sucks the bloody snow off his fingers.

"Sorry if I scared you just now," he says. "Nothing for it but to press on. When we meet the other traders up ahead, I'll get it out of them who did this."

We do our best now to spread out our remaining food as far as it can go. We peel the bark off trees and boil it to make tea. We drink as much of it as our stomachs will hold, hoping to quiet the growls. The hard biscuits we brought have gone soft and blue with mould. Moisture from freezing in the cold and melting beside the fire. All the survival provisions we brought, though, don't seem to me that they last especially long. You're just stuck eating them anyway, once they're all you have left. My lips are chapped even worse than my knuckles. I'm always licking at them, which makes them chap worse. The hours and days are hard to tell apart now, as though time is getting away from us.

And after who knows how many of these blurry, smeared-together days we come to a spot where two rivers meet. There is no town. No outpost. But it does seem as though it's a place where a great many things meet. Snow and frozen water and blank sky overhead. But the place doesn't feel blank. The tree line is far in the distance. I can see it across the flat and empty land. No living things at all.

"Where is it?" Laird shrieks. This frenzy is worse than the one before. He looks as though he may rip his own arms out.

"I've come this way dozens of times. Dozens! It's here. It should be here." And I believe him. He kicks away at the snow, searching for the ice underneath.

"Here's the river," he says. A small triumph. "We're right on top of it. But there's nothing here. There's no wreckage. They wouldn't just leave. It was almost a god-damned city. It's like it was never here at all. There's nothing here!"

Though I can't see it, I do feel this city he mentions. A large fort. Many traders, some from the Hudson's Bay, more from the tribes. They have come far, very far. I look out and see nothing, no living things, and yet I can feel where they should be. It's as though Laird and I have slipped under a sheet of ice, all the life I feel on the top, us stuck underneath. We're on the side with nothing, just empty air and snow and cold. And we have been drifting deeper in for a long while. Ever since the empty traps, something's been leading us farther in. And this far deep, nothing ever has been here before.

Laird screams more. First for help, then just cursing. He slumps to the ground. Looks up at the blank, white sky.

"We'll wait here until dark," he says. "The stars, remember I told you. The constellations will show us where we are. That will get us back on course." I don't say anything, but I know it won't work. Though I'm not upset. I don't mind it here, so far.

We make camp in the middle of the wide clearing. Laird insists on keeping the fire away from the trees and out in the open, where anyone that might come along will see us. This leaves us open to the full force of the wind. The gusts are so bad that we can't get the tent to stay up. We dig a small pit in the snow for the fire, deep enough that the tiny flames don't blow out. They don't give off much warmth. Uncle Laird turns his face away and inches closer, trying to warm his back, and his coat singes and catches and I have to stomp him out. Overhead the dark grows and spreads until all is black. There are no stars tonight. Laird doesn't scream this time. He pouts and says nothing.

After a long while, a few hours maybe, Laird is slumped over in the snow, snoring. There is a dull moon but no stars. The fire is long burnt out, my eyes adjusted to the dark. I press my fingernails into the heel of my hand. Hard. The pain keeps me alert. I chew at my dry lips, pulling away thin strands of skin until I can taste the rawness underneath. When I am sure uncle Laird will not wake up, slow and quiet I move away and pull the rags from between my legs. This is the most blood yet, dark under the moonlight. Not just liquid but there are also clumps and clots cradled in the cloth. Like when I seen the gore-spattered traps, my stomach rumbles; something primal awakened by the blood. Before I can think I've shoved the cloths to my mouth. I gobble at the clots first and then suck the liquid blood out of the fabric. And put them back into my pants, wet now with spit. My stomach is a little quieter. I put handfuls of snow in my mouth, hoping it will wash the shame from my tongue.

And though it is a great distance away, I see something at the very edge of the tree line. I see the antlers first, barely noticeable against the tangle of empty branches behind them. Then I see the rising mist of hot breath. It could be a deer coming out of the forest, the first living creature either me or Laird has seen in ages, but the antlers reach so high. I can't imagine an animal being so tall. Or still. As though it isn't even there. I stare a long time, trying not to wake my uncle. I hold my breath. And then, out there in the dark, it blinks. It snuffs a great burst of air and rears even taller as it turns and slinks back into the trees. I stand unmoving. Eventually the dark fades and there is only blinding sun reflecting off the snow.

Laird awakens, confused and sluggish. He looks around and I can see the memories building on his face. Where we are, where we should be, and how far apart those two things are. Before too long, his purpose returns. We'll keep out in the open and we're sure to find someone eventually, or someone will see us. So we start walking again. The sun lasts unnaturally long. It seems we are days and days walking, but the light never dims. The sun never moves across the sky but hovers, looking down with menace. Or indifference. Which of those is worse?

Finally, neither of us can walk any further, and we stop for rest. Fall asleep in the daytime with our arms over our faces to block out the light, and eventually awake to pure black. It's as though time has come unstuck here. The dark threatens never to lift. We drift off to sleep again, and still it is dark. There is light when we wake up, but though we have been in near constant motion for what should have been days, we don't seem to have travelled at all. Still we can see the meeting of the two rivers, the trees in the distance. And nothing else.

We try again to leave and the same occurs. We make no progress and the cycle of light and dark is unpredictable. Soon Laird loses all desire to try and leave. He throws the sledge over on its side and makes camp right where we stand. Someone will just have to come across us, he says. He refuses to move from this spot. We find our same small firepit from days before. I venture as far as the tree line and gather wood. We burn the fire in the same place so long that it melts deep into the hard-packed snow and we have to climb down into a hole to get near the flames. I feel terrible cramps and pain under my belly somewhere. I check the rags frequently but there is no more blood.

While the night grows to its darkest point, while my uncle sleeps, I look up at the stars, dig my nails deep into my palms, chew at my sore and ragged lips, and I wait for the loping approach of the antlered monster. It doesn't come right to the fire but close enough that I can see it clearer now. Even at this distance it still towers over me and I have to crane my neck to look at it. The antlers reach so high, the points of hard bone like a cradle for the stars. Its arms and shoulders are covered in thick, coarse fur but its belly is bare flesh turned black by frostbite. It walks slow laps through the clearing and around the fire before receding back into the cover of the trees. After a time, I feel safe enough to leave the ashes of the fire and follow after it. I crisscross over its tracks, trying not to lose the trail in the dark. I never do catch up to it. Night after night I follow it to the edge of the woods. I awake to daylight, not far from the fire, the only tracks in the snow from my small snowshoes.

I never tell uncle Laird what I am seeing. After dumping the sledge, he doesn't care much for anything. He no longer cares who cleaned out his traps. No longer cares to find the outpost. No longer cares to leave. No longer cares that the food is all gone. He lies in the tent and waits for someone to come along and lead us out. His body begins to take up less and less space in the tent.

I pull the bark from the trees and eat it, never minding to make it into tea. I boil the bootlaces, the webbing from the snowshoes, the ties from our packs, our belts. The leather froths into a gummy paste that I skim off and suck from my fingers, drip into Laird's mouth as he lies on his back. I gobble handfuls of snow to quiet my belly.

Uncle Laird sees me poking at the heel of my hand with a knife, checking the depth of fat the way my father would do to a pig before we slaughtered it. He says nothing, just goes back to the empty branches—the nettles all chewed away—to sleep and wait.

The hunger is getting so bad that it's all I can think about. Eating. I find it hard to talk because my lips are so chewed up. What little I do say is about food. I dream of feasts and banquets. "I see long tables, heaping with bowls and cups," I say aloud. "There is roast duck and goose and turkey, all shiny with grease. There are bowls spilling over with nuts. Berries soaked in thick cream."

"Shut up," I hear from inside the sad little tent.

"I want to eat all the snow," I say. "All the way down to the grass until I crunch something green in my teeth."

"Shut your filthy, bleeding mouth!" he screams at me, bursting out of the tent and flopping soft to the ground.

"I am eating the trees, eating up all the forest," I say. "I start at the bottom and grow tall enough to reach the high boughs at the very top. And there, suck in huge bites of the clouds and reach past the sky, into the darkness that holds the stars." And then I loom over my weak uncle, gibbering into his filthy sweat-sodden clothes, a tiny little thing cradled in enormous shadow, swathed in dark points like stars, and I eat and eat and taste blood and meat and feel hair and green things in my mouth, tickling my throat, and I eat up all the world.

WE DRAW THE LINES

Will J. Fawley

An emptiness blossomed in Terry's stomach as he bussed home. The prairie scrolled past outside the window, flat snow-covered fields full of horizon and sky blinking into granaries and industrial buildings as he approached the city limits. He'd lived in Winnipeg all his life and still sometimes forgot what it was like outside the city. It was as if the earth had been rolled out to eliminate any quirk or deviance from the perfect, sterile sphere. His stomach churned, a sharp pain echoing through the hollow parts of his bowels. A festering ulcer threatening to grow until it consumed him. Then one day—*poof*—he would be emptied into the void.

As the bus pulled Terry back toward the suburban sprawl, the pain became a heaviness that weighed him into the seat, and his skin suddenly began to tingle. The tingle grew, becoming a warm energy that consumed every particle of his being for a brief moment, and then escaped him. Terry took a breath and told himself he was just exhausted from a long day. There was his breakfast/lunch double shift at the Inland Seafood Restaurant, followed by the emotional strain of bussing out to his boyfriend's house only to catch said boyfriend with another guy.

As he breathed the air through his lungs, the warmth faded and the weight returned. *I can't be one of them*, he thought. The woman across the aisle looked up and stared for a moment before turning away. She fanned herself with her book and looked at him again before focusing her gaze out the window at the snow. The guy behind her removed his coat and studied Terry through thick-framed glasses.

Were the other passengers besides the woman and man staring, too, or was Terry just being paranoid? He was breathing fast and shallow, and his vision blurred. Terry got off at the next stop. The aura of energy burned hotter than before, and his skin itched with heat. His body was not his own.

As he started walking away from the bus stop, a burst of energy rippled the air around him like a stone tossed in a lake, and Terry slid outside of himself. A second later he returned to his body and the ripple dissipated. A warmth washed through him, and then he saw the snow inside a three-metre radius had melted; two drivers within that range panicked in their cars.

Terry turned around to make sure no one had seen the burst of energy. The bus had vanished, dissolving into the vertical lines of downtown in the distance, but the guy with the thick glasses was standing there, even though Terry hadn't seen him get off the bus. Their eyes met for a second, and then the guy turned and walked away. *He knows*, Terry thought. *Maybe he's one of them too.*

When Terry got home, his mom was in the kitchen, baking. He snuck to the bathroom before she noticed he was home. Then he pulled off his clothes and turned the shower on as hot as he could stand.

Though he was clean and warm, Terry was shaking when he was done. Wrapping himself in a towel, he walked back to his bedroom. The books on his desk rattled from his phone, and he picked it up to find five texts from Jeremy.

Sorry.
I didn't mean to hurt you. :'(
I didn't want you to find out
like this.
I still love you.

A tremor shook Terry's body and he dropped the phone on the floor as a second burst of energy shot through his nerves. It radiated out from his gut and then burst through his veins and muscles until it escaped from his body and rippled through the air, ruffling his sheets and fluttering the skateboarding posters on the walls. The window rattled in its frame, and when Terry turned toward the sound, Glasses Guy from the bus was out on the sidewalk, looking in at him.

What did this freak want? If he kept hanging around, people might think that Terry knew him, they might suspect that Terry was like him.

There was still a faint hum to Terry's skin as he covered himself in layers of clothes: undershirt, hoodie, jeans, Vans. It wasn't enough, so he pulled on a coat and wished he could keep covering his body until he lost himself in layers. He ran downstairs to tell the creep to stop following him before people started talking.

Terry ran down the street, and when he got to the next block he was out of breath and realized he hadn't seen which way Glasses Guy had gone. It was -40c and the air was jagged in his lungs. He tried to keep his mouth closed as he panted for breath on the walk home.

Arcs of energy sparked across his body like tiny lightning bolts until it burst out of him again in another invisible ripple that melted the snow around him. His consciousness seemed to shoot out of his body with the energy, and for a moment, he was free from the cold. But then he snapped back into it like an elastic, and Glasses Guy was standing in front of him. He had short black hair and thick eyebrows that crawled atop the glasses like fair-trade caterpillars.

"Come with me," he said.

"Who are you?" Terry asked.

"I'm like you."

Terry looked around to make sure no one was watching. But the snow-filled streets were empty.

Glasses Guy made Terry feel strange, and not just because he was spying on him. There was something else, something that numbed the churning in his gut. So Terry followed him as they walked past his house and down the next block. "Where are we going?"

"I'll explain everything soon, but we can't talk about it here."

So the boys walked in silence, their footprints following them through the snow until they were filled in by more flakes.

Glasses Guy led Terry to an unfinished house at the edge of the neighbourhood. None of the houses on the street were complete, and they tapered off into a prairie forest that was now, in winter, just a field of naked trees. Terry looked into the forest as they approached. The spaces between the trees created flashes of falling sunlight that stung his eyes, but he kept staring, mesmerized by the way the spaces followed him as he walked, becoming nothing and then filling in with light and trees.

"This way."

Glasses Guy opened the front door of a castle-like house with two peaked towers and a second-storey porch that wrapped around the house like a turret.

"Are we allowed to be here?" Terry asked, though he was already entering the house.

"We're allowed to be anywhere we want. Come on."

The inside was as incomplete as the exterior. Hardwood floors had been laid but were still coated in their own dust. Drywall had been hung and covered in an initial layer of thin white paint. But the rest of the house was empty. Wires stuck out of holes in the walls and ceiling, and there was no furniture. An old boombox sat on the bare floor, pushing a calm song into the air to fill the negatives. Terry recognised the tune, but couldn't name it.

They walked down a set of stairs to the basement.

"We can talk here," Glasses Guy said.

In contrast to the empty house above, the basement looked lived in. Two beanbag chairs sat in a corner beside a space heater, which Glasses Guy cranked up to high. There were posters on the walls and books stacked on shelves. Scraps of carpet were stretched across the concrete floor in a patchwork pattern, and electric lamps hung from the ceiling beams. Glasses Guy switched a couple of them on and sat on a beanbag, motioning for Terry to do the same.

"So now can you tell me who you are?" Terry asked as he warmed his hands over the space heater. His skin tightened as it thawed, and the bones in his fingers ached. He made a fist and the dry skin of his knuckles cracked into red lines.

"Drink?" Glasses Guy asked.

Terry shrugged, and Glasses Guy pulled two cans of orange soft drink from a box and rolled one toward him.

"My name's Malcolm," he said. "Sorry I didn't say anything before, but we have to be careful with our power."

"Our power?"

"Yeah. Magic is a dangerous force. Not everyone can see it, and even fewer can channel it. I had a feeling about you. I've been watching you for a while now, but I had to be sure."

"Be sure of what?"

"That you felt it too."

"Magic?"

"Magic, energy, the life-force, the Universe—whatever you call it."

"Do I feel it?"

"You tell me." Malcolm chugged the rest of his soda and tossed the empty can in another box.

"I feel something. Like a buzz of energy that takes me outside of myself." The pain was mostly gone from his fingers, and Terry flipped his hands over, studying the palms, then the cracked backs of his hands.

"Yeah. Exactly. I know this is weird, but I'm not trying to freak you out. It's just that I know what you're going through, and I want to help." Malcolm leaned in toward the space heater, closer to Terry. "And I don't want to be alone anymore."

"So help me. Tell me how to get rid of it." Terry stared into the orange can and squeezed the aluminium so it shaped to his grasp.

"You don't have to get rid of it. Nothing's wrong with you. You're just figuring yourself out, and that's always hard, isn't it?"

Terry nodded.

"If you want, I can teach you what I know." Malcolm closed his eyes and the ripple of energy rolled out of him like before, making the lanterns flash on and off. The air around them grew warm—not hot, but more like a tropical ocean breeze.

A tingle crept through Terry's body. "Okay, teach me to control it, so I can make sure it never happens again."

"I can't."

"You just said you could."

"I said I could teach you what I know. Control is not part of it. That's the key, actually. Control is an illusion. You have to reach out and let the space between us guide you."

"What?"

"I know it's hard to understand at first. Think of it this way: the Universe wouldn't exist without the space. Or maybe it would all come together in a big crunch and then a big bang, cycling without beginning or end."

"Huh?"

"Sorry, it's hard to explain. It's just … okay, how about this: when you look at the night sky, are you seeing dark or light?"

"I see the stars"

"And what do we see in the stars?"

"Constellations?"

"Exactly. We instinctively want them to connect. Thousands of years ago, our ancestors envisioned lines between the bright spots in the sky, creating these fantastic creatures. But you can connect them any way you want. There are no actual lines, and so there is an infinite possibility of connection."

"I could redraw the lines to make the sky into a poem."

"Sure." Malcolm laughed. "You're a natural."

"Because I want to make refrigerator poetry in the sky?"

"It's not just the stars. All matter is like that. We can connect it any way we want. Because we draw the lines. Here, close your eyes and put your palms out in front of you."

Terry did as he was told. He took a deep breath through his nose as he tried to feel something other than the black hole in his stomach that was dissolving him.

"Where do you feel yourself being pulled?" Malcolm asked.

There was nothing at first, but then Terry took a second breath, and a warmth washed over him. It came in through his nose and dripped down his neck and chest, soothing him. The electricity sparked through his body again, and like a magnetic pull, there was a tug in the space between him and Malcolm.

It felt amazing for a moment, but then like he was turning inside out. "I have to go. My mom's expecting me for dinner."

Malcolm nodded slowly. "You know where to find me."

♦

When Terry had walked in on Jeremy and whoever the other guy was, it had sparked something in him. There was a burst of energy that rattled the walls and flipped the pages of a book on Jeremy's desk. It was an autographed copy of *Breakfast Bees* that Terry had given him for his birthday. They stopped mid-fuck and Jeremy looked up at Terry standing in the hallway, freshly ricocheted back into himself.

"Shit!" Jeremy said.

Terry ran, but Jeremy caught up with him in the hall. Jeremy was naked, and his hair was pasted to his face with traitorous sex-sweat. He grabbed Terry's arm and Terry went limp, a bouquet of flowers falling out of his hand and onto the floor.

"Shit. Were those for me?" Jeremy asked.

In his mind Terry was already back on the bus, passing straight through the city and across the endless stretch of plains to the Rockies, and maybe even the coast. Maybe he wouldn't stop there, maybe he'd get on a plane or a boat in Vancouver and just keep going, passing it all by, the whole world turning against him beneath his feet until he'd travelled all his life and gone nowhere.

"Terry?" Jeremy said, shaking him by the shoulders. "Terry, I said, are you okay."

"No," was all Terry could get out, the air within him weak and small enough for only one short sound. He heard the plastic of the flowers' wrapping crinkle under Jeremy's feet behind him. But Terry was already out the door.

✦

Two days later, Jeremy called and begged for another chance. The wanting and the anger and the hurt welled up into bile that burned Terry's throat. He wished it was as simple as forgiveness and moving on, but the idea of being with Jeremy now reminded him of the distance between them that would never close, that horrible feeling of being deceived. The worst part was not the desiring of someone other than himself, but remembering all the times Jeremy told him they were soulmates, that when they were together nothing and no one else mattered. In those moments Jeremy was talking around the truth, speaking in holes instead of wholes. The truth would have hurt, but he could have moved on.

The emptiness was hot in his stomach and Terry let his mind wander to Malcolm because he'd become the only distraction that could make the feeling go away. But Terry didn't want another boy to fill the hole in his life. Love was temporary and would inevitably lead to another hole that would fuse with the first one into a giant chasm that would consume him.

Weeks went by, and Terry stayed busy helping his mom with a 3D puzzle of the Taj Mahal, playing video games, doing anything to convince himself things were normal, that he'd forgotten Jeremy and that he had only dreamed about Malcolm and the warmth. Maybe there never was a Malcolm or a brilliant buzz that grew out of the hole inside him. Terry started attending a poetry workshop in the basement of a Unitarian Church where he could write about this dream and further push it toward abstraction.

He was at the poetry workshop on a Wednesday night after a long day waiting tables, listening to an older guy with wispy, grey hair read a poem about a dog's perspective of the world. Then Malcolm walked into the room.

They made eye contact, and the buzz echoed through Terry's skin. The energy radiated from his body and the feeling returned, the same one he had in the basement of that unfinished house. Like his insides were turning. Terry ran out of the church and to the bus stop, but he couldn't stand around and wait for the bus, so he kept running until he caught the one that was just arriving at the next stop.

That night, Terry tried to work on a poem, but the words all ended up rhyming in a disgusting way and none of the letter combinations on the page ever became the unwordable feeling inside of him. He gave up around eleven and got into bed, but only tossed and turned. When two A.M. came and he was still awake, Terry got up and dressed. If he didn't do something about the feeling now, find some way to let it out, it would consume him.

His breath hung in the air as he walked to the unfinished house that had become a refuge in a world where all emptiness had been filled.

It was dark, and there was a thickness to the air, and when he closed his eyes he could feel a current, just like Malcolm had said, an intangible thread connecting him to the house. He let the pull of the air guide him to the forest at the edge of the development. The space between the trees was invisible now. It was all just a patch of blackness in the distance.

There was a light on in the basement when he arrived, and Terry looked in the window. Malcolm had his eyes closed, but he wasn't sleeping. He was buzzing with energy, just like Terry did.

Terry knocked on the window and Malcolm opened his eyes and waved. A few seconds later, the front door opened. Malcolm was still vibrating faintly when he led Terry down to the basement.

As they walked down the stairs, Terry finally understood the feeling Malcolm gave him: safety. And right now he needed that comfort, needed Malcolm. Once they were in the basement, Terry closed his eyes and tried to lose control, to give himself over to the helplessness he had felt earlier, but he didn't buzz this time. "I can't do it," he said.

Malcolm put a hand on Terry's shoulder and looked inside him. "It's okay, it takes practice."

"But shouldn't there be some natural instinct that takes over?"

"Yes, but you have to learn how to listen to it," Malcolm said as they sat lotus-style on the bean bags. "Magic in this world is made from the space between things. But it's not the empty space. We are. And in our emptiness we hold the potential do anything, to be anything. We think we have control over ourselves and the world around us, but that control is an illusion. Without the space between things, we couldn't float, couldn't swim, couldn't be kept separate from anything else long enough to exist in the sense we think of things existing."

"How do you know all of this?"

Malcolm downed the rest of an orange soft drink. "My aunt taught me."

"Do you know any others?"

"Other than my aunt? I've never known any personally. I haven't wanted to risk outing myself."

"But you must know who they are, or have an idea?"

"I guess?"

"Come on, we can't be alone," Terry said. He stood up and began pacing around the room.

"Well there is this group, they pretend to be a homeless shelter for queer youth or something, but it's kind of a front for magic. Because some people have taken the term queer to mean, like you and me."

"People who can ..." Terry searched for words to contain the unnameable transformation.

"Change stuff. Yeah." Terry's heart raced at the thought of being part of something instead of just apart. He examined one of the lanterns hanging from the ceiling beams, and it glowed in his hands.

"When can I meet them?"

"You can't," Malcolm said. He rested his face in his hand and closed his eyes. Terry imagined he was looking in at himself.

"Why?"

"Terry, it's not safe for people like us to just come out of hiding. My aunt, she disappeared four years ago."

"Like, poof?" Terry made a gesture with his hands.

"I mean, there's no proof or anything, but I'm pretty sure she was kidnapped."

"Shit."

"It hasn't always been this way, you know. In ancient times people born with magic were celebrated. They were tribe leaders."

"Do you think it can be like that again?"

"Maybe one day? I mean we have to hope, right? Otherwise, how do we keep going?"

"Yeah, but nothing's going to change if we keep hiding, is it?"

"Look, you're welcome to go. But I'm staying here. And if you hang out with me here for a while, I can help you. Whatever you do, you have to learn to manage it."

"I know."

Malcolm took off his glasses and set them on the ground beside his feet. He patted the beanbag across from him. Terry looked around the room, wishing he could just let it all out for once, but Malcolm was right, he had to learn to manage his new power. So he sat down on the beanbag again.

"Let go of everything," Malcolm said. "Don't try to see the space between us, let it observe *you*."

Terry closed his eyes and listened to Malcolm as he continued.

"Even things we perceive as physical objects are mostly space. Which means everything is connected in a sea of molecules. When you stop thinking as a single body, you realize that giving up control means speaking through everything. Once you do that, anything is possible."

Malcolm snapped his fingers, and Terry opened his eyes. A flame shot out of Malcolm's fist and then melted back into his body. His eyes sparked with blue energy, and then a wrinkle across his forehead split open to reveal a third eye. "Let the feeling overtake you. Your molecules are the same as the ones in the air between us, all part of the same sea. Let the current take control."

Terry closed his eyes again and felt the current. He let it pull him into its undertow, taking his life and pouring it into the Universe. It tugged him forward until he felt something soft against his lips. His mouth opened to receive Malcolm's kiss.

The buzz crawled across their skin, and it moved through Terry's body like heat. When it reached his stomach, he pulled away and jumped to his feet.

How could he both want something and be completely terrified by it? His phone vibrated in his pocket and he pulled it out to discover a text from Jeremy. Why couldn't he just move on with his life and be happy like everyone else? All he had to do was forget the piece of himself Jeremy had carved out.

Terry turned to leave.

"Where are you going?" Malcolm asked.

"To meet the others," Terry said, realizing his purpose for the first time. He deleted Jeremy from his phone. "Maybe they know something about your aunt. Maybe we don't have to be alone."

"Wait."

"I have to do this, Malcolm. I'm sick of being afraid."

"That's not what I meant. You've made me realize how I've let fear keep me from living, from finding out what happened to my aunt. I'm going to regret this, but I'm coming with you."

Terry pulled Malcolm to his feet and they walked up the stairs hand-in-hand.

The emptiness vibrated within Terry's core, all the pieces of nothingness becoming. Emptiness was never the feeling, he suddenly realized. Not emptiness, but a potential of molecules. A potential to arrange them any way he wanted—not a void, just unshaped. Maybe he couldn't forget the past, but he could accept it and the future. If only he could accept the present, accept the magic.

As Terry closed the door behind them, he looked through the trees and saw the light bending around something. The something was invisible, only the light around it visible, as if the colours of everything it touched were enhanced for a moment before it disappeared, creating a ripple of energy around it. The ripple travelled through the forest, and when it reached Terry it filled him with warmth. The hole inside him would never be filled. But it also wasn't empty. It was part of him now, another possible connection between points in the Universe. There were infinite ways he could connect himself to the past and future. Once he opened himself to the Universe, anything was possible.

JUDITH

Jonathan Ball

Scott refused the machines. But then Judith.

Who wanted to go skydiving. Who found a company that would drop them over Hawai'i Volcanoes National Park, where they could see the ocean, volcanoes, and lava fields on the way down, and then land just beyond this glorious but hazardous scenery.

A beautiful, once-in-a-lifetime thing. The perfect way to begin a honeymoon.

Scott balked. What if something went wrong? A shame to survive the wedding only to die on the honeymoon.

She didn't laugh. So they fought.

Too risky, too worrying. She wasn't worried. They'd book it now, he'd have a year to worry about it, but then they *were* jumping out of that plane.

And if something happened? Nothing would happen. But if he was so worried he could ask the machines.

He stalled. "What machines?"

"You know." She lit a cigarette. She was quitting as a wedding gift but not for another month.

The death machines. They drew some blood, analyzed it somehow, and spit out a piece of paper explaining how you would die. No one knew how the machines worked, but they worked. They were never wrong, though frustratingly vague.

"It'll ease your mind," she said, "when it doesn't say *skydiving* or something like that. You'll see there's no reason not to go."

He said the machines were dangerous. That they worked by suggestion, crafting random but self-fulfilling prophecies. She scowled and told him that was crap, a conspiracy theory. Besides, it didn't change things. They were never wrong, and whatever fate the machine outputted, be it *gunshot* or *choking* or *tsunami* or *sex with pitbull*, it wouldn't be *skydiving* and that was that.

And if it was, well, then she'd give up and they wouldn't go. Although it wouldn't make any difference. If the machine said *skydiving* then *skydiving* would get him in the end.

But he didn't want to know.

"That's nonsense. You're just afraid. Everyone wants to know. It's freeing."

Judith had gone herself, years ago, when the machines were first released for public use. *Bus*, the machine said, and since then she'd cultivated a taste for things like skydiving. And though she didn't believe you could escape your fate, she avoided public transit.

She was right. He was afraid. But he denied it, so they fought some more.

In the end, though, he gave in. The perfect wedding gift. And though he couldn't admit it, she was right. He wanted to know.

✦

The machines were in all the malls, so Judith took him to Polo Park. She let him pick out something from Victoria's Secret as a thank you for agreeing to go.

"Don't think too much about it," she said, hoisting the small bag. "Think about this instead."

He asked what it was like, when she went. She twisted her purse strap.

"I'll be honest, at first it's terrible. A real shock. You want to know more, but the machine won't tell you more. If you do it again, anytime, at any machine, it's always the same prediction. After a few days, though, it feels great. You feel helpless, but the flip side is that you don't have to worry so much about other things. And you realize that there's also no point worrying about your fate. I don't even notice the buses anymore."

He was distracted and anxious all day, so she told him jokes and smiled her best smiles. He thought about the lingerie, tight against her tanned thighs, and how happy she'd be in the air, the lava fields spreading beneath them.

They shopped and ate some pizza while they moved in a narrowing spiral around the mall's death machine, putting it off. He felt sick and the pizza made him feel sicker and he decided to stop putting it off.

The machine looked like an instant-photo booth, black and orange like some child's toy, but marked with the grey image of an ancient stone face. A Greek mask of Apollo, painted on the side—Apollo's face severe, his mouth a gaping O.

Thick dark cloth hung over the booth's entrance. Scott parted the black and stepped inside.

He hadn't told Judith, but it was his second time inside this booth. When the machine was first installed he came to it, alone. Before they met. He waited for a long time—the line stretched halfway down the mall that day—and when his turn came he sat inside, looked at his hands, and went home.

Now, he looked up into the mask of Apollo, also painted inside the booth on the wall in front of him. Apollo's flat eyes stared into his own. The wide mouth a black hole he was meant to put his hand inside.

Judith swept back the curtain and leaned in through the entranceway. She kissed his forehead, then swiped her credit card through the payment slot.

Scott stuck his hand into Apollo's mouth. Something jabbed his palm and he pulled his hand out. The machine whirred and a small slip of paper appeared from a slot to his right.

It was done.

He couldn't believe it was over so fast. He looked up at Judith, then down at the paper. He picked it up and turned it over. Some blood from his palm soaked into its white edge.

The paper said: *Judith*.

He stared at the word, his mind blank.

His first thought, when thoughts came, was to hide it from her. But he had looked at it, unbelieving, for too long. She'd dropped the lingerie bag and staggered backwards. The curtain slung down to separate them. He crumpled the paper and rose, her name in his throat, but by the time he made his way out of the machine she was gone.

✦

He didn't know what to do so he shambled to the food court and sat down. He thought of nothing and after a while decided to go home.

He went to the parking lot and spent a long time looking for the car before he remembered they'd taken hers. He walked to the bus stop. When the bus came he realized he didn't have the proper fare and overpaid with a five-dollar bill.

He almost missed his stop because when he got close he realized he still held the piece of paper, crumpled tight in his clutching, stiff hand. He smoothed it out. It still said *Judith*, a smear of blood at the bottom of the *h*. Somehow, he'd thought it would say something different.

He shoved the paper between the cracks of the seat and exited the bus. Judith's car wasn't in the driveway and she wasn't in the house.

He didn't know what he was supposed to do now. The dishes were dirty, so he did the dishes. Judith had been drinking a glass of orange juice that was still half-full and on the counter. She'd left it out, like he kept telling her not to. He moved to finish it and wash the glass but decided to put it in the fridge instead.

He tried to watch television but there was nothing worth watching on television. He went to the bedroom and saw that her clothes from yesterday were on the floor. He picked up the clothes and put them in the laundry hamper, then realized her new lingerie was still at the mall, in its bag beside the machine.

He thought about the lingerie and how good she'd look but it didn't excite him. He felt detached from the image, like he was looking at her picture in a magazine.

He began to read, a book she'd left on the nightstand. She didn't live with him but slept over most nights. The book was *Timeline* by Michael Crichton. He thought the book might help him understand something he was having trouble understanding. It had waited here for him, it should offer some insight.

But it was not the book he needed at the moment, and it seemed shameful that nothing in his life, not even a book, had anything to say to him right now.

He closed it, keeping her place, and went to sleep.

✦

The next day Scott called the office to say there had been a death in the family and he would be taking some time off. He called in the morning before anyone arrived so he only had to talk to the machine. His manager called back but he didn't pick up the phone and didn't listen to the message. He ate breakfast and went back to bed.

He wanted to call Judith or maybe show up at her place unannounced, but that seemed wrong somehow. Instead he left her alone.

He thought about what the machine might have meant. Would she cause some accident, make some mistake, which would somehow result in his death? Would she pass on some sickness, some disease she would survive but to which he would succumb? Would she murder him? It seemed insane. But the machines were never wrong.

They were mindless and vague, mysterious. But they were never wrong.

He spent the week in limbo. In bed or wandering through the house. He didn't shower, afraid of missing her call.

He spent a lot of time cooking. Grand, five-course meals, more food than he could eat. It relaxed him, gave him something to do, instructions to follow. He filled the fridge with leftovers and listened for the phone.

Then she called.

"Judith?" His voice cracked. He hadn't spoken to anyone, not even himself, for days.

There was a pause, and then her. "Scott?"

"Judith, come over."

"No." Her voice soft. "But I'd like to see you."

◆

Scott arrived at Stella's Café before her and turned the pages of *Timeline*. He'd brought the book to kill time (*haha*) and because he thought she might want it back. She could never start a new book until she'd finished the last one, and who knew when she would return to his house?

He wondered about the wedding and whether the wedding was off. He was thinking about this when she arrived and it showed on his face.

"Don't." She sat without saying hello. "What are we going to do?"

"We don't need to do anything. It's just your name. It changes nothing."

"It's not just my name." She was wearing her sunglasses indoors but he could still see her eyes. They crinkled at the corners as she fought to stay composed. "It means I'm going to kill you."

"It doesn't need to be so dramatic." He wanted to take her hand but thought it might make her more anxious. "Maybe you catch a cold, and I catch it too. When we're old. Maybe you lose control of a car. It doesn't mean you'll grow to hate me and poison my food."

"I suppose so." She swirled the coffee he'd ordered for her. She'd arrived late and it was cold. "But, somehow, I'm responsible."

"It doesn't matter. We don't need to do anything drastic. It's like you said: it's shocking, but something we need to accept."

"I can't accept this." She sipped her coffee and grimaced. "I just can't."

"If the machines are never wrong, then there's nothing we can do. We keep living our lives, just like before."

"You don't get it." She fumbled for her cigarettes, even though it was illegal to smoke indoors. "I can't accept it. And I can't go on like before. It's like the buses. I know that it's pointless not to take the bus. No matter what, one day the bus will hit me when I'm walking, or driving, or whatever. Somehow, a bus will end up killing me. Whether I ride the buses or not. So why not ride them? I know this, but I can't. I just can't."

"It might not mean that. Maybe someone named James Bus is going to hit you with his car. Or maybe somebody *else* named Judith is going to end up causing my death. It doesn't have to be you."

She was quiet, playing with her cigarette. He handed her the book. "I thought you might want to finish this."

She looked at the book like it was a UFO, something she'd never seen before and never expected to see. But then she took it.

"Thanks."

"Look, you don't need to decide anything now. Let's just have coffee."

She nodded. "I suppose it could be someone else."

"Let me order you a new coffee. And a piece of cheesecake. We don't have to talk about it anymore, we can just talk. Think about it some more, but don't jump to conclusions."

"Okay. But just the cheesecake. I don't need more coffee, I'm jumpy enough."

He smiled. "There's a long line, I'll order while you have your cigarette." He moved to the counter and she went outside.

When his turn came he picked out the biggest piece of cake, the one that would take her the longest to finish. He motioned through the window for her to come back inside. She held up a finger and pulled hard on the cigarette while he looked at the cover of her Crichton book, thinking about the story so far.

They relaxed a little and talked until the cheesecake was gone, careful not to discuss the machine's prediction. It reminded him of their first date, tentative and awkward.

When she said she wanted to go home he didn't argue.

"Can I walk with you?"

"Not today." She pulled herself into her coat.

They left together and she pulled out another cigarette. She was chain smoking, which he hated to see, but he said nothing.

They stood outside for a while, looking at each other and looking away. She sniffed at the cold air.

He scanned her face. "It was good to see you. Call me later, okay?"

"Okay." She gave him a sad smile, but it was still a smile, so he took it. She turned and stepped into the street.

◆

Something hit Judith hard then, slamming into her back. She fell forward, gasping, breath slammed out onto the pavement.

A loud thud and screaming. Screaming and the sound of brakes.

◆

The machines were never wrong. Were never wrong. But, dying, he wondered if he beat them.

Was that the bus? Had he saved her? The machines were never wrong, but maybe he saved her. Or would it happen again? Someday, in a future without him, when he couldn't push her out of the way?

Her book had fallen in the street. Her juice was still sitting in his fridge, which was full of food that was going to spoil.

Meals that he made for her. Judith.

EATING OF THE TREE

Chadwick Ginther

That goddamn squirrel left his nuts in my coffee cup.
Again.

There are things that don't exist for the daytime world. Things you only see when you work nightshift security in Winnipeg. Of all the strangeness Marie Belanger had encountered, the worst—the fucking *worst*—was that squirrel.

"I will get you for this you furry-tailed, piss drinking, pack rat!"

Marie scanned the break room. She couldn't see her rodent nemesis. She sighed and dumped the acorns into the trash. She washed her cup in case the squirrel had left her any other surprises.

She'd assembled quite the collection of "gifts" in her cup over the last few months. Beads. Buttons. Feathers. Wingnuts. A weird looking dead lizard. Lately it had been Scrabble tiles. So far, she had two each of R, A and T, and a single O, S, and K, respectively. At least she knew the squirrel couldn't spell worth shit. Sometimes Marie believed the squirrel talked to her and she thought she was going crazy. Other times, she thought the squirrel plotted against her.

On those days she *knew* she was going crazy.

✦

An ash tree grew in the centre of Union Station. No one knew who'd planted it, but it'd grown fast since last November when something had blown the roof off the station rotunda. The tree had been a wispy five feet tall then—little more than a broom handle—but in the months since, it had more than doubled in size.

The tree—and the wishing well constructed around it—were the source of most of Marie's problems. They'd become a symbol of hope for some. People turned up at all hours to drop coins and ask for … whatever idiots without train tickets wished for. Cleverer, less scrupulous idiots showed up later to steal those same coins. The thefts had ramped up lately, but Marie had seen no sign of the culprits.

Do we blame the dayshift, Marie?
Yes, we do, Marie.

Before the tree, nights were a great time to do Sweet FA. There were the occasional drunks or sightseers who wandered in from the nearby Forks Market, but those were few and far between. Mostly, Marie's job was peaceful. Quiet. Except now she froze her ass off eight months a year because some idiot had decided to leave the rotunda open-air after the repairs.

She gulped more coffee and headed to the rotunda to make certain it was still clear.

It wasn't.

A crowd encircled the tree, holding hands. They wore embroidered cloaks and chanted in a language Marie didn't understand. Maybe *they* were her thieves.

Marie yelled out, "Security!"

They ignored her. One, a woman, broke the circle, and dropped something in the wishing well. A coin? The circle closed hands behind her while she ladled water from the well onto the tree's trunk with her hands.

Still ignoring Marie, the woman said loudly, in English this time, "Grow powerful and strong."

There was a shimmer, like a heat mirage in summer, and fog rolled off the well engulfing the tree. *Are they putting dry ice in the well?*

Marie blinked—was the tree taller? Broader? It looked to be. Had to be a trick of the light. Edges of night and caffeine jitters.

She tried again. "What's going on?"

They still ignored her.

"I've got bear spray, and I'm not afraid to use it," Marie said.

That got them. They turned as one and stared at her like she was crazy. Maybe she was, but not because she wanted them out of her building.

Make them think you're crazier than them, Marie. Or they'll never leave.

"Go on, shoo!"

That probably isn't going to do it.

The last wisher addressed Marie with the haughty tone of a River Heights soccer mom. "We are not leaving Yggdrasillsson unprotected."

She couldn't make out the word—presumably their name for the tree. Why would they name it? Did they expect it to answer?

Probably.

Weirdos.

"Your ... sick Iggy ... dress tree is in good hands," she said, brandishing her bear spray. "It's my job to protect it. Now leave. Before I call the cops."

The woman narrowed her eyes and pursed her lips as if she wanted to ask for a refund without a receipt. "And what can the police do to keep the tree whole? What can *you* do?"

"I've also got handcuffs and a good left hook."

And a stun gun and telescoping baton. Not perfectly legal, so she wasn't about to bring it up with them. Just because they were trespassing didn't mean she had to go down with them.

"Not enough," a cultist said, shaking her head.

Something shrieked from above. Marie flinched and hoped her fear hadn't shown. The last thing she wanted was these weirdos knowing she was frightened.

A squirrel—*the* squirrel—leapt from the roof. The squirrel hit the thin top branches of the ash and the tree swayed so violently, Marie worried its trunk would snap. She didn't want to be the one to explain why, and how, it'd happened. The squirrel scrambled down the ash and bounded through their ranks, darting between Marie's legs. She tried not to squeak. It would diminish the badass pose she'd struck to intimidate the trespassers.

You totally squeaked, Marie.

Quiet, Marie.

The squirrel circled round and came to a stop beside her. Red as a cartoon devil, and *big*. The little prick looked like the offspring of a drunken night between a raccoon and an Irish Setter. It *stared* at her.

"I see," the lead weirdo said, inclining her head to the squirrel. She looked ready to bloody bow. "It appears you do have matters well in hand."

Because of the squirrel?

Don't look a gift horse in the mouth, Marie. Move them along.

"Right," Marie said, giving them a brisk nod—which she hoped conveyed a confidence in her statement she didn't quite feel. "Leave it to me."

They bobbed their hooded heads emphatically in return. "If you need us." The leader passed her a business card for Ashes to Ashes, some holistic health store in the city's Little Italy area. "Don't hesitate to call."

"Got it," Marie said, tucking the card into a pocket. She stole another look at the squirrel standing at attention beside her. She didn't like the way it looked at her. Also: she was glad she didn't need to wear skirts to work. "We see anything, we'll holler."

The cloaked figures spun their finery off their shoulders, rolled up their cloaks, and tucked them into their oversized purses. Absent the renaissance fair garb, dressed in skinny jeans or yoga pants and blouses or sweaters, they looked strangely normal. Without another word, they filed out, leaving Marie alone with the tree.

And the squirrel.

The tree *seemed* fine. Coins peppered the wishing well, a few shining silver in the moonlight. It was mostly pennies. *What wish do you expect for a cent? Seriously.* She shrugged. No other use for pennies since Canada had decommissioned the copper.

"Foolish thing, putting a wishing well near that tree," a male voice said from behind Marie. She jumped in surprise and wheeled around, but no one was there.

Only the squirrel, still standing on its haunches.

Looking at her.

"Worse: not specifying *who* you're wishing to grow powerful and strong."

Marie blinked. The voice … it'd come from the squirrel. It couldn't have come from the squirrel.

"Shitshitshit."

Deep breath—don't show fear. You've talked down meth heads and wrestled bikers, Marie. You can do this.

"Destiny and fate can get … confused where wishes abound," the squirrel said. Then: It. Smiled. "Hello, Marie."

Stay calm.

Must I?

No.

"Ahhhhh!"

That wasn't calm, Marie.

The squirrel picked at an ear, as if in discomfort. "*Must* you?"

"Ahhhhh!"

Apparently, I must.

The squirrel winced. *Can squirrels wince?*

"Please stop," it said.

It said, "please," Marie.

"Ahhhhh!"

The squirrel waited for her to finish yelling. That took a while.

Eventually, voice hoarse, Marie sputtered out, "You … you can talk."

"Obviously," the squirrel said, looking up at her. "Surprisingly, so can *you.*"

"Oh, don't be a dick."

Okay, Marie, the squirrel is talking to you. No avoiding that.

With a shaking hand, Marie took out her phone and pointed it at the squirrel, fumbling with the camera app, and tried to hold her bear spray steady in her other hand.

"Say something else."

The squirrel raised a tiny paw ... *was he? Yup. He's flipping me off.*

"Aww, c'mon. No one will believe me if you don't talk."

The squirrel asked, "Why do you care if they don't?"

"*I* won't believe me if you don't."

It nodded. "Fair."

The squirrel scampered toward the tree, and Marie backpedalled away from him. He tested the water with a paw, dabbing it several times before he raised it to his lips.

"This water tastes like bull piss."

Marie's first thought was, *Really?* Followed by, *You've tasted bull piss?* She said nothing.

The squirrel pulled a bug off the tree and ate it. He chewed noisily before turning around to address Marie. "I remember when Odin wished for wisdom. And what did *that* get him? No peripheral vision and a blind spot for Loki to exploit," the squirrel said. "'Grow powerful and strong.' Be careful what you wish for, meat bags."

Marie eased her stance but didn't put away her bear spray in case the squirrel was rabid or it wanted her wallet. She kept her phone out too. Marie was pretty sure she hadn't drunk a forty before work, or eaten a bag of mushrooms, but in the morning she'd need proof this'd happened. The big red bastard looked at her, cocked his head, tsked, and bounded away.

Toward the break room.

Marie turned to the tree. Smoke, or fog, rose from the well. Hoarfrost crusted the tree's trunk. Whatever was happening, Marie hadn't seen it before. Somebody ought to look into that.

Somebody who was paid to care.

That's you, Marie.

She sighed. *It is, isn't it?*

'Fraid so, Marie.

Well, *shit.*

Marie followed the squirrel. She could use some more coffee. She looked over her shoulder and saw a black shape, like a lizard, peel a strip of bark from the tree. Another held a shining coin in its jaws. The coin thief disappeared into the well in a flash of steam and a splash of water. *There's not enough coffee in the world, Marie.* Bobby always kept a mickey in his locker. She shrugged. Maybe she'd make her coffee Irish.

✦

The tree is dying," the squirrel said, hopping onto the counter and rummaging through the cupboards.

"Looks fine to me," Marie said. "Growing, even."

"Looks can be deceiving." The squirrel sipped coffee he hadn't paid for and grimaced at the taste. He rubbed his little chin thoughtfully. "Especially since the tree is being devoured. From below."

"By those lizards?" Marie paid for the squirrel's coffee. That meagre gift was the last of her change, but she was unlikely to need caffeine to stay awake with a talking squirrel doing a ride-along.

"They're *dragons*." The squirrel's voice held surprising graveness. Marie still wasn't convinced any of tonight's events were happening.

"Of course they are." Marie shrugged. If talking squirrels could exist, why not dragons? She'd call the Church of St. George. Maybe she'd get to ride one! "Why haven't I seen them before?"

"They used to be content to chew the roots. The ablutions those weirdos provide, and their wishes for the tree to grow strong and tall abate the damage. Somewhat."

"They believe in it. In the power it has. The power it *could* have. *If* it grows strong enough. If it lives long enough."

"And what power might that be?"

"To reconnect the remnants of nine broken, shattered worlds. To return your world to an age of legend."

"That might explain some of my Friday night shifts. 'Legendary.'"

The squirrel huffed and jammed its fists into its haunches. "Be serious."

"*You* are telling *me* to be serious?"

The squirrel wrinkled its nose. It looked cute when it scowled.

Don't get distracted, Marie.

"Unfortunately, the dragons figured out what these would-be wise women are doing, and they're stealing the wishes, and they're growing along with the tree. They hate it. It came to be after their brothers and sisters died."

Marie wasn't sure if she wanted the squirrel to be right, or wrong. She'd read legends. They didn't work out well for most people. Even heroes had a hard time. It was a rare hero who got a fair shake where gods and magic were concerned. If the squirrel was wrong, she was sharing a coffee with a giant talking squirrel. If she was imagining all this … *Not better.*

"If you can talk—and I'm not crazy—I guess I should know your name."

Yeah, knowing the name of the talking squirrel you're imagining is real helpful, *Marie. Bravo.*

The squirrel scowled. A cute look. She took a picture. It'd make a great animal meme. After she picked a celebrity to compare him to.

But who?

Kevin Costner?

You'd call him *a celebrity? What has he done lately?*

What have you *done?*

Low, Marie. Real low.

The squirrel's scowl hadn't abated. He really had expected her to know who he was. Marie shrugged, and the squirrel held out his hands as if pleading. "I gave you my name. Thor's nuts, I *spelled* it out for you."

Marie scrunched her brow. Spelled ... "The Scrabble tiles?"

"Yes."

Marie tried to make a word—a name—out of the letters the squirrel had left for her. "Rostarkat? What kind of name is that?"

The squirrel let out a peeved sigh. He rubbed at his nose with little paws. Another photo opportunity wasted. "The name is Ratatoskr."

Marie repeated the name in her head. It sounded more like someone clearing their throat than a proper name.

"And that's supposed to mean something to me."

"Gods damn it, woman, haven't you heard of Google?"

"Obviously."

"Well if you'd tried *that* you'd know what's going on."

The squirrel stood on his hind legs and leaned against the counter like an office raconteur. He reminded her of Bobby, whose funny stories always ended in a creepy compliment or request for a date. The squirrel was only missing the polo shirt (and pants).

Don't look there, Marie.

Too late.

The squirrel winked.

Yeah, just like Bobby.

"You're right," Marie said. "I'm sorry."

"I need more coffee," the squirrel said. "*Good* coffee. Where do you keep the espresso?"

She needed to de-escalate this ... Ratatoskr. Squirrels were trouble enough. A talking one hopped up on caffeine ...

Marie tried to convince herself she'd dealt with worse. Plenty of times. Especially when she'd worked loss prevention at the Bay downtown. Something about that place brought out the weirdos. She'd had people come at her with switchblades, drywall saws, whatever they could get their hands on. One guy'd kept a full set of kitchen knives down his pants.

She muttered, "I can't believe I'm talking to a fucking squirrel."

"I'm not *a* fucking squirrel. I'm *the* fucking squirrel, thank you very much."

"But ... why are you ... why would you? Why are you?"
Bravo, Marie.
I thought we handled that superbly.
The squirrel rubbed at his face and took another sip of coffee. "Okay, here's the deal: I need you to save the tree."

She shrugged. "I'm not sure what *I'm* supposed to do about it. I'm a security guard, not an arborist."

"*This* is your call to adventure."

"This is my call to go to the hospital," Marie said, rubbing at her eyes. *How many hours can you go without sleep before you hallucinate?*

"How about this? You will be visited by three—"

"No."

"Aww, c'mon."

"No."

"Fine," the squirrel said, crossing its arms and sulking.

"Why me?"

The squirrel snorted a laugh. "Why does everyone given a quest ask 'why me?' Boo-fucking-hoo. Life's unfair. I'm sure you've seen the shoe commercials. Just do it, Marie."

"I'm not complaining, you bushy-tailed dick. I'm curious. Why me? Why does it *have* to be me? What do I bring to the table?"

"You control the tokens," the squirrel said, holding a loonie he'd pilfered from the staff coffee fund. "You control the wishes."

"And you're what—a furry genie?"

"Wrong pantheon. How would you understand it?" The squirrel puffed himself up, straightened his shoulders and loomed. The action looked ridiculous. Marie felt ridiculous. "More like your Gandalf. Or Obi-Wan," he said.

"I don't need either," Marie said, wondering why all the film references, and also where squirrels went to movies. Did they go alone? Or did a bunch of them climb into a trench coat so they only had to pay one admission?

Ratatoskr continued rummaging through the break room cabinets. "What did you do with those nuts I gave you?"

Marie blushed. "I threw them in the trash. I ... I didn't know where they'd been."

The squirrel cast some serious shade and maintained his angry stare. He lashed out with a foot, kicking over the garbage bin. He rummaged for a minute, fished one of the nuts from the trash and gave his head a disappointed tut-tut shake. He also held up a half-eaten egg salad sandwich.

"You gonna eat this?"

Marie shuddered. "All yours."

Ratatoskr nodded his thanks and crammed the whole thing into his mouth. He pressed the acorn into her hand.

Dealing with after-hours drunks was more adventure than she'd ever had—or needed. She'd pulled a woman from a moving Jeep. The Jeep kept moving and the would-be thief lost control of her bladder while they'd tousled. Marie had been scared before, but she'd never feared for her life until today.

Ratatoskr kept talking, cheeks bursting as he spread garbage *everywhere*. "Here's the thing ..."

Marie rolled the acorn around in her fingers. It had scratches that looked like they might be letters, only not in any alphabet she recognized. Had to be a coincidence.

He passed her the other acorns. "Keep these with you."

"I don't want any of this."

"And yet," the squirrel said, now stuffing its cheeks with *her* lunch, "here we are."

✦

The squirrel hadn't helped her clean the break room. Said he needed to check on the tree, since she wasn't doing her job. Marie decided to refute the little red shit by doing the job she was getting paid for.

He'd said his name was Ratatoskr. The name didn't mean anything to Marie—she could barely pronounce it—but on a whim she'd Googled it while making her rounds, looking for dragons and elves and trolls and any and everything she knew and—not quite—believed to be real. Her results were filled with Norse mythology links. In between checking doors and sipping coffee, Marie read on her phone.

Myths being real made less sense than talking squirrels.

There was a tree, also an ash—*the* ash, Marie supposed. An eagle. A dragon. The illustrations looked like that weird lizard the squirrel had left her. A baby dragon? No more outrageous than anything else that'd been happening lately. It was all there. Well most of it. There was a bunch of other stuff mentioned too. Fortune tellers and wells of wisdom. Cows. Other worlds. None of that had shown up yet—unless you counted those weird ladies at the wishing well. Nonsense.

Ratatoskr appeared to be on the level. As on the level as a shape-changing talking squirrel *could* be.

What if he's a guy who turns into a squirrel?

Why would he choose a squirrel and not a wolf, Marie?

Or a bear?

Exactly.

Can lycanthropes choose what they turn into?

More squirrels in the city than wolves or bears. Easier to hide.

True.

And he could've Googled all this Norse shit as easily as I did. All his "proof" is right there. He might just be fucking with us.

Still doesn't explain the lizards, Marie.

Dragons.

Right. Dragons.

Or the tree. Or the weird cultists …

It could be a long con. Like something out of Ocean's Eleven.

For pocket change? Unlikely.

Maybe myths being real made more sense after all. She didn't know why she was trying to make sense of it instead of drinking until the squirrel was quiet. Marie's phone rang.

Ratatoskr's voice, several octaves higher and a hundred decibels louder than Marie remembered, screamed, "Where *are* you?"

"Doing my job," Marie shot back. "How'd you get this number?"

"Hurry!"

Marie didn't want to believe the squirrel, but she ran anyway.

She fished out the weirdo's business card on the run, hoping she wasn't about to make a fool of herself. Thinking, backup would be great. She fumbled her phone, and as it was either phone or card, she dropped the card and kept running.

The Union Station rotunda was centrally located, but she was about as far away as she could get and still be in the building. And on a different floor. It took her longer to make it back than the squirrel—or she—would've liked.

Fog still rolled off the pool. Marie's breath misted as if the temperature had dropped twenty degrees. Something dark and obscured by the fog clawed at the tree. She heard hissing and scratching. The tree was dying. Its branches drooped, leaves wilting and falling into the wishing pool. Tiger stripes of eaten bark criss-crossed its trunk.

And Marie had thought the talking squirrel and the tree-worshipping cult were weird. Distracted by the fog and what was inside, it took a moment for her to notice the creature wasn't alone. Lizards circled the rotunda, darting towards the tree and hopping backwards as if afraid of it.

Dragons, Marie.

Yes, of course. Dragons. *Best not forget that.*

They'd grown. Now they were larger than dogs. Big dogs. Almost as big as her.

Too big.

One saw her and scuttled forward, hissing. The others continued to gnaw at the tree. Marie drew out her baton, snapping out the telescoping rod from her belt, extending it with a flick of her wrist. She didn't think that would be enough to keep the dragons from destroying the tree.

The dragon came at her in a serpentine undulating dash. She wasn't sure who screamed louder—her, or the squirrel. The dragon's motion made it hard to track. She swung, striking its side. The baton rebounded like she'd struck a wall and almost hit her shoulder on the backstroke.

She had to get to the tree. Get the dragons off it.

She skittered back to get space, prodding the dragon on the snout with her baton to keep it at bay. The dragons had a manic, hopping gait. When their bellies weren't pressed to the floor, they ran atop one another like a stream of snakes. Their hisses sounded like steam escaping a kettle. She yelled and waved her arms. One dragon leapt off the tree, splashing through the pool toward her. The others scuttled around the hind side of the ash, watching as they ate its bark. They grew larger with every nibble.

Now she had a dragon on either side of her. Tonight was going to get worse before it got better.

"Ratatoskr, help me."

"I'm a lover not a fighter. I run messages. That's it."

"What are you, a *yellow* squirrel? Help me you fucking coward!"

"That's the spirit! Do that to the dragons."

"Do what?"

"Insult them. They *have* to react."

Marie wasn't sure she wanted the dragons to react to her any more than they already were. She had nothing else to lose. "You suck, dragons!"

"Do better."

"*You* do better. I'm busy."

It would be a cold day in hell before Marie would listen to a squirrel again. It should be too cold for reptiles—the snakes wouldn't be out of their dens in Narcisse for another month or two—but these little buggers were rolling in the freezing mist and basking in the moonlight as if it were sun, pleased as piss to be out in the cold.

"Go on," Marie hollered. "*Shoo!* Get!"

As one they turned. Dull yellow eyes staring. Tongues darting. What did reptiles do with their tongues? The memory came back to Marie in a disgusting rush. They tasted the air with their tongues.

Oh, God. They're tasting me.

Marie bit back a scream. Acting would help with the fear. There were a lot of them, but she could handle this.

Something landed on her shoulder and Marie did scream.

"Be careful," the squirrel said, smaller now, the size of an actual squirrel. "They're venomous."

Of course they are.

"Thanks for the tip," Marie said through gritted teeth.

"That's why I'm up here. The longer you stay upright, the safer I'll be."

Typical.

The weirdos had been splashing the trunk with water from the well. They'd believed it'd helped. First Marie had to get the dragons out of the water and off the tree. Or the cavalry couldn't ride any further.

Marie struck the lizard to her right and dashed for the pool, splashing through the icy water and swinging wildly at the dragons on the tree and in the pool even as she avoided their hissing strikes. Where water hit the tree, Marie saw the bark grow over its scars. She still saw wounds, but the tree *was* on the mend. If only she could get the dragons angry enough to follow *her* and leave the tree behind.

"Your insults aren't strong enough," Rat said. After a peeved squawk from Marie, the squirrel looked back to the rotunda's open roof and hollered, "They aren't, and you know they aren't."

"Seriously?" Marie shook her head. "*You're* plenty irritating. Why don't you try?"

The squirrel scowled. "I'm the *messenger*. Why don't *you* try since my entire life offends you so much?"

She shrugged. Couldn't hurt.

Unless you succeed, and they come after you and hurt you.

Thanks, Marie.

"You're ... uh ... too fat to fly," Marie said.

Ratatoskr rolled his eyes. "Tried that one."

"Try it again."

The squirrel cupped his paws to his mouth and yelled something at the dragons in a language Marie didn't understand. They didn't even look up.

"Shit," she muttered.

"You're looking pale."

"Shut up, squirrel."

"You'll have to do better than that." The squirrel looked at her. "They say your uniform isn't very flattering."

It wasn't. Marie didn't care. Okay. She *did* care. But not about a lizard's opinion.

"Tell those jerks go fly a kite."

"You'll have to do better than that too."

"You look like worms with frostbite!" *Nothing.* She turned to the squirrel. "Any advice on how to make them want to fight?"

"Thor would usually call folks cock-gobblers and threaten them with his hammer. Loki accused people of incest and farting during sex."

I'll definitely have to get more creative.

"Imagine they're me," Ratatoskr suggested. "You always had good insults for me."

"You heard those?"

The squirrel nodded, and Marie smiled, turning back to the dragons. "You lamprey-pricked corpse-gobbler!"

As one, the dragons turned away from the tree and stalked out of the wishing well.

"That did it!" Ratatoskr yelled gleefully. "I didn't need to translate that one!"

Great. Careful what you wish for, Marie.

She bolted from the pool and the dragons clipping her heels and ran toward the cafeteria. She flipped tables and chairs behind her to slow their pursuit.

Ratatoskr asked, "You still have those nuts I gave you?"

"Yes."

"What are you waiting for?" The squirrel shook his head. "I can't help those who won't help themselves."

A dragon swiped at Ratatoskr.

"Hey," Ratatoskr squeaked, "*I didn't say it. She did!*"

The dragon didn't seem to care.

Marie didn't know what to do. The tree wilted faster, and she couldn't get to it to change that. To say nothing of the fact she and her squirrel mentor were about to be eaten.

Rat believed the nuts he'd given her mattered. Could she trust a squirrel? He said she'd guarded the wishes people had put in the wishing well. She rummaged in her pocket and drew them out.

The dragons' attention perked up.

Well, that's interesting, Marie.

Sure is, Marie.

"*I'm* the guardian of the tree? Like a Valkyrie? Or She-Ra or something?"

Ratatoskr nodded.

She took a deep breath. "You can do this, Marie."

Sure, Marie. It's like riding a bike except you have to steal the bike first, and its owner is a dragon and the bike is on fire.

She cracked the nut between her teeth and snapped out her telescoping rod, yelling, "I have the power!"

This wasn't *Masters of the Universe* and she wasn't She-Ra, but she felt something change. It'd been a clear sky, fog in the station notwithstanding, the stars were out, and out of nowhere there was a bright flash, and thunder boomed, shaking the station.

She caught her reflection in a glass door.

"Ah!"

She was smoking. The lightning strike had turned her rod into a sword and her bear spray was a round oaken shield. Twin braids contained her hair now, rather than a ponytail. Her uniform had been replaced with boob cups and furry bikini bottoms; her boots with strappy sandals.

Oh, come on.

She tried to cover herself. The squirrel was watching—and a pervert.

"Hey, this is your idea of what a lady warrior looks like, not mine. Do some research."

Yeah, his probably only needed the sandals.

Marie muttered, "I clearly should've said, 'I have the power—and the clothes.'"

She liked the braids. They were pretty. She'd have to get her roommate to teach her how to do them. Now wasn't the time for updating her style. She had dragons to fight.

This is a bad idea, Marie.

Tell me about it.

Hurry up or we'll never go through with it.

She gave the sword a test swing. "Let's do this."

"Little help," cried Ratatoskr. A dragon had pinned him. Sickly yellow saliva oozed from its jaws.

"I'm coming," Marie yelled, rushing to the squirrel.

The dragon squatted, covering Ratatoskr. It reared up, ready to fight, tail swaying behind it, a whip waiting to snap.

Marie yelled, "Get off him, you fucker!"

The dragon snarled, but other than the motion of its tail, it didn't move.

"Do better!" Ratatoskr yelled.

"Get off, you ... you ... shite-eating tree fucker!"

The dragon hissed. Its claws loosened. Marie rushed it. Her feet closed the distance faster than she'd expected. She felt taller, not just stronger. She slashed at the dragon. Its tail lashed out to batter the blade aside and the sword sliced neatly through it. It shrieked, jaws darted for her, and Marie grabbed it by the throat. Its claws were still free. Marie needed space. She shoved her shield against it and reared back, hoping to free Ratatoskr with a kick so the squirrel could help her.

She kicked, and the dragon soared into the air taking Rat with it. It crashed into the second-floor balcony, rebounded off the stone and plummeted onto the food court tables. Ratatoskr skittered out from under the debris.

"Thanks," he said, dusting himself off.

"You're welcome."

"I was being sarcastic."

"So was I."

The dragons circled Marie, but at least they were leaving Ratatoskr—and the tree—alone.

That's great, Marie. I'm so happy you've made this happen.

Quiet, Marie. We have monsters to fight.

We'll discuss this later.

Of course we will.

She had to keep them away from the tree. She had to keep them from destroying the rotunda. She'd have a hard time explaining what had happened to the dayshift as it was. They already thought she was crazy.

Crazy like a fox who knows what's really going on in the chicken coop.

That makes no sense, Marie.

Neither does tonight, Marie.

You've got me there.

Damn straight.

She was the guardian of the wishes as well as the tree. The magic acorn had turned her into one of the *Masters of the Universe*. If she'd made her own wish, maybe she could get rid of them for good. Only problem: she had no cash. Rat's coffee had taken her last quarter. Worse: she had nothing to pay for her next cup of coffee.

The coffee money!

"Rat! Get me the coffee fund!"

The squirrel gave her a quizzical look, but understanding quickly dawned. "On it!"

She needed to hold off the dragons long enough for the squirrel to get back. Assuming her plan would work.

It had to work.

You're the guardian of the wishes, Marie.

I'd better be.

As the squirrel scurried away, Marie yelled imprecations, hoping to keep the dragons' attention on her until Ratatoskr returned with the coins. For the life of her she couldn't think of an insult. She *needed* an insult. She searched through a pouch on her belt for her phone, hoping it still worked after whatever power had turned her into a monster fighter. Her baton had become a sword, what if her phone was no longer a phone?

It was.

She typed frantically, the dragons rushed forward.

Insult generator.

"Gorbellied full-gorged maggot pie!"

"Spongey ill-breeding codpiece."

"Wimpled trash-eating barnacles."

"Loggerheaded treacherous egg!"

The dragons hissed back at her. They weren't charging. It was as if they were answering her, insult for insult. She couldn't understand what they were saying without Rat there to translate. She wasn't sure she *wanted* to know.

Rat was back, and a ring of dragons separated them.

"I'll piss in your chimneys!" Marie didn't know what that meant. But it worked.

Ratatoskr darted through the line of dragons, coffee can of coins held high. One of the dragon's tails slapped Ratatoskr aside. The can rolled away, its lid popped open, and the coins spilled onto the rotunda floor.

Marie dove for the coins, scooping up as many as she could.

"I wish you couldn't hurt the tree." Marie tossed one coin for each dragon. They looked back and forth between her and the tree, worried. She tossed in more coins. "Or anyone else."

The dragons splashed past Marie and into the pool, lunging for the tree, but they couldn't touch it. The dragons shrieked, scratching, trying to bite, stab. Nothing they did had any effect.

Marie shook her fist. "Nuh, uh," she said. "Scoot!"

The dragons hissed.

Marie shook her fist full of coins. "My next wish'll be a doozy."

The dragons bolted for the train station exit and towards the riverside market. She should let them be The Forks Market security's problem. That would teach them.

But she was the tree's guardian, and this was *her* problem. "I wish you'd go home."

The fog caught up with the dragons and dragged them into the well. With a muffled *whump* they, and the fog, were gone.

The squirrel beamed at her, puckering up as if awaiting a kiss. "Now about my reward …"

Marie shook her head. Never trust a squirrel.

Or his nuts.

A FISTFUL OF WOOL

Darren Ridgley

Dawn cursed as she struck one of the many potholes that dotted westbound Route Fifty. She was coming back, at Mom's urging. She didn't plan on staying any longer than she had to.

She had just turned off of Fifty when she saw the sign, more harbinger than herald for her now. She was less than ten kilometres out of Alonsa.

She made it into the community, not quite a town anymore, and let her rusted Crown Vic come to a rest outside the diner that had changed ownership so many times, Dawn never bothered to memorize its present name. The menu was always the same no matter who ran it, anyway. She should go home, check in on Nellie. But she preferred to hide out with the old man for a minute, and since it was before noon on a Saturday, this was where he'd be.

She opened the rickety storm door separating the patronage from the dust-ridden wind. The smell of grease hit her first, but it soon blended with the stink of sweat-stained flannel as the room filled with aging farmers, in for a bite after a morning's work. Just like every other town she'd ever visited in this province.

She hated how dark it was, considering summer was just starting and it was a wonderfully sunny day out. Over in the corner by the register, was the old man, sipping what was probably his sixth mug of cheap joe.

"There she is," his voice was hoarse from years of cigarettes. A few days' worth of stubble sprouted from his skinny, loose-skinned face. "My little girl, come to buy me breakfast."

"I think you still owe me from last time." Dawn pulled up a red vinyl-covered chair, the back of it split open, and took a seat across from him. "Good to see you, dad."

"Been home yet?"

"Just got into town. How are they?"

"Oh, God. You'd think the world was ending."

Dawn recalled the phone call she'd received from her mom a few days prior. Nellie—her younger sister and mom's Permanent Golden Child—had broken her leg after tumbling down a flight of stairs at work. She'd be off her feet for a while the leg mended in a cast, but she'd heal up fine. To mom and Nellie, though, it was the end. Nellie had been such a strong runner in high school, Mom had whined. Now, the injury might endanger Nellie's chances of taking part in future events. Never mind that Nellie hadn't run a race since Grade 12, eight years ago, except for some jogging to stay reasonably fit. To Mom, this was Muhammad Ali getting diagnosed with Parkinson's. Dawn resented their bond. Not that she wanted it reversed, but she remembered how it used to be different—how she had been mom's favourite for a while, after which the focus was placed solely on her younger sister. Dawn never knew why. She knew if she asked, all she'd get would be denial. As she mused, a teenager in an apron dutifully filled her brown mug with bad coffee, assuming that everyone who came in here wanted some.

"Is mom, like, aware that Nellie isn't dying?"

Dad rolled his eyes. "You know the two of them. They get each other going and there's no talking to either one of them."

"I know, right?"

"Ah, well," Dad leaned back in his chair. "She's still your little sister, Dawn. You stuck up for her all the time when you were kids. I know that changed over the years, but she'll always need you there, somehow, someway."

"You're getting soft in your old age."

"Ah, shut it." Dad gave her a brusque wave-off. Dawn smirked.

A plate of shredded hash browns and sausages was placed in front of her dad, and the conversation stopped.

◆

Dawn and her mom had been smiling at one another in the living room for several minutes, their teas cooling in their hands, before Dawn decided to just abandon politeness and start the argument she knew was coming anyway.

"There is absolutely no reason for Nel to move in with you for a while. None. You're being"—a host of profane and insulting terms crept to Dawn's mind but it was still Mom—"silly."

"I am not. Your sister is in a huge amount of pain right now. The injury is still fresh, and she needs my help. That medicine they gave her is good for nothing."

A groan escaped from the upper floor of the house, followed by a whimper. Dawn rolled her eyes. Nellie should've been in drama class, not on the track team. She was probably eavesdropping on their conversation through the vent in the floor up there.

"That may be the case today, but she'll be just fine. Honestly, you baby her so much."

Dawn's mom said nothing. She sipped from her tea, looking away from her daughter.

"I'm her mother, Dawn. I will always look after my babies. If it was you I would—"

"Tell me to suck it up and move on?"

"Good Lord, Dawn. Are you ever going to get over that?"

Dawn smacked the bottom of her mug on the table a bit too hard, sending a geyser of orange pekoe roiling out of the cup and onto her fingers. She held in a yelp before it escaped her mouth, sucked the warm liquid off her fingers. Her mother took on a hard expression.

"Dawn?" Nellie's voice bored down the staircase and the hall. Her pain hadn't halted her projection any. "How long are you going to make me wait? Come see me. Please."

Dawn sighed, pushing away the mug, and stomped adolescently up the stairs. The upstairs bedrooms had been converted into a kind of miniature loft back when they were kids, forcing the two of them to share the space. Only one bed remained in the room, reserved for the child who visited more. She occupied it again now, still in her pajamas, the TV softly droning with reality TV schlock.

"It's good to see you, sis."

Nellie's voice was pained. She probably was in quite a bit of discomfort, but even so, Dawn was hesitant to dote on her too much and feed into any exaggeration that might be there. "You too. So you've come home for a bit, huh?"

Nellie reached for the remote and shut the TV off. Dawn felt her IQ return to normal levels as the nasal droning of real housewives dissipated.

"Dawn, I've come home for good. I'm never leaving this place."

"Oh, come on. You're going to milk Mom and Dad forever based on this? You've taken advantage of them plenty of times, but this—"

"You don't understand. This is it for me. I'm not going to make it through the week."

Dawn rolled her eyes. She figured Nellie would overblow her problem to garner sympathy with Mom and Dad, but didn't expect Nel to try the same thing with her.

"Give me a break. You want me to buy that you have gangrene under that thing or something? Maybe flesh-eating disease?" Dawn rapped her knuckles against the cast.

"This isn't about the leg. The leg I could deal with. This is about something else. Something I did a long time ago."

Nellie's hand seized Dawn by the forearm and gripped it tightly. Dawn noted how wiry Nel's arm looked, how strong she still appeared to be.

"Do you remember," Nellie continued, "the man in the long grey coat?"

Dawn felt a knot in her stomach. "I'll always remember the man in the long grey coat."

It happened in the early '80s, when they were little girls playing on the outskirts of town. Dawn had been the stronger one then, Nellie scrawny and sick most of the time. Dawn had been following a family of frogs as they hopped through the tall grass around a culvert. Nel had fallen behind, as usual, and when Dawn turned around to check on her, she saw Nel talking up a stranger. Everything about him had screamed "stranger danger," so she'd run at the two of them and grabbed Nellie, trying to pull her away. The stranger kicked Dawn in the torso, winding her and breaking a rib. She passed out just as he took Nellie's hand in hers. When she woke up, she was in the hospital, Nellie was still around, just sitting there with Mom and Dad as if nothing had happened. She never saw the man again.

When Dawn was recovering from her injury, she asked Nel why she'd been speaking to the man, and Nel's response had made little sense to her then: "He promised to help me catch up."

"I'm surprised you remember, Nel. You haven't remembered all those years. I tried to save your life and you told Mom I had climbed a tree and fallen. I was attacked! And you lied about it to protect some stranger? Mom said that I was reckless and irresponsible and I deserved the pain for being stupid."

"I know Mom was always hard on you and I'm sorry, okay? But I had to protect myself. I wasn't protecting him. I gave that man something. Now I know I'm not going to get it back. Not unless you help me."

"Nel, what could you have given him that would be so important? You were just a kid."

"He's coming to collect now. I know he is. I've seen his ... messengers. I want you to go talk to him for me, to try to help me out of this, Dawn. Please. I'm begging you."

Dawn paced the room, her arms crossed defensively across her chest. Nellie had soaked up all the attention, all the glory, for years.

She'd treated Dawn with disdain during their teenage years, actually expecting deference from her, to idolize her like their mom did. And now she wanted help.

She looked at her sister and saw her eyes, red from crying, watched her face as she winced while moving herself into more of an upright position. She had already tried to save her little sister, once. But like Dad said, they were still siblings. She still needed someone to look out for her, especially now. Who knew what the man in the long grey coat was after?

Dawn muttered something dark. Then she made up her mind. "How do I find him?"

"I learned back in second grade how to call him. It'll still work."

"Give me the number."

"Not a phone number. A song. You won't believe me until you sing it and he's there."

✦

Dawn sat back in the same table she and her father had occupied the day before. She'd considered trying it out in a field somewhere, away from prying eyes, but her gut warned her not to be entirely alone during the attempt. And if this worked, she didn't want it happening at home.

She waited until the staff was occupied in the kitchen. She kept her eyes on the table—Nellie had said to be looking down when it started—and sang.

Hey hey hey, old Jack Grey
Won't you come and make your way
To make my wishes all come true
And let the chase begin

She looked up and there he was, sitting in the corner, his back turned. A great grey overcoat, the one she remembered, was draped over his shoulders. But now, having grown up herself, she realized just how thin he was, and how his scant frame made the coat seem that much bigger. His hair was as black as it had been when she met him all those years ago.

"Aren't you going to come sit with me, Dawn?" he said, the words oozing from his throat.

Dawn stared at him a moment longer and winced. She looked at her palm to see she'd dug her fingernails through her skin, little lines of red marking their place. Her rib started to nag her for the first time since she was a child. She rose from her chair and took small steps until she was seated in front of him. He looked like a normal person, which surprised her. She'd had years to mutate his features in her mind, so his ordinary looks almost felt anticlimactic. His moustache was as black as the hair on his head, and the bags under his eyes suggested he didn't sleep much. He could have passed for any middle-aged farmer in the area, if it weren't for the alarm bells blaring deep within her making it clear she was not safe.

An oblivious server came by with two empty mugs and a pot of coffee, right on time. Jack Grey motioned for them both to be filled. He gulped his as soon as it was set down. She watched the muscles in his neck move as he drank, forcing down the hot liquid. When he was done, he motioned for a refill.

She couldn't tear her eyes off him to consider the mug in front of her. Finally, she found some nerve.

"You did something to my sister," Dawn said. "Whatever it is, whatever this is, I want you to stop."

"I didn't do anything to or for your sister that she didn't agree to. But then I'm guessing she didn't tell you the whole story, hm?"

Dawn nodded.

"But I'm betting after singing that song and calling me here, you're a little more open-minded?"

She nodded again. He drank the second half of the cup in one mouthful. Trails of dark brown fluid trickled out the side of his lips.

"Your sister sang that song not even believing it would work. I guess I have Bloody Mary to thank for that. You kids and your summoning rituals, you don't even know what's real and what's not, anymore," Jack scoffed, pushing the mug away with his fingertips. "But when she saw I was there, she knew exactly what she wanted."

"Which was?"

"To surpass you. Kids are so fickle, and jealous. A completely typical case of a younger sibling's envy of the elder one. You were taller and stronger and quicker on the draw, intellectually. And you were the first-born, which brings with it a certain household status. So, as power-ups go, it was easy. A wave of my hand and her muscles got a little bigger, her asthma disappeared, her IQ went up twenty points. Immediately she was ahead of the game, and as long as she kept up the good work it would stay that way."

The knowledge made Dawn angry. Nellie's grades had skyrocketed around grade three. She became more athletic. From middle school on, she was bringing in gold medals left and right. All to show her up? All this time Dawn had felt outclassed by her younger sibling, and had resented her for it, and now she knew that success hadn't even been earned. Nellie had rigged the system against her. But then what about the present?

"But Nellie didn't stay successful. She hasn't competed in over a decade. That doesn't sound like the deal you made."

Jack defensively shook his head and wagged a bony finger at her. "Not my fault. You humans, you're too complacent. I didn't make her stop competing. If she'd kept it up she'd have been Olympics material for sure. But like all kids, she changed her dreams once she got older. She wasted her gift. Now, the time has come to collect."

"About that. She said I was supposed to get you to stop from collecting something."

Jack considered that for a moment, but then his eyes went wide and he laughed a loud, booming laugh, startling the server at the register. "Oh, that's good. I see."

"Illuminate me." Dawn's posture grew more relaxed as her initial fear of him waned.

"Do you even know what I am?"

"I don't know if I care. I'm just trying to help my sister."

"Oh, you ought to care. What your sister is asking of you very much concerns you."

Jack reached out and brushed her cheek with his finger before she could react. In a moment her mind was flooded with fear, pain, and an aching, bottomless loneliness. Her hands gripped at the surface of the smooth table but found no purchase. Several of her nails broke in the effort to grasp it. She contained a scream and instead released a heavy sob. The server made a move for their table, but Dawn shot her hand up to wave her off. Her mind tried to find a word for what she felt.

"You're the devil."

"No. A devil. Well, an angel, technically. But devil works."

"Nellie sold ... sold her soul to you?"

"Almost."

"What do you mean 'almost?'" Tears welled up in Dawn's eyes. The emotions triggered by the demon's touch were taking their time dissipating.

"Well, sure, let's have some Sunday School while we're here. I seem like the guy for that." Jack rolled his eyes at her. "Children *can't* go to Hell. They're fundamentally innocent and therefore can't be damned. But they're also incredibly gullible and, as I said, eager to barter something long-term for something short-term. It was a goldmine waiting to be tapped and no one was tapping it. So I did."

Jack took Dawn's coffee from her, taking deep gulps before continuing.

"I make the deal, right? Your soul for whatever you want. And then you get it, immediately. But I wait until you're an adult to collect, after you've a chance to *lose* that childhood innocence. But sadly, it's not even as simple as that. Since the deal was made with a child I have to make my mark re-agree to the terms as an adult, so it's all on the up-and-up. Honestly, the worst thing about the other side isn't the holy wrath or the predestined outcome of Armageddon—it's all the *bureaucracy* they make you deal with."

Dawn tried to think of what he could mean by "re-agree to the terms," and the song came back to her head.

"And let the chase begin," Dawn whispered, newly worried someone might be overhearing, somewhere.

"You have to have a fair chance out of the deal, to make up for the fact you were naïve when you signed. It's all chances within chances within chances. When I collect, I send a messenger. Three times. Twice to warn you the time is near. The second and third visits will occur the same day. The third time you see it, the chase is on, and you have your chance. My messenger will flee, and if you can lay hands on it before it disappears from view, you get your soul back, no harm no foul. If you can't, you're dead before you know it, and I have you. You're in Hell before you've had time to blink."

"Just like that?"

"Just like that."

"And what if someone refuses to chase your messenger? You said they have to re-agree to the contract. What if they just say no?"

"Well," he swirled the coffee around in its mug. "That was a problem, at first. But you know, I'm happy to be vague about what constitutes 'agreement.' As of the third visit, the chase is on. You're free to stand perfectly still and never go after it. You're free to turn your back and leave."

"But?"

"But it will just keep reappearing. Every day, day and night, in your waking hours, in your dreams. You can keep ignoring it, if you want, but eventually, you'll wear down. You'll get tired of seeing it in your face all the time. You will chase, even if you have to lose your mind first to do it. Might as well buck up and get it over with."

Dawn watched as he finished the other cup. She hadn't noticed until now how fast her breathing had become.

"Now do you realize why you're here, Dawn?"

She nodded. She did.

"You bastard. You waited until Nel couldn't chase your stupid messenger. Speed was her whole thing, and you broke her leg, then sent your goons."

"Whoa, whoa, whoa, I didn't break her leg. That was just bad luck for her. It would have violated the contract for me to rig the game like that, but if it works out that way by random chance ... hey, I'm not complaining. Lots of people go their whole lives without breaking one of their legs. Hell of a stroke of luck for me."

"And now, Nel needs someone to run the race for her. She wants me to do it for her ... to agree to the contract on her behalf."

"And do you agree? Will you?"

She thought back to that day, in the ditch, back when they were girls. Dawn had failed to protect Nellie at the time. Her sister had been a dumb kid, filled with a child's jealousy, and had spent the rest of her life dreading exactly what was coming. Dawn's feelings about her sister were powerful, a sibling rivalry that had simmered, and sometimes boiled over, for years. But she didn't want her sister to lose her soul.

She felt sick. All those years ago, she'd tried to keep Jack Grey away from Nellie and failed. She could hardly comprehend what was on the line, but she saw a second chance in front of her. Nellie didn't deserve this fate, however much of a pain she might have been, and Dawn knew she didn't either—but Nel didn't stand a chance, and she did. There was only one choice to make.

She nodded again.

"I'll do it. One condition, though. No matter what happens, we're not playing for Nel anymore. It's me you get if I lose."

Jack hopped in his chair a little bit with faux excitement, as though he hadn't anticipated her decision. She hated that he was mocking her, but knowing what she knew, was unsurprised.

"Such a good sister you are. I'll be in touch. Soon."

Jack rose from his chair and left the restaurant. Dawn never saw him walk past any of the windows. He was nowhere in sight when she left soon after.

◆

Dawn and Nellie sat across from each other at the kitchen table while their parents worked in the garden outside. Dawn looked out over her mother's rock gardens and enjoyed a moment of peace, the first she'd had since her meeting with Jack Grey. Dawn had been glad to escape her rural confines and take up the metropolitan life in Winnipeg. She liked her Wolseley townhouse, so close to a great coffee shop, and the bustle of downtown and the shops of Osborne Village. But when she was here, the colours in the flowers just seemed to pop more. Birdsong reached her ears more easily. Sometimes she wondered if she could return to quiet, pastoral Alonsa, maybe when she was older. She wondered now if she'd have the chance.

Nellie knew what she'd asked Dawn to do. She knew from the moment Dawn walked in that she'd accepted the deal. Dawn couldn't help but pity her sister: all of her success early on, all of her accolades and the love from her parents, all of it had been beneath the shadow of Jack Grey, looming overhead her entire life. She wondered if Nellie had really enjoyed any of it. No wonder her attitude had sucked.

"How many times have you seen it?"

"Just once. Before I came out here. Right after I broke the leg."

"How did you know it was the messenger?"

"It gives you the same feeling he does. But even just seeing it ... to me it looked like a jet-black ram. It was standing in the middle of downtown Winnipeg and nobody reacted. It stared at me the whole time I was looking at it, and then it just vanished. I knew then he was coming for me."

Dawn nodded. A ram. A little on the nose, symbolically, but then this was a demon who dealt with children, so maybe he wasn't afraid to go broad. She'd have to keep her eyes open.

"Dawn, I don't know what to say," Nellie choked on her words. She gripped her cast tightly, funneling some anger into the plaster, as if she wished she could heal the leg and bust the cast open through sheer frustration. "I don't think there's anything I can say. I don't even know if I understand what I've asked you to do. I thought I knew, but the closer we get to the moment, the more real it becomes … Dawn, what did I do?"

"You've asked me to go to Hell for you. Potentially."

Nellie covered her mouth. They hadn't thought about heaven, or hell, for years. Not since they moved away from home. Neither of them had been much for religion—Dawn had been agnostic at best. She longed for those days.

You've asked me to go to Hell for you. When the words had come out of her mouth they tumbled out easily, like she was reading about quantum gravity out of a textbook—a concept beyond her understanding, easily put into words made empty by ignorance.

Nellie tried to say something, but the words caught in her throat. She spun in her chair, walked along the kitchen counter one-legged over to the sink, and vomited, bracing herself on her elbows. When she finished, she wept, spit and puke reaching down from her chin to the drain in a thick tendril.

Dawn heard her mother call to them through the open kitchen window. She looked out and staggered back. Standing amid the marigolds, next to her mother, was the ram. It looked straight at her, not moving a muscle. Dawn's mother didn't seem to notice anything.

"There it is," Dawn found herself whispering again.

"I don't see it. God, I don't see it. He really did it. He passed it on to you. Dawn, I'm so sorry," Nellie wiped her mouth with a dishtowel, then went still, unsure what to say next.

Dawn looked at her watch. It was one o'clock. Something told her the chase would begin in the evening, something more than a gut feeling. Her survival instinct, maybe. She looked back at the garden, and the ram was gone.

❖

Dawn and Nellie both grimaced as the Crown Vic struck potholes along the highway again. She knew the ram would have to come to her wherever she was, so she found an open field to set up shop. The longer she kept the thing in her line of sight, the better her chances would be. Out here, she could see for miles. She pulled over onto the shoulder and got out, helping her sister out of the passenger side and onto her crutches. She handed her a cellphone and her keys.

"Call mom and dad to come get you and take the car home if I don't come back. Take care of it, at least as well as you can. It's a real junker."

Nellie leaned forward, placing her forehead on Dawn's shoulder.

"I love you."

"You too."

Dawn stepped back, feeling the cool evening wind on her skin. She had been able to borrow some of Nellie's old track clothes, which blessedly fit fairly well. She'd need the range of motion.

"Any advice?"

Nellie thought for a second. This wasn't like anything she'd ever had to do. "Don't ease up for a second. Don't ever assume you're about to win. Go as hard as you can until it's all over. Don't quit even half a second before that. Your brain is going to tell you that you're tired, that your muscles are too sore. Don't listen."

Dawn nodded. "What's the time, Nel?"

Nellie looked at her watch. "It's seven."

Dawn took a deep swallow. Anticipation, in anything, was always the worst. "I don't know if you can hear me, Jack. But it's like you said … Let's just get this over with."

They waited, the wind whistling past them, rustling the growing soybean crops and forming small cyclones of dust on the gravel shoulder. Dawn surveyed the landscape, and twenty yards to her right, in the field, she saw it. They locked eyes. The ram ground its hooves backward, kicking up clumps of freshly-watered earth. It took off in the other direction, and Dawn pursued.

She gained on the ram rapidly, but as they got deeper into the field she realized its ability to traverse the terrain gave it an edge. Running through the crop was getting harder. She tried to regulate her breathing. She expected the ram to be impossibly fast, but it wasn't. It wasn't easy, but she was at least keeping up with it. The demon had been truthful in this: winning was within the realm of possibility. It gave her hope. She pushed harder.

The ram took a sharp left turn, back toward the highway. Dawn wondered if it was tiring, running through the crop, and hoped to get on smoother ground for more speed. She turned with it. As she ran, the feeling the ram gave off crept back into her, the fear and pain and loneliness that infused Jack Grey. She tried to block it out, to keep running. But the feeling slowed her for half a second—a half-second which she already knew would cost her.

She went into a sprint to try to catch up. She started gaining again. They got to the edge of the field and the ram turned again, running parallel to the highway. Dawn finally saw what it was doing. Sitting at the edge of the field was a long-abandoned tool shed, its white paint peeling in the sun. The doorway was open, the door swung inside the structure and the interior was cast in shadow. If the ram got inside, she'd be unable to see it.

Her lungs were burning and her calves were beginning to cramp up. She growled in protest and ran harder, knowing that if she failed, her lungs would be no good to her anyway. If she ran until she had a heart attack, it would be worth it to save her soul.

She gained on the ram again, close enough to see flecks of dirt in its wool. She got closer and swiped at it, but her hands snatched at empty air. The ram bleated angrily and picked up its pace. Dawn tried to mount once last sprint.

Her right foot lifted off the dirt. It caught on something hard, and she fell to the ground with a crash.

She didn't look at what it was, whether a root or a discarded tool, or something else altogether. She couldn't afford it. She scrambled to her feet, feeling the sting of new cuts on her knees and shins, and ran again.

She started to lose hope as the ram neared the shed. She remembered Nellie's advice. Don't stop pushing. Don't stop pushing till you're over the line. She ran without breath in her lungs. She felt her heart beating, pulsing in her head, sweat dripping into her eyes.

The ram made it into the shed, but she was close enough she could still see it in the shadows. It stopped and looked at her. The ram nudged the door with its horns, pushing it closed.

Dawn sprinted again as the closing door covered more and more of the ram. The ram bleated, gloating already. The door closed slowly, but steadily. She reached the shed.

She wasn't sure if she could still see the ram's tail when she slammed into the wooden door. Her mind was too busy, too overloaded by adrenaline and exhaustion, too oxygen-deprived. Her shoulder struck the door, still open by half an inch. She barreled through an empty space and cracked her head on the shed's back wall.

The door slammed shut behind her. The ram was nowhere inside. The chase was over.

Dawn took a breath and felt a change in the air. A fierce wind howled through the wood walls, an obvious change from the calm summer evening she'd just left behind. She could see the interior of the shed, knew it was the same physical place she'd run into. But there was something off. The windowless storage space blocked her from seeing what was outside, but she knew. She could already feel it creeping into her. She cursed the demon's luck: if Nellie hadn't been hurt, she'd have caught the ram. The demon knew it.

She sat on an overturned bucket and caught her breath. She knew any moment of solitude in the shed might be her last. She was already in Hell, but it seemed like her humanity hadn't entirely drained away. She looked at the rusted, brown knob of the shed's door. The energy kept seeping through the walls, compounding the feelings it generated in her—the same ones Jack Grey had put in her heart just yesterday.

She thought about Alonsa, the place she visited rarely, and appreciated too little, too late. She'd never go back into that greasy spoon. She longed for the stink of sweat. She tried to picture her mother's flowers, but they were already fading. All of it was fading. Loneliness seeped into the places once occupied by faces, names, the different sounds of their laughter.

She looked around again, at the inside of the shed, at her own clothes. Another change. It wasn't that the world was without colour—she could still see red, and white, and brown, and green—but it was as if colour stopped meaning anything. As if it didn't matter whether anything shone or not. Light and dark, it made no difference. If there was a sun in Hell, and it shone yellow and warmed the days, Dawn didn't care. She couldn't, even if she tried. The loneliness was front and centre, and it flowed out freely from a cavern inside of her.

A knock came at the door. She stood up, dusting herself off. Her very last thought containing any humanity at all was, oddly, one of gratitude that she had spared her sister this bleakness. She'd done what she'd set out to do.

She grabbed the knob and twisted it.

INSECTUM

Adam Petrash

Mark stared at the cabin in front of him.
Neglected for years, the building was in dire need of repair. The eaves were filled with debris and covered with moss, the roof was tattered and needed replacing, the paint peeled and weathered after years of harsh Manitoba winters. It was a fixer-upper, but his grandfather had left it to him. It was his now, for better or for worse.

His grandfather had bought the land, building on it shortly thereafter, when he first emigrated from Australia back in the '50s. His grandfather had moved out there permanently after the death of Mark's grandmother; stayed there until he had fallen too sick to be on his own, and he was put into a home. He never made it back before he passed. Mark's parents were too busy with their careers to put any time or effort into a humble little shack, so no one had been out to tend to it and it showed.

"This is your cabin?" said Beth, her lip snarled upwards as she stepped out of the car with Molly, her Yorkie, cradled in her arms.

"Sure is."

Mark stepped onto the shifted steps, wobbling as he tried to balance their luggage and open the door, but when he turned the lock it didn't budge.

"The jamb must have shifted," he said, putting his shoulder into it. The door swung open with such a force that it stirred the dust inside.

Mark launched into a coughing fit, his lungs agitated by the stuffiness of the room.

"See? No problem."

Beth stared.

"Well, come on, then."

Inside, the curtains were drawn over all of the windows. Mark fumbled for the switches on the breaker and hit the lights. Beth screamed.

"What? What is it?"

He turned to see Beth.

"What are those?"

Mark looked to where Beth was pointing. The walls were lined with picture frames. Inside them were all different kinds of preserved insects. The shelves were lined with books on the subject, old ant farms, and specimens preserved in jars of liquid.

"Oh, that. Sorry, I should've mentioned that. He was an entomologist ... loved insects ... collected them from all over the world."

"It's creepy," she said, bending over to put Molly down.

Mark scanned the room, feeling only nostalgia for the many summers he had spent here, his grandfather teaching and quizzing him all about the different species of insects he had kept, when he saw the broken glass on the floor.

"Don't put Molly down yet. There's broken glass here and I'll need to pick up the rat poison first. It could kill her if she gets a hold of it."

Beth righted herself and held onto Molly tighter.

"What? There are rats in here?"

She babied that dog. Said she'd rather Molly have a personality than be well-behaved, but this meant that she chewed everything at floor level: fallen paper and pens, shoes. Mark thought it was cute at first, too, but the novelty quickly wore off when he found tooth marks in his new pair of Allen Edmonds.

"No. There shouldn't be. It's just a precaution. Wait here."

Mark grabbed the broom and dustpan out of the closet and swept up the pieces of broken glass. He saw that one of the many ant farms his grandfather had owned was broken. It was about the size of a large aquarium, and had long cracks that ran parallel to the many empty tunnels housed within.

Mark put his fingers into the exposed dirt and inspected it. It was bone dry, and absent of any nutrients whatsoever. He figured it must've shattered from one of the many cold winters. Anything living would be long dead by now.

He then found the old container that housed the poison and began combing through the rooms being as thorough as possible, peeking in the nooks and crevasses for the teal-coloured cubes.

Once when he was little he had come out there for a weekend with his family and his grandfather's dog, Bugger. Bugger managed to find a missed cube, had chewed it up into gnarled little pieces. He remembered his grandfather had to force a whole bottle of hydrogen peroxide down Bugger's throat to induce vomiting.

To avoid a repeat of that situation, he continued checking, double-checking, checking again until he got to the last bedroom where he saw a small heap of fur tucked in one of the far corners. There lay two dead rats, ossified, the flesh looking like it had been chewed. Maybe that's what the poison did to their insides.

Mark remembered his grandfather telling him about all the rodents looking for a warm place to hibernate and survive the cold winters. Squirrels in the old cast iron stove or rabbits under the floorboards. His grandfather said these things were commonplace if you lived out here.

Not wanting to scare Beth any further, Mark used the side of the pail and scooped the dead carcasses inside, closing the lid. He was sweating now from his cleaning and scavenging work, surprised by how warm the cabin was for not having any running heat source. He never remembered it being quite like this.

"We're all good," he said, returning to the door where he had left Beth. "How about we open up all these windows, get some air in here, then go to the water, pop some bottles of wine, and watch the sunset?"

Beth smiled at the romantic gesture, her mood warming.

✦

They both sat down on the bulging granite that tapered into the water. It was one of many rock faces that scarred the earth in this part of the Whiteshell, stretching as far as Mark's eyes would let him see. The sun hung low, suspended, turning the sky a palette of fiery oranges, delicious popsicle-coloured pinks, and deep crimson-purple magentas.

"It's pretty," said Beth, before sipping on her glass of white wine.

Molly roamed close by, investigating the nearby fallen trees and vegetation.

"It sure is."

"But that cabin is a disaster, Mark. You should sell the land and be done with it. Think of the money we can get for a lot like this. The land alone has to be over half a million."

Mark swirled his glass of Tempranillo, put the glass to his nose, and took a long drawn out inhale before sipping and swishing it in his mouth.

"I can't do that. Not right now at least. Besides, we could rebuild. Make it better, bigger."

"We? You mean you."

"Okay. I could rebuild. And when we have kids—"

"If."

"If we have kids it's a place to get away as a family, a real family, Beth."

Mark paused. He knew Beth wasn't fond of kids. Said she hated the idea of something growing inside of her, but he was still holding out hope that she'd come around.

The sun was behind the trees now, the water had changed to grey, and shadows stretched over its mirrored surface and where the two of them sat.

"You know I didn't have that with my parents," he continued. "It'd be nice."

Beth stood up in front of him and undressed down to her underwear.

"What are you doing?"

"It's dark enough now. No one will see. Come on," she said, wading into the shallows at the foot of the ridge.

Mark guffawed as she shivered from the initial cold. "What? You thought it'd be like the water when we went to the Bahamas?"

"Shut up and get in here."

Mark undressed and dived head first off the ridge.

"Mark?"

He could hear Beth's voice muffled beneath the surface and swam toward it, his arms stretched out blindly in front of him.

"Mark?"

He slowly emerged behind Beth so as not to cause a stir.

Molly yipped and growled from the ridge to the water below, only adding to what Mark assumed was Beth's anxiety.

"Mark, it isn't funny."

That's when he grabbed her from behind, and she screamed.

Mark burst out of the water and launched into a fit of laughter.

"Jesus," she said, splashing him with her hands. "You're such an asshole."

"Come here."

He took Beth into his arms and kissed her as she wrapped her legs around his hips, the water making her body weightless.

Molly continued to yip and growl, concerned that the two of them were in the water away from her.

"Molly, enough, go," said Mark.

She didn't listen.

"Molly," said Beth.

The dog whimpered and walked back to the cabin on her own.

Mark pulled Beth out of the water, gently laying her down beneath him, the ground soft from the surrounding lichen and moss. They both shivered from the air on their wet bodies.

"I can hardly see you. Come here," she said, putting her hands on his chest, slowly moving them downward.

Back at the cabin Beth called out for Molly, but the dog didn't come.

"It's been a while since we've seen her. I'm worried."

"I'm sure she's fine," said Mark. "She's a dog. She's probably still out exploring."

Seeing Beth agitated, Mark changed gears and suggested they wait a little longer, watch a movie. She sat on the pull-out couch, her eyes looking out the window toward the ridge that overlooked the lake, as he went through the stack of VHS tapes beside the old boxy Panasonic TV until he found one he had loved as a kid.

"*Breakfast Club?*"

"Never seen it."

"What? How have you never seen *Breakfast Club?* How are we even together?"

"I wasn't a '90s kid obsessed with '80s movies like you."

Mark knew that much was true. He had felt disconnected to the '90s: lost. The '80s had *Breakfast Club, Ferris Bueller's Day Off, Pretty in Pink, Sixteen Candles, Some Kind Of Wonderful* and *Weird Science.* In other words, the '80s had John Hughes, and John Hughes got how Mark felt growing up. As a kid he would watch them for hours on end when they aired on TBS.

He turned the lights off, the room dark except for the glow of the TV screen, popped the movie in and sat down next to Beth, letting her cuddle in underneath his arm. The audio on the tape buzzed from years of multiple re-watching.

Mark jerked, slapping his neck, startling Beth.

"What's wrong?"

"Mosquitoes."

They went back to watching the movie, but Mark's skin felt like it had things crawling all over it, so he brushed his legs, swatting away at the invisible, psychosomatic things.

A pitter-patter could faintly be heard over the TV.

"Is it raining?" asked Beth. "It sounds like rain."

The Whiteshell was known for its overnight thunderstorms: quick, violent and loud, but calm by tomorrow morning's first rays of sunlight.

Mark got up off the couch to the window to see. It wasn't raining, but from the roof it sounded like it was raining, lightly.

He went to the wall with the light switch and hit the lights. Beth screamed.

The rain they heard wasn't rain, but footsteps. Thousands of ants were flooding into the room through cracks and knots in the roof's wood panelling. They didn't look like the carpenter, pavement, or thief ants that were native to Canada. They had dark-bluish abdomens, a reddish thorax and head, and had the largest needle-like mandibles Mark had ever seen.

He stood on the coffee table and slapped the roof. The ants surrounding his hand dropped to the floor, and Beth wasted no time lifting her feet up.

That's when the ants started biting Mark all over, repeatedly, hanging on with their jaws.

Mark screamed, lost his balance, and crashed onto the coffee table, breaking it in two. He convulsed on the floor as if he were on fire, slapping all the parts of his body he could reach, but the ants kept coming. The walls changed from their original colour and began to move. The cabin was a gigantic anthill. Pulsing and throbbing.

Beth sobbed and then screamed. From the floor, Mark could see she was covered in ants, the places where she had been bitten already swelling and red. She got up, stepping on ants, and waved her arms around in a panic. He stood up, too, and helped swat the ants off Beth as she continued to wave her hands and stomp her feet, but the ants kept coming, crawling over their feet and up their legs.

"Oh, God," she said. "Molly."

She ran out of the lighted room and into the dark toward the front door calling Molly's name. Mark chased after her, but soon caught up with her where she was kneeling on the front porch, a lifeless Molly cradled in her hands.

Mark tried to ignore the pain from the stings and put his arm on Beth's shoulder.

"We need to go," he said.

Helping Beth to her feet, they quickened their pace to the car. Mark opened the door for Beth, got her in safely before getting in and starting the car, his hands shaking as he turned the key. Mark took one last look at his grandfather's cabin before leaving it for good. Beth was right. He would sell the land.

They were on PR 307 by the time he looked over to check on a sobbing Beth. She refused to let go of Molly's body, as if hugging her closer meant she wasn't truly gone. His heart sank at the thought of how Beth must feel, but then she started repeating the word "no" over and over again, shouting it.

"What? What now? What is it?"

Beth was slapping at Molly. Her fur was covered in ants that were coming from the open cavities of her body. Mark reached a hand over to help, but more ants kept coming, and they hung on with their mandibles, biting the both of them.

Both screamed. The burning agony of the ants' attacks took over Mark's sense and he lost control of the wheel. The car veered across the yellow line, jumping the road, the headlights illuminating the Jack pines they were about to hit.

LIMESTONE, LYE, AND THE BUZZING OF FLIES

Kate Heartfield

The summer we were twelve, nobody asked my best friend Tom and me to wear bike helmets, because it was 1989. If they asked where we were going, we just said, "Bike ride."

They would just nod and go back to whatever they were doing. My dad would go back to the bar; my mom would go back to staring at the TV. Tom's mom would go back to screaming at Tom's older brother.

So we would ride fast in the sunshine. River Road had a few honest-to-goodness hills, a wonder in rural Manitoba. We used to kick our legs out wide and put our hands in the air and let our bikes rattle down, around the curves, knowing there might be cars coming, though there never were.

We always went to the same place: our little kingdom. A green slope between the highway and the river, with a limestone fort squatting on it.

When we got to Lower Fort Garry, we'd park our bikes and walk in through the back gate. Nobody ever made us pay. Nobody swore or wailed at us. It was the one place we knew where we got to choose whether to talk to people. You walked up and talked to the pretend fur-trader or the pretend shopkeeper, or you didn't. We would sit on the grass and listen to the crickets, or watch the lazy Red River glitter in the sun until our eyes hurt.

I think that's why we heard what others did not hear, saw what others did not see. Something whispers in every silence and there is writing on every wall. One of my sisters said that to me, once, when we were chained together in a dungeon barely larger than a grave.

No—that is the wrong memory. That didn't happen. Not to me.

I was a girl in 1989, in Manitoba, and my friend Tom and I would go to our fort. At times when there was hardly anyone else around, we would walk inside the square fort itself. We would sit on the barrels in the fur-storage room, stick our tongues out at the pelts that still had snarling faces attached, and try to make things out of trap wire. The pimply girls in their heavy nineteenth-century dresses would give us ice cream sandwiches out of the staff freezer and one of them taught me how to smoke a cigarette.

The only one who never broke character was the blacksmith. If a visitor said something about TV or telephones he would pretend not to know what they were talking about. It was always 1850 for him. I never knew his name. The smithy was just outside the fort walls and I hated going in there because a fire was the last thing I wanted on a July afternoon. But Tom liked to go there to get nails for his collection. So I would lean against the shoeing apparatus just outside the door and listen to the smith bang and hiss and twist.

"Now you be careful of this one, young sir," the blacksmith said to Tom once when they were on their way out into the sunshine. I flipped my sunglasses up onto the top of my head so I could see the two of them. The smith had his thumb cocked at me.

Tom blushed and I rolled my eyes.

The blacksmith talked about the fire a lot: how hot it should be, what kind of wood, that sort of thing.

"This is no ordinary fire," the blacksmith said the last time we visited. "It began from a spark struck off the anvil of the first Scottish smith to work on this spot, in 1815, and has never gone out since."

"Really," I said, humouring him.

He nodded. "It's a need-fire. It protects this place. So long as there is a smith to tend it."

"Protects it from what?" Tom asked.

"The smith's wife. She came here first, tried to claim this place and all the souls in it, but he followed her from across the ocean. As long as he has this fire and red iron in it, she'll never have dominion here."

"But she's long dead," I said. "She might even be dead in 1850. Do you mean her ghost or something?"

He shook his head. "As long as there's a smith there's a smith's wife."

"Oh," I said. "Well, what if the smith isn't married?"

"It's just a story, Daphne," Tom said.

We had all the history plaques memorized and when it got too hot we would go into the museum and watch the twenty-minute heritage movie just so we could sit in the air conditioning. The fort was built in the 1830s by the Hudson's Bay Company, which controlled the fur trade in those days and was pretty much the government of Canada back then, too.

There was a lot of history they didn't tell us: like the fact that Governor Simpson had eleven children by seven women and insisted on having a personal bagpiper with him when he circumnavigated the globe in a birchbark canoe. Or that Louis Riel's secretary Honoré Jaxon, a wannabe Métis who was born a white Methodist, was locked up in Lower Fort Garry's isolation chambers in the 1880s after the Red River Rebellion, when the place became an asylum.

They showed us maps and dramatizations and pretended like all these sad, weird white people were so brave for snowshoeing or paddling out into a wilderness where they weren't wanted. Like they weren't all running with dogs at their heels.

✦

The summer we were fourteen, Tom and I got jobs. We didn't go to the fort anymore.

I worked at the hot dog diner near the locks. I sold slices of soggy cherry pie that we were supposed to say was homemade if anyone asked, and ice cream out of big plastic tubs, and bait worms. I came home at night with my uniform smelling of hot dogs and pine cleaner. My fingernails were brown from cleaning the grill and my wrists were sticky because the fishermen liked to put nickels in the bottoms of their Coke glasses and watch me fish them out.

◆

The spring when we were sixteen, Tom and I didn't hang out much anymore, but his locker was close to mine.

"How do you like waitressing, Daphne?" he asked one day when the hall was empty because we were both late for class.

I shrugged. "How do you like the gas station?"

"I hear they're hiring for the summer at Lower Fort Garry."

"For what job?"

"You know, dressing up and talking to the tourists. Acting or whatever."

I had never thought of that as an ordinary job, as a job that I could do. But Tom was right. They hired us and even paid a few cents over minimum wage. We could hardly believe our luck.

Tom got hired as the assistant to the very blacksmith who used to make him nails. I filled in wherever they needed a girl. The first week, I baked bannock and bread in the oven at the back of the governor's mansion. I hated the heat and the flies there, the buzzing always in my ears, and the sun glaring off the limestone. If I listened for a few minutes, the buzzing seemed to fall into a pattern.

Joanne, a woman in her forties, played Anne Maxwell Colvile, the governor's wife, mistress of the Big House. Joanne was always tired because her kids were brats. One day I was listening to the flies and kind of humming along to myself, and Joanne had to ask me three times if I'd seen her parasol.

Then one of the girls who worked in a settler house got mono and I asked if I could move there. The settler houses and teepee were outside the fort, just down the white-stone path from the smithy. It was quieter and cooler there. I could pour beef-fat candles into tin moulds in the shade of the farmhouse doorway while visitors watched. I memorized how the line of the shade would move from the doorstep to the carrot patch over the course of my shift: my own personal sundial. I could almost hear a ticking in it. I'd watch the line and say to myself: One o'clock, two o'clock, three o'clock, four.

I made a little game of it. *One o'clock, two o'clock, three o'clock, four. Rattle the windows and knock on the door.*

My clothes smelled of lard and lye and I learned to make things.

My first day in the settler house, Tom wandered onto the path when there were no visitors around, and I wandered over to say hi. My skirt swished as I walked, and I could see myself as he must see me: an image, a sunlit woman against a green and blue background. He smelled like fire.

We said things like "hello" and "how are you finding it here?" We talked differently to each other in costume. Me in my leaf-green dress, with my hair all done up under a cap, and he in a loose white shirt, trousers that tied at his waist, and a blue cloth tied around his dark hair. We were dressed up like a man and a woman and we talked that way, like we were in a play, even though I tried not to.

The blacksmith watched us from the doorway with a poker in his hand.

The next day, he went away somewhere and they made Tom head blacksmith. Tom had been watching for years. He knew what to do.

◆

The pretend-wife in the other farmhouse was an eighteen-year-old named Amberly. Her fake name was Mrs. Grant. She was nice, but she couldn't get the hang of things. I offered to show her about candles on a slow, grey afternoon.

"You have to pour it smoothly, like this," I said, showing her. As I filled each tin tube, I said a little rhyme to keep my work in rhythm:

Mulleins and murrain
Candles and kine

Gone is the leman
Who once was mine

"What's that?" asked Amberly.

"I don't know. I must have read it somewhere."

My hand started to shake but I managed not to spill the tallow. I kept saying the rhyme to myself, to keep myself grounded, even though it scared me. I hadn't read it anywhere. I didn't know what half those words even meant. But I knew that each word came with a mark on the flagstones where my shadow-dial ebbed and flowed. That crack was *mulleins* and that weed was *murrain*. The shadow taught me the words.

Amberly asked me to teach her the words and I did.

After that, Amberly came to me for advice on just about everything. She pinned her cap with two hidden safety pins just like I did. She broke up with her boyfriend when I told her to.

Soon I had rhymes for many things. The butter churning had a fast rhyme that I learned from sunlight on limestone. The bread kneading had a slow one that I learned from the buzzing of flies. When I planted the late carrots, I knelt down looking at the river beyond, the quick ripples of the waves.

I taught the other girls. Nobody had ever listened to me before. But somehow I seemed to remember, like the memory of a dream, that girls had once listened to me, had once taken my advice, had begged for my secrets. Those were not real memories; those were not these girls.

Once they had learned the words to any of my rhymes, once they had repeated the words to me, they would listen to whatever I said. They would follow my advice. Even Joanne, the pretend governor's wife. I told her to loosen up about her daughter's curfew, and she did.

I liked the patterns in my mind. I told myself I just liked to make up things while I sat and thought. There was plenty of time for sitting and thinking there, after all.

Tom got an assistant blacksmith, older than both of us. Gareth was a quiet man with a big beard. He looked the part. He looked like he ought to be carrying an axe or a tree trunk all the time just in case it was ever needed.

One quiet morning when it was still cool, just before we opened, Tom and Gareth came by the little willow stand where we demonstrated things for the kids. It was close by the smithy. I was getting things ready, putting out the sticks for fire-starting. The willow trees were bending as if they were doing a little dance for me, teaching me.

"What's the coffee can for?" Gareth asked.

"Making charcloth. When you light a fire with a stick and a board, you need something to take the spark. So you burn the cloth, see?"

I held out a bundle of squares of off-white linen.

"But you don't want the cloth to actually catch fire. So you put it in the coffee can and nestle the can in just the right spot and leave it there for hours. You have to make sure that there isn't much air in the can, too, so you can't be checking it all the time. Kind of like making rice."

I used my bright steel Zippo to get a fire started, flipping the Zippo's top on and off a few times, idly, just like I had seen the smokers at school do. Then I put the square of ivory-coloured linen in the coffee can, setting it just in the right place, with a little singsong:

Here is the hill and here is the dell
Here is heaven and here is hell.

"Here," I said, holding out another coffee can. "You do one, Gareth. But you have to say the rhyme."

He laughed a little, nervously.

"You don't really have to say the rhyme," Tom said. I liked the way his shoulders looked in that olden-days shirt, but even thinking that made him seem like a stranger. I didn't know what happened to the skinny kid who used to park his police-auction bike out at the gate next to mine.

"You do so have to say it," I argued. "Come on, Gareth. It won't work otherwise."

Gareth laughed again, because he was shy.

Mrs. Boggs, the missionary, whose real name was Stacy, came by with my Coke from the machine.

"Is there anything else you'd like?" she asked.

I shook my head. Tom watched her. He put his hand to his forehead to keep the glare out of his eyes. We weren't allowed to wear sunglasses and he didn't get a straw hat because he was supposed to be in the smithy most of the time. He looked at Stacy in her lace yoke. He looked at me.

It just made sense that if I was doing the work to get the fire-kits ready that someone who didn't have any set up to do would bring me a Coke. It's not like I was asking her to do all my homework for me or throw herself into the river or something. It wasn't like that at all.

◆

Amberly and I did a bannock tea for Canada Day in July. We set up the tables in one of the storerooms and put out china tea cups and little dishes of jam.

"Did you go on that date with the shopkeeper?" I asked. Sometimes we called each other by our pretend job titles instead of our names because we were so used to being in character.

She shook her head. "I got back together with Keith."

"No," I said. I put a butter dish down on the table. "I hate that guy. He's no good for you. Dump him. Call him tonight and dump him."

She shook her head, not looking up from the table. She kept putting little silver knives down, *clink, clink, clink*.

"Amberly," I said. "Say you'll do it."

She shook her head. *Clink, clink, clink.*

I whispered, looking up at her, waiting for her to join in.
A hooded crow on a frosty night
Sold me a child with an eyeball bright
Husha, husha, sang I to him
Dance while you can ere your eyes grow dim

She kept her pink-stained lips together. She pulled something out of her apron pocket and rolled it around in her fingers. A black iron nail.

✦

Soon everybody had one. Joanne kept hers on a loop around her waist, which looked ridiculous. Gareth had one on a chain under his shirt. All I could see was the chain and the shape of the nail, but I knew what it was. Stupid heavy things to carry around.

I walked into the smithy on a July day, passing right under the horseshoe because I wasn't superstitious.

"Why are you turning everyone against me?"

Tom was alone, as if he was waiting for me. He had a bar of iron in the fire.

"Nobody is against you. Don't be ridiculous."

"You could have fooled me."

"They aren't yours, Daphne."

"So, whose are they? Yours? This was always my place. I found it first."

I had. I remembered. We were rivals before we were lovers. Smiths have always thought it their business to hunt my sisters and me. He had wielded his accursed craft in that Scottish hamlet long before I turned up there, singed and hoarse from the flames, the screams of my dead sisters in my ears. I only wanted a quiet life, a safe place. I feared the iron, but I loved him, and he said he would not harm me. He said God would forgive me.

When our baby was born blue, I said a little rhyme over him. Just one little song, a bluebell song for my bluebell boy. My husband snatched him away and put me in iron, weeping over me as if he were driven to it. I had cheated death before. I freed myself and I sought a quiet place.

Tom shook his head as if he was trying to get the memories out. "Would you like me to make you something?"

He pulled the bar out of the fire; it was red at the end. I took a step back, into the sunshine.

He dropped the bar on the ground with a clang and he grabbed my wrist with his gloved hand.

"You will not shackle me!" I yelled. I remembered the cage of black iron, how it had burned and bitten. I hung from that gibbet for far too long, exposed to all foulness, before I found the words to burst those broad black bands gilded with weather. It was a wonder I had survived, after a fashion.

I ran from him before the blacksmith could cage me again.

✦

On the August long weekend, the staff held a bonfire.

I got there late but they had still not set it alight. There was still enough light to see by. Tom was telling people where to put the wood, where to set up the coolers and mosquito coils.

Everyone obeyed him.

"Hi, Amberly," I said.

She looked away as though I had said something awful. He had turned them all against me.

My fortress by the river still whispered to me, but it no longer needed to lend me words. I could not make them repeat the old rhymes after me, not with his iron binding them. But I could get into their heads.

I sang the first tune that came to my lips: "Bizarre Love Triangle" by New Order. Amberly giggled. The iron nails grew heavy; they twisted and bent, some of them went red.

Joanne was a woman of experience. She knew when to let go. She untied her nail from the bit of rope at her waist and threw the horrid thing into the wood pile.

The others threw theirs, then. They were free. I freed them.

Tom pleaded with them, but I did not hear what he said. He moved his lips like an actor in a silent movie. One by one they came to stand at my side and stare at Tom, and sing. We all knew the words. In our dresses and trousers we sang, as if the song were an old song. I made it an old song. I pulled my Zippo out of my pocket and flicked it a few times. I walked toward the pile of wood.

Then Gareth approached, a silhouette against the last light of the sky. He was carrying a long poker before him, and on the far end of the poker was a flat piece of iron, like a paddle. And on that iron rested an ugly pile of coals. Coals from the need-fire.

I stopped singing. We all stopped.

I remembered the screams of my sisters, their hair curling crisp while their legs cooked, their coughing and weeping.

If they could not cage me, they would burn me.

✦

Open ground under a Manitoban sky at twilight has its own kind of silence, a silence loud like the hum of an airplane. I ran headlong in that silence, under that grey sky, feeling as though if I stopped running the world would keep moving anyway.

But I did stop when I reached the back gate. No one came after me. No one made me pay. I disentangled my bike from the others. I had to hike my skirt up to my hips, because Daphne—I—did not ride a girls' bike. I had no time to change. I had to get away, to safety. I had to get away from the fire.

I rode fast. When I came to the hills I did not lift my feet. I pushed until my pedals spun and whacked my bare shins.

This time, there was a car at the bottom.

✦

Tom visited me in the hospital, in jeans and a T-shirt. It was one of those wild dark days that come to the prairies in August and the rain lashed wordlessly against the wide hospital window.

It seemed like nothing more than a campfire story. But Tom and I couldn't look at each other. The silence between us was uncomfortable, filled with the gentle beeps of machines, the nattering of nurses in the hallway. A sterile silence with no memory in it. Nothing to listen to, except the unspoken words in our minds.

"Gareth is taking over," he said. "I'm going back to the gas station."

I nodded. "Will they get another girl to play Mrs. McTavish?"

He shrugged. It didn't matter. I—she—would find someone: Amberly, Joanne, hell, maybe governor Colvile himself—Matthew—or Ben the shopkeeper. Maybe she didn't even need to be a woman. Or maybe she'd find a way to get far from the need-fire, far from the smith.

I doubted it, somehow. I'd left her behind. When I got free she didn't come with me. I wondered how the smith had found a way at last to cage her, to keep her there, with him.

My head ached. Tom frowned. He seemed to be thinking of the right words to say, and I was just hoping he wouldn't say it. I was listening hard to the rain.

That's how I remember us, when I remember us, now. I moved to Montreal and Tom moved to Vancouver. Opposite directions. As if to show each other we had no intention of ever seeing each other again.

WISAGATCAK'S JOURNEY

Wayne Arthurson

Wisagatcak came to her the way Wisagatcak always did: in a dream. Technically, it wasn't a dream because you weren't supposed to dream in hypersleep. And in theory, no one was supposed to be able to access their cerebellum while they were in hypersleep. But Wisagatcak was as close to a god as one could get. Well, at least a version of one. So various laws, be they those of physics or source code, didn't really apply.

Wisagatcak appeared as a Cree man in his twenties with shoulder-length, unbraided hair. He wore denim trousers, the knees torn and frayed, a black short-sleeve shirt with a faded image of a boat on water, the words *Norway House Cree Nation* wrapping around the top and the Cree words *Kinosao sipi* along the bottom. He wore a denim jacket with a fur-lined collar over that. Images had been hand-drawn on the jacket in some kind of black ink or pencil. He drank liquid from a red metal can and sucked on a white, thin tube that Vianne knew was tobacco but didn't seem to be any traditional conveyance of tobacco that she had seen before.

Based on the squalor of the location, she guessed he was projecting an image of the latter part of the Settler Period, somewhere around the False Reconciliation, a couple or so generations before the True Reconciliation and the Renewal.

Wisagatcak sat in an old brown armchair, the upholstery so worn that bits of the chair's wooden frame and springs were exposed. The chair sat on a piece of material that technically could be called a carpet but was so thin that weeds—dandelion, thistle, purple loosestrife—grew through.

The rest of the domicile was similarly decayed: walls of plaster punched with holes, window openings covered by sheets of plastic, bits of food and garbage strewn about the floor, and an old-style view-screen encased in a wooden box, the screen cracked and blank. A prevailing sense of dank hung in the air, irritating her nose and clinging to her skin.

He blew out a cloud of the tobacco smoke, the scent a mix of sweetness and harsh chemicals. Even though she instinctively winced as the smoke floated her way, she was impressed. All in all, it was a very masterful tableau. Most tableaus focused on sight, the way light and shadow made a space look, the visual details like an old-style 2D cartoon. Sound got a lot of play in tableaus as that quality (and sometimes volume) played a key role in creating realism. Touch had the next priority, especially when there was action, or something to be had to be picked up or felt. Erotic tableaus focused much on touch. Taste and scent were almost considered secondary senses in the majority of tableaus, usually only used when there was something to eat or to cook.

But rarely did a tableau feature the subtlety that Wisagatcak offered: the condensation on his drink can, the random drifting of the smoke and its smell, the way the humidity of the air felt on the skin. She acknowledged that, and his presence, with a nod.

"Tanisi, Wisagatcak," she said in Cree. *Hello, how are you, Wisagatcak.*

"Hey, how's it's going?" Wisagatcak replied in the colloquial English of the time. He smiled a toothy smile. He gestured with his hand holding the shiny metal can. "Have a seat."

Vianne turned but there was nothing behind her.

"Sorry," Wisagatcak said with a blink. A second later, a solid wooden chair appeared behind her.

She thought about standing, thought about not being so accepting of Wisagatcak's hospitality. But that would only play into his hand. Or distract him. As a trickster, Wisagatcak liked being challenged, liked playing mind games with people, even when there was something more important to impart.

So Vianne sat down. Wisagatcak smirked but seemed slightly disappointed she wouldn't play games. But with another suck of tobacco and drink from his can, he moved on. He leaned forward, elbows on knees. "It's good to see you again, Vianne. You've been away for a long time. Your people miss you."

"I was away for a long time because of the work I do for my people, you know that."

"Of course, and your people do appreciate your work. But they miss you."

"I miss them, too," she said. "But are you here as a representative of my people or on your own?"

He smiled. "Probably a little bit of both. I know you don't wish to be disturbed as you travel—"

"No one wants to be disturbed when they are in hypersleep; that's why we do it." Interrupting Wisagatcak was a sure-fire way to antagonize him, a challenge that brought his trickster instincts to the forefront. His eyebrows furrowed and pushed up. He aged a decade in a second. Vianne was pleased she still had the power to annoy him in this way, but held back a smile. Then she made a peace offering.

"Although I must admit your tableau is amazing," she said waving an arm in a circle. "The sense of decay and rot is incredibly detailed. I've never seen anything like it, even at Kanonsionni they cannot come up with detailed modules like this."

When Wisagatcak leaned back in his chair and smoked his tobacco, she knew that he was appeased. He would be playing no tricks on her. At least no extra tricks on top of the one he may be working at the moment. Wisagatcak never appeared in this way to Vianne unless he had something brewing. And after all her time at the Confederacy, all the time playing games that many called politics, she was tired of it all. Which is why she took a Slow ship. Still, it was time to find out what Wisagatcak wanted.

"Although I'm pretty sure the resources you're taking up for this kind of work will be noted, registered and shut down by the ship's AI. So if you have something to tell me, you better make it quick."

Wisagatcak shrugged, unconcerned. "The ship's AI has a more important concern than little ol' me at the moment. Which is why I showed up and said hello."

"What are you talking about?" Vianne asked, a hint of worry rising in her voice. Something shook, and she felt her chair sway. The tableau shimmered for a moment but then regained its presence.

"What have you done, Wisagatcak? This is not the place to play those kinds of games. A few tricks are fine, but not this."

"This has nothing to do with me. What's happening outside this room is outside my skill set. And it's not fun at all."

Another shake, this time it rocked the room, almost knocking Vianne off her chair. "What the heck is going on, then?"

Wisagatcak drank from his can and sucked on his tobacco in a dramatic pause. He blew the smoke in her direction and this time it reached into her lungs, clawing at her breath. She coughed once to clear her lungs, but it didn't work. The coughing became more intense, and she fell off the chair onto her knees, hacking and retching as Wisagatcak's smoke tore at her insides.

"Time to wake up, Vianne," he whispered in her ear. "You're under attack."

◆

Vianne woke out of hypersleep, her body racked with pain, muscles twitching and jerking as each spasm rolled through her body in deep, cutting waves. She fought for breath, each cough an agonized retch, mucus and hypersleep fluid spewing out of every orifice in her body. This was not the way it was supposed to happen.

Waking from hypersleep was a calm, luxurious experience, like rising after a long, restful sleep. All the fluid and tubes that had been injected into your body already removed. Your skin clean and dry, white-suited attendants waiting on you hand and foot, ready to fulfil any request while soft music played in the background.

That was one of the key reasons why Vianne usually chose Slow ships to return home after time in Kanonsionni, the Long House, the place where all the representatives of Haudenosaunee met to discuss the issues of the League. The Cree were not one of the original five members of the Haudenosaunee, but the League of Nations had always been open to new members to gather around the fire. The Cree, along with many nations of the Earth and later the stars, were just one of many additional members.

But after all those months of politicking, nothing beat a long comfortable rest followed by first-class attention in the finest accommodations available to humankind. There were other perks, but the luxury hypersleep offered was one of them.

And this was the first time she had ever experienced an emergency wake up—probably the first time anyone had ever experienced an emergency wake up, because the safety records for Slow ships, especially those with government functionaries, was impeccable. Sure, they might be minor problems from time to time, like shortages in a type of food or drink. Or towels that weren't as warm as the last trip. But never enough to cause the implementation of an emergency wake up. Well, at least, she had never heard of one.

And it was one of the most unpleasant experience of her life, agonizingly so, disgustingly so, almost unbearable to experience. She wanted it to stop. She wanted to just lie down and die, forget everything that ever happened, forget everything and everyone in her life so she could escape from the pain.

And she almost did, until something hit the ship, something explosive, and the resulting shockwave knocked her hypersleep chamber off its pedestal, dumping her onto the floor. More fluid surged out of her body, as tubes that had been inserted in order to initiate and maintain hypersleep were jerked out of position, their ends flaying like waving hoses, spraying fluid everywhere.

Some of the fluid splashed on her face, the cold wetness snapping her out of inertia. The pain subsided slightly, her muscles still ached, her head throbbed to the beat of an off-rhythm pow-wow, and she still continued to gag.

Most of the tubes had been ripped out in the fall, save for one—her feeding tube. It prevented her from breathing. The lack of oxygen made her start to panic. She clawed at the tube but was unable to find purchase. Her brain started to shut down, her hands became more frantic, reaching, grasping, slipping. She was not far from collapsing when the voice of her father rose from her memory:*Panicking never helps anything, Vianne. Think before you start freaking out.*

She froze for a moment, remembering her dad: solid and soft, quiet and angry, hilariously silly, sometimes cool, many times not, but always there. Always. Even when he would leave home, he would always stay in contact with her, asking her about her day. It annoyed her as a child, this ever-present presence—not an intrusion, Dad would never intrude on her unless it was necessary, but there nevertheless, always there. It made her feel safe.

And when he left for the final time, she missed him terribly and grieved for weeks. She soon discovered that even in death, he was still with her. His voice, his words of advice, his dumb jokes, almost all the things he told her and did with her, lingered in her mind. His voice was one of the three voices that spoke clearly in her head. Sometimes his voice would mingle with hers.

So whenever his voice arose from the clamour of her thoughts, she listened to it and acted accordingly. She set aside the panic and quickly evaluated. She knew she was in a terrible situation. Something bad was happening on the Slow ship, something so bad that in the end, she might not make it. But it was not time to focus on what might happen; it was time to think about the here and now. On what she could do at this moment. Then she would move onto the next moment.

The tube. The one in her throat. It was restricting her breathing.

If she didn't remove it, she would die.

She centred herself, willed herself to grab the section of the tube hanging out of her mouth, and yanked on it. The outside of the tube was covered in fluid, so her grip slipped a couple of times. Using an edge of her robe, she wiped off the fluid and tried again.

Her grip held, and she could feel the tube move, advancing slightly as she pulled on it. But every time she got it a little bit out, there was a spasm in her throat, pulling the tube back into its original position. Panic set in again but she controlled it with thoughts of her dad.

She would have to induce vomiting in order to force it out. As a kid she hated throwing up, even now the wrenching of her stomach and the burn of the acid pushing through her throat and mouth made the little girl inside of her scream and feel like throwing a tantrum.

But the adult in her realized that she was in charge of her fear, and letting her fear take control of her now would kill her. This time, when she yanked on the tube, she coughed a little, trying to engage her gag reflex. After a frustrating three attempts, the reflex kicked in and her stomach lurched. The tube—and a smattering of bile, acid and saline fluid—burst out of her mouth, spraying her hands and the floor below.

Vianne didn't let her disgust get the better of her; there was no time. She had to get to an escape pod. She tossed the long plastic tube onto the floor, got to her feet and looked around to orient herself. She was surprised how much of the safety demonstration the crew did before every flight was stuck in her mind; she found it annoying and tended to ignore it as much as she could, but repeated demonstrations had engrained enough of the procedure. A voice rose up in her head: *In case of evacuation, please follow the instructions of the crew. If the crew is unable to assist you, in-floor lighting will guide you to an escape pod.*

There were no crew members in sight. But a line of blue light pulsed on the floor, directing her to the door. She followed the light and it told her to go left. So she did.

But Wisagatcak came back into her head. A soft voice, female this time, like one of the crew members of the ship, friendly, helpful, but somehow, a bit bored. "No. This way."

The pulsing blue light disappeared, and another light, this one orange, told her to go right.

"But the escape pods," she said out loud, her voice raspy.

Wisagatcak threw up an image inside her head. It was brief: a half-second of fast-cut scenes, barely sufficient to register in her mind, but enough. People jumped to escape pods, crew members of varying types, passengers, someone's pet dog. Fear on everyone's face, even on the crew. Escape pods ejected from the Slow ship, their rockets firing to push them away. The ship itself seemed to be slowly breaking into three or four major pieces, the debris tumbling and flaring as explosions ignited, creating even smaller pieces. And finally, the engines for the escape pods fired their second-stage rockets to boost them further away, but then they imploded, the outer shells of the pods sucking into themselves like a fast deflating balloon, crushing anything and anyone inside.

"What the fuck!" Vianne shouted when she returned to the present, inside the ship where the orange light pulsated, telling her to go right.

"This hasn't happened yet, Vianne, but it will. Very soon," Wisagatcak said in a sterner voice, almost imitating her father. Even though Wisagatcak was a trickster and could be dangerous sometimes, there were certain lines he wouldn't cross unless it was necessary. Him invoking the memory of her father at this time told her she should listen to him. "Move fast, Vianne. Docking bay is your only hope. Follow the orange."

She shook her head, pushing the thoughts of all those people on the pods, now dead. Or soon to be dead. Killed by something that had the power to take out a Slow ship and all those aboard.

"The Warrior faction of the Mohawks has been rattling spears lately, so to speak. And the Mayans have always been interested in more power," Wisagatcak said, answering Vianne's unspoken question.

He was right on both counts, although Vianne couldn't fathom either one of those nations actually using that power. Killing people in this way.

"And the Settlers have been way too quiet," Wisagatcak added. "That's never good."

The Settlers? Were they getting a more expansive nature again? Hadn't they learned anything from the past?

The ship rocked, knocking her against the hull, breaking her out of her contemplations. "Follow the orange," she muttered, pushing away all thoughts save for ones related to her survival. "Follow the orange."

She turned right, as the orange light on the floor told her to. A long shudder, like an earthquake, flowed through the ship, knocking her to her knees, creating cracks in the hull and the floor underneath the carpet, but she got up and continued in a half run. Smaller aftershocks followed the heavy one, causing her to weave and stumble down the hallway like a drunk.

She made another left, a right, then a left, moving away from the guest areas to the spaces where the crew lived and ran the ship. The walls were hazy grey, a holdover from the earthbound naval ships; there were more exposed panels, some of them now emitting sparks into her path; and the floor was chilling her bare feet, and getting colder as the in-floor heating started to cut out. The corridors were littered with scattered bits of debris—the glass from shattered view screens, shards from broken ceiling tiles, bent sections of metal from broken control panels, and the flotsam and jetsam of discarded tools and possessions that had probably been dropped by crew members racing to escape pods.

She gingerly stepped through the debris field, trying to move as fast as possible, but with care so she wouldn't cut open her foot. Underneath, the orange light beckoned her on and she followed it, just as Wisagatcak had told her to.

It wasn't easy to trust a trickster like Wisagatcak. He loved games, loved leading people on merry chases into nothingness, even into danger, because he thought it was fun. But something about the way he had contacted her, in a dream during hypersleep, something he had never done because he respected her need for rest, made her believe this was actually happening, that it wasn't some kind of trick or game he was playing.

And while Wisagatcak liked games and pranks, he was always a friend to Vianne, to the Cree. And his tricks were always didactic, used as a means to teach a lesson of some sort. So while Wisagatcak might lead people into danger, that danger would never be life-threatening.

So she followed the orange lights, getting deeper in the bowels of the ship that no guest ever saw. Lights flashed and alarms blared, and when Vianne turned another corner she almost stepped onto the body of a crew member. His body lay across the floor, neck bent at an unnatural angle. Her stomach heaved slightly at the sight, and she briefly wondered who this person was, what his role on the ship had been and if he had family that would now be missing a member, like a limb being cut off.

"Move, Vianne," Wisagatcak shouted in her head. "Don't linger with the dead."

She shook off her thoughts and moved away. "*Cistemaw*," she muttered. One always left behind a bit of tobacco with the dead to help in communication with the Creator and she hoped that invoking the Cree word for a pouch would be a suitable replacement for the real thing.

"A nice touch," Wisagatcak said to her.

"I had to leave something for the dead."

"But don't leave yourself. You're almost there. Just behind this hatch."

While all the hatches in the ship had been open during her escape so far, this one was closed. "Can you open it?" Vianne asked.

"Working on it," Wisagatcak said, his voice now more like a female robot.

Another shudder went through the ship, deeper than the other one. It knocked Vianne to the wall but she remained on her feet. A long metallic groan roared through the corridors, as though the ship was vocalizing its final moments. It was the sound of the spine of the ship, the hull bending past its breaking point. Soon the ship would tear apart like it had in the images Wisagatcak showed her. And if she did not escape in time, she would be dead, exposed to the vacuum of space with only the soft cotton of the long sleep robe to protect her. Her body would last longer than the robe, but not by much.

Another groan. This time the lights flickered off, leaving Vianne in the dark. Her childhood fear of darkness flared in her mind, but she could control that fear. Besides, the dark couldn't kill her unless it was the darkness of space.

Then her stomach gave a light heave and she felt her feet lift off the floor. Along with the lights, the internal gravity system had also shut down. Since she had stopped at the door and had no real momentum, she knew that if she stayed still, she would remain by the door. She reached out and grabbed the handle to keep herself in place.

She could breathe, so life support systems were still online, but the temperature was dropping quickly, so it was only a matter of time before that would fail. It would take some time for the oxygen to completely deplete, but it wouldn't last forever. Neither would the pressure. If that failed, then it wouldn't be long before the ship, like the escape pods in Wisagatcak's images, would collapse violently inward, crushing everyone.

"Wisagatcak," she said with a tone of desperation.

"Working. Soon."

"Hurry."

"There was a fire in the docking bay, so the door sealed itself shut. Also, be aware that fire retardant was employed so once I open the door, the release of pressure will create a wave of retardant into the corridor. I suggest you hold on."

"I've got a grip on the door handle."

"Excellent, then I will endeavour to open the door inward to help with your forward momentum."

"Anytime would be good."

"Working." After a second, when another groan stretched through the ship, this time in conjunction with a deep shudder, Wisagatcak spoke. "Here we go. Opening. Be ready."

The door slowly opened inward, pushing against the fire retardant, pulling Vianne backward as she hung on. White chemical foam flowed past her, enough to fully envelop her body and a space the size of the door opening. It didn't rush out in a torrent but in a sluggish flow, like magma from a volcano. Also like magma, the flow was powerful, tenacious even, and the retardant pulled on her, trying to break her grip and tow her out into the hallway. She gripped the handle as tight as she could, fighting the pull of the current, knowing that if she let the retardant succeed, she would not have enough strength and time to get back to the door.

Hang on or die, she told herself.

It felt like a forever moment, but that was just *kakayesitipahikan*, a false time or measurement. It reality it was probably a few seconds, no more. Finally, the torrent subsided and Vianne pulled on the door, using that momentum to force her into the room. In the dark, she collided with the wall, but it wasn't a hard hit. She took it with her shoulder and though there would be a bruise, it was nothing compared to what would happen if she did not escape.

"Where am I, Wisagatcak?" she said out loud.

There was no answer, and this time the *kakayesitipahikan* seemed even longer than forever, though it was barely five seconds. Dying alone in the dark was one of her worst childhood nightmares.

"Wisagatcak?" she said again, her voice small and piteous. There was little she could do to push aside the small girl inside of her.

"Turn around," Wisagatcak said, filling her relief. The voice of the young Cree man from the tableau returned. She might die, but she would not be alone. She did what she was told.

"Reach out," he said.

She did, and her hand touched some kind of fabric. She explored it, feeling shoulders and arms. A suit.

"An EVA suit," Wisagatcak said, telling Vianne that she had spoken that thought out loud. "Put it on, quickly."

It had been a long time since she had worn an EVA. As someone who travelled through the Confederacy on a regular basis, she had been given training on how to put on an EVA suit. But that had been long ago. The newer models were simpler than the one she had trained on, but she doubted she could remember all the steps in order for it to work properly.

"This will be a bit … disconcerting, strongly involuntary," Wisagatcak said. "But since this is an emergency, I am allowed to breach protocol."

"What are you talking …" was all Vianne got to say before her limbs started to move of their own accord, her hands pulling the suit from its locker and her body making movements to get it on. She fought for a moment, but quickly realized that Wisagatcak had taken over and was putting on the suit for her so she would survive. It was a major protocol breach, almost blasphemous. Even a trickster would not cross this line unless it was completely necessary.

She relaxed and let Wisagatcak do what needed to be done in order to save her life. It was one of the most odd and uncomfortable feelings she'd experienced in her entire life, letting a foreign intelligence assume control of her body and bend and move it as it wished, but Wisagatcak was so smooth and gentle that it felt like she was still and the EVA suit was sentient and was putting itself on her.

Finally, the transfer to the EVA suit was complete and her body was her own again. She felt her bladder release itself, a release of tension, but the liquid was easily collected by the suit to be recycled later.

Moving in the EVA suit was simple, no different than walking in regular clothing. Although it would protect her once she was out in space, it was designed to be light, to allow for natural movements. She had seen actual suits from humanity's early forays off the planet and wondered how someone could move in such bulky gear.

But even though there was no gravity and the suit felt like nothing, she could sense a mass on her back, something Wisagatcak seemed to have added.

"Opening outer hatch," Wisagatcak said.

The door opened, and Vianne stood at the edge, staring at the infinite dark in front of her. Oddly, with the ship about to break apart, this was the safe place for her now. But it didn't feel like that. It went against every single human instinct inside of her. Her mind told her that she had to leave to live, but her animal mind told her that space was dark, cold, and empty. And full of death.

But then in the dark, she saw spots of light, stars in the distance. In the dark, cold and emptiness of infinite space, there was also life. So she stepped out, pushed herself away. She desired to turn back and see the ship behind her, but the ship only meant death. The star she focused on in front of her was the symbol for life. And the further she got from death, the closer she got to life.

"Prepare for acceleration," Wisagatcak said.

There was a flash behind her, a tiny bit of heat felt through the suit, and the weightless feeling was instantly replaced with acceleration. Pain racked through her muscles as she rushed forward. Visually it seemed like she wasn't moving at all because there was no frame of reference. But the pressure on her body and the pain in her muscles told her she was hitting at least five Gs and accelerating. The pain increased, and her vision turned grey and then the periphery got smaller and smaller until she could see nothing.

Wisagatcak gave a half-second visual of what was happening: the ship behind breaking apart, the glow of escape pod rockets bursting away from the ship. And on the other side of the ship, another glow, almost imperceptibly small, moving away from the ship at great speed.

She instinctively knew that was her, that he had attached some type of propulsive device onto her EVA suit in order to get her away. But was it enough? Would she be safe from debris? And if she survived this, how would she continue to survive out here with just an EVA suit?

"I'll do my best to protect you, Vianne," said Wisagatcak. "It won't be easy, but I will do all that I can."

"I'm hoping you're just playing a trick on me, Wisagatcak."

"Sorry, Vianne, this is no trick," he said with a small laugh. It was not a joyful laugh, more of an expression of discomfort and worry. "But I have many tricks to keep you alive, you can be sure of that."

"I want you to use all of them."

"I will, and then some. But first, I need you to sleep. To keep you alive, I need to shut down many of this suit's systems so it lasts longer. To do that I need to shut down your body's systems save for the essentials. To do so, you will have to sleep."

"Don't let me die in my sleep."

"Not letting you die is my primary directive at this moment."

"Yeah, but if all your tricks don't work, I don't want this to be my last thought. If I'm about to die, I want you to wake me before I do."

"*Nipâwin*," Wisagatcak said to her in Cree. *Sleep.*

"If I'm going to die, promise to wake me up before I do."

He said nothing in return, but after a long time, just before she lost consciousness, she felt him nod. That was enough.

ANNE BLAINE

Craig Russell

"The library is closed, ma'am."

Anne looks up from the yellowed pamphlet she's been studying for the past hour. A young woman, about the same age as Anne's own daughter stands across the table from her.

A nametag gives her name: E. Mason. She's blond and soft-spoken, and her clear gaze leaves Anne feeling tongue-tied.

"Sorry, um, sorry. Found this. Inside the *Britannicas*." Anne holds out the folded paper. "It's handwritten, and the text is awfully hard to make out."

"That's all right, ma'am," the librarian says. "Let me scan your faculty badge and you can reserve it for tomorrow."

"Oh, I'm not a professor. One second. Here." Anne produces her student card.

The young woman passes her hand over the ID. "Welcome to the University of Manitoba, Ms Blaine. May I have the item?"

"Thanks. I'm so excited to be here. I really like your library."

"The Elizabeth Dafoe is one of a kind." The woman turns the paper over twice. "That's odd. There's no title, author, or catalogue number. And no RF tag."

"I've been trying to decipher the text." Anne says, "Hard to imagine people ever wrote like that, isn't it?"

"Looks like a steel-nib." The young woman smiles. "Sort of my specialty. Pre-Victorian written texts. This looks quite old. Where did you find it again?"

"Inside the *Encyclopedia Britannica*." Anne carefully pulls over the heavy volume, "Here, you can see the mark it left on this page, in the 'P' volume, on the entry for 'Pitcher Plant.'"

"Yes, I see. The 1768 first edition."

"I've never seen such an old encyclopedia before. I used to read the ones at school when I was a girl," Anne explains. "It doesn't look like this one's been opened in a long time."

"No, I suppose not." The librarian returns the pamphlet to the inside the book. "Look, can you hold on for a minute? My link can't identify the document's place in the collection and I have to call in my supervisor."

Mr. Phillips has a parchment look, and Anne can see from his coat and hat that he's been caught on his way home.

"*Quid hoc est?*" the man says to the young woman.

Anne isn't sure if he's just the sort of academic who actually prefers Latin, or if this is meant to keep her in the dark.

"An uncatalogued item, sir."

He turns to Anne. "Found by …?"

"I'm a mature student. From Brandon. My kids are grown. I thought I'd finish my—"

"Yes, yes." His tone suggests that she ought to have better manners than to find anything out of place in his library. "It won't be available to students for quite some time, if ever. And certainly not until after you've left us."

It sounds like he thinks expulsion is more likely to be her fate than graduation.

The inconvenient mystery is handed over to Miss Mason.

"Archive this tomorrow, Elizabeth."

•

The next day, Anne sees the young woman puzzling over the pamphlet in a windowed staff-only workroom. Her friendly tap on the window brings a shake of Miss Mason's head. Clearly Mr. Phillips' instructions are taken seriously here. Then the man himself appears and the window blinds drop like guillotines.

The snub hurts more than she'd like to admit, and Anne retreats to find a cup of solace at a nearby canteen.

Fortunately, she'd had the forethought to take phone shots of the pamphlet before she was interrupted the previous night. The first line starts "*A mound, secret and sacred, waits in northern Manitoba ...*" and so, though she's sixty and not really one for adventures, she decides she can set her studies aside for a day or two.

But no tourist guidebook shows her a mound at the location described, and no roadway even passes nearby. Online, the few places that dot the area are shown as abandoned.

She supposes that the villages disappeared when a mine went broke. The evaporation of small communities is a common enough occurrence on the prairies.

Her new roommate, Georgie, is a sweetheart, and lets her borrow her Land Rover for a drive in the country with a promise to return in two days. And although she had intended to keep the promise, it was soon long past due.

Anne hadn't imagined that after she left the main road the cross-country trek would be so difficult. But her previous encounters with the Canadian Shield had been in cottage country.

The landscape here is rugged enough on its own. But she discovers that the old signposts have all been vandalized and the road is more pothole than pavement. Fallen trees often block the track.

If not for the power winch mounted on the Rover's front bumper and her own pure stubbornness, she would never have made it across some of the streams.

She'd brought extra gas, but that is gone. She won't have enough for the full return trip. At some point she'll just have to leave the Rover and walk out. The thought makes her knees ache.

The abandoned buildings along the way are sad to see. What should be quaint cottages are piles of rubble, overgrown with bracken.

A few blackened beams jut like compound fractures, the roofs burnt long ago. She wonders how long it has been since anyone has walked these lanes.

Now, on a remote hillside, she pauses, camera in hand. The slope is steep, so she is on foot. The borrowed Land Rover waits in the shallow valley behind her.

Near her feet is a splash of purple vegetation. She plucks a plant and sticky fluid clings to her fingers. Glancing around, she sees the slope is covered with them. Hundreds of tiny pitcher plants.

"Jesus. That's weird."

She wipes her fingers on her jeans and wonders at the synchronicity. The pamphlet's shadow on the encyclopedia page had underlined a passage—*the bottle leaf, oft mistaken for a blossom, allows the plant to survive where others cannot.*

A sense of unease settles on the back of her neck. She turns to scan the view across the valley and a hilltop figure catches her eye. It stands motionless atop a nearby crag.

"Hello!" Anne waves, but gets no response.

She brings up her camera and presses zoom. The picture focuses.

"Darned eyes, playing tricks." She sees that it's not a person, but a wooden Celtic cross, mounted on a dry-rock cairn.

The circle and intersecting lines put Anne in mind of the scoped crosshairs on her dead father's hunting rifle.

The winter she had turned sixteen, Anne had used that rifle to put meat on her mother's table.

Her Mum had been so proud. She cooked venison every day, three times a day, for a month, while the dressed carcass hung in their empty barn like a war-crimes victim. Venison sausage for breakfast. Cold roast venison for lunch. Broiled venison steaks for supper.

And as all good mothers do, she insisted that Anne eat every scrap of the wretched, greasy stuff that she cooked for her.

"God loves a clean plate," Mother said.

Anne looked for that one in the family Bible, but gave up at "Honour thy mother and thy father."

With only the two of them to feed, it seemed like the carcass would last forever. Then Anne cut the damn thing down and let the dog at it.

The memory provokes an unwelcome thought.

"Is this what a deer feels like, before the bullet?"

Talking out loud feels crazy too, but it's what she needs.

Searching the rugged horizon, she discovers three more on nearby hilltops. Two crosses to the left and one to the right of the first; all of them face in her general direction.

Turning back and forth to triangulate, she grows certain that the crosses don't actually face her, but the low barrow mound on the hillcrest above her.

Anne dusts off the seat of her pants. Perhaps the crosses were erected as penance by some errant missionary.

She faces the hill, examining the mound. It only rises a few metres above the hill's plateau and would be scarcely noticeable from the air.

A sharp puff of wind raises dust. Blinking, she sees there's an opening into the interior of the barrow. No door bars the way inside. It waits for her to enter.

Her mouth feels dry. She looks at the meadow of pitcher plants that surrounds her and takes a backward step down the slope. A second step back and loose stones skitter. A new, gentler breeze reaches her from the hilltop. It smells of fresh-baked bread.

Another step back and she slips on something soft and wet. Her knees hit the scree. She scrambles up, purple paste stains her jeans.

She wants to run, but can't turn around.

Her backward pace down the hillside grows faster and more reckless. She doesn't know what to think, just wants to get back to the Land Rover and get out of here.

The bread smell sours, reeking like overturned manure.

She turns and flees downhill, heedless of the ankle-breaking rocks. Tears blur her sight as she careens onward. Her tongue feels huge in her mouth, coated with bile. She needs to reach the Rover.

Then she's there, leaning against the driver's door, gasping for air. The solid presence of metal and chrome gives her the courage to look back. She is beyond the curve of the hill, beyond view.

Her shaking fist holds the key. It takes both hands to hit the unlock button. Stupid. Why had she locked it at all?

Once inside, she relocks the doors and the key finds the ignition. She puts the Rover in gear and gives it gas.

"Not too fast."

She turns in a tight circle, ready to get out of here, to head for home. The turn takes her a little further west into the valley.

There's no reason to do so, but habit makes her check the rearview mirror and something familiar catches her eye. She looks again with the dreadful certainty that what she sees is no illusion. There, behind the hill, where she couldn't have seen it before, is another vehicle.

Cautiously she turns around, drives closer and stops. It's another Land Rover. No one is inside. She shuts off the engine, gets out, leaving her sanctuary, her armour, and stumbles across a half-dozen metres to the other Rover.

She can see it's a newer model but with plenty of fresh mud and scrapes.

The driver's door isn't locked. Why would it be, way out here?

She climbs inside and pops the glove box. A rental slip gives up the driver's name—Elizabeth Mason.

Now what? Anne feels uncertain about what she should do, like maybe she shouldn't even be here. Is she an interloper?

"I'll call Georgie. Get her advice," she says to herself

She's left her smartphone off to save the battery. Now she stabs the power button. It beeps, and balloons dance above a message—"Not in Service Area".

Useless. She stuffs it back into her pocket.

From here she can see the mound again, innocent in the plain morning light. The young librarian must have been as excited as she had been to find it.

Miss Mason must already be in there. Maybe something she did caused those smells. Perhaps she'd opened a crypt and released that foul odour.

The girl has left the keys in the ignition. Why not? Only paranoids worry about car theft in the middle of nowhere.

Which Rover to take up the hill seems like six of one and half-a-dozen of the other so she turns the rental's key.

The engine catches on the first try. Anne engages the four-wheel drive, clips the seat belt and cinches it tight. Unaccountably, that makes her feel better.

She'll just drive up and find the girl. With a bit of care, she should be able to coax the rented Rover up the hill.

She tentatively presses the gas pedal. The four knobby tires grip the sod. Slowly the Rover bucks over hummocks and rocks. She reaches the base of the hill and starts climbing. Her speed is dead slow. Two, maybe three miles per hour at most.

The scene ahead is static. A couple of times she hits the horn, hoping for a response. Nothing.

Cresting the slope, the sight of the green barrow mound fills the windshield. She's only a few metres away. The steering wheel is solid in her hands and she does not want to let go.

She honks the horn again and cracks the window open, hoping for something, ready to laugh at her flight of fancy. Nothing.

Trembling, she kills the engine, pulls the key and jerks the door handle. She steps out onto the turf.

"Hello!" she calls, still hoping for a cheerful, reassuring call back from the young librarian. "Hello, it's Anne. Anne Blaine."

But the voice that responds is male.

"I say."

It's Mr. Phillips, the senior librarian, standing to her left, on the level ground near the mound's curved perimeter. But it's not the Mr. Phillips of starched shirt collars and embroidered waistcoats. No, this Phillips is dressed in khaki, calf-high boots, a bush jacket and a pith helmet.

It makes Anne want to laugh in relief and call him "Bwana."

His right arm comes up in a jaunty wave, jerking like a marionette. "I say," he repeats. "Come. Help." The words are each an individual effort.

Anne's thigh muscles twitch.

"Sure," she calls back.

The pith helmet on the man's head squirms and panic touches her stomach. This morning's cereal threatens to splash against the back of her throat.

She steps back and sees red flow down the librarian's temple.

He stumbles and falls to the ground. His limbs jump and flex without rhythm. He's having some kind of fit. She can hear his teeth grind and gnash. He needs her help and she's frozen in place.

The thrashing slows. First his arms, and then his legs quiver in dynamic tension. His body goes rigid, then relaxes.

He rolls to his stomach and starts to rise like a broken doll. Then, moving less like a puppet with each passing moment, he walks toward her. Suddenly his arms and legs begin pumping like a twenty-year-old, heedless of whatever it might cost his body. The helmet is lost in the rush and something dark and stringy writhes on his bald pate.

Anne runs, but half-buried rocks threaten a twisted ankle. The man gains ground, and fast. At the edge of the hillcrest he slams into her, a hard, sharp shoulder. They tumble, entangled down the talus slope.

His knee smacks her square in the nose. The blow snaps her head back and exquisite pain blooms across her face. At the end of their final gyrating bounce Mr. Phillips is below her when they land.

Anne sees it all. The jutting granite boulder. The back of the man's head laid open to the bone, a great ragged flap of scalp skinned off like a piece of mandarin orange peel. They lie on the ground, separated by a few feet. Loose rocks slither down the slope behind them.

Anne is flat on her back. She coughs. Blood from her broken nose trickles down the back of her throat. She's never been hit in the face before.

The man's grip has been broken, but her abdomen is scored by ugly fingernail tracks. The smell of crushed plants and the copper taste of blood are the only sensations that don't involve pain.

Then something probes insistently against the back of her skull. She jackknifes onto hands and knees, her stomach a blaze of pain.

Where her head had lain is the ragged scrap of the man's scalp. Entwined in the torn flesh is a horror. Flatworms with tick-like mouths. Some broken, some whole. Down the length of each segmented body, tiny moving filaments connect and re-connect each worm with its neighbours. Tiny pinhole eyes examine her with sharp intelligence.

Her hands scramble at the back of her head, raking at the hair, pulling, pulling desperately.

Her hands come away, dirty but nothing else. No headworms.

Heedless of the mess dripping from her nose, she snatches up a stone and smashes the flap of scalp, pushing with all her weight. The sound of fleshy pops is more satisfying than anything she ever imagined. Deep in her monkey brain she hates these things. She wants to kill them all.

She lurches to her feet. Phillips doesn't move. The old man's shirt is dark with blood where his bones have splintered. More blood stains the plants that surround his head. Anne can't tell if he is alive or dead, and nothing is going to make her approach. She can only leave him there.

With the toe of her boot she flips the rock back. Underneath, the scrap of skin is black and oily with the broken parasites. Her flesh crawls, and she rakes her fingers through her hair again.

One worm starts to rise from the mess, and her boot heel comes down hard, twisting back and forth, crushing the thing into paste.

She's got to find Miss Mason. Hope that what has happened to Mr. Phillips hasn't also infected the girl.

It's crazy to try, but Anne can't help thinking, what if this were her daughter? Wouldn't she want another woman to try everything she could to save her child?

"Need to look. But not on foot. Stay inside the vehicle. Lock it. Drive around the mound. That's smart."

She looks back up the hill at Miss Mason's rented Rover. Walking up there holds no appeal. Safer to retrace her path down the slope to Georgie's vehicle.

It's a quick hobble down and she's back in the driver's seat. Windows closed, doors locked tight, she keeps her distance and circles the base of the hill, honking the horn. There's no response, and she can't help but think that time is running out. The thought of Elizabeth Mason's imaginary mother hounds her.

She drives up the slope again, passing close to the old man. Blood continues to seep from his lacerated scalp. He must be in shock. He needs help, but she can't imagine having him inside the SUV with her. He was too strong, too dangerous.

She circles the summit. There's only one entrance to the mound. If she's going in to find Elizabeth Mason, there's one choice.

"Shit."

She manoeuvres Georgie's truck closer and shines the high-beam headlights through the open doorway. The passage is lined with stone and quickly curves away to the left, sloping down into the hill itself. She holds down the horn for a solid minute.

It takes all she has to step outside the vehicle. Letting go of the door feels like stepping off a cliff.

"Hello!" she calls again and dreads a response.

Then she's in the doorway, and a smell like low tide penetrates her awareness. Her stomach lurches and the mound's slab walls change.

Solid stones flex and bloom hundreds of thin grey fibres. She falls backwards, scrambling crab-wise, away, hands and feet flying. One fibre catches at the tip of her hiking boot.

"Shit!" She kicks frantically. The fibre comes off and she skitters until the back of her head hits the Rover's front bumper.

Metres long, both from within the passageway and now all across the mound's entire external face, the grey fibres strain toward her.

Anne waits for a hundred stings to penetrate her skin or the tendrils to lash her flesh, but the trap has been sprung too soon. She is out, and the longest doesn't quite reach her. Her shoulder touches the power winch on the front bumper of the Rover and she uses it to lever herself back to her feet.

She edges across the front of the grill, more grateful to reach the corner of the truck than for anything in her life. She climbs back into the Rover and quickly pulls back. The doors are relocked and she keeps it in gear, ready for a hasty retreat.

The tendrils withdraw. The wall is motionless again. Her mouth tastes acid green with hatred.

The library girl has to be caught inside this thing. God only knows what that means.

"What can I do? I can't …"

But there's no one here but her to stop whatever is going on.

She has no weapons, and even if she did, what good would a gun do? All she has are the two Rovers.

Maybe with gas from the one she can get back to the main road with the other. It's not very far, but it will take hours no matter how fast she drives. She still has to cross those streams and the winch can only run so fast.

The winch! Oh, yes. The big cable winch. The one on Georgie's has two thousand kilograms of pulling power. The one on Elizabeth Mason's looks bigger and stronger. That's the one she'll use.

One cable won't be long enough, but she can use both. Together they should reach all the way around. She's in the fight.

"Okay, Miss Mason's mother. I'm trying."

Maybe if she can really hurt the thing, it'll let the girl go. Who knows, what other chance has she got?

Holding hard onto this new plan, she steps out of the Rover.

"No time to lose. Keep it simple. And move."

It's surprisingly easy to remove the steel cable spool from Georgie's truck. God bless the engineers at British Rover. Watching for trouble, she grabs the heavy steel hook and pulls a dozen metres of cable off the spool. The scratches Mr. Phillips left on her stomach are raw, but she crawls between the rear wheels of the rented Rover.

She hasn't wriggled on her belly like this since her kids were small. Oily mechanical scents penetrate her broken nose and she manages to avoid contact with the hot exhaust pipes.

Two loops through the frame to make the cable fast cost her skinned knuckles, but there must be no weak link.

Careful to stay well away from the wall, she pays out the cable, moving clockwise around the mound as far as it will reach. Just over halfway around, the spool runs out.

"So far, so good." Anne drops the end and walks back. She's got no more running left in her. The fisherman's splice she uses to connect the cable ends would make her old 4-H leader wince, but the hook makes a satisfying *clink*, and completes the loop around the barrow.

"Got you. I think."

Anne walks back around the curve, back once more to the Rovers.

The girl is waiting for her, of course, standing next to the rented Rover.

In Miss Mason's right hand is a fist-sized rock, humanity's fall-back tool. But she hasn't yet smashed in the window.

The girl's face looks like a Hieronymus Bosch triptych. One part as serene and beautiful as a Buddha; the other, a battleground of facial tics and contortions, and Anne wonders what the headworms are doing to the girl she met in the stacks.

"Let me through, Elizabeth. I don't want to hurt you."

"No." The single word is exaggerated, slurred like a drunk, fighting to look sober. The fist and rock come up. There's no mistaking the intent.

"Keys." The girl mouths the word like a stroke victim.

That frightens Anne all the more. If the headworms had only wanted to stop her, the window would've been smashed by now, the hood popped and the engine disabled.

But perhaps they understand what the vehicles represent. Mobility. The chance to go out into the human world, to travel, to spread.

Anne digs into her pocket and finds what she needs: the keys for Georgie's Rover, the one that's *not* hooked up to the cables. She dangles them, a black and silver set, like a doggy treat. She wants the girl to see that they are the real deal.

"You want them? Go get them."

She turns and throws the keys as high and as hard as she can, out toward the valley. They twinkle, twisting around the keyring, a pair of escaped pixies handcuffed at the wrist.

But their flight is short. The plastic and metal are too light. They fall and bounce once, lying in plain sight, well shy of the plateau's edge, not ten metres away.

For Anne what follows is a moment of pure tableau. The contorted side of Miss Mason's face relaxes, shifting from committed resistance to perfect compliance, and Anne knows the headworms have the girl. As completely as they controlled Phillips, they have her too.

And as fast as Phillips was, Miss Mason is faster. The girl is past Anne before she's taken a step. There is no time to look back. Anne is committed. The important key, the key to the *rented* Rover is in her fist. She thumbs the unlock button and launches herself at the driver's door. From behind comes a shriek of feral delight as Miss Mason and the flatworms find the thrown-away keys.

Anne is at the unlocked door. A howl of rage and jealousy meets her success with a sound that scores her nerves like a flensing knife.

Miss Mason sees her. Anne has what the flatworms want. They are coming.

Heaving the door open, Anne flings herself inside.

Close the door or start the engine? She tries both at once. The Rover's engine catches and roars to life, a defiant war cry, overmatched by the screaming girl at the door.

The girl has both hands on the doorjamb versus Anne's one on the handle. It's no contest. She can let go or allow herself to be pulled out of the Rover, like a snail sucked out of its shell. She lets go and scrabbles for the winch control.

Anne has used the winch in Georgie's Rover dozens of times in the last few days and knows exactly where it should be. So when she toggles the switch and the rear hatch pops open she curses car designers and the pointless changes they make to justify each year's new model. Hats off to you, Mr. and Ms. New-and-Improved.

Elizabeth has no such difficulties finding a grip on the front of Anne's shirt and the girl hauls her out like the trash. Anne pulls at the young woman's hands but can't bring herself to strike at her.

Miss Mason pushes Anne backward, toward the barrow mound, and there the tendrils have her. Strong as piano wire, they hold her immobile, lifting her off the ground. She senses movement behind her. Something is coming from within the mound, just for her. Her own special package of headworms.

She sees Elizabeth Mason climb into the Rover. Her movements are limited, awkward; the paucity of human joints is not to the worms' liking.

The girl's right hand moves to the ignition, ready to kill the motor. But new facial tics corkscrew across her face and both sides now are in remission. Some part of this brave human woman yet survives and fights on.

That's when Anne understands. The person who wrote the pamphlet, and placed it just so, was the same person that seeded the slope with pitcher plants. Someone fighting the headworms for control, in the only way they knew how. Someone very much like Elizabeth Mason.

"The winch!" she screams. "The winch!"

But the girl must already know. She'd seen the cables encircling the mound. She and Mr. Phillips must have used their winch too, just to get here. The girl's right hand, out of her control, claws at the ignition. She throws her head forward, smashing a pert and perfect nose into the steering wheel. In that moment her left hand engages the winch.

The low-geared grind of a turning metal drum is an angel's choir. Near Anne's feet the steel-wire cable jerks, tightening; it smooths a narrowing arc of trampled heather around either side of the mound.

Inside the Rover the violence continues unabated. Blood streams from the girl's broken nose, and now she and Anne have a matched set.

Anne sees Elizabeth arch her body, foot planted on the gas pedal, pressing her skull into the hardtop roof, squealing with terror and glee, popping a few ripe and unready worms against the dome-light, keeping the ignition out of her own reach.

Anne's own struggles are futile, but the tendrils begin to drop away from her as more and more of them reach down to seize the cable, trying to hold it back. She falls out of their grasp and tumbles onto the raw, scrambled earth.

Now all slack is gone from the encircling winch cable, the straining tendrils hold it away, then push up; and the Rover jumps up, suspended in mid-air, tires not touching the ground.

Tens of thousands of tendrils shift their grip. The cable and Rover both rise again, half a metre higher. Anne understands. It's shifting the noose, to lift it up. Up and over before it closes. The mound is low. Two more lifts and it's safe.

She tears a rock out of the turf and scrambles in through the Rover's open rear hatch. It rises again, higher. Her added weight is nothing to the entity.

The passenger side of the Rover is buried in a wall of pushing grey fibres. The engine's roar drops, fades to idle. Elizabeth's foot is off the gas pedal. The winch drum stops.

Anne strikes at the top of the girl's head. A tentative, apologetic blow. The rock comes back clean, the worms burrowing into Elizabeth's skull unaffected.

Anne strikes again. Harder. Elizabeth snaps her head back to meet the blow, anxious for the contact. Anne's jaw clenches in sympathetic pain, but the girl's feet, both of them this time, find the gas pedal again, planting it with a snarl.

The winch, power renewed, grinds on relentless as time. Overpowered, the tendrils surrender and the cable bites in the thing's crown.

Using the rock, Anne jams the gas pedal down and Elizabeth lets herself be pushed out the open driver's door.

◆

It's a bit embarrassing to find out that her phone works from the hilltop. Her 911 call brings an emergency helicopter, and a few days later, after Elizabeth and Mr. Phillips recover from the worst of their injuries, they're very gracious about it.

Everyone, from *Time* magazine to Colbert cover the story, and at first theories about the thing's origin and purpose run the gamut, from "duck blind" to "doomsday weapon."

Anne favours the "alien life raft" hypothesis. It makes the most sense to her. The thing wasn't a world killer. It was meant to blend in with its surroundings and use the local biosphere to keep itself and a few stranded survivors alive in a hostile environment; long enough for help to arrive.

The autopsy proves her right. Deep inside the carcass, like ovarian cysts, the hibernating passengers are found. Censored video of the creatures makes the headworms look like baby seals. That stops the tinfoil-hat crowd from sending her more death threats.

She avoids most of the demands for interviews, but consents to a request from CBC Radio. It seems like the polite thing to do.

The host is a bit dense though.

"Why would honest-to-god aliens want to eat people?" he asks. "That's so sci-fi."

"I think it's like Clarke's Third Law," Anne says, "but turned on its head."

"I'm not sure I follow," the man says.

"There's a famous quote from Arthur C. Clarke," Anne explains. "He said 'Any sufficiently advanced technology is indistinguishable from magic.'"

"And?"

"And perhaps the opposite also applies. When a civilization reaches an advanced level of development, do all primitives start to look like animals?"

"Surely not. We're people."

"With mankind's history as an example, it's no great leap of logic. Humans would look like stick-wielding apes to stranded aliens. I wonder how a cynical Arthur C. might have put it?" Anne feels a moment of empathy for the creatures. "Or maybe you just make do with what's available."

"There's speculation," the man says, "that an interstellar rescue party might arrive any time, looking for the castaways. What do you suppose they might do?"

"Fiction offers no eloquent law on that point." Anne smiles. "But people like Elizabeth Mason give me hope. We can learn, even from a lifeboat. And when the time comes, I'm sure we'll be prepared to use the tools at hand."

SUMMER FRIEND

Chris Allinotte

Come on, take it, thought Michael. He was lying prone on the Fairly's old dock, fishing line threaded down through the gap in the boards, and willing a dark green rock bass to take the hook. With the practised twitch of the fingers that Brian Fairly had taught him last summer, Michael brought the baited line a fraction of an inch closer. It was enough. With a barely perceptible flick of its tail, the fish darted forward and seized the scrap of raw bacon. The excitement of the moment almost cost Michael the catch. A large part of him hadn't expected anything to happen, so when it did, he was shocked. He jerked the line straight up. The fish thrashed, trying desperately to retreat into the slime-covered boulders beneath the dock, but being no more than five inches long, it came easily up out of the water. It was the last six inches that was the tricky part, when he'd need to manoeuvre the fish through the gap in the boards.

Michael's phone squished into his thigh through his pocket as he pressed his body into the dock for stability. It was his first real phone, and he was thrilled to have it. Brian wouldn't believe Michael had caught anything, but with a photo, there'd be no doubt. Brian and his brother were the only other kids on this stretch of Winnipeg Beach and it was getting boring without them—even though they picked on him sometimes.

Just a little further now and he'd have the fish out.

"What are you doing?" asked a voice directly behind him.

Michael screamed, his whole body jumped, and the stick fell out of his hand. Turning over, he saw a girl standing with crossed arms and a peculiar grin on her face. She looked about the same age as him, but shorter, though it was tough to tell for sure from his level.

He found his voice, "Fishing. What does it look like?"

"Like you'd lost something down there."

There was a tiny splash from under the dock. Michael peered through the crack again, seeing only the naked black hook in the pale yellow-green water. He rolled up the line on its stick, saying "I *did* lose it," under his breath, but loud enough that she could hear.

"It's not *my* fault you don't have a real fishing rod," she said.

Michael frowned and stood up, finding he *was* taller, by a bit.

He studied the girl more closely. Dirty brown hair was falling out of a sloppy ponytail, and her pink and white T-shirt had a large stain on the shoulder, but she still managed to look as if she was doing him a favour by talking to him.

"I've never seen you before," said Michael.

"I just got here," replied the girl. "So. You want to play or what?"

Michael, still getting over his initial surprise, finally settled for, "I guess. What do you want to play?"

Her smile widened. "Tag. You're *it!*"

On the word 'it,' she shoved Michael off the dock. He landed feet first. The water was waist deep, but the momentum carried him backward in the soft, sucking silt of the lake bed. Though he flailed valiantly, he fell further back and went all the way under. Tendrils of seaweed caressed his exposed skin and he half-staggered, half-jumped to his feet. On the shoreline, the mystery girl was laughing.

"The expression on your face," she said, giggling. "It's swell."

Michael charged. He was wet, there was mud in his pockets, and he was going to make this girl pay. He ran with huge, ungainly steps through the water and promptly fell down face-first again. Sputtering and trying to get the water out of his eyes, he heard her speak again.

"Geez, if you just wanted to go swimming, why didn't you say so?"

Michael bellowed, storming up onto the beach, but the girl had already started running. In his wet clothes, it was tough to keep up.

She remained just out of reach all the way to the grass line and up onto the lawns of the lakefront cottages. At some point in the chase, Michael's anger at being soaked became a simple desire to catch up to this strange person. *Besides*, he thought, in a mental voice that seemed to be panting as well, *you weren't supposed to hit girls—even when they pushed you in the water—and who* was *she anyway?*

Suddenly, she stopped, and he almost tripped over her. She was crouched down at the edge of the woods that separated his parents' cottage from the next one over.

"Whoa. Stop. *Stop.* I'm sorry about the water," said the girl, whispering. "Get down here for a second."

"Good," replied Michael, not whispering.

"Come on," she said. "Pretend we're in the jungle and a jaguar is stalking us. If she hears even a single breath, it's all over."

"Pretend games are stupid," Michael replied, but he crouched and whispered anyway. "And I'm still mad."

"And I'm still sorry," she said.

Something in the bush crackled, and the girl cocked her head to the side, listening. In the low light near the edge of the foliage, her skin looked paler than he remembered.

Upon looking at her again, taking in her filthy-kneed jeans and messy hair, Michael didn't see any of the gleeful cruelty that he'd suffered at her hands just minutes ago. He saw a lonely kid his own age. Skinnier, too, if that was possible. He wondered if she was sick.

"Are you okay?" he asked. "You look like you're going to throw up."

Her body stiffened, and she didn't reply right away. Michael waited for a few seconds, and was about to repeat himself when she stood up, stopping to dust soil off her knees.

"Are you still here tomorrow? she asked.

"Yeah," he said. "I'm here all week."

"Okay." She turned to leave.

"Wait," he said. "What's your name?"

"Karen. What's yours?"

"Michael."

She started through the bush. "Cool. See you tomorrow Mikey." The bush seemed to close in around her as she went.

"Are you staying with the Duncans?" he asked after her, but she was already gone.

◆

It was dinnertime when Michael returned to the cabin, and Dad was in the kitchen. Once, Michael had overheard his father talking on the phone, referring to weekends out as "kid shift." Dad in the kitchen meant two things: Mom had already left for the city, and they were having grilled cheese sandwiches for dinner. As Michael stopped inside the porch to take off his sopping shoes, Dad called from the kitchen, "That you, Mike?"

"Yeah," he replied, and, after taking one step toward the living room, decided to take his socks off too.

Sure enough, when he went inside, Dad was standing at the olive-green stove, flipping buttery brown bread.

"I thought we'd do hot dogs on the fire later," said Dad. "This'll hold you over 'til then, right?"

"Sure," said Michael. He walked through the living room, trying to slip into his room to change his clothes, but it was no good. Dad was in a conversational, three-beer mood.

"So how was your day?" his father said, turning around.

His chipper expression fell as he saw Michael for the first time.

"What the hell happened?" he asked, gesturing with the spatula.

"I fell in the water."

Dad didn't say anything for a moment and Michael could see him working out whether to be pissed off or not. Finally, Dad just sighed and said, "Go change. We can hit the laundromat tomorrow, I guess."

When Michael didn't immediately start moving, Dad gestured again, "Move it, Soggy. Dinner's ready."

Wouldn't want my grease sandwich to get cold, thought Michael as he walked down the short hallway to the smallest bedroom and, with relief, peeled off his damp, gritty jeans.

◆

After dinner, Michael turned on the TV and Dad turned on his laptop, promising to be "twenty minutes, tops."

An hour later, TV had given way to an old paperback, and though he still wasn't sure who *Christine* was, Michael loved the way the characters talked, and cursed. It was just getting really good when Dad slapped his computer closed.

"Done. Now how about that fire?"

Bonfires were the one thing Dad got excited about. They went outside and, after a few minutes' work, had a good fire going. Michael used a mostly dull paring knife to whittle the leftover carbon from the hot dog sticks.

Movement near the shoreline caught Michael's eye. Backlit by the rising moon over the water, it was hard to make out who was there, but from the shape of the silhouette, he thought it was Karen. He waved. The silhouette stopped.

"Who are you waving to?" asked Dad, squinting to see past the flickering fire.

"This girl I met today," said Michael. "I think she's staying at the Duncans' place."

"There's no one in the Duncan place," said Dad, but his tone was distracted as he fit a wiener onto his cooking stick. "Unless someone bought property over the winter," he added.

Michael looked again. The shadow was gone.

◆

The next day Michael was sweeping out the boathouse, trying not to focus on the dozens of spiders he was trapping in the corn bristles of the broom.

"Hey," said Karen. Michael turned around.

"Hey."

"You done?" she asked.

"Yeah," said Michael, and put the broom down after banging it straight up and down a few times to maybe kill some of the spiders. "All right. Done," he continued. "What do you want to do?"

"Let's go catch frogs," replied Karen.

"You're not going to kill them, are you?" asked Michael, ready to argue.

"Ew. No," said Karen, "that's sick."

It was good enough. He grabbed a bucket and they set off.

An hour later, they had been through three of the deepest, most stagnant roadside ditches and had five small green frogs hopping in the bottom of the pail. Just a little further up the road, past the last of the cottage driveways, they reached the final ditch in the system.

This ditch was deep and mostly dry, except for a foot of odorous brown water along the bottom. The corrugated metal conduit at the far end of the ditch was a black hole in the green, weedy earth. There were no more cottages from here until the other side of the creek, and this drain led under the ground of an empty lot to finish up above the dirty brown stream. Mike had already slipped and soaked his shoes again, so he was the first to trudge through the wild grass at the bottom of the ditch, wincing as more water seeped in through the sides of his shoes.

"We're sure to get some in here, Karen" he called over his shoulder. When he didn't get a reply, he turned to see that Karen had gone thirty yards further up the road, just past the Duncan place. Michael had to call her twice more before she turned around.

"What?"

"I said where are you going? There's a huge one near the end there," said Michael, pointing to the area near the conduit at the end.

"No," said Karen. "Not that one." She turned and started walking up the road. He staggered up the slope of the ditch as quickly as he could to follow but slipped back into the water. Mud slurped at his heels.

"Shit!" he cried. Between the muck today and the lake yesterday, his shoes would never be white again. He clambered up the ditch and jogged after her, wincing as his shoes squished with each step.

"Karen," he called, but she wasn't answering.

"What happened?" asked Michael, finally drawing up next to her.

"I don't want to do this anymore," said Karen.

"What, catch frogs?"

"Yeah." She didn't meet his eyes, and there was something weird in her voice that Michael couldn't figure out.

Starting to walk away, she added, "I have to go now, anyway. Bye." Karen turned abruptly and ran off the road onto the beaten dirt driveway of a nearby cottage.

They were past the Duncan place now, and it was impossible to see the cabin from the road. Counting the shadow last night, if it had indeed been Karen, she'd now left him abruptly three times.

Michael's curiosity got the best of him, and he started down the path after her.

The road was overgrown, the beaten dirt path barely discernible. It was a wonder that Karen's parents could get a car down here without scratching it.

Ducking under a final low-hanging branch, Michael suddenly stopped. Karen was nowhere to be seen, and the cabin in front of him could not possibly be where she'd gone.

Overall, the impression Michael had of the little cottage was that someone large—Paul Bunyan perhaps—had sat down hard on the roof, giving the entire building a sway-backed appearance. It would be easier to count the remaining shingles on the roof than the ones that littered the ground, and the windows were covered with cracked plywood.

Michael made his way around the side of the cabin. Karen had to be here *somewhere*. As he reached the front of the cabin, the sun, already filtered through dense brush, seemed to retreat further behind the gathered dark clouds, and Michael shivered. The door to the cabin was closed, but not all the way. It seemed like the weather had swelled and warped the wood so that it wouldn't close.

Standing at the threshold, hand outstretched to push the door, Michael paused. Did he *want* to go in? Who was to say Karen had gone in? She may have cut through to the beach to go somewhere else. Looking in the direction of the lake, it did seem the more welcoming of the two options. At the same time, his curiosity was piqued and, if he was being totally honest with himself, he was more than a little interested in Karen's long hair, big eyes, and the fit of her T-shirt. He started to blush. Taking a deep breath, Michael pushed the door.

It didn't budge. The warped wood stuck fast in the jamb. He gave another hard shove. This time, the door scraped backward a little in the frame. One more push would likely do it—but had Karen done this, too? She'd only been a little ahead of him—surely he would have heard the heavy scraping of the wood. Unless there was another way in.

Or she didn't come in here at all, he thought. He turned to walk to the beach, but on a final, crazy impulse, shoved the door again. It cleared the jamb with a woody "pop" and swung back into darkness.

The clammy air inside the cabin seemed to cling to Michael's skin. The door opened into a large main room with two doors at the back, leading to a bedroom and bathroom, he supposed. It was a similar setup to his own cottage, but it looked as if it had been neglected for a decade. There was no sign of Karen anywhere. *Good*, he thought. *I can leave.* As he turned to go, he heard crying coming from one of the back rooms.

"Karen?" Michael stepped further into the room. He wanted to be able to see into the back rooms without going closer, but it was too dark.

The crying continued. He went closer to the room on the left.

"Go away Mikey." It was Karen's voice, but it sounded different, thicker.

"Are you alright?" Michael stepped closer.

"Go away!"

Michael could just see inside the room now. Karen stood with her back to the door. Her hair looked wet.

"You ran away so fast, I just—"

Karen turned around and Michael's voice dried up in his throat.

It was hard to make out details in the shadow, but Karen's face looked *wrong*. Her features were swollen, and her skin was even paler than it'd been before—almost white.

"Go away," she screamed now. Her voice lost all trace of humanity. Instead of the girl he knew, there was only a Karen-shaped monster in the room.

Michael backed up. He wanted to run. His stomach felt like a shrivelled nut and he had to pee. Still, he didn't leave. Behind the awful voice and the distorted face, there was still a girl that had taken time to talk to him when he was lonely.

"I don't want to go," he said, voice trembling. "I want to help."

"You can't," said Karen, but her voice seemed less harsh, more human. "This is what I am. This is *all* I am."

Michael couldn't help the question, "Why?"

"This is what I looked like when I died," she replied. "In the drainpipe."

They were silent then. Michael's mind raced, putting together the rest of the story. Was this what happened when *everyone* died? It couldn't be. Karen stood in the shadows, looking at him.

He cleared his throat. "That's really awful."

"Yeah," she agreed. "It is. You can go now. Tell all your friends."

"No," Michael said, walking closer to the door. "You're my friend."

"I don't want to be here!" Karen slammed her hand against the wall, but it passed through.

Swift, light tapping on the roof told Michael that it had started raining.

A thought occurred to Michael, but he didn't say it aloud. Instead, he let it burn his ears bright red. It was stupid to compare Karen's situation to dumb things he'd read or seen on TV.

"What?" she asked. She moved closer. "You're thinking something. What is it?" Despite his best intentions, Michael stepped back. There was a fetid, swampy odour about her in this place that was hard to be around. She backed up too, and Michael saw the hurt in her expression.

"It's nothing," Michael mumbled. "It was a stupid question."

Karen sighed. "I've got time for stupid. Give it."

He cleared his throat. "Just. God. This is dumb. Do you think there's some purpose or task that you're supposed to do before you can, you know, move on?"

"What? Like revenge?" Karen gave a bitter chuckle. "I did this to myself. Just a stupid mistake."

Michael soldiered on with another fiction-induced suggestion. "Did they find your body? Maybe that's what has to happen?"

"Yeah," Karen replied. "They found me about a day after the flooding went down."

"Shit."

"Yeah."

A breeze was blowing through the door. Michael shivered. "Could we keep thinking about it outside? I'm pretty cold."

"I look worse in direct light."

"That's okay," said Michael. "I think better when my nose isn't cold."

"It's raining."

"It'll still be warmer out there."

Karen smiled, and even through her distorted features, which Michael was surprised to find he was getting used to, she looked a little happier.

"Race you," she said, and passed through the wall.

Outside, Michael found Karen looking the same way she had when they'd first met on the dock. Thinking about the dock reminded Michael of something else.

"I thought you couldn't touch anything," he said. "But you pushed me in the water."

"I *scared* you in the water," she corrected. "The rest was just your brain making stuff up."

They walked through the few trees near the front of the cabin until they reached the beach.

"How come you don't still look, you know." Michael started.

"Dead?" Karen finished. "I don't know, I guess I'm feeling better right now."

They walked a little way along the lakefront. Rain pattered down around them, making tiny neat circles in the sand.

"So, any other ideas?" Karen asked.

"Um," Michael replied.

"Gotcha. Nothing." Karen spit on the sand. The gob of liquid disappeared as it struck the sand.

"What were you doing in the pipe?" Michael asked. "Maybe that has something to do with it."

As much as it was possible, Karen blushed. "I was playing hide and seek, and I thought I'd be *sooo* smart by hiding in there. Then I got stuck."

"Didn't your friends come looking?"

"Turns out I won at hide and seek," she said. "Forever."

"What if I find you?" Michael blurted out. He didn't know he was going to say it, but now that it was out, it didn't sound any weirder than anything else he could have come up with.

"What do you mean?" Karen stopped walking.

Michael heard hope in her voice. It made him direct his gaze out onto the lake. He didn't want to see her expression if his idea upset her.

The rain was picking up, and the sand had turned dark around them. Michael rushed to get his idea out before it got too bad.

"Maybe your soul, or ghost, or whatever, was just waiting for your friends to find you," he said. "Maybe you died feeling abandoned, and that didn't let you move on, or whatever happens."

"So what are you suggesting?" Karen's hand came over his

shoulder far enough that Michael could see it, but he couldn't feel anything except a bit of a numb itch.

He turned his head back, and met her eyes which, though she looked like she might cry, still looked pretty human.

"Let's play hide and seek," he said.

✦

"Are you sure about this?" Karen asked as she looked down the length of the ditch. Already water was running freely into the pipe. It was only a rivulet, but Michael could see how quickly it would get dangerous.

"I'm not sure about anything," Michael admitted. "In fact, why don't we do this tomorrow?"

"No," said Karen. "It was raining that day too. Maybe that's how it has to be."

Michael took a deep breath, then let it out. The rain had soaked his T-shirt through and was doing a pretty good job on his jeans too. Now or never.

"All right. One, two, three." He put his hands over his eyes.

At fifty, Michael stopped counting. It was certainly enough time for Karen to have hid. His teeth had begun to chatter at "forty".

He went right to the pipe and looked down its black interior. Unlike last time, though, he couldn't see all the way to the other side. Now, there was something in the way.

"Karen?" he shouted down the pipe. "Found you! Come out!"

"I can't!"

"What?" Michael's breath was steaming. Now his heart began pounding.

"I can't move," Karen's voice sounded panicked, desperate.

"Sure you can," Michael called. "Just stand up, you can pass through stuff, remember?"

"I *can't!*" she screamed. "I can't do *anything*. Oh God, I'm going to drown in here again!"

"You don't breathe!" Michael yelled back.

"No. Oh no," Karen was crying out, seeming oblivious to him.

Michael moved, knowing in his head that it was crazy to worry about a ghost drowning. At the same time, his heart only felt that a friend was in trouble and needed help.

He put his hands down inside the tube and moved a little way inside. His body further reduced the amount of light, and Karen was now just a black shape moving against a sliver of light from the other end of the pipe. The water was already up to his elbows.

"I'm here," he called. "Can you see me?"

"I can't see anything," Karen said. "It's so dark."

"Okay," Michael said. He moved forward, and his feet left the ground outside the pipe. Immediately, the space seemed smaller. The rain splatting into the ditch outside was an echoing din in the pipe. Michael moved his leg back, wanting to feel the ground again. Karen whimpered ahead of him.

"Listen to my voice," he shouted, and then winced at how loud he sounded. "I'm moving closer, but you need to move this way. Just one step forward, okay? Start with that."

The water continued to climb. If the nearby creek got too high, the level in the pipes might get much higher in a hurry. He didn't like the thought of water coming up to his mouth. Karen's shape moved.

"Just come on," said Michael again. "You can do it."

"I can't."

"I can't pull you," Michael said. "You need to move on your own. But I'm here. I'll stay with you. Just start moving."

The water continued to rise. Despite his instincts, Michael made himself crawl forward, further into the pipe.

"Come on," he tried again. "You can do it."

"I CAN'T!"

Karen's voice changed to the same monstrous scream he'd heard before. It startled Michael, and he pulled backward swiftly. The motion wedged his body back on top of his calves, and he could feel the corrugated metal pipe along his back, as well as pushing into his shins. He was stuck. Karen was still crying.

"I'm stuck, Karen!" Michael couldn't help the panic in his voice. The water was climbing higher, nearing his biceps now. Soon it would be up to his chin, and he thought that at that point he'd *really* freak out.

He took a deep breath through his mouth, and grimaced at the rotten plant flavour of the air in here.

"I need you to help me," he called. He tried moving forward again. His back and shoulders ached, and his legs were cramping in the cold water. "You have to go get my dad."

When she didn't answer, he added, "please."

The water climbed higher.

"I don't want to die too! Help me!"

"Help *me*," Karen cried.

"I know you're scared," Michael called. "I'm stuck at the opening. If you back up a little, you can get out. Please."

Karen's crying slowed, and Michael could hear her shifting around in the tube, moving. She was coming toward him.

Michael remembered what she'd looked like in the cabin and could *feel* her getting closer in the pipe. In that moment, he forgot about his friend and could only see the hideous, bloated thing that had shown itself to him in the cabin coming for him. He jerked back, and this time, he managed to pop a leg free. It was all he needed.

He shoved his other leg back, though Charlie-horse spasms screamed out from his calf, thigh, and butt. His shoes touched the bottom of the ditch, and he slid free of the pipe. At the last foot before he'd be all the way out, his feet slipped in the muck and he fell forward and down. His hands caught the edge of the pipe, but he still managed to catch his chin on the sharpened metal. Then he was under a foot of ditch water, and he jerked up to his feet, spluttering.

Michael's chin stung. He put a hand up to his face and it came away full of blood, which started to disappear immediately under the pouring rain. It wasn't until he had pulled the hem of his T-shirt up to stanch the flow that he remembered to look for Karen.

Looking back at the pipe, he saw her. She was somewhere in between the two forms he'd seen. Her skin was sickly blue-white, and her lips were swollen, but she wasn't quite the bloated dead *thing* that had chased him out of the pipe either. She crawled out and stood before him in a series of quick, jerky motions that made him step back.

"You're out," he said, for lack of something else to say.

"Yeah." She smiled, but it was a sad smile, full of thoughts of something else.

"Are you all right?" he asked.

"Still dead," she replied, her smile warming. "But I think it worked. I feel *different*."

"Like how?" Michael wadded more shirt under his chin, caring but not caring that he was exposing his bare chest to Karen. His curiosity burned.

"Like I can go now."

Neither of them said anything then. Rain splattered around them. Michael took his shirt right off and held it to his chin. He thought the blood might be coming a little slower now, but he couldn't tell. Dad would be angry that he'd hurt himself. The rain on his bare flesh made him shiver.

"Am I ever going to see you again?" he asked.

"I don't think so."

He took a deep breath. "I'm going to miss you."

She nodded. Her face blurred as she did, and when it stopped, she looked like she had the first day. "You were a good friend, Mikey."

Before he could say anything else, she leaned forward and planted a kiss on his lips. It was cold, and wet, and her breath smelled like seaweed, but Michael thought it was the best thing he'd ever felt.

When the kiss was over, he looked at her for a long time. "I thought you couldn't touch stuff."

She shoved him back hard and he fell butt-first into the ditch. "*That's* what you have to say for yourself?"

He shrugged.

"You're an idiot," she said, and she started to fade away. Michael could see trees and powerlines through her body.

Before she was all gone, she whispered, "I'll miss you too."

Michael watched the empty space for a few moments, his heart still pounding. How would he even begin to tell anyone about any of this? Even as he had that thought, it was replaced with the knowledge that he wouldn't have to. What had happened was something that was just for him. His life. His friend. His first kiss.

He turned around and walked home with his lips tingling and his shoes squishing all the way.

MY MOTHER'S FAMILIAR

Gilles DeCruyenaere

I read all the books. I took all courses. *Dealing With the Impending Death of a Companion Creature, Caring for the Long-Lived Guide of a Departed Loved One, When a Family Member Leaves Its Second Spirit Behind.* Hell, I even signed up for *Advanced Care and Feeding of Large North American Felines.* I thought I was ready. I really did. And I'm not talking "pretty ready," or even "ready enough." I'm talking I absolutely one hundred percent totally freakin' got this.

Truth is, there was nothing, absolutely nothing, which could have even begun to prepare me for the day when my mother's familiar left.

◆

I've always loved Bird's Hill Park. Some of my best childhood memories come from our family's numerous trips there. We'd usually make a fire in one of the rusty pits nestled in the forest by the road, cooking hot dogs and roasting marshmallows under the watchful eye of the forest's many eager little inhabitants. After lunch we'd head out to one of the fields and my brother and I would chase after our balsa-wood gliders, making machine gun noises as we pretended to shoot each other out of the sky. Everything about it was amazing. The enveloping heat coming off the sandy soil, the incredible smell of wild sage, the buzz and hum of a billion tiny creatures going about their unknowable lives—these combined to awaken in me the very essence of pure joy, the very best of childhood's fleeting gifts: the thoughtless, guiltless experience of simply being. Of course, I was not the only one to enjoy our outdoor excursions.

The companion creatures in my family were generally a fun little bunch: there was my fox, Nestor, my dad's turtle Blou-Blou, my brother's deer mouse Max, and my mother's lynx, Myriette.

I got Nestor when I was four. He had arrived at our doorstep as a pup, and when we let him in, he had immediately curled up at my feet and instigated the strong psychic bond which would connect us for the rest of our lives. That same day my dad had begun construction on a small screened-in habitat in the backyard, with a little pet door connecting it to our kitchen.

My father had been coupled fairly late in life, at the age of six. His family had been on a camping trip when he had suddenly felt drawn to a small boggy area near the campsite. When he had come strutting back, proudly holding a small red-eared slider before him, his parents had initially been uncertain, fearing that his anxiety at having not yet found a familiar may have led him to a bout of wishful thinking. They had asked him repeatedly if he was sure, and had even suggested that he return the turtle to the bog so he could think it over for a while. If, the next morning, he was still certain that this unusual creature was in fact the one, he could go back and retrieve it. My father hadn't needed to think it over, however. The fact that amphibian companions were considered a little odd had meant nothing to him at the time; this creature was his, as sure as the sky was blue. Sadly, a combination of peer pressure and failing self-esteem had eventually led him to be embarrassed by his familiar, seeing it as one of many unfortunate and unfair things with which he had been burdened in his life. Nevertheless, his bond with Blou-Blou stayed strong, and the little turtle remained steadfast in its duty to guide my father in every way possible.

My brother had found Max by the Red River Floodway, as he, my father, and I were out flying balsa-wood gliders. He'd had to chase the little rodent at first, but his persistence paid off, and he was eventually able to ambush it under a stand of dead grass. Once caught, the little mouse had nuzzled into the three-year-old's hand

and fallen asleep. Recognizing the importance of the event, my father had packed us up and driven us home, stopping on the way to pick up a large mouse habitat and supplies at the pet store. Wanting desperately to stay and fly airplanes, I had been fairly upset at the time. Fortunately, I quickly grew to love Max the deer mouse, and our aborted aerial shenanigans were all but forgotten.

The story of Myriette was a little less clear cut. My grandfather claimed they had picked her up in the Whiteshell when my mother was three, while my grandmother swore the lynx had been found cowering beneath a pile of wood between their house and the neighbour's. My mother herself claimed to have no recollection of the day she and Myriette had come together.

Though the details of her appearance remain a mystery, this I can claim with absolute certainty: Myriette was by far the bravest, most loyal and steadfast familiar I have ever known.

She was also the only familiar ever to have killed one of her own kind.

◆

It happened the afternoon of October 7th, 1977. Star Wars had been released earlier that year and, being the eleven-year-old boy I was, my mind was drifting off to a galaxy far, far away.

My father had bought me an X-wing fighter model kit that very morning. Though he was not a fan of the movie (he claimed the characters' lack of familiars was unnatural), he could not resist the power of a small boy grasping a cellophane-wrapped box in his pudgy little hands, gazing up at him with a look of need and excitement which was at once heartbreakingly sweet and, frankly, just a little bit frightening.

I was in my bedroom, happily rummaging through this newly acquired box of white plastic joy, when Nestor jumped onto my bed, panting and whining, and practically radiating anxiety. Startled, I put the box on my desk and sat next to him, stroking his soft red fur and doing my best to project calm despite my Star Wars-induced state of excitement. The little fox was obviously trying to tell me something, but our usually strong connection was fading in and out, like a satellite signal on a stormy day. The little I did sense from him was jumbled and inchoate; his normally well-controlled telepathic emissions were now coming at me like stray bullets, punctuated here and there by frantic little balls of confusion and panic. After a moment he jumped off the bed and ran to the door, where he stopped, back arched and hackles up, a low, dangerous growl emerging from his throat. I got up to try once more to calm him, then paused when I heard the sound of breaking glass, followed by an angry shout from my father. I followed as Nestor yipped and ran out of the room into the kitchen, where my mother stood next to the sink with a ceramic bowl in her hand, eyes blazing.

"What's going on?" I shouted. "Nestor's freaking out!"

"Mom's been into the painkillers," my dad replied, looking both angry and overwhelmed, "and now she's smashing things."

I took a quick look around as my father tried in vain to appease my mother, who had begun uttering vile things in an unhinged yet dopey and slurred voice. On the kitchen table lay empty packages of codeine-laced acetaminophen, her weapon of choice for fending off the horrifying hallucinations and delusions which had tormented her for years. Unfortunately, the codeine usually just pushed her nearer to the edge, counteracting what little relief her prescription medication could offer her.

As the standoff between my mother and father continued, Myriette crouched by the fridge, panting, hackles raised and ears flat against her head. My mother's episodes had a terrible effect on the lynx, whose need to help her conflicted with her wish to protect the rest of the family. Even worse, Myriette's connection to my mother made her susceptible to the same terrifying visions and emotions which had assaulted her since her late teens.

I turned at the sound of Nestor whining by the stove. He was clawing frantically at the space between the oven and the counter, jumping away when my mother lashed out at him with her foot, only to creep back and once again resume his scratching.

At that moment something in my chest clenched, and I was nearly overwhelmed by the need to locate the other familiars in the house. I quickly poked my head around the corner to see Blou-Blou, who was standing on a branch in his tank by the telephone, anxiously waving his head back and forth. I then glanced toward the cage on top of the fridge, where Max spent much of his time when my brother was in the basement drawing, as he was now. The habitat appeared empty, though it was hard to be certain without getting closer and peering into Max's little plastic hidey-hole.

I stepped toward the fridge, then froze as I caught a glimpse of something darting towards the desk by the window. Nestor howled, my mother screamed, and Myriette pounced, turning towards my mother a second later, her feline eyes smouldering with anger, confusion and pain.

The quiet pause that enveloped the room couldn't have lasted more than half a second, but to me it seemed to stretch on and on. I don't know if I was the first to process what was happening, but I was the first to speak.

"Max!" I cried in my shrill, child's voice, "Myriette has Max!"

My mother's familiar backed away slowly, the little deer mouse struggling frantically in its jaws. My mother screamed again as my father darted forward, kicking Myriette in the ribs as hard as he could. The cat dropped Max immediately, then slinked away, looking back and growling low in her throat.

Sensing that this was more than one of my mother's all-too-common crises, my brother darted up the stairs in time to see his little Max run frantically along the wall and under the fridge. He reeled momentarily as he was struck by an intense wave of fear and grief, then quickly kneeled down and tried to coax the mouse out. My mother, eyes glazed, sat at the kitchen table and lit a cigarette as my father stalked into the living room, casting a somehow accusatory glance at Blou-Blou as he passed.

Max emerged a few minutes later, quickly jumping into my brother's trembling, outstretched hands. Though obviously shaken up, the little rodent seemed, at the moment at least, to be more or less unharmed by his misadventure. As my brother and I huddled together studying Max, my mother suddenly snapped out of her psychotic state—a startling transformation the likes of which I had never seen before, nor would ever see again.

"I'm sorry," she whispered, as tears began to flow down her cheeks.

"I know," I replied, as my brother, pale and shivering, placed Max onto a bed of shavings in his little habitat on top of the fridge. Glaring at my mother and swearing under his breath, he gently lifted the cage and carried it with him to his bedroom.

For as long as I can remember, there's been a lonely old oak tree on Highway 59 by the floodway. Every time we drove by it my father (who had a bit of a romantic temperament), would say, in a low and solemn voice, "I salute you, brave and steadfast oak." We buried Max there the next day.

✦

It's been two years now since my mother passed away. Towards the end of her life she and Myriette had shared a small room in a care home where, thanks to advances in anti-psychotic drugs, her life had been relatively peaceful. The staff there had been quite fond of my mother and her familiar, and had offered to continue caring for the lynx after my mother had passed. As we had all expected Myriette to follow my mother in short order (as is usual with familiars) we had agreed, thinking it would be best not to put the lynx through the stress of a move at this late point in her life. When Myriette showed no signs of slowing down after six weeks, however, my wife and I had decided it would be best to bring her home to live with family. Myriette had settled in quickly, happily reuniting with Nestor and taking an immediate liking to Ginger, my wife's northern saw-whet owl.

Things were tranquil over the next two years. Myriette, who at first had been viewed as a curiosity, was soon embraced by our friends and neighbours as something less than a familiar, but much more than a pet. She was especially beloved by the children, with whom she would tussle and snuggle at every opportunity. My brother even came to visit once from Toronto, along with his new familiar, Beaker, a beautiful whiskey jack. Beaker spent most of his time here perched upon Myriette's head, which seemed to suit her just fine.

Then, on June 17th, 2016, everything changed. My wife and I were awakened by our familiars, Nestor scratching and whining by my pillow, Ginger fluttering around the room with a kind of spastic, reckless abandon. I was suddenly assaulted by an intense wave of anxiety from my little fox, and was immediately transported back to that terrible day thirty-nine years ago. I quickly raced into the kitchen to find Myriette huddled under the table, crying softly. I crawled to her on my knees, anxiously petting her thick fur and doing my best to comfort her as Nestor paced back and forth behind me, occasionally sniffing the soles of my feet. As Myriette's cries began to abate, I received a second strong signal from Nestor—a peaceful, joyful impression of my mother, father, brother and I picnicking at Bird's Hill Park. The image filled me with sensations of peace and sadness so strong they were nearly devastating. Tears rolled down my cheeks as I turned towards my wife who, struggling not to cry herself, simply smiled and nodded.

We got to the park two hours later, and set up a blanket in a small clearing just off the road. Nestor and Ginger stayed close as we ate the small meal we had packed, while Myriette paced back and forth near the edge of the forest, pausing once in a while to sniff the air. When the food was gone, we sat and watched Myriette for a while, then began packing the dishes.

As I moved to load the cooler into the car, Nestor bounded up to me and began scratching at my feet, whining excitedly. I quickly turned towards Myriette, who was walking in slow, tight circles, ears down, tail puffed out and twitching. As our eyes met, the world around me seemed to disappear—the insects went silent, the colour drained from the grass and the trees, the myriad scents of nature evaporated. All at once I was aware of nothing but this beautiful creature, who had loved my mother unwaveringly and had suffered so much by her side.

I was suddenly filled with a terrifying, exhilarating mix of grief, fear and elation which sent wave after wave of chills up and down my body. I fell to my knees, my heart thudding violently in my chest, just barely aware of the fact that I was sobbing uncontrollably.

As both Nestor and my wife rushed to my side, Myriette crouched down, emitting a low, mewling growl from deep in her throat. Then she rose, turned toward the forest, and walked out of our lives forever.

As my wife held me, my sobbing abated and the world gently seeped back into existence. The sun brightened, its rays warm and comforting, as all around us a billion tiny creatures buzzed and hummed, and the wondrous smell of wild sage rose from the hot, sandy soil.

And, for the briefest of moments, I felt it: the thoughtless, guiltless experience of simply being.

About the Contributors

CHRIS ALLINOTTE was born and raised in northern Ontario and spent most of his formative years going to the cottage on Lake Superior. Many years and many moves later, he found himself married with children in Winnipeg. He has been writing for publication for just over fifteen years. His stories have appeared in the anthology *Unquiet Earth and Creepy Things*. He has edited four volumes of the *Days of Madness* anthologies of psychological horror, and is working on a novel.

WAYNE ARTHURSON is an Edmonton-based Indigenous writer/musician, whose family hails from Norway House Cree Nation. He is the author of six novels: *Final Season*, the award-winning and bestselling Leo Descroches series (*Fall From Grace*, *A Killing Winter*, *Blood Red Summer*), and the new Sergeant Neumann series (*The Traitors of Camp 133* and *Dishonour in Camp 133*). *Fall From Grace* won the Alberta Readers' Choice Award in 2012.

JONATHAN BALL holds a PhD in English and teaches writing, literature, and film at universities in Winnipeg. He is the author of the poetry books *Ex Machina*, *Clockfire*, and *The Politics of Knives*, the co-editor of *Why Poetry Sucks: An Anthology of Humorous Experimental Poetry*, and of the academic monograph *John Paizs's Crime Wave*. Visit him online at JonathanBall.com, where he helps others tell exceptional stories in exciting ways.

S. M. BEIKO currently works in the Canadian publishing industry as a freelance editor, graphic designer, and consultant. Her first novel, *The Lake and the Library*, was nominated for the Manitoba Book Award for Best First Book, as well as the 2014 Aurora Award. She is also the author of the Realms of Ancient series: *Scion of the Fox*, *Children of the Bloodlands* and *The Brilliant Dark*. Alongside Hope Nicholson, she co-edited *Gothic Tales of Haunted Love*, and wrote the story (with Maia Kobabe on art) "A Heritage of Woods."

SHELDON BIRNIE is a writer, community journalist, and the author of *Missing Like Teeth: An Oral History of Winnipeg Underground Rock 1990-2001*. A terrible golfer, Sheldon lives in Winnipeg with his wife, Clara, and son, Jack. His writing has appeared in the *Winnipeg Free Press*, *Vice*, *Noisey*, *Canadian Dimension*, *lichen*, and *Descant*, among others.

KEITH CADIEUX has had short fiction appear in *Grain*, *Prairie Fire*, ELQ, and the *Exile Book of New Canadian Noir*. He is also the co-editor of the anthology *The Shadow Over Portage & Main*. A French translation of his story *Donner Parties* is forthcoming in the anthology *TransLit 11*. He grew up in Manitoba except for a brief stint in Nova Scotia during his high school years, and completed an MA at the University of Manitoba.

JENNIFER COLLERONE has called the northwest corner of Winnipeg home for the entirety of her life. A passion for writing has stuck with her since elementary school, where she wrote the classic (at least in her young mind) *How Penguin Learned to Fly* using those weird Crayola stamper markers that made animal shapes. She's been published in the anthology *Manitoba at Christmas: Holiday Memories in the Keystone Province*, and wrote and drew several comics for *The Manitoban*.

GILLES DECRUYENAERE was born and raised in Winnipeg, where he now resides with his wife, Joanne, and their fur-baby, Yogi. In his spare time Gilles enjoys reading, watching movies, creating art and experiencing nature, as well as collecting rocks, minerals, antiques and Star Wars paraphernalia. A graduate of the Digital Media Design program at Red River College, Gilles recently served as Assistant Film Editor for the feature-length animated film *Ozzy*. Gilles is also the author of the sci-fi novel *I Dreamt of Trees*.

WILL J. FAWLEY holds an MFA from George Mason University, where he was assistant fiction editor for *Phoebe Journal of Literature and Art*. Originally from Virginia, he moved to Winnipeg in 2012, and the prairies have shaped both him and his writing. His speculative fiction has appeared in *Unburied Fables, Expanded Horizons, The Northern Virginia Review, Another Place: Brief Disruptions,* and *Sassafras Literary Magazine,* and his book reviews have appeared in *The Winnipeg Review* and *As It Ought to Be*.

DAVID JÓN FULLER'S short fiction has been published in *On Spec* and in anthologies such as *Tesseracts 18: Wrestling with Gods; Long Hidden; Kneeling in the Silver Light* and *No Shit, There I Was*.

CHADWICK GINTHER is the Prix Aurora Award-nominated author of the *Thunder Road Trilogy* (Ravenstone Books) and *Graveyard Mind* (ChiZine Publications). His short fiction has appeared recently in *Tesseracts Nineteen: Superhero Universe, Those Who Make Us: Canadian Creature, Myth, and Monster Stories* and *Grimdark Magazine*. He lives and writes in Winnipeg, spinning sagas set in the wild spaces of Canada's western wilderness where surely monsters must exist.

KATE HEARTFIELD grew up in St. Andrews, Manitoba, a short bike ride from Lower Fort Garry. Her first novel, *Armed in Her Fashion,* was published by ChiZine Publications in the spring of 2018. Tor.com Publishing will publish two time-travel novellas by Kate, beginning with *Alice Payne Arrives* in November 2018. Her novella *The Course of True Love* was published in 2016 by Abaddon Books and her short fiction has appeared in several magazines and anthologies. Until 2015, she was the opinion editor at the *Ottawa Citizen*, where she was a columnist and member of the editorial board for more than a decade. She now makes a living as a freelance writer, editor and teacher in Ottawa.

PATRICK JOHANNESON writes science fiction and fantasy. His work has been published in *Daily Science Fiction*, *The Arcanist*, *On Spec*, and *Tesseracts*, among others. He won the Manitoba Short Fiction contest in 2004. Other fascinations include website programming, judo (which he teaches), Canadian and indie cinema, and Norse mythology. He lives in Brandon, Manitoba, with his wife.

LINDSAY KITSON was born and lives in Manitoba. Her work has appeared in *Microhorror* and the anthology *Athena's Daughters Volume Two*.

CRAIG RUSSELL's first novel, *Black Bottle Man*, won the 2011 American Moonbeam Award gold medal for Young Adult Fantasy. It was a finalist for the Prix Aurora Award for Best English Science Fiction or Fantasy Novel, as well as for two Manitoba Book Awards in the same year. His second novel, *Fragment*, was published by Thistledown Press in 2016. He's a lawyer, supervising the land titles system in southern Manitoba, and lives with his wife in Brandon, where they're restoring their 1906 Victorian heritage home.

J. M. SINCLAIR was born and raised in Winnipeg, but has also lived in Mie, Japan and St. John's, Newfoundland. When she isn't writing, she has worked as a teacher and an archaeologist. She is currently a third of her way to her goal of being able to speak 13 languages. This is her first fiction publication.

CHRISTINE STEENDAM was born and raised in Manitoba and currently lives just outside of Winnipeg. She is the author of seven works including *The High-Maintenance Ladies of the Zombie Apocalypse*, which she co-authored with Melinda Marshall Friesen. She's also been featured in the anthology *Expiration Date*.

About the Editors

DARREN RIDGLEY is a journalist and speculative fiction writer originally from Killarney, Manitoba, and now residing in Winnipeg. His work has previously been published in anthologies such as *Fitting In: Historical Accounts of Paranormal Subcultures* and *Endless Apocalypse*, and magazines including *Polar Borealis*, *Empyreome* and *Fantasia Divinity*. *Fantasia Divinity* later selected his work for its Best of 2016 anthology, *Memories of the Past*. He's not always a grouch, but he does have a brand to maintain.

ADAM PETRASH is a writer from Winnipeg. He is the author of the indie novella, *The Ones to Make it Through*, and his work has appeared in the anthology *Fitting In: Historical Accounts of Paranormal Subcultures*, and in places such as *After the Pause*, CHEAP POP, *Devolution z*, *Lemon Hound*, *Spacecraft Press*, *WhiskeyPaper*, the *Winnipeg Free Press*, and other publications.

Editors' Acknowledgements

The editors would like to thank:

Great Plains Publications, for giving this project their confidence; our editorial director, Catharina de Bakker, for her eagle eye and insight into the stories which make up this collection; our marketing director, Mel Marginet, for her enthusiasm and being a champion of this project from the very beginning; and to everyone else on the Great Plains team who had a hand in the project behind the scenes: thank you.

Relish New Brand Experience for the stunning cover.

We would also like to thank Keith Cadieux, whose insights were invaluable as we began the early work of making *Parallel Prairies* a reality; and to all of our other contributors, without whose stories this book obviously would not be possible.

Last but not least, we would like to thank Lindsay and Sarah for their love and support.